SHATTERED VOWS

SHATTERED VOWS

USA TODAY BESTSELLING AUTHOR
SHAIN ROSE

PAGE
&
VINE

Page & Vine
An Imprint of Meredith Wild LLC

Paperback ISBN: 979-8-9877583-7-3

Note on Content Warnings

As a reader who loves surprises, I enjoy going in blind with each book. Yet, I also want to give my readers the opportunity to know what sensitive content may be in my books. You will find the list of them here: www.shainrose.com/content-warnings

For Lily Alexander and Danielle Keil.
We write together; we die together.
Write-or-dies for life.

CHAPTER 1: MORINA

"Let's take this shot with a dare." My best friend, Linny, lived on the edge of reason, ready to take life by the horns and make it her bitch. I think she'd accomplished it, too, with a successful travel blog that allowed her to fly around the world as some sort of influencer.

"What do you mean?" When I tilted my head, my long dark wavy hair fell to the side of my bare shoulder. It was all I could muster for this night out. The black crop top hinted at my tattoo of the sun and matched my black jeans.

I hadn't even tried to put on heels after our limo delivered us from our small town to this big-city hotel. My boots provided comfort, and I needed it, considering I didn't venture out much.

"I'll give you a dare to complete by the end of the night, and you give me one." Linny bounced about in the limo, the seat's leather creaking under her. Her boyfriend, Chet, had put us up in a hotel so Linny could visit him at a club in Miami tonight. He'd also sent a limo our way for the drive.

"What if my dare was that you have to cheat on Chet?" Pushing the boundaries of her game was my attempt to shine a light on her risky behavior.

Still, Linny wasn't a party pooper by nature. She shrugged. "I'd make do. Plus, your heart's too good to make me do that."

A disgusted sound came from my throat. I hated being pegged correctly. "Fine. I'll play. I dare you to figure out your boyfriend's job and invite him to dinner in our town."

Her eyes narrowed, the makeup around them looking

even smokier. I guessed my blue eyes had the same effect, considering she'd lined them with dark shadow before we left. It was probably her attempt to make me look somewhat presentable with my unkempt hairdo. "That's playing dirty. You know no one likes our little Coralville town."

Coralville was made up of about two thousand people and ran off the oil terminals that belonged to a corporation in the big city next to it. Tourists flocked in and out but never stayed long.

I shrugged. "I love our town. If he's legit, he'll like it enough."

"Fine." She pointed to my shot, and I downed it. "My turn. You find the guy you're most attracted to in the club tonight." She paused and I smiled, thinking that would be easy enough. "And you talk his ear off. Have a full-blown conversation for at least thirty minutes. And the first place he invites you to, you go. No hesitation."

I wrinkled my nose immediately. Mentally scrolling down my list of guys I'd been attracted to in the past few months, I cringed. "That's probably going to be impossible, Linny."

A laugh burst from her, and the bottle of vodka sloshed in her hand. "Why?"

Before I could answer, a laugh bubbled out of me too. "Oh, God. All the guys I hook up with can't hold a legitimate conversation!"

She pointed and laughed more while the city lights streamed into the limo and we fell apart at my expense.

Some things were downright funny when you accepted them and that was it. For a while now, I'd gravitated toward big men with small IQs. I didn't have a reason for it. They just felt safe, easy ... uncomplicated.

Sobering, Linny leaned in and clinked her shot glass with

mine. Her red nails were a hard contrast to my unpainted ones, but her dark eyes were genuine and full of love when she said, "Cheers to hearing your laugh, Morina. It'll get easier after it gets terrible. I'll be here for you whenever you need me."

I sighed and downed the shot with her. The terrible taste made me cough, which only made me chuckle at how inexperienced I was in comparison to her. "God, I'll never get used to the burn of liquor. I'm going to need it in the next few weeks. I just know it."

"How's Grandma Maribel?" she whispered and her dyed black mohawk curl fell onto my shoulder.

I let my head fall onto hers as we slumped down together in the leather seats. "Not good. She's refusing further treatment. The lung cancer's metastasized, and the doc said two weeks ago that she had two weeks to live."

"For fuck's sake." She breathed out. "You need this night out more than me."

"I need a button to pause time. I've wished on it, but the damn stars don't care what I have to say. My horoscope read like a girl's with bad luck for the next week."

"Oh Jesus." Linny rolled her eyes.

"Hey, I didn't wear any bracelets or bring crystals tonight. Be proud."

"I'll be proud when you complete my dare." She poked my bare stomach.

"In my defense, the men I hook up with are normally very nice and amazing in bed."

"Are they though? Like, what's amazing in bed if you have no connection?"

Linny loved every man she dated, and I envied that about her.

For me, it was just about sex. I didn't need an emotional

tie. No complications. "If they can work their stick, I'm not complaining, okay?"

Linny laughed and turned toward her window to point at the club as our driver pulled up. "That's us. Get over here for a selfie before we go in, you little player. I need one before we get all sweaty from dancing—or, in your case, talking—in the club."

I leaned in and stared at us in the glow of her phone screen. Our eyes were ringed with makeup and our straight smiles looked damn good on our contoured faces. Linny was a louder, more-in-your-face beautiful, but my hair was pushed to the side with a bunch of long waves. I'd always been able to snag a guy or two—probably from my oversize chest and butt. I had an hourglass figure because I'd never been any good at counting calories.

Linny snapped two photos.

"Enough?" I asked between smiling teeth.

"One more!" She tilted her head and took another.

"Please tell me we aren't going to document every second of the night?"

She shoved her phone in her clutch and rearranged her shirt before opening the door. "Oh, get over your camera phobia. I have to catalog you dressed this hot and out with me. When was the last time I caught you in something other than a swimsuit and with makeup on?"

If I sighed, I'd probably be without her as a friend.

I ushered her forward as the club's bouncer waved us up. "We're with Chet," she announced so loudly I was sure people at the club across the street heard.

The bouncer appeared twice my size, and I wasn't thin. He glared at us with his thick dark brows down over his eyes, then he lifted the cord to the inside and pointed to our hands.

I glanced at Linny, not sure what he wanted. The local tiki bar was my scene—the one I frequented even as a minor. There, Bradley waved me in with a smile and no questions asked.

She held her hand up, fingers curled, and he stamped the back with a large, capitalized font.

VIP.

Right away, a man with spiced cologne beckoned us down an aisle that only a few select people seemed to be admitted to. We took stairs that lined the club and watched the sea of people below dancing to the pumping music. The second floor held a beautiful dark oasis of men and women who indulged both in alcohol and people watching those downstairs.

As I stepped toward them, the man with too much cologne shook his head and pointed to a dim staircase. "Another floor."

I narrowed my eyes, but Linny shrugged and waved me on.

As we ascended to the third floor, I could barely make out the steps. Thank God I'd worn combat boots.

When the door opened, diamonds and glass and crystal glittered like the ocean at sunset on black everything. I gasped as I walked forward—even the floor was made of glass. We stood directly above those on the floor below.

"Interesting," I murmured to Linny and pointed down.

Her eyes lasered onto her man, though. She'd scanned everyone and squealed when her gaze landed on a tall man with hollowed-out cheeks and ghostly eyes. He lit up when he saw Linny, though, like she could cure him of whatever caused his distress.

He hugged her when she jumped into his arms and murmured something into her ear. Laughing, she pointed to me. "That's Morina, Chet. She accompanied me. So I'm not on my own."

"Morina." He held out his hand. "You both should have a

guard for how good you look."

What was I supposed to say to that? The comment threw me off. "Thanks. We're not really that important."

"Anyone with Linny is important to me." He snuggled into her neck. I didn't know much about love, but his smile with Linny was genuine, infectious, and doting.

Too many romance novels and movies made me long for something I didn't need.

Linny turned to wink at me. "Remember the dare, Morina." Her eyes got wide as she ticked her head at a guy in a navy suit walking up behind Chet.

He wasn't really walking so much as gliding, like he couldn't be bothered by the restriction of gravity. His dark eyes read me, the room, and all his surroundings, but his face drew everyone to him. He was tall and well built, sure, but he had bone structure that cut through all the others. His strong jaw and plump lips had my mouth dropping open.

The problem was his suit. It held all the information I needed to know I would never see him again. A man who wore something that well-tailored wouldn't be in one place for long. Money pulls people in all sorts of directions. He'd have been a nice conquest. Except this time, Linny expected me to chat his ear off, and I was seriously concerned his IQ was as striking as his looks. He peered up and down at me as if taking all of me in and then glanced away, like I wasn't worth his time.

I completely accepted that.

To him, I probably didn't meet some standard that wealthy businessmen who have a model on their arm at every event lived by. Instead, I took on a guy here and there who stopped on his way through our town to talk business regarding the plant.

Chet turned and nodded to him and the other man I'd noticed stuck by his side. "Bastian, meet my girl, Linny."

Bastian's smile flew across his face, welcoming even, as he extended a hand. "Pleasure to meet you, Linny."

She tilted her mohawk my way. "Also a pleasure. That's Morina, my very best friend. Out to enjoy a night with us all."

"I figured," he whispered almost to himself before his hand slid out of hers to shake mine. This time, his smile dropped, and he glanced back at the man on his shoulder. Immediately, the guy ducked into his phone.

My eyes narrowed. Were they wary of me for some reason?

"I'm going to go get a drink," I mumbled, but Chet waved a waitress over. She wore leather booty shorts and flirted shamelessly with all three men who stood near us. Bastian took a moment to talk with her while I concentrated on not rolling my eyes. She'd get a big tip and probably a date by the night's end.

Instead of idling, I stepped around them to talk to the man behind Bastian. His smile was gentle when he looked up from his phone, and his greenish eyes popped against his tanned skin in such a unique way. I might have stared a bit too much.

"Want a picture, Morina?" His deep voice rolled out, soft and comforting like a warm tide creeping in.

"Jeez. Sorry." I shook my wavy hair from my face. "You have really pretty eyes."

A glare came over his face. I almost took a step back from the way it plowed through me, so mean I wasn't sure if I should cower away or try to ignore it, if only to save myself. Then, his face cracked into a smile so bright I thought I had whiplash. Yet I found myself smiling back. "I'm Dante. And I get that a lot. I'm messing with you."

I bit my lip and relaxed enough to tease him back. "Can't you buy a girl a drink before you start with jokes?"

"I bought the drinks instead." Bastian's voice rushed

through me, loud and lethal this time. It was nothing like a warm tide washing over me, but instead, a cold wave crashing onto me, taking my breath away. He had all my attention immediately.

Bastian's big hand held a small glass filled with clear liquid, lime, and ice. The gold ring on one of his fingers matched the very expensive watch that peeked out from under his cuff. I'd learned to judge an escapade by his attire and accessories because that's all he'd be to me for an evening or two.

"We good, Dante?" he asked his friend without looking at him. Instead, our gazes held over our drinks like he searched for something more from me, and I definitely tried to read way too much into our interaction.

And there was the stupid dare. Should I talk to him or Dante for the next thirty minutes? I broke our stare to look over at Linny. She was already on one of the chaise lounges with Chet.

"All good, Bast." Dante nodded at me like I was the topic in question.

"Well, Morina, seems you're a legitimate friend of Linny's," Bastian announced and took a sip of the liquid in his tumbler.

"Um, what?" I sputtered, my eyes wide. "Are you researching me?"

Dante patted my shoulder but didn't say anything before disappearing into the crowd like he wanted nothing more to do with my gaping mouth.

"You've got to be kidding," I murmured and glared up at Bastian. "I'll have you know I'm a stand-up friend."

"Seems that way." Bastian's finger tapped his glass a few times as he glanced around to find Linny and Chet. Then he sighed and motioned toward a table and chairs. "It also seems our friends are occupied for the time being."

I could have told him off for doing whatever weird background check he'd run on me. I could have left him in the dust too. Yet, I had a very serious problem.

I was nosy.

I walked toward the barstools and sat down. "Why are you running a check on me? And how?"

"Unique name and face."

"Face?" My voice squeaked.

"Technology is crazy these days. I don't know how, but Dante does." He was already bored with me as he looked around the club. "Anyway, I know Linny's history. It was easy enough for Dante to work a little magic. It's his job."

"To vet all the people that hang out with you?" I set down my drink and crossed my arms.

"Essentially."

"Why? That sounds like it's no fun."

"What's not fun about it?" He rolled the crystal tumbler in his hands so the liquid swirled.

"There are no surprises."

"Oh, I find enough surprises to last a lifetime in the people I associate with."

"Probably," I grumbled and picked up my drink. "So, what's the deal with Dante?"

Scanning the crowd, I set my sights on someone who looked likely to have less baggage. Bastian's appearance far outranked anyone else in the club, but Linny didn't need to know that I felt that way.

"The deal with him?" Bastian cocked his head.

"Yeah, like is he single?" No harm in cutting to the chase.

"You're interested in him and not me?" He sounded completely shocked, and now his focus was directly on me, with no sign of that wandering eye.

"Bastian, I'm much too simple for your tastes." And he was much too complicated for mine. "Dante seems nice."

"Well, I'll be damned if a girl looks at my security team instead of me tonight." He rubbed the stubble across his chin. "What's your story, Morina?"

"I don't have one. We're in Miami for a night and then back to the grind. I work, I eat, I sleep. I'm sure it's a much more boring life than you live. One your friend would probably be more interested in."

He sighed and brought his glass to his lips. I'd had too much to drink in the limo, and that sloshy feeling came over me. I knew right as he took a swig and my eyes trailed down his neck. The liquid flowed down over his full lips, sat on his tongue and then probably rolled down that thick throat of his. His mouth looked so pillowy, I wondered if he could possibly lead with such soft lips.

One side of them tipped up, and my gaze snapped to his. He murmured, "I lead in everything I do."

"I—" I didn't even know what to say as I slapped a hand over my mouth. "I'm really embarrassed that I said that out loud. I drank ..."

"The liquor can catch up to you when you don't drink a lot." He nodded, not making fun of the fact that I had totally been considering him sexually.

"So, about Dante ..." Back to the real matter—the safer matter.

"I don't think it'd be a great idea to hook you up with one of my closest friends after you've hit on me, Morina."

"I'm not hitting on you. I was admiring your face," I threw out and then slammed my mouth shut with a wince. He chuckled, and I shook my head to motion for him to stop. "This is not normally how I am. I'm better at hiding my attraction to

14

someone."

"You're attracted to me now?" He leaned on the table, a twinkle in his chocolate eyes, and I found myself wanting to lean in.

I turned to the crowd. "I'm attracted to your friend too. He seems like a safer bet. More realistic."

"What makes me unrealistic?" he asked in my ear and a shiver ran over me, making me aware of how close he'd come.

"For one, your suit probably costs more than my whole wardrobe."

"I have no idea how much combat boots go for. You very well might be more expensively dressed." He shrugged in his suit.

"Oh please." I waved off his joke, both of us knowing my shoes were for comfort and not a fashion statement at all. "Second, no one's bothered you since you've been up here, which means you probably are the one who commands the whole room, and you all probably do illegal things."

"What if I told you only one of those things was true?"

"I'd ask which one." I shrugged, but my mind had run away with another idea already. "What are you doing in Miami?"

He nodded and sat a little straighter, like he was ready to give his elevator speech. "I'm scoping out companies my father owned. He squared away a lot of his business dealings when he was more involved in his investments, but then the economy took a dive. Anyway, he's been gone a long time and now I've taken over a lot of those dealings."

I nodded, trying to sound interested. "Really?"

"No, not really." He shook his head, and then his long lashes lowered over his eyes. He studied me like I was a Rubix's Cube. "I don't know why I want to tell you the truth, but it might just be I'm sick of Miami, and I need some excitement.

My business dealings aren't exciting."

"They sound great," I said with about as much enthusiasm as I could muster. I didn't want to sound bored with his business, but my mind takes off easily if I I'm not fully entertained.

"It's boring as shit and you know it." He dragged a finger down my nose, and my eyes met his immediately. His touch was like a zap to my system. He seemed to know the pull he had when he did something like that because his smile flashed like lightning across his face.

I leaned back out of his reach. "It doesn't matter. I'm sure someone else would be more interested in your work. I'm more interested in your friend."

"What for?" He crossed his arms.

"He's safe!" I huffed, annoyed he hadn't heard me the first time.

"What's with you and being safe? You can't live any type of life if you're safe."

"I live just fine where I'm from."

He peered behind me, stared at Linny, and then glanced back at me. "Have you been outside of where you're from ever?"

"I'm here, aren't I?"

"I could take you somewhere else though."

"Oh, are you offering to take me back to your apartment or hotel? Show me how you really work your magic stick?" I laughed at my own joke, sure he was about to use it as a pick up line.

He narrowed his eyes, and his next words came out cold, almost condescending, but still he gave me a question, not a command. "Do you think I can't show you a good time, Morina? That I couldn't show you something new?"

"Of course you can't. You're just another guy wearing a suit." I'd had my fair share of them come through the tourist town I'd lived in. I knew his type.

Sort of.

Something behind his dark eyes, that wolfish smile, and all the perfect angles of his face made him different. He was nice enough, soft lips—or so I guessed—and was saying everything right, like he really was an accommodating gentleman ... right up until he closed the door to his lair and ripped you apart.

"I've been with a lot of men like you before." I searched the room for Dante.

"Like me?" The corners of his mouth lifted, but the warmth in his smile was gone. Bastian's sheep clothing sagged, and the wolf was coming out to play. He had power, confidence, a sheer knowledge that he was greater than all of us.

It made me want to back away and lean in at once.

Maybe it was that particular evening and how I knew my grandma was about to leave me. Linny lived on the edge for fun, but I teetered on it. I was about to be alone in this world and at twenty-three, that seemed a little unfair. Cruel, even. I questioned a lot on my good days, and on my bad, I grabbed my crystals and hoped the planets and stars would align in my favor.

Tonight, the edge was close for a lot of reasons, but not for fun. The voice in my head echoed that we were doomed, like we tiptoed through a valley of razor-sharp rocks, about to trip at any moment.

I shut my eyes and tried my best not to spiral and fall. "Look ... Bastian, right?" He nodded. "Bastian, you're older, wiser, probably have a lot more experience with women. So, I'll tell you. I'm probably not like a lot of women you meet. I'm like the really eccentric ones you usually avoid. I watch for full moons. I've been known to sage my house. I'm a believer in signs. I'm not your thing. I read my horoscope yesterday, and my week is supposed to be filled with a lot of the same. It told me to avoid that and go down a rabbit hole."

"What sign are you?"

"Oh, do you actually know signs?" I'd never met a man in a suit that wanted to discuss astrology.

Maybe, just maybe, our stars would align.

CHAPTER 2: BASTIAN

A large part of the business deals we were tying up required both of us working together. Dante, my security and distant cousin, could reach out to Cade continually for intel, but it wasn't as smooth.

When your father was the head of a dirty mob family, cleaning it up took precision, finesse, and fucking attention.

Cade knew this was a team effort. Years ago, we'd put out a hit on our father, brought him down, and made the conscious decision to clean the family up. One painful business at a time. Every one of them was a mess—drug imports, sex trafficking, and illegal money laundering.

I wouldn't leave a legacy of filth though. My empire would know a different type of power. But I needed my team. I relied on them and built trusted partnerships with each of them. That included my brother working alongside me so I didn't stumble through communications with a company. I needed Cade to run checks, give me background information, and confirm dealings as I shook hands with businessmen. Today, instead, Chet had waited for Dante to sift through information, making our communication stilted.

The deal wasn't done. With all that waiting, Chet didn't trust me enough to sign those papers yet.

So here I was, drinking at the boy's night Chet proposed when I could have been back on the jet, flying home.

The only silver lining was that it would be done soon and maybe I'd find a woman to relieve some of my stress before the night was over.

But it certainly wouldn't be this one.

This one was a train wreck waiting to happen.

One I would glance back and stare at, maybe tell the person on the phone about because of how ridiculous said train wreck was.

Quite frankly, the whole city of Miami was full of ridiculous people with ridiculous needs.

And hobbies.

And beliefs. Like crystals.

I worked night and day in my city to close deals. Here, they partied and read their horoscopes.

Morina checked every one of those boxes, I was sure. Her eyes lit up like Santa was coming to town when I showed an interest in her sign.

Did she think that shit was real?

Absolutely absurd.

"Nope." I cut our conversation about astrology off. "Don't even know what my sign is."

Now, those big blue eyes fell like a wounded doe's. She did have that going for her at least. They were a dark blue, like the color of the sky at midnight. Unique, honestly.

She scoffed, "Figures." Her gaze scanned the room again and landed on Dante.

For some reason, her picking Dante over me felt ridiculous too. Why want someone who believed in hocus pocus? Were stars what really matched people?

I couldn't begin to fathom that someone would write off a whole person based on the day they were born. "Do you intend to ask my friend his sign?"

"Well, not if you know his birthday. Was he born in—?"

"I don't know his birthday," I cut her off.

"Well, that's rude of you." She humphed.

She could think I was rude or a liar. I knew Dante's birthday because we all made it a mission to never celebrate them. His had been a few months back, and he'd been away. Probably on purpose.

"Do you want another cocktail?" I asked, changing the subject.

"Not a good idea."

I nodded. I'd had too much already, and she definitely didn't need any more. "Drink enough on the way over?"

She studied me again, like she was sure I was judging her. "How much have you had to drink tonight? Or was it just this one?"

"Would it matter if I had more?"

"I happen to think you didn't have much at all."

"Why not?"

"Because, like I said, you seem older. Wiser."

"Morina, don't you know that means I could show you a thing or two?"

She stared at me for about five seconds before answering. She took in my suit again, my shoes, probably even my hair before she mumbled something like *To hell with it* before saying, "I'm kind of in the mood to see if you can really do that."

"Meaning what?"

She sighed. "It means I want to get out of here with you. This isn't my scene. This"—she waved in front of me, then around the room—"isn't really living. It's a boring second to a lot of what the world has to offer. Linny of all people should know that. She's a travel blogger, you know."

"Linny is also a woman in love. That seems to trump a lot of things to most people."

She looked her friend's way and winced. "Right, and I

hope it works out. But I'm not here for love. Just a good time and maybe to forget life a little."

I wouldn't tell her that I hoped it didn't work out, that Chet wasn't a man to be associated with, that I wouldn't really be associated with him after this deal, whether I closed it tonight or tomorrow.

It wasn't my place. I was getting out of this town and moving on to tie up the rest of the deals in the state.

She sighed and turned back to her glass. "Maybe I do need a drink to pass the time."

She was so damn bored.

And she'd lumped me into the boring category with the rest of this club where people thought they were somebody.

Truth be told, I was bored too.

Bored with my existence and the fact that I was probably living the same damn life my father had. Sure, I was trying to clean up the dirty businesses he'd invested in and make a better name for the family, but maneuvering numbers and partnerships wasn't of interest to most.

It wasn't even of interest to me.

"Do you think Dante knows signs?" she asked quietly, probably more to herself than me.

"He knows a little of everything." My friend, who was also my second cousin removed, was well traveled. He claimed that going around the world centered him.

I needed centering too, but I didn't really believe in any of the bullshit that came with deep breathing and yoga and star signs.

"How did you two meet?" she asked, like I was going to sit there and give her tips on how to date Dante.

"We've known each other since birth. Our families are distantly related."

"Huh." She narrowed her eyes at me and scanned my body. "I don't really see it."

"See what?"

"You're so ..." She waved at me like it was obvious. "Unapproachable and ... broody, maybe?"

I rubbed at my jaw and stared at her, trying to figure out her angle. "I'm neither of those things."

"In your line of work, do people come up to you and talk like they aren't scared of you?"

"No, because they are scared of me. I'm the boss."

"Well, then my perception of you stands. Unapproachable, broody, and I'll add that you probably don't frequent clubs like this unless you're working."

"And you do frequent clubs like this?" I eyed her again. Her outfit downplayed her figure, but she wasn't hiding that she was good looking. Admittedly, if you got past her belief in horoscopes, she was probably one of the better looking women in here tonight. Lower maintenance with a body that was real, curvy, and appealing.

She shrugged and turned, leaning her elbows on the tall bar table behind us. We both stared at the clubbers buzzing around. She tapped her boot on the ground. "I probably shouldn't wear shoes like this in VIP, especially when I'm standing on glass that overlooks two floors of people."

"Are you concerned that we're on glass?"

"Maybe more concerned that we think we have the right to be standing on others." She shrugged and scuffed her boot back and forth. "I'm wearing cheap shoes and have a good friend who has a connection. What makes me any better?"

Her words shot through me. I'd said the same thing time and time again to my father growing up. I was just like everyone else. He'd remind me that I wasn't. I was an Armanelli, and I'd take his place one day. That made me much more important in his eyes.

In mine, I'd wanted equality. Always.

Yet here I was, standing over Miami, ready to take on another business deal. This one would solidify a power shift that I'd known was on the horizon. I'd become the most powerful man among my business associates. It put me in a position where I wouldn't be mixing with people like her. I frowned at the physical discomfort I felt as my gut twisted thinking about it.

"Your shoes are fine."

"Your shoes probably cost more than my car." She pointed to my Italian leather Oxfords.

They'd been custom made and shipped directly. "They're just shoes."

She wrinkled her nose. "Come on, how much did they cost you? More than five grand?"

I scoffed at the small number and her eyes widened.

"Oh my God. They do. Why? What is wrong with you?"

There wasn't a reason for me to be defensive and yet ... "Most women in this club would be happy to see I'm well dressed."

"Most women in this club are looking at you precisely for your money."

"And what are you normally looking for at a club like this, Morina?" My eyes narrowed on her but not because I questioned her identity anymore. Dante normally reached out to our tech guy and my brother who were able to hack into any criminal database. I knew she was clean and a real person.

Still, I couldn't pin down her motives for being here or her intentions in talking to me. She didn't fit the mold of the normal woman out. She was beautiful in a unique way with her wavy hair askew and not properly brushed. Her curves were real, and I knew her ass would barely fit in my hands if I gripped it now.

My dick stirred more than it had with the women who'd made their way over to me earlier tonight.

Interesting.

And she was appealing in a weird, ridiculous way, and yet, I hadn't been interested in much in a long time.

Her gaze darted around the club, like she was looking for Dante again. "I'm looking for a nice guy—someone who gets me—to have fun for a night. Nothing more, nothing less."

"A one-night stand?" I murmured, surprised.

"So?" Her head snapped back to glare at me. Cold fire in her blue eyes. That look on her was straight out of a fucking magazine. She was one of those brilliant-when-being-fucked-with types.

"And you think Dante is going to do that with you?" I pushed her to see where her head was at.

"He seems laid back enough to have a good time. And frankly, I have every right to a good time. Don't I?"

She didn't know my friend whatsoever. "You realize he's my security, right? So he has to be trained to fight someone if they were to approach me aggressively."

"So he's got a banging bod?" She took a deep breath. When she breathed it out, the fire in her eyes had extinguished. She hit me with a big smile and waggled her eyebrows at me. "I could get down with a good bod."

Why did I suddenly want to prove to her that I worked out too? "You do this a lot?"

"One-night stands? Well, no. Not really." She shrugged. "Linny's my friend, so I said I'd come out with her, but honestly I don't think there's anything in this big city world that will bring me much more happiness than what I've already found in my own town."

"Not even a miraculous one-night stand?"

She looked me up and down, trying to act like she didn't see anything appealing. Yet I saw the shiver, the way she licked her lips. "If you're insinuating that I'd find that with you, I don't think so."

"Really?" I lifted a brow. "You'd be surprised the things I'd show you."

"What? With you being older?" She crossed her arms. "I find that affects stamina."

I chuckled at her indirect slight. She looked younger than me but only by maybe ten years. This girl wasn't someone I would normally entertain, but her words, the way she dismissed me, and the way she pegged me so quickly were the last straws on my shitty day.

"Let me show you then."

"Show me what?"

"What you've been missing by staying in that small town of yours."

CHAPTER 3: MORINA

Linny's eyes narrowed when Bastian said we were leaving. "I don't think you've done near enough talking to go anywhere."

Was she insinuating that I was losing the bet or that she was nervous about me leaving with a man I'd just met? "We'll talk more on the drive."

"Drive to where?" she asked, leaning away from her boyfriend. So, definitely the latter.

"I—"

"Totally right for you to be concerned about your friend. Here's my card." Bastian handed over a business card that was all black but had his name and contact information on it.

I peered at it and lifted a brow. "Sebastian Armanelli? Fancy name."

One corner of his mouth lifted just a hair. I couldn't quite tell if he was amused or irritated with me, yet I liked that look all the same. He continued as if I hadn't said a word. "If something happens and you can't find her in twenty-four hours, hand that over to the police. And call the number now."

Pulling her phone from her purse, she punched in the numbers. His phone rang instantly.

"You have my personal line, and I promise, your boyfriend would help you find me. He likes you more than he does my family."

The man was trying more than most men would, and I wasn't quite sure why. I'd surrounded myself with a lot of people who didn't go against the tide. If it pulled them, they went. I didn't find fault in that, but now that I had a man going to such lengths to spend time with me, it shook something in me.

I studied Bastian's arm when he offered it to me. "Maybe I shouldn't go. This is a lot of fuss to prove my statement wrong."

"Yet, I'm the one making the fuss. So let me decide how far I'm willing to go."

Effort.

Why was it so attractive? And why was I so scared of it?

If curiosity killed the cat, I guess I was about to find out exactly how. There was something behind his dark eyes that pulled me in, like he was searching for something more than the club had to offer, and he wanted to show me that we could find it together.

I sighed and waved to Linny. "I'll put my location share on for you, okay?"

She nodded and motioned for me to call her.

Leaving the club was much faster than entering. Bastian beelined through the VIP crowd and pulled me down a different darkened staircase. A car waited at the bottom, right outside a back door. "Well, that's convenient," I mumbled.

"Perks of my lifestyle, I guess." He waved off his driver and opened the door for me.

I didn't know the make of the car, but I immediately knew it was more expensive than the limo. The leather was stitched precisely and felt like butter instead of alligator skin to the touch.

He paused outside the car and spoke to the driver, maybe giving directions, before taking the seat beside me.

"Where are we headed?" I asked, aware that I'd gotten into a car in a darkened alley with a man I didn't know. The thought sobered me up more than a little.

"One of my favorite places to go—a little island off the

coast. The sunrise over the ocean is like a painting."

"Interesting," I murmured. "I pegged you differently."

"Assuming? I figure you know the saying of what it makes out of you and me."

"I do, but you have to admit everyone does it. It's part of our makeup to try and piece things together to avoid being caught in a surprising situation, don't you think?"

"I think you don't mind a surprising situation, considering you're sitting here with a man you barely know on your way to a place unknown."

I stared out the window. In the distance, I saw lights I knew very well. His driver was heading straight to the airport, and I pointed to the planes taking off. "Showing me the sunset with planes flying by?"

"Something like that."

"Hm." It was different, something I'd never watched, at least not close. "I decided I liked airports when I was young. I went to them a few times with my parents and got to people watch long before I was ever concerned about germs or security or anything like that. I used to love staring out at the big machines."

"How many times have you flown?"

"Not many. Just enough to know I'm not a total basket case in the air but that I still have a fear of landing."

The corner of his mouth lifted just a hair. "You said you like your little town. Did you fly here?"

I smirked at him. He'd gotten more information from me than even the men in my town did. We'd been talking much longer than thirty minutes, and if Linny asked, I'd have to admit it was intriguing to build a bond with another human that I might hook up with.

Yet the feeling tugged on me, warning me to run or to shut

up and not say another word.

So I leaned in and whispered, "Does it really matter where I flew from, Bastian?" and took his full lips in mine.

He kissed with precision and a languid sort of lead, like he didn't want to push too far, even though I was the one who'd started it. I scooted closer and grabbed the lapel of his jacket for leverage. His hands gripped my hips as he let me climb on top of him, and I felt his excitement even if his mouth was all control.

I rolled my hips against him and could tell he was bigger than most men I got with. The rigidity of his muscles under my hands told me he must be feeling the bolts of pleasure I felt too. I moaned. We would work out just fine. This was what we both wanted anyway.

Watching a sunrise with the guy wasn't going to happen. I'd meet Linny back at the airport early in the morning, and we'd be on our way home. At least I'd have this little adventure to remember our trip by.

He gripped my arms and eased me away when the car stopped at the terminal. "We're here."

"Should he just drive around?" I shrugged.

"You're borderline insulting with just wanting to fuck me here, Morina," he teased me. Then he quirked his head, like he couldn't figure me out.

I huffed out a breath. "No, it's just ..." I poked his shoulder. "That's not what I mean. I don't normally do all this talking, and I think the sunrise sounds nice but ..."

"You said I couldn't show you a good time."

"I take it back. It will be a good enough time in the car."

"No. This would be a time you've had with many other men."

"Excuse me, not *many*." I tsked and corrected him. "Some.

Just what I need to fill a void. I don't—"

"I don't fill voids, love. I obliterate them." His dark eyes narrowed, and it was the first time I saw what Bastian hid underneath his calm demeanor—dominance. "I'm not like any other man. I've had a shit day, and you comparing me to everyone else is pissing me off."

Fire in his eyes was not what I expected. The Bastian I'd met in the club seemed so controlled, yet his grip on my arms tightened a touch. But he must've realized it, because a moment later, he smoothed his palms up and down my skin and goose bumps popped up. My heart fluttered like I cared.

I didn't.

This was a bad idea.

Still, the fire lured me in. Trying to read him more deeply, I found myself shrugging and getting off his lap. "I don't see why you'd want to compete with the boys I normally hang out with."

"Because they're boys and I'm a man, huh?"

"Well, you're definitely older," I taunted, and he squeezed my thigh as he smiled.

Before I could say anything else, he called to his driver, "Drive to the back, please."

"Sir?"

"You heard me. Drive around."

We sped through the terminal drop off and made a sharp turn onto a private road that the driver had to use a keycard to access. I glanced at Bastian and then at the driver. This wasn't something I'd seen before. This was straight out of a slasher film.

Grandma would be pissed if I died here.

"So, you know my location share is on, right?"

"You were about to ride me in the back of this car, and now

you're concerned for your life?"

"Well, this is a private road."

"I'm aware you have location share on. Feel free to call your friend or text her where you are if you want."

"Where exactly are we going then?" I grabbed my phone and waved it at him as if suddenly I was being responsible.

"To the back of the airport where the jets are located."

"Jets?" I practically screeched as they came into view. "Please don't tell me you own one."

"I own more, but one is here."

"Oh my God. You're filthy rich. Like disgustingly rich, aren't you?"

"Does it matter?"

I sort of wanted to hyperventilate. People like this made my skin itch and put me on edge about everything I did and said. They had to be intelligent to have so much but also ruthless or mean or something just as terrible. "Sort of! I mean, people like you should be like giving back to the poor or whatever. Don't you feel greedy?"

"Greedy that I've worked for all this?" He waved to the huge jet we pulled up to.

"I don't understand this side of living."

"I'm not asking you to. I'm asking you to come on a ride with me."

"I wanted to ride you, not come *on* a ride with you!"

He stared before he started laughing. "I think I'm finally different than all the other men you've been with."

"I mean, maybe. I don't ever talk to them enough to see if they're flying around on jets. They come in and zip out of my town. I don't ... this is ... this is stupid rich, Bastian."

"All right, all right." He waved away my gobsmacked shock. "Come for a quick flight to the island. It's a thirty-minute ride."

I was stunned. Speechless. The alcohol must've left my body faster than ever before.

"Come on, let's see if I'm as boring as the VIP club in Miami."

He opened the door and stepped out, then turned back and offered his hand to me. I took it.

Why the hell not? I'm already this far in.

What's the worst that could happen?

CHAPTER 4: BASTIAN

"Big private jet, Bastian. You must be making up for something very small." She laughed at another one of her absurd jokes.

Morina had a whole vibe to her. She was scared of manmade things and money—or maybe didn't really like them. Yet, she was curious enough to walk up the jet stairs with me and talk the pilot's ear off about how to fly the plane. He smiled at her the whole time as if she had some enamoring quality.

When she saw the flight attendants, I witnessed what made her so likable as she said, "I think you're absolutely beautiful. Hopefully he pays you to sit here and wait for him while he gallivants around Miami."

Spitfire. She was absolutely okay saying the first thing that popped into her head, barreling straight into whatever emotion was on the tip of her tongue, and not thinking about the consequences. It was unique. Around a man like me, most people mulled over their words, practically chewing them up before letting them creep from their mouths.

The flight attendant was one of the women I'd had the pleasure of knowing time and time again. She didn't hesitate with her answer. "He pays me very well, in more ways than one."

Morina's eyebrows rose. "Well then. Good for you both."

The flight attendant made her way up to the front where she talked to the pilot. Morina whispered, "So, big plane, hot flight attendant that talks you up. You're for sure making up for things, I think." She smirked to herself.

Her insults and the way she doubted me added to my dick's attraction to her. I'd barely been able to stop from fucking her in the car on the way over. This woman with her messy waves and lush curves wasn't my usual type, but damn, I wanted to violate that smirk off her face.

"You want to find out, *piccola ragazza*?"

"What does that mean?" Her deep-blue eyes squinted.

"Little girl."

She was young, but the Italian I didn't use much anymore had slipped out.

"Little?" She giggled as we taxied down the runway. "Your flight attendant is small. I'm not. And I highly doubt I'm small compared to the women you normally date."

"Shorter, that's for sure." I assessed her. "And younger, definitely younger."

Why the fuck had I brought her here? She'd goaded me a little, but something about Miami had me doing stupid shit I never normally did.

I didn't indulge in women the way I used to. I'd learned my lesson time and time again. They disappointed me like most everything in the world.

And Miami was no different. I remembered being there as a child, remembered my father telling me to learn from the dark nights on the streets where he exchanged briefcases and deals.

Miami was somewhere I'd felt nothing. Been nothing.

Did I need to prove myself to her all of a sudden? To the city?

She scoffed like she wasn't the least bit swayed. "I think I would have been more impressed if you'd fucked me in the car."

I didn't answer her. Instead, I let the flight attendant bring us each a glass of water, as she went over her normal lines with guests. We could have food made, but this flight was short, and we had to be sure to buckle for landing when the pilot made the announcement.

I looked Morina up and down. She *tap-tap-tapped* her boots on the carpet of the plane as we flew higher and higher into the clouds. We would be over water soon, but darkness would cloak the view. Not that it mattered. We were both looking at one another, and her gaze was daring, like she wasn't even sure I'd take her there.

"You know fucking in the car is never that comfortable, Morina."

"And an airplane is comfortable?"

"This one can be. There is a bed in the back."

"Of course there is. You're accommodating then? That's all this is? A business gentleman?"

"I can be." I mulled over her assessment. "In most things, yes, I'm accommodating. And let's be clear, there's also the possibility that maybe I simply wanted someone to see the sunrise with." It wasn't exactly true, but she didn't have to know that.

"But you kissed me."

"I returned your kiss," I corrected her. "There's a difference."

"Are you saying you don't want to sleep with me?"

"I don't think any man would say that to you truthfully."

"Oh, there have been men who have." She chuckled to herself. "Which is fine, because I'm here for a good time. And I don't know if you get down and dirty like the rest of us. All signs point to no."

"*Piccola ragazza*, I'm dirtier than the rest of you. I was born into it." I didn't wait, I closed the gap between us and took her mouth with mine. This time, there was less restraint. I wanted to take something rather than be a part of it.

If she was here for the good time, I would be too.

I needed to let off steam. I bit her lip, sucked it hard, and she moaned. I wound her dark hair around my hand where I could fist it tight and pull her head back to gain better access. With a gasp, she opened her mouth further like she was ready for the unhinged side of me.

But I wasn't.

I pulled her away, my breath heavy. Something was unraveling after being in that city today, and I needed to get a grip on it.

Yet, Morina searched my face before she smirked. "Welp, I'm not sure you'll live up to the daddy expectation I have of you now after calling me little girl. That kiss was mediocre at best."

I hummed and the air shifted between us. Most women would have praised me, worshiped me. This one wanted something raw, and she was digging for it.

"Get on your knees, love." The words slid like silk from my mouth. "I'll show you how much of an expectation you're about to take."

She licked her plump lips, and it acted like a beacon for my dick. Something about her screamed pure and innocent while another part of her purred like she was a sex kitten waiting to be pet.

Her hands went to my trousers, and I unbuckled her belt as I devoured her mouth. It was nice and full—full enough to wrap around my cock.

When she gripped my dick and gasped, I pulled back and flexed it in her hands. I almost lost myself to her right then. Something about that open mouth making sounds for me pushed all the right buttons. "Knees, *ragazza*."

She stammered, but her hands slid from my pants, and she

slowly kneeled, obeying like I wanted her to.

Morina's jaw dropped when I took out my cock for her to see.

I brushed a finger down her cheek. "Open wider, love. Let's see if you can take it all like a good girl, huh?"

She did as she was told, with a glint in her sapphire-blue eyes, and I slid my dick right where it wanted to go.

When her lips closed around me, I gripped her hair, trying to pace her and myself. But damn, it wasn't easy, not when she was so warm and wet around me. "Shit, I knew this mouth was fuckable."

She looked up at me, her dark-blue eyes suddenly so innocent that it almost made me come right down her throat.

I needed her to remember this was only a fuck, not us connecting or anything like that. "Come on, pretty girl, let's see how good you are." My voice was ragged as I flexed in her mouth. "Handle me better than my flight attendant, huh?"

Fire sparked in her eyes, and I thought I might have pushed too far, lost her, but then she took her time, taking me fully down her throat. Her tongue lapped at the bottom of my dick as she dragged me back out. This time, I moaned a "Fuck" and pulled back before she could continue. "Get up," I commanded, and she did exactly that with a triumphant smile on her face. "Lose the shirt."

She raised it over her head, and I was struck still by the sight of her in a bra. I knew she had to have great tits, but they were full and real and begging for me to hold them. A small tattoo stood out against the tanned skin of her shoulder and every part of her appeared delicate against the black ink.

The red lace of her bra strained to hold all of her in, and the vivid color told me she'd known exactly what she'd get herself into tonight.

I smiled with that knowledge.

"You want me to fuck you in that seat or go back to the bed?" She shrugged, but her eyes were still on my cock. "Want another taste before I have you, Morina?"

CHAPTER 5: MORINA

I should have said no. Jesus, he was massive though.

I'd felt it in the car, and I'd been inclined to go down the rabbit hole of the night, not because of that but because he'd refused to screw me right there.

Bastian wanted to be some sort of gentleman, but his cock told another story.

The way he looked at me now told another story too. He was all constraint, slowly unraveling, whereas I'd unwound long ago.

And I didn't get on my knees for just anybody. I could count the men on one hand.

I'd never even swallowed. Yet, I was between his legs and lowering my mouth to his cock faster than I ever had in my life. For a second time.

I couldn't believe that after him comparing me to his flight attendant, I was doing this. I hated being compared to others, and his statement was one I'd make him sorry for by being the best. But that wasn't why I was here.

His kiss had pushed every button I hid from other men I'd been with. Most men were a nice lay, but Bastian's kiss had been vicious, like he'd unleashed a beast. He hadn't held back that second time, and I wanted to know what sex would be like without any constraints. Could he go to the limits I wanted to? Did I even have limits at this point?

No man had the audacity to push all the boundaries on a quick fling. And I'd never wanted more than that.

Bastian might have the confidence though. And I was willing to take the risk.

Plus, I wanted to see him come apart when I tried my best to take him all in my mouth.

His fingers tangled in my hair as I licked the tip of him once more, pre-cum already coating my tongue as he whispered a string of obscenities.

I took him in my mouth nice and slow, one inch at a time, my hand at the base of him, pumping.

My tongue explored where it could, but he was only halfway in before I was completely full. So full I knew I'd gag as my eyes watered from his size.

He ran a finger down my cheek and murmured, "You're beautiful with my cock in your mouth, love. Keep looking at me just like that."

His hands in my hair took some of the control as he pulled me back, and I was able to swirl my tongue around him and flick the tip.

Big, hard, and overwhelming. Just what I wanted.

With his legs caging me in and the next row of seats to my back, he controlled the moment. When he gyrated forward and pulled my head back down his length, more of him slipped in my mouth, more than I'd ever taken.

"This too much, *ragazza*?" he asked as tears streamed from my eyes.

But I shook my head because I saw the way his neck strained, the way he was breaking a sweat.

"Fuck," he moaned when I took a bit more of him and gagged. "I want to come in you and have you take it all. You'd be so good at it. I see how you like it. Jesus, so good."

I thought he was about to. I was ready for it but then he yanked my hair back again. "We finish this in the bed. You're mine for the night, pretty girl."

A little giddy, lips tingling, I followed him to the back of the jet where a shiny oak door opened to a room that looked straight out of a luxury hotel. Crystal glasses sat atop a granite bar. The cream carpet was lush under my feet, complementing the soft-beige walls. The bed was a king because of course this man needed everything to be the biggest and best. "Guessing these sheets are Egyptian cotton."

Bastian laughed behind me before he bent down to my neck and sucked my skin. That spot was one of my most sensitive ones, and I couldn't help but moan. When his arms came around me, I dragged his hands up my stomach and let him knead my boobs.

God, he was good with his hands, and his dick against my ass felt like one I would enjoy riding all night. I pushed my ass out, and he ground hard into it.

"You like teasing me, Morina?"

I smiled. The truth was I thought Bastian liked it, so I continued. "Honestly, I should probably stop the teasing. You're big but I don't know if you can keep it up and play all night."

He squeezed one breast harder. "And why is that?"

"Well, the men I've been with—"

"Were just boys, Morina."

I glanced back at him with faux innocent doe eyes. "But boys know how to play for a long time, Bastian."

"Men don't play. Now." His dark eyes changed. Gone was the fun. Gone was the toying around. Bastian Armanelli grabbed my attention by the throat and dropped the veil he kept up for everyone else.

Behind me stood the king of monsters, commander in chief of a vicious army. His stare raked over me, leaving a trail of heat over my neck, stealing my breath. "Bend over." He pushed at my back, and I fell forward, catching myself on the bed. My ass pointed right toward him, and he didn't wait in lowering my pants. He growled when he saw my red panties, but he yanked those down too.

I heard him rip a condom wrapper and waited for him to come up behind me and plow in.

He didn't.

I finally peered back to see what he was doing, and as soon as our eyes made contact, he brought his large hand down fast on my butt cheek. I cried out at the sting but pleasure shot through every nerve.

He shook his head. "Not enough."

His large hand, calloused and hard, came down on me again. I gasped out his name.

"I'll punish you every time you compare me to someone, *ragazza*," he growled out his warning as he kneaded my reddened flesh.

I whimpered at his touch, my pussy already clenching for more punishment. That edge most men wouldn't go over during a one-night stand? Bastian flew over it unapologetically, and my body loved him for it. This wasn't a kink I thought I'd ever have, and yet the words that flew from my mouth confirmed it. "Better make it a good enough punishment to remember then, daddy. I'm still not convinced you'll last through the night."

One hand slid to my hips and his other one pinched at my clit before he tested my entrance. White-hot pleasure raced through my blood faster than a riptide could take me under. "So wet. Are you sure you'll last?"

I bit my lip and moaned as he worked two fingers into me. I was drowning in him now, losing myself in the feel of him.

"Wet and tight. Guess it is just boys fucking you, huh?" I wasn't in any state to keep up the game. I was on the verge of unraveling into ecstasy. "That's right. Moan like my good girl," he murmured close to my ear. "Tell me who you really get wet for."

Before I could fall over the edge into oblivion, he pulled his fingers from me and reddened my ass again. "Morina, I expect my name on your lips when I ask for it."

I glared up at him, furious he held my orgasm hostage. "I could have got wet for a lot of men tonight."

He grabbed me by the jaw and held my gaze as he dragged a thumb over my bottom lip. "I'll fuck your mouth again for the way you talk. You'll take me again and again, love. You're so fucking good at it."

Then his cock plowed into me. I didn't have time to consider the spanking or the words. The sting on my ass along with the pleasure of his dick stretching me was too much.

The way my blood rushed to my ass and how my pussy clenched around his pulsing length left my head spinning. I could barely breathe, never mind speak.

Bastian fucked me like he owned me and the world. He'd been considerate of everyone else throughout the night, but here, he was different. I witnessed the unyielding domination where he didn't adjust for anyone.

That didn't stop me, though. I met him thrust for thrust, pushing back onto him, screaming his name over and over.

When I hit my high, he growled and rode it with me, yanking my hair back so my ass arched further into him.

Breathless, I fell against the sheets and disappeared into the darkness of ecstasy.

When I awoke, no idea how much later, a streak of sun peeked through the window. The plane was still and quiet, signaling we'd already landed. Bastian sat up in the bed, one tattooed arm behind his head as he stared out.

He didn't turn my way, so I wasn't sure how he knew I was awake when he said, "I'm happy we distracted you from the landing."

I shrugged away the warm feeling in my chest that he might care about something like that and grumbled, "Sure."

He nodded toward the window. "This is a place that hasn't been marred by man. I bought the island just to watch the sun rise. It's by far the most ridiculous thing I've ever done ⬚ and the best."

Soft. Gentle. His voice was back to smooth businessman.

I sat up and wrapped a sheet around myself. "Then we'd better get out onto the sand to really see it, right?"

His stare melted as he looked at me, and the smile that crossed his face wasn't at all the ruthlessly delicious man I'd had the night before.

I left my clothes on the floor and opted for wrapping the sheet around me as Bastian slipped on boxers to tell the pilot to lower the stairs.

The sun shined on the beach and made the sand sparkle. The water swayed in like it always did on every other beach, and I breathed the air I loved best. I'd grown up going near the ocean every day with my dad who'd come from the Caribbean and had a bit of Samoan mixed with his Haitian roots. Loving the ocean was in my blood. "I'll never think there's a more beautiful thing in the world than the beach."

"You may be right about that," Bastian murmured.

I knew he was staring at me as he said it—I saw him from the corner of my eye. It made me feel special enough to lean into him while watching the waves and the sun for a little while longer.

We made our way back to the plane and lost my sheet and his boxer briefs along the way.

The lovemaking we did then was softer, and my one-night stand rolled into another morning where I got lost in a make-believe world.

CHAPTER 6: MORINA

The low hum of the motor almost lulled me back to sleep.

Until the night's events flashed through my mind like a bad movie.

"Fuck." Eyes wide, I jumped up.

The man's big arm fell off my waist from my forward momentum. He'd been cuddling me?

Oh my God.

This wasn't just a bad movie. It was a trash one. Complete and utter garbage. I scooted off the bed and grabbed my top off the floor of the jet.

The jet!

"Morina, you really fucked up this time," I grumbled, scrabbling around the room completely naked looking for my bra. It was red. Of all the colors, how could I not find a red bra?

It had been a spur-of-the-moment addition to my outfit last night. I didn't fluff things, and I didn't dress for clubs, but I'd prepared for some extra fun after my horoscope said something along the lines of "pleasure awaits you and then death."

The horoscope had been right about that.

The aftermath I'd thought was my grandmother's. I'd spiraled. Completely willing to follow my self-destructive pain off the cliff that was Bastian Armanelli last night. Yet, I'm pretty sure this was the death of my self-respect.

I'd jumped on a jet with a questionable guy to get fucked into oblivion.

I had to admit, he'd done it. My daddy fetish was probably

at an all-time high right now. The way he'd commanded the room and taken everything he wanted from me but still managed to make me feel good. The man had known what I wanted more than I had.

Still, it didn't matter. I wasn't hanging out with him again. This was not a happily ever after waiting to happen.

This was a shitshow and a half. The walk of shame of the century.

A flight of shame.

As I shoved my boobs back into the dumb lingerie that should have fit much better than it did, his sleep-laced, gravelly voice sounded from behind me. "You're scrambling to get ready like we don't have to fly at least half an hour back to the airport."

I froze, trying to calibrate everything he was saying. I wasn't a morning person, especially after more than a few good rounds of fucking someone during the night and early morning.

"Shit!" I grabbed my panties and wriggled into them, then raced to the front of the jet before Bastian could stop me. Finding the pilot lounging at the front of the control area, I blurted, "Can you get us back to the airport in thirty? I have to get home. I think Chet's sending a limo for us. I need to get an Uber back to the hotel."

He almost fell out of his seat when he turned and saw me in underwear. His wide eyes popped up but within a second they'd flicked back down as Bastian appeared with a sheet and wrapped it around my body.

"Get us back soon, huh?" he said before turning me around and pushing me back toward the jet's private room.

I rolled my eyes. "Thanks for the sheet, I guess."

"Better to not scare my pilot," he murmured, his voice calm, calculating. Almost accommodating. This Bastian was nothing like the one last night who'd ordered me to bend over.

"I have to meet Linny back at the hotel," I explained.

"Do you know what time it is?"

"Well ..." I hesitated and glanced out a window. "No, but it feels like it's late."

"It feels, Morina?" He chuckled as we re-entered the private suite.

"Yes." I pulled the sheet tighter, thankful to be covered while I took time to locate my pants. I didn't need to though. They were folded on the bed where they hadn't been a minute ago.

I slid my pants and crop top on. "Well, what time is it?"

He glanced at his gold watch. "It's 8 a.m."

I hummed. "Okay, my checkout is at eleven. So, we'll be fine."

"I could have driven you home," he said, almost to himself.

"God, no," I blurted out. Rude. I winced. "I mean, it's just, I ... this was fun."

"Fun?" He chuckled and lifted a dark brow.

I studied him while he studied me.

Bastian Armanelli was a sight in the dark of night in a suit, a vision on a plane with that suit unbuttoned and unbuckled with me on my knees, and he was beautiful while watching the sunrise on an island with me standing in the sand beside him. Yet, Bastian with bed head and no shirt on first thing in the morning was a priceless work of art that would be sought after for centuries to come. Women would call him timeless with his sculpted muscles, strong jaw, full head of dark hair, and broad, strong shoulders. I wanted to lick every part of him.

Instead, I looked away. "Yes, it was fun. I don't think we could have had much more fun than we did, though, right?"

"You so sure?" Ah, there was the real man. He dropped the controlled mask he wore so well and his eyes grazed up and down my body. "For someone who rode my cock all night and screamed my name, you're sure in a hurry to get back to your regularly scheduled programming, *piccola ragazza*."

I took a deep breath, trying not to be tempted by the Italian falling from his lips. "Bastian, night's over. Can't call me that anymore."

He chuckled. "So, I shouldn't expect that *daddy* nickname to continue either?"

I face planted into my palm. "Oh, God. Please, let's not talk about the night."

"Why not?"

"Because it's over? I don't normally have to do this morning exchange." I straightened my clothes as the jet moved. "And we're headed back to civilization. You'll go back to where you came from, and I'll go back to where I came from."

"You're very territorial of this little hometown, aren't you?"

"Isn't everyone territorial of their home?"

He thought about it for a minute, and we let the plane take us high into the sky in those moments. The flight attendant didn't have the audacity to come back and tell us to put our seat belts on. Thankfully, the pilot seemed to navigate the skies well.

"I guess I'm territorial of what I own. A home could potentially be a part of that."

That was a weird sentiment. I didn't dive into it though. It wasn't my intention to know more about this man. I'd already learned way more than I normally liked to.

The feeling made me itch, made me antsy. Maybe skydiving wasn't such a bad idea ...

I probably did have some sort of commitment problem. I was faced with the sad fact as I sat there knowing I'd be stuck on the plane with him for another twenty minutes.

"So, I'm going to go sit in the seat up front," I said almost to myself as I stared down at nothing on my phone.

This was too awkward. I was being forced to basically have a morning-after with a one-night stand when all I wanted was a quick walk of shame home.

He didn't come to sit next to me. I heard him answer his phone and breathed a sigh of relief. If he was working, it meant we wouldn't have to have a morning-after conversation. I pulled up the horoscopes for the day and started reading mine.

"You're a Sagittarius," he murmured, standing over my shoulder.

I jumped and clicked my phone off immediately. "I like to read all of the signs. Not just mine."

He narrowed his eyes, then motioned for me to scoot over so he could take the aisle seat and I'd be at the window.

I glanced across the aisle, and he caught my subtle hint quick enough to take a seat there instead. "I'm guessing we're not exchanging numbers."

I fiddled with the edge of my crop top. "I don't mind."

I totally did. Normally, men didn't ask and I didn't disclose. That was the problem with a jet back home. This was too much time to fill space with unnecessary chitchat.

He smiled at me. "I think you do. It makes me want to ask again for some reason."

"That's pretty twisted, Bastian."

"I agree, especially because I'm in the business of forming connections that everyone feels comfortable with."

I hummed but didn't push further. Bastian was in another business dimension that I was sure would kill the cat if it was curious enough.

I'd met my limit with him.

I'd crossed enough limits too.

The plane began its descent, and my breathing started to

normalize.

"Thanks for the flight to that little unknown island." I nodded out the window.

"Thanks for watching the sunrise with me," he said back. "It's a different type of experience next to a beautiful woman who appreciates it."

"I think most women would appreciate a flight and a sunrise, Bastian." It'd be absurd for him to think I was the only one.

"You stare at the ocean like a mermaid who belongs there, little girl. It's a different experience with you."

"No, I don't."

"You don't?" He crossed his arms over his chest and tilted his head as he looked me over. "How would you know? You look at yourself in the mirror every time you're at a beach?"

I chewed my cheek, trying to hold back a snide remark. "For someone in the business of connecting with people and making them feel comfortable, you sure don't have a way with me."

"We connect differently. That's for sure."

I rolled my eyes. "Well, that connection is about to be over."

He didn't say anything back. We disappeared into our own phones, our own lives, and our own priorities.

CHAPTER 7: MORINA

I made it back to the hotel in time to sit with Linny in the limo home. We slept mostly, considering we'd both had long nights.

Once back in Coralville, my grandma wanted to go for a walk on the beach. We wandered down there as often as we could. Sometimes daily. Sometimes only weekly. Yet, we enjoyed each time all the same.

"Grandma, I'd feel better if I could spread your ashes into the wind or something instead of keeping them in the house."

"Well, I'm the one who's going to be dead in a few weeks. So, shouldn't I get to pick?" she shot back as her wiry gray hair flapped in the wind as we walked down the coastline.

I took in a deep breath of salty air and tried to stay calm at that inevitability. "It's not good for anyone's spirit to keep you locked up in an urn above a cupboard in your old kitchen."

"Who says?" She looked up at me. Somehow, she'd shrunk in the past ten years, and now I towered over her. I'd always been tall but so had she.

Then lung cancer had taken over, and her posture had suffered. The last doctor's appointment wasn't any news to us. She'd refused treatment months ago and the cancer spread rapidly. She wanted to die in her home, then have her ashes sit there.

With me. Because I would be living there still.

I shuddered at the thought.

"Well, I guess I say." I folded my hands in front of myself and squeezed them together. It'd taken me years to stand up for myself like that. I'd been a quiet little girl, always running off to the water and beach, a loner who didn't really get along with anyone after my parents had died in a car accident. My grandmother had raised me ever since and had let me disappear into my own mind until high school.

Something had shifted in her then, and she'd pushed every limit I had, debating with me and not letting me back down.

"Ah! That's what I wanted to hear." She smirked. "You telling me you don't want my ashes?"

"No! Of course I don't want them. It's weird. Your spirit might hover and feel trapped or something." My stomach rolled with the feeling, and I twisted the beaded bracelets on my wrists. They were a reminder to feel every feeling and go with the flow.

Her cackle came out like a witch's. With her black flowy dress and frizzy hair, she probably looked like one to the little kid who ran past and jumped at her laugh.

She laughed harder at their fear but didn't taunt them. "Fine, Mo. I won't haunt you, I guess. Throw me wherever you want to."

"I'm not just throwing you out."

"Oh, I'm dirt at that point anyway." She waved me off. "If I have a spirit, it'll be long gone. I'm going to fly up into space and go check out those other planets you always talk about. Maybe, I'll come to you in a dream and tell you all about them."

I couldn't help but grin at that. "I'd like a visit in a dream."

"Just not in the middle of the night in the kitchen, right? When you're pouring yourself a glass of milk and I creep up behind you?" Her shoulder bumped mine, and I wrapped my arm around her small frame as we walked in sync together.

Maybe it was the waves at our feet or the wind in our hair, but I felt at peace with it all. We'd done the crying when the doctors had told us. We'd been through the pain. Or at least I had.

Grandma didn't seem to fear death. She'd just shrugged and said she was surprised she'd lived this long. The doctor had mumbled the same thing.

The woman had numerous lives. I kept to myself when I saw her meeting with people dressed like hitmen and didn't ask many questions. I was nosy, but I wasn't stupid when it came to my grandmother. Nobody outright said she was ruthless, but she could snap at you quickly if you weren't careful. She'd outlasted her husband, brothers, and even her younger sister. To me, as a child, she'd been invincible. But now …

"Any other wishes?"

She stopped and turned to look at the body of water. The Gulf of Mexico reached out across the horizon, covering half the world in its melodic and chaotic movements. "You're going to be tested, child. I've protected you and shielded you from what I probably shouldn't have."

I took a deep breath. She wasn't saying anything I didn't know. I knew I'd lived a sheltered life. We had lived humbly, but I think her and Grandpa's savings had kept her afloat. For me, I'd have my food truck and her little house. I'd be just fine.

"Just remember, when the time comes, you'll have to make choices. Make the right ones, the ones I laid out for you, and you'll be just fine." She patted my hand. "Most of all, I wish for you to stay strong in your views, embrace the oddities, and be happy."

I took a deep breath. "Happiness is on the surfboard and in the truck for me."

"I don't know if my passing will allow for just that anymore. You'll have a house, Morina, and you'll have bills and the men in this city—"

I snorted. "I don't care about all the men."

"Well, you should. You can't enjoy life without someone, Mo."

I rolled my eyes because my grandma loved to matchmake. "When exactly did Grandpa pass?"

She scoffed. "That Irish fool wasn't someone to enjoy life with. He passed from the heart attack that he had coming for years."

"So, you've lived without someone for a very long time. I can too."

"No. I had your mother, and I had you."

Her statement shot through my heart. I couldn't let her see that though. "I'll be fine."

"A man would be good for you."

"I don't need to deal with the men in this town. They're all struggling for power and measuring ..." I trailed off.

"Their dicks?" She raised an eyebrow at me. "I don't know how I ended up where I am, but I can tell you, it's all they're doing. Try to remember to enjoy the small things. And ignore the big dicks."

I laughed at her advice and that night, I let one or two tears fall at the idea that I wouldn't have her to walk with soon.

Our time was running out. I was okay with it. She'd molded me to be. But I'd miss her. I'd miss my carefree life.

The water lulled me to sleep, like I belonged to it. I hoped I always would.

CHAPTER 8: MORINA

Like the ocean rocking me to sleep, the sun's warm rays nudged me awake. I watched it rise as I carried my board to the water. I nodded at two of the guys I always met early at the surf. We didn't talk much. We were there to wake up with the water, not with other humans.

The water washed over me as I dove in. It pushed my wild hair away, naturally smoothing it back the way the wind couldn't.

The waves approached, and I ducked one after the other. Into the breeze, then into the deep. Air and water. Air and water. A rhythm the ocean created or maybe the wind did. The sun warmed us as we took our first wave, and the ocean cooled us as we fell back in before we hit the sand.

The water wasn't a place I went to think.

It was a place I went to escape and be held hostage at the same time. I needed this. I was addicted to it but it was one of the only places I felt free.

As the air got warmer and warmer, the town came to life and I rode in my last wave.

"You done for the day?" Bradley asked, not that he cared at all other than he wanted me to make him a smoothie soon.

"I'll get the truck open soon. You can't be that hungry." Bradley was about my age and had been a loyal customer since I started working the truck.

"Not like the smoothie is going to curb my appetite anyway."

"Then go to the cafe down the street." I knew he wouldn't.

He scrunched his nose at me. "And deal with the line? Nah."

I rolled my eyes and wrung out my hair as best I could. "You'd wait in line all day for me."

He eyed me up and down in my bikini. Although I could have lost the extra weight on my ass, he stared at it every chance he got. "You bet I would." He winked.

I chuckled. We had a good friendship. Comfortable. And when we were both single, we'd indulge every now and then. With a full head of dark hair and a buff body, Bradley was a good amount of fun. The butterflies weren't there, and I'm sure his heart wasn't connected to mine in a passionate way, but we scratched one another's itches when we wanted.

Except this last week, no one could seem to scratch the itch the way a certain man in a jet had. "Give me ten, and I'll have a Pink Princess ready for you."

"Can you consider changing the name of that?" he yelled after me as I rushed away. I saw a few people idling by the truck, which meant they wanted a morning fix too.

It wasn't the norm.

I usually had time to open and get dressed in some of the wrinkled clothing I stashed in a ball somewhere in the truck. I waved at a couple of guys I knew, one was a surfer, and then did a double take when I saw a black Rolls-Royce idling in the parking lot.

One I'd seen before. One I'd ridden in just a week before.

My stomach flip-flopped and a wave of queasiness followed. Not good. Sweating, I avoided the itch to duck down and hide.

As embarrassing as it was to admit, I actually gasped at the sight of both Dante and Bastian exiting the vehicle. Tall, built, and all straight lines in their black suits. Their shoes shone like they were made of diamonds, and as my eyes trailed up, their faces didn't disappoint either.

Both faces I knew.

Both faces I thought I'd never see again.

Bastian smiled like he'd heard my gasp. My mouth snapped shut.

I scoffed and rolled my eyes but not before witnessing how when he smiled it didn't really meet his eyes. Not the way it had that night. His face had held youth and some sort of humor and connection with me on that jet. I'd felt like we belonged in the same universe.

But now, he was devoid of any emotion.

He could have been on Jupiter, light years away, with the look he'd plastered on his face. Then his eyes cut away from me and I saw him scan the beach, like he was making mental notes.

My grandmother dealt with men like that. She said it was business, and the part of me that was happier being in the dark let it slide.

Those men walking toward my food truck were nothing but bad news. Bad news and a one-night stand I wanted to forget.

Instead, he walked toward me, more lethal in the sunlight, like the night had cloaked his danger. He was ready to haunt me in the daylight rather than my dreams.

As I opened the metal back door into my little sanctuary, I didn't bother grabbing the ball of clothes in the corner. It was hot enough that I could make smoothies in a bikini anyway. It might be one of the last warm days, even with the chill in the air. The seasons were changing, just as my life would be soon.

I threw some strawberries, yogurt, pineapple, and ice into the mixer as I leaned back to see who was in the window. My first customer was an older surfer who switched up his drink every other day. "Jonah, what can I get you?"

"What are you making there?"

"The Pink Princess for Bradley. He likes them prissy."

Jonah chuckled and turned to wink at Bradley who flipped him off. Then he shrugged and nodded toward the mixer. "I guess I like them prissy too. Add another to the blender."

I dropped in all the ingredients and threw in two bags of my spice. I ground up cinnamon sticks, both chia and flax seeds, agave powder, and other nutritional additions that added a pop of flavor. After adding a cube of frozen wheatgrass, I pressed the button.

As a longer line formed and I took down more orders, I spotted the suits moving slowly toward my truck, waiting their turn. Both of them scoped out the area like it was for some sort of sale. They'd soon learn this place was priceless, owned only by the water and the land. The seagulls may have had a few pieces of it too.

I handed another Pink Princess to the next customer and grabbed my hanging chalkboard sign as the beautiful men descended upon my food truck.

Suddenly my little window was letting in too much sun.

Scribbling a few additions to my chalkboard, I didn't look up as I said, "What can I get you?"

Normally when I got a newcomer, I'd welcome them and offer the list of special drinks, but men dressed so nicely where the sand dirtied you up and made you one with the beach irked me.

Especially when one of them was a man I'd slept with and hoped to never see again.

"I don't know." Bastian's hair curled every which way. Did he style it to look that good or had he been born with that rich color and perfect wave? "You don't have a menu written out yet for me to choose from."

I shrugged as I kept writing. "Well, most everyone got the Pink Princess smoothie today."

"The owner of this company probably wouldn't like to know that the girl he hired isn't giving customers her full attention or all the options."

"The owner of this truck is just fine with it. She thinks guys in suits who come and demand all the options are sort of rude," I deadpanned. Then I leaned through the window enough so they would both have to step back. Hanging the sign to the left, I pointed theatrically. "Oh, look, a menu!"

"Pink Princess, Kiss of a Rainbow, and Black-Suit Pricks?" Bastian hesitated on the last one. His smile after was swift, though, like he had a sense of humor after all.

That smile dimmed everything else on the beach that day. It was deadly, brilliant, and quite frankly, the most beautiful thing I'd seen besides the ocean water. His dark eyes sparkled just like it when he smiled, but the darkness hid something deep down that I knew I didn't want to find.

"Pick your poison, boys." I folded my arms over my chest, and his eyes flicked up and down my body.

"Morina." He said my name, and it sounded like it had in the plane right after we'd slept together. He'd pushed my hair from my cheek and murmured it softly like I was the only woman in the world.

Maybe I had been that night.

This was reality though, far from sunrises and private jets. And he wasn't supposed to be in my reality.

At all.

"How did you find me, and why did you even look?" I glared at him.

His eyes widened, clearly shocked with my question. "I

didn't come looking for you. I'm looking for the owner of this truck."

"That's me," I threw back.

"No. That's impossible. Maribel owns this truck."

My grandmother's name rolled off his tongue with ease but it hit me like a bullet. "Maribel Bailey is my grandmother. She gave this to me."

His gaze whipped to Dante who immediately started tapping his phone screen.

"What's going on?"

But Bastian was already shaking me off and dismissing me. "It doesn't matter. We'll handle it," he growled.

"Oh, daddy can't share anything with little old me now?" The question shot out before I had time to think about it.

His eyes widened, and his jaw flexed.

I stepped back, suddenly realizing that Bastian and I were not in the territory of playful taunts anymore. Our realities were mixing, and they weren't ones to be toyed with.

I turned to the blender, not giving them time to choose anymore. "Smoothies it is."

"Tell me, is it sanitary for you to be making these in a bikini?" he asked softly.

I can't help wanting to reply, "I'm not making them in a bikini. I'm making them in a blender."

He couldn't come to my place of business, throw around my grandmother's name with no explanation, and then on top of everything else, comment on my attire. I wasn't good at hiding my emotions. It was the Sagittarius in me. I cleared my throat and my frustration away when he didn't respond. "If you're so concerned, go elsewhere."

"See, that's the interesting thing about this place." Bastian leaned into the window of the food truck, put his elbows on it like he owned it, like he owned everything. Just with that movement, I knew he was important. Someone my grandma probably knew, and someone I didn't want to know at all. "You're the only food truck for three miles up and down this beach. We had on file that was your grandmother's doing. Tell me, how did you and her manage that?"

I didn't like to admit that I was naïve. I didn't really consider myself flighty either, but his words were a kick to the stomach and a reminder that I was. I never really thought much of it. I'd taken over the food truck at fifteen. I'd worked it nights, weekends, and summers during high school. When I graduated, I'd taken it on fully.

Business had always been good enough.

"Haven't you ever considered that, *piccola ragazza*?"

"Stop with the *little girl*." I sounded just like that as I said it.

He chuckled, and I spun back to make the smoothie. These two men had waited for the line to go before them. They wanted to be last, which meant they wanted more from me than a smoothie.

Bastian would never get more from me ever again.

I didn't enjoy one-night stands coming back to terrorize me.

I poured blueberries into the blender, spices that would turn the banana and ice black, and, just as Bastian started to speak, hit the power button.

I smirked at him and winked. His response was to lift an eyebrow.

Welcome to Mo's Food Truck, jerk. Here, I rule.

He looked toward the sky and sucked on his teeth. It gave me a good look at his strong neck—at how tense it was—and the little bit of black ink that peeked out from his shirt. I'd run my hands over those tattoos while he'd dragged a finger over mine just a week ago. What a reminder that he wasn't all stuck-up suit but something more underneath.

Once the whirring morphed to a soft hum, I knew I had to turn off the machine. I grabbed two Styrofoam cups and took the big pitcher off the stand to pour the contents. The fruit complemented the spice in this mixture well. I'd made it a million times before but I usually called it Midnight on the Beach. Today, I would add the little twist just for them. "You need to be calm or energized today, Dante?"

"Does it matter?" Bastian grumbled.

Yet, his friend behind him with the piercing green eyes responded quickly, "We need energy."

"Well, then. I guess Mr. Difficult will have what Dante's having." I grabbed a citrus oil with a touch of lavender and shook in a couple drops to top off their drinks. I handed over the cups and straws.

I was about to say the total when Bastian laid a fifty on the counter between us. "You own this truck then?"

I stared at the money, not at all sure I wanted that big of a tip. I had men come in and out of my little beach town all the time. They threw money around like it meant something, like they could attach all the strings in the world to it too. "So what if I do?"

"I need to know if your grandma has partnerships with other businesses in the area." He nudged the money my way.

I narrowed my eyes at him, rang him up, and pushed the change back his way. "I don't have information for you."

"Oh, come on. You're sitting here in the only food truck in town, practically the only small business if I'm being honest, and you don't know that she's made some deals?"

"I don't make a lot of money here, Bastian," I said softly,

my eyes darting between him and his accomplice now.

A seagull cawed overhead, and the water crashing on the beach sounded much louder than before.

"You could make more if you answered my questions." His voice was calming now, almost hypnotic, urging me to go ahead and obey. He pushed the extra change my way.

I wasn't that naïve.

I shook my head. "I don't want your money."

He narrowed his eyes at me, and I could see him clenching his jaw. Then he slowly unwrapped the straw, never taking that gaze from mine. He dipped it into his drink and brought it to his lips. Full lips. Ones that wrapped around the straw and sucked in my creation.

I shouldn't have been turned on. He looked like a stuffy god, a ruler who needed to unwind.

It had me curious, nervous, fearful, and turned on all at the same time.

All things I shouldn't be feeling. The one feeling missing that should have been there was regret.

He cleared his throat, and I jumped, lost in my own thoughts and focused directly on his mouth. It quirked up before he immediately let it drop again. "Your shake is really good, Morina."

"It's out of this world." Dante stepped around him and put his large hand out as if he wanted to be friends. "Nice to see you again. Wasn't aware we were going to. Your name is Morina, right?"

I narrowed my eyes. "Why, Dante? Find something in my file that is questionable?"

"Your file says you reside in the town over and have no relation to Maribel."

"My mother was quirky with birth certificates. My dad's

the only name on mine."

He lifted a shoulder and turned to Bastian. "Can't expect me to know that."

"Cade would have."

"Cade's had his head in a computer since he was born. I was fighting for our country. Want to weigh the two?"

"Not really. Considering my brother can start a war in 2.5 seconds on a computer, there's not much to weigh," Bastian shot back.

Dante laughed, so easy in his confidence even when it was being threatened. "You're right. That guy is chaos waiting to erupt."

"Tell me about it," Bastian grumbled.

Dante's green eyes cut to me again, and he lifted his shake with a smirk. "Guess we're going to be getting to know each other much better, Ms. Bailey. We can start with what you put in this shake. Is that lavender, citrus, and chia seeds?"

I heard the passion in his voice and saw the blatant disregard he had for his boss when he had a question about said passion. Bastian scowled behind him.

"You're right," I said. "I hide a lot of good stuff in there. I'm hoping you get an energy boost from the citrus but that the lavender keeps you calm."

"Oh, I already know I will. Tastes like the right mix," he mumbled. "I'll be back for more for sure."

I laughed at the way he vigorously nodded at his drink. I loved seeing people happy with something I created.

Bastian tapped his friend on the shoulder and Dante immediately stepped aside as he nodded to me and walked off toward the car. Good, they were going. Hopefully only Dante would come back while they were in town.

Once he was out of ear shot though, Bastian dashed

my hopes. "You know something about this town and I have business in it, Morina."

"Well, it's a small town. Everybody knows something. Ask anyone."

"I want to ask you though. I have business with your grandmother. You seem to have figured out a little trick, and I need to understand why."

"What do you do, Mr. ...? Armanelli was it?" I waited for him to confirm.

"You know you can call me Bastian."

"Sure it can't be daddy anymore?" I couldn't hold back. If he was going to throw *little girl* in my face, I was going to bite back. I turned and grabbed the large pitcher to take it to the sink.

"Oh, it still can, *piccola ragazza*," he growled low enough that I almost didn't hear.

My body reacted immediately. Jesus. He jumped from gentleman to alpha male so fast. I knew he was dangerous and into something questionable now more than ever. Still, I was stupid enough to find him attractive.

I flipped my hair over my shoulder and glared at him. "No thanks. I'll go with Bastian."

We stared one another down. Maybe this would be the farewell battle, the one where he left me alone after.

Instead, he asked, "Care to share why you're so defensive?"

"I don't like you insinuating I've done something shady with my food truck. I've been here for years. My family ran this truck, and it's been a staple of the area. There's nothing odd about it."

"Except that you're the only one."

"We don't make much money. Maybe people decided they wanted to make more in an actual building. The beach isn't for everyone."

He hummed low like my explanation didn't make much sense. It did to me because that's what had happened. I made just enough to get by because there wasn't much overhead. I'd inherited the thing. We kept with tradition and this was part of it. Might not have been the smartest idea, but it didn't matter.

"I have to clean up and get ready for the day."

"Hmm. Finally getting into work attire?" His gaze drifted behind me to where most of my clothes were together with a lot of other knickknacks.

Suddenly, I felt the urge to clean and that infuriated me. I couldn't control my eyebrows slamming down. "If you think your smoothie is contaminated, I'm happy to take it back."

As I reached for it, he backed up immediately. Ah, he liked it as much as Dante. "I'm keeping the smoothie."

"It could be full of germs," I singsonged.

"It's surprisingly good ... for a black-suit smoothie. Nice even."

I smirked at him. "Am I supposed to say you're surprisingly nice even with that black suit you're wearing now? Because I won't. This meeting has not been enjoyable."

He finally stepped back, like he realized he'd overstayed his welcome. His shoes sank into the sand a little, looking completely unnatural in it. "I'll see you around."

"Please don't," I grumbled once he was out of earshot. I turned and washed out the blender. I scrubbed it harder than I should have but it was the only way to take out my frustration. The man was an entitled piece of work. What business did he have in this area?

He probably wanted to open a smoothie shop down the street.

I knew a shark when I saw one—in the water or out of it.

They snuck up on you, circled and circled, watching for your weakness. I wasn't giving him any information though.

I spun back around and made myself a smoothie. I poured way too many strawberries in with strawberry yogurt and added some strawberry syrup too. My smoothie didn't have to be nutritious. It was feeding my mental health instead, right?

I let the machine whir as I stared out at the beach. One of the guys lifted his smoothie to me in a cheers motion and I smiled.

This was my town.

My beach.

My oasis. And no one could take that away.

CHAPTER 9: BASTIAN

She was supposed to be older, or more mature.

Not my one-night stand.

Jesus, Morina looked damn good on the beach in her natural environment.

Not that it mattered. She was dealing with a different side of me now. This was the last place I needed to tie up my father's illegal business doings. I'd been at it for years.

The Armanelli Family, the most infamous Italian Mob in the United States, was almost legal.

I knew Miami and this small town was my last loose end, the frayed thread that I needed to tighten up or cut off. Maribel had been dabbling on both sides of the fence. She paid for protection from an Irish family to keep that food truck up and running. Then, she'd partnered with my Italian family, my father mostly, for the oil company.

Two partnerships with opposing families meant she was fucking one of us.

Morina knew something.

She had to. Except given the way her eyes fell, that deep-blue sapphire suddenly a little misty and confused about her grandmother, I wasn't sure she did.

My one-night stand in Miami was turning out to be a fucking problem.

"What do we have wrong here?" I asked Dante in the car later that day.

"It's just a blip on the radar. We're scoping out the city and

Maribel, not a food truck. We'll take care of it if necessary."

"This little town connects to oil terminals, the farms, and the corporate area, Dante. That company brings in millions, and if the majority voter is dabbling in different partnerships, that's a problem. My father always invested here, not the company itself."

"Ah, your father maybe liked Maribel then."

I laughed at that ridiculous statement. "He was a fucking prick who loved no one but his money. We both know it. You remember my mother. If he couldn't love her enough to stop doing the shit he was, then he could love no one."

Dante didn't respond to that. He knew my mother. She'd showered the world in Italian love with her cooking, her singing, her passion for life. My father stared at her like she was beautiful, but he walked past her time and time again to go kill a man, to make a deal, to continue building his empire of wealth.

And he'd dragged me along with him.

I remembered the first time I'd asked to stay home with Mother instead of go out on business with him. He'd pulled a gun from his suit jacket and told me to be the man he'd raised me to be.

It was just how Mario worked, how he'd built us up from a young age. Mario Armanelli groomed me to be ruthless, forceful, and greedy.

I tried to be the complete opposite.

I stared out the window at the palm trees. I felt the warm sun that leaked through them. This town was quaint, understated, and probably underutilized. Still, I'd been providing protection and partnership to so many over the years based on my father's illegal doings. I wouldn't do that anymore. Maribel would have to let me take over her shares and run a clean business or I'd pull my protection.

The mindset was one I didn't enjoy particularly. Allies were always good to have, but I needed them to be legitimate. My father had dirtied our hands time and time again. My family deserved to run everything legally, within the law, and still maintain the level of financial stability we'd always had. We'd earned that through years and years of hell.

I rubbed my chin. "We go to the source then."

"Maribel only wanted virtual meetings because of her health."

"Not doable, Dante. You and I both know that. I can't read her when she's on a screen."

He sighed and texted away.

We planned a surprise visit for that night and pulled up to a house very near to the coast, close enough that the older woman could make it there by foot if she had the mobility.

We exited the car onto a dirt driveway. The plants around it weren't enormous nor was the home. It didn't seem as though the person who lived here was doing so lavishly or hoarding money I didn't know about.

Her porch had been painted white fairly recently, and as I stepped up onto the wood, it felt sturdy enough, even where the winds and the rain could potentially ruin it.

"What the hell are you doing on my porch?" an older woman with deep wrinkles croaked at me through a screen door.

"We have business to discuss." I pulled at my tie, seeing her brow furrow.

"I only discussed business with your father, Bastian." She sighed like she'd known I was coming.

"I haven't introduced myself," I said as I took in her stance. She hadn't opened the door yet, and I would wait for the invite before I entered.

"No need to. We both know who each other are. You look like your father. And I'm sure I don't look anything like how he didn't describe me. I say didn't because we all know he didn't drop my name to you once."

I schooled my facial features as she waited and studied me.

She smiled when she realized I wouldn't let anything slip in my expressions. I'd trained myself to never give a thing away. "I'm thinking I've met my match in you because your father would have started talking already. Even so, I just said it and I'll say it again—I only discussed business with your father." She smoothed the white nightgown she was wearing. The woman wasn't at all concerned about her appearance. She brushed away my visit, lessening the importance by focusing on her pajamas.

"My father's dead, Maribel." Her gaze shot up, and she scanned the scenery behind me. "You know I ordered a hit on him."

I molded myself at the time of his death. I called that shot to kill him and watched him bleed out, watched the beginning of our sins leak away with him.

She scoffed but glanced past me to my security. Dante was a good friend, a man who I trusted to stand by me while I made house calls like the one I was making now.

The old woman's eyes narrowed. "My granddaughter is here. Don't say a word about my shares in the oil company. You got it? And I'll sell them to you fair and square. You keep my city running. That's the deal."

I hummed and rocked on my heels. I met her stare, and we watched each other with the legacies and traditions flying between us, weighing us down, ripping at our trust in each other.

"I won't bend on that. You make good on this town,

Bastian."

"You paid some Irish to have that food truck on the beach, not us."

She scoffed. "One time. It keeps my granddaughter happy. It wasn't a slight to your family. Not like what your father's done to mine time and time again. Now, let me get dressed." She slammed the door on both of us.

Dante chuckled behind me. "Not our warmest welcome."

"Fuck me," I grumbled. Morina hadn't known.

Shit.

"This is getting more complicated by the second," I muttered.

"We got eyes on the place in case she's planning anything," Dante told me.

"She's not." That wasn't what I was worried about. "She doesn't trust us because my father probably fucked her over."

"Mario wasn't nice to anyone unless he had the motivation. He did what he had to do in order to get what he wanted for our family."

"You don't make alliances that way. Sometimes it takes family sacrifice for the good of all your partners."

"I wouldn't argue with that." Dante cracked his knuckles, and I glanced back at him. His light eyes contrasted with his bronzed skin and the tattoos across his neck. "We'll have to keep levelheaded. I've heard about her through the underground channels."

I checked my watch as the fall breeze picked up. It wasn't enough to keep us cool in the Florida air, the humidity weighing everything down with it suffocating warmth. "I need a vacation."

"You're never going to get one."

"Why not?"

Dante didn't respond. He knew as well as I did that the head of the Mafia didn't ever get to rest. That wasn't an option.

I'd never had one to begin with.

The door swung open again, but instead of an old woman, there stood the young one. Morina had the exact same shape of eyes as her grandmother. My mind didn't calculate fast enough, but I knew the end result was going to be one I didn't want.

"You've got to be kidding. Did you follow me here?" Her voice came out high pitched.

I took a step back with her statement. "I'm here to see your grandmother."

"My grandmother?" she screeched. "You need to leave right now."

I ignored her. "My father never mentioned Maribel had a granddaughter."

"Probably because Maribel and I don't tell suits like you our family business."

Her grandmother hollered from down the hall to let us all in. I straightened a cuff link while she decided whether she wanted to obey. "We're coming in either way, Morina."

Her eyes narrowed, and I knew a snide comment was about to whip out of her mouth. "I'm definitely regretting the decision I made last week now."

That would make two of us, piccola ragazza. I didn't say it out loud. There was no need to fan the fire.

She backed away as I stepped in and took in the quaint home. A few plants lined the entryway, and straight ahead, in the kitchen, a scuffed wooden table told me that Maribel was hiding her wealth. If my family knew, then most cartels, gangs, and other families did too.

Yet, Maribel hid it from someone in plain sight and that was her granddaughter.

Morina waved at the table. "Well, take a seat or don't. Grandma will be out in a minute."

"We don't intend to stay long," I mumbled, hoping she'd leave. I didn't want to discuss business in front of her.

"You intend to take our money, don't you?" She tilted her head, her big eyes narrowed on me.

"What?"

"You're here to collect on the town's payment for protection and allegiance to you, right?"

"I don't think that's a conversation you and I should be having."

"My grandmother's dying, Bastian." Her voice was quiet, whispering the pain of love for someone I'd never felt. She dragged a fingernail on the table and then over some beaded bracelets she wore. "She's leaving everything to me. Including her debts and alliances. So that sort of is the conversation we should be having considering I'll be paying you soon."

I glanced at Dante who pinched the bridge of his nose and then ran a hand through his short curly hair.

"She's smarter than I give her credit for, you know," Grandma Maribel said as she appeared in the doorway. The woman had changed into a black dress with intricate pleating and layers.

Dante and I scanned her immediately. She most definitely was carrying but I wasn't sure exactly where—I doubted Dante was either. "When I said I was sick, I meant very sick. Mo will take over business proceedings whether she likes it or not."

"I don't like it." The younger woman's eyebrows pulled together as she sighed and ran a hand through her long wavy hair. "I didn't ask to be a part of the ridiculous—"

"No one asks for their lives, Mo," her grandmother cut her off. "I didn't ask for it either. You inherit it and you run with it."

"I'm not made for"—Morina waved at me and Dante—"dealing with suits. I just want to run the food truck and ..."

She stared at her grandma. Maribel's eyes glistened, and she rubbed her chest. Her other hand held the back of one of the wooden chairs so tightly her knuckles turned white. "It's only a few other loose ends, Mo."

"I'm sorry, Grandma. I'm sorry. It'll be fine." Morina went to her side and put an arm around her. They stood with their heads bowed for a moment.

I was born into the business. I didn't have the love they shared. Yet, I understood Morina's struggle. I'd never wanted the business handed to me either.

I'd taken what was mine in the end though. I accepted that I'd been born into a life of sin and greed. I figured I'd change what I couldn't live with and learn to live with what I couldn't change.

I cleared my throat, and Morina glared up at me. "You've done this to us."

I crossed my arms and studied her. "Your disrespect and accusations aren't exactly the way to start a welcome meeting."

"You're not here to be welcomed." Morina leaned her head on her grandma's shoulder and dragged her eyes over both of us. "You don't want a friend. You want a business transaction."

I rocked back on my heels. She wasn't wrong. Yet, most of my father's business partners had taken kindly to our partnerships with no need to force their hands. I'd made a lot of alliances where my father couldn't because I was strategic in dealing with families.

I treated everyone as one of our own.

Even if they weren't.

"I'm under the impression you'd both like to continue a partnership with the Armanelli family."

"Do we have a choice?" Morina raised an eyebrow.

Her grandmother chuckled and patted her cheek. "You'll be fine when I'm gone, I think. So much fire in you, even when you let the wind and water take your mind away half the time."

I didn't understand what she was alluding to. Nor did I care. Morina needed to be present and available for business proceedings and that was it. Outside of that, I didn't care what the girl did. "Just make sure you hold up your end of the bargain, Maribel. I don't know what's going on with that food truck."

"It will be done with. Everything else will stay the same if that's done with, right? When I'm gone, Mo will need protection too." Maribel raised her eyebrows, hopeful.

"I don't need protection," Morina pushed back. "No one cares about me. I'm secure enough with the sheriff and deputies around town."

Grandma Maribel coughed and the sound almost shook the room. Instead of clearing her throat, though, the congestion rattled around and caused a fit of sorts. She gasped for air as Mo pulled out the seat for her to take at the table. Her skin grayed, paler than before.

She gripped her granddaughter's hand and wheezed out, "No one's safe around here once I'm gone."

Morina glared at us like the coughing fit was our fault and rubbed Maribel's back.

Dante spoke up from behind me. "Can I get a cup of water for you, Maribel?"

Pointing toward one of the pine cupboards, she nodded. Dante always wanted a balanced atmosphere. He said when the energy of the room was off, explosive things happened.

In a weird way, I agreed with him. "We'll secure the area, Maribel. Same stipulations."

"It won't be enough," she murmured and that one soft

comment had me sitting down at the table.

I needed all the information if she expected me to help her. "What won't be enough?"

"Oh, your father knew as well as I did, once we were gone, you'd all have to fend for yourselves. You're fine. Mo, here, she's as flippant as a hurricane. She'll go full-speed one day and slow the next." Morina tried to argue, but Maribel pulled her wrinkled hand from Morina's and shushed her. "You know it's true. I don't care. We've always loved that about you. It's why I paid the Irish for your food truck area. It was the one thing that could keep your attention."

"Fuck me," I grumbled, and Dante sighed.

"What?" Morina whispered.

"You can't mix allies like that," I said, my voice ominous.

"It wasn't meant to be found out." She shrugged. "Just a little payment for one food truck to stay open."

"They respect you I'm guessing," I offered, my mind working it all out.

"Of course. They do it for me because I'm old. I have that power. I'm meaner than Mo too. I'll chop a hand off—"

"Grandma!"

"Oh, child. It's just a hand!" Dante chuckled but I watched Mo. She wasn't laughing. Her blue eyes widened to saucers, and I knew right then she wasn't made to lead an area of mine. She wasn't like the women in the mob. She was young, fun-loving, and completely naïve to violence. "Anyway," Maribel went on, "with me gone, she goes into witness protection, dies, or ..."

The silence stretched, and I let it hang in the air waiting for her request. I was used to discomfort and the absence of noise. It heightened everyone's awareness, made them really think about their intentions and contemplate their gravity.

"You could have her marry one of your top guys for a

while. Put her in a position of power so they fear harming her enough."

"Are you kidding me?" Morina stood abruptly as the question whispered out of her. Then it bellowed out. "Are you kidding me, Grandma?"

"Oh, it would only be for a few years," replied Maribel. "It'd save your life!"

I raised my hands before either of them got too angry or too worked up. "I won't put my guys in that sort of position." I shook my head. Her hand in marriage wasn't an option.

"What sort of position?" Morina asked, ready to unleash her anger on anyone.

"Don't, *piccola ragazza*." My voice cut through the air before I had time to contain the outburst. "I'm saving you from an arranged marriage."

Instead of her shrinking in fear, she seethed, lifting her chin. "Your men would be happy to have me."

I looked her up and down. "My men want women, not girls. You're too young for most of our tastes."

Her jaw dropped. She paced up to me as if ready to slap me. And I found I wanted it. The way her fury boiled over into my space and burned me in just the right way had to be wrong. Still, I wanted her.

Shaking her head after a minute of us staring one another down, she paced away to the window and glared outside. "What planet is in retrograde right now? There has to be something off today."

Her grandma groaned, and I heard Dante shift behind me. "You must be a Sagittarius."

She smiled at him. "That I am. And you must be a Leo. I get along with Leos."

"I think we're going to get along just fine." Dante smiled

like she was right. Was she? Did I need to research the damn signs now?

My neck muscles tensed, like a fucking feral dog wanting to claim her all of a sudden. "We'll be in touch. Maribel, I expect this to be put in your final will. I don't want anything left out that will cause me to do anything illegal."

"A true Mafia gentleman." Her grandmother laughed and stood from the table. "It'll all be there."

We didn't stick around after that. We left with only Dante waving goodbye to them.

CHAPTER 10: MORINA

The rest of the evening, I waited like prey ready to be slaughtered any second. I jumped at the slightest sound, and my grandmother even scolded me.

"Mo, is this so scary to you? What's got you so tense?"

"Oh, I don't know. The mob being in our town, for one."

She sighed and rubbed a hand over her wrinkled brow. "It's not like you think. I fluff my own ego by acting as though we're still at war. Like a soldier wounded in battle who remembers those days as some of the bravest ones he ever lived, I like to talk as if it still might happen, huh? Don't get your panties in a bunch. They're mostly businessmen now. Like I said, gentleman mobsters."

I took a deep breath. "What do you mean, Grandma?"

"Ach. They have hearts now. They live by new rules. They make clean money instead of bleeding those who crossed them." She waved toward the big city. "They know how to move things without death now. I think it's better this way but maybe more cruel. I've heard of how Bastian works. He'll cut off dealings with those he doesn't want to work with and let the wolves underground rip apart those he doesn't protect. He wants everything legal but still holds all the cards in his hand."

"That sounds just as scary." I shivered as a breeze passed through.

"Maybe. But there's ethics now. Code he lives by more than his dad ever did. It'd serve you well to marry into that."

Sighing, I dug my nails into my hands so as not to jump down her throat right away.

Grandma meant well. In her mind, marriage could smooth over many things. She thought Bastian would be protecting me with his name, but she didn't understand. "They love me here, Grandma. You know that right? Jonah is out on the water every day with me, Iago is at the food truck bright and early, and I've worked at the humane society for years. Dr. Nathan—"

"Don't be naïve, Mo. Men love a pretty woman to look at. They won't risk their lives for you. And who's going to take care of you when I'm gone?" I stumbled at her question in shock. I tried to school my expression, but she caught it. "Oh, I know. You think you take care of yourself, but I pay the bills. I run the numbers of the real businesses we have. I'm your protection."

Her words were like a punch to my gut. "I'm perfectly capable of doing all of that, Grandma."

"We will see," she murmured and went to her room.

* * *

She died that very night, and her last words loomed, now ominous with their weight.

There wasn't a sound made. No glass fell to the ground, no cry for help, not even a great sigh from her bedroom. She went the way everyone hopes they will—quiet and warm in her bed.

My grandmother had taken life by the horns and maybe she'd wanted to ride out of it softly. Either way, I liked to think she chose it. She'd always been able to steer things her way. Why not death?

I'd taken one breath, two breaths, and then maybe fifty more as I stood over her the next morning.

In the end, we'd planned her funeral, wake, everything.

It was all planned perfectly.

Except what I would do the day it happened.

I was alone, the only sound in her room was my breath, not hers. The gulls outside, the waves, their rhythm was with my breathing.

Not hers.

Just mine.

Life was too quiet without her rattling breaths. The room was so empty with only my own.

The sun shone in through the window as if mocking me, and I turned the bracelets on my wrist for far too long before deciding to call the nonemergency line.

They came right away, much like if I'd called 911.

Yet, no sirens. No sound.

Maybe that was the benefit of a small town. The sheriff pulled me in for a hug. He'd heard from the nonemergency call and decided to come with. He told me to swing by the tiki bar later, that he'd tell Bradley to have a drink waiting for me.

I didn't go.

I sat in that empty house and listened to the new silence.

I was silent when I cried that night too.

And the night after.

And the night after that.

Complete quiet except for the rhythm of my breathing and the rhythm of the waves.

We worked together to get me through those hard days.

Losing my grandmother was like losing my life. She'd been both of my parents for so long. When they'd passed, she'd stepped in.

She'd always stepped in, even when they'd still been there.

Losing her was bigger, more detrimental, and much more heart wrenching.

I'd planned for it all, but I couldn't plan for the pain and for the loss of myself.

So many gifts arrived those next few days. Flowers and more flowers and pies and food, as if I wanted to eat and have a nice-smelling house.

I set it all next to the urn I had to hold on to until the funeral.

I ignored calls and the doorbell ringing until that day.

It was the day I had to pull on my big-girl dress and face the music.

The world still turned, and Grandma was gone even if I didn't want her to be.

The funeral home was small and dark. It was not a place my grandmother would have ever enjoyed. I didn't enjoy it either, not with the fabric of the wooden chairs yellowed and worn from so many people coming to say goodbye to their loved ones, so many people who'd sat in those same spots.

So much pain.

So much death.

Over the past few days, a beating had started in my soul. Angry. Sad. If you could imagine a drum of death and darkness, that was exactly how it sounded. Sometimes the thump was so roaring, it sounded like thunder, so loud in my ears I couldn't hear anything else. Maybe it was my heart.

It went up and down, up and down like the ocean, like my breath.

"Morina." Bradley's hand on my shoulder made me jump. He yanked it away and winced. "Sorry."

"No, no." I shook my head to try to right myself. "It's fine. I'm on edge today."

"As you should be. It's a hard burden to carry yourself," he blurted out and then immediately followed up with, "I mean, not by yourself. We're all here."

"Of course you are." I patted his back and kissed him on the cheek. His kind eyes searched my face. Bradley would have provided me comfort any other day, his muscular frame always dwarfing mine and making me feel protected. Today, though, no one could protect me from the grief.

He hesitated from saying anything more, and I squinted at his awkwardness. "Don't tiptoe, Bradley. It was never your strong suit."

He sighed, but his shoulders relaxed a little. "It's a hell of a day, Mo. Everyone's going to walk on eggshells around you."

I turned and found the whole town piling into the funeral home. "Don't I know it," I mumbled.

I gripped my bracelets, one a deep, earthy green color with spots of bold red. Bloodstone for courage and bravery. I wore another made of howlite for patience and compassion. I'd also slid a rose quartz crystal in my black dress's pocket. I would grip it when I needed the confidence and calm that I surely wouldn't feel today.

People filled the seats or bustled around the empty spaces, and most of them weren't idly talking. They moved flowers around, waving in others, hugging the ones who cried, laughing with the ones who shared memories.

The town was a family, and I smiled because Grandma had been a big part of it.

The director came to talk over logistics, but Grandma had said she wanted a speech from the priest, nothing from me, and wanted one thing played before they ended the ceremony.

Nothing from me. A part of her probably always wanted me to do nothing. She'd never ever wanted to be a burden. Today, more than any other day, I appreciated that.

I sat next to Bradley, and he put his arm around me while

the priest spoke of Grandma's love for the town, the work she and my grandfather had done, and how every moment spent with her was a joy.

Everything he said, people nodded along.

I didn't let a tear escape as he talked. I'd cry alone in the silence tonight.

Today, I'd let the town cry for her instead.

The priest announced that there was one song she'd chosen and motioned for the funeral director to play it.

Grandma hadn't let me know this part but as the beat started up, I think I was the first to chuckle. We'd always played and laughed at Eminem, so when "Without Me" started, I laughed.

The words were absolutely ridiculous, and those who knew them started laughing too.

We sang along, and the tears that streamed down my face were happy ones.

When it ended, the funeral director hurried forward but I stopped him. "I want to say one thing." My breath shook as I took it in. "I'm not good with words. We all know I'm mercurial by nature. I'm a product of my parents, right?"

Most of them laughed at my joke.

"Maybe my grandma was a little perturbed with my mom marrying a guy that bent with the wind. And when the accident took them, I think she was a little mad even. Still, she never bent to anything—the wind, the water, this town could have tried to push her, and she would have stood her ground. We were lucky to have that, I think."

I took a shaky breath and tried to smile instead of cry. I caught Bradley's eye and he nodded for me to continue. "We knew we could count on her in anything. Bradley even counted on her to take down more moonshine in the tiki bar than anyone else. I'm pretty sure she made you thousands with the bets you won every time a businessman stopped into town."

Everyone laughed at that.

"I guess we all know with me, you can't do that. I'm always doing my own thing." More chuckles. "Except for the food truck, our puppies at the humane society, and the ocean—you know I'll always be there for you when it comes to that. So, she's gone, but she'll always be a part of the city, and here's to hoping that her spirit flying through here will make us all a little more like Maribel."

Bradley whooped and everyone clapped.

I stepped down from the podium and went to lay a hand on the urn. Some heavy weight lifted from my chest. I believed in spirits, in things of the atmosphere shifting, and if she was there, I think that weight lifting was her spirit sighing in relief. "I'll be fine, Grandma," I whispered.

That moment marked the exact second that I finally felt I would be. This town was going to be the place where I'd never feel alone.

When I looked back into the crowd, the air around me changed. I don't know if it was because I'd slept with him or if it was because of the aura he carried everywhere, but Bastian tampered with my atmosphere every time he showed up. What the hell was he doing here?

I finally needed the rose quartz in my pocket. I squeezed it.

I glanced at the beads on my wrist and eyed my newest addition up against the bloodstone and howlite. Pure black tourmaline for protection, confidence, emotional stability, and strength. But I also wore it for Grandma. She was strong, and I wanted that strength with me always.

His eyes met mine as he looked up at me on that stage near the urn. I shot daggers his way. He nodded, turned, and left.

Good.

This was for our town today. Not an outsider.

I received more condolences, hugged more members of the community, and accepted more gifts.

Bradley stayed through most everyone leaving and through the funeral director letting me know the next steps.

Then, we stepped out into the sunshine together.

I thought fatigue would set in, that I would want to go home and curl up with a glass of wine, but outside stood Bastian in a navy suit. His Ray-Bans covered those dark eyes that always pierced my soul. He had one ankle crossed over the other and his hands in his pockets as he leaned against his Rolls-Royce.

The sun shined down on him like not a thing had gone wrong today. The birds still chirped, cars still drove by, the wind still blew, and in the distance, I could still hear the waves rolling in and out.

In and out.

Was I breathing the same way? Or was it faster, more furious than before?

I knew my heart beat more rapidly too, because the thudding was deep, hard, and mournful.

I fisted my hands and Bradley asked beside me, "You okay?"

I nodded, not looking at him. "Yes. I need to handle something. I'll call you later."

His lips pursed but he kissed me on the forehead and told me to call if I needed him. Then he left me as I walked toward Bastian. "What are you doing here? Why didn't you leave?"

"I came to say I'm sorry for your loss." He didn't attempt to come any closer. He didn't even take his hands from his pockets like he wanted to give me a hug and share his sympathies.

We weren't friends. We didn't know each other. My

grandmother had wanted us to meet again after she passed away—she'd given me that information at least. Bastian said he would be in touch. But this was not the time nor the place. "I appreciate that. But the wake is only for family and friends."

"I understand. The reading of her final will's tomorrow. It seems we're both on it. I thought I would stop by to let you know it's scheduled for ten."

Final will? Both of us? None of these words made any sense. "Isn't it a little soon?"

"I requested that we get business taken care of as quickly as possible so I can get out of your hair and everyone else's. I need to confirm partnerships with the ports will stay the same and that she honored her side of our arrangement." He shrugged like his callousness was completely warranted.

"My grandmother just died," I practically hissed as I glared at him, the crack in my voice a surprise to even me.

He jerked back at the fury and pain that laced my words. "My condolences, Morina," he said softly. His hand lifted a little like he was about to pat my arm, but then it dropped just as suddenly. "She will be missed."

"Not by you," I threw back. "You're here to circle like the shark you are. I'm not in the mood to be accommodating to that."

"Morina, come on now." The gentle coaxing from him wasn't going to work.

"'Come on'?" My hands went to those beads on my wrist that I could pull energy from. Courage. Poise. Strength. Maybe the black held fury too. "You need to leave," I almost shouted.

"Don't do that. Don't make a scene with me." He said it quietly, like he had the audacity to try to calm me with a smooth command.

"Or what?" My eyes widened at my own boldness.

"Or you'll learn who owns this little town and the whole state very quickly. Don't disrespect me, especially in public, unless you want the punishment to be served in public just the same, *piccola ragazza*." The name flew from his mouth like a menacing laser, not at all a sweet term of endearment anymore.

"Is that so, daddy?" I shot back. Maybe I wanted a reaction. Maybe I was spiraling. Because I wasn't stopping. "You wouldn't know the first thing about punishing me and getting me back in line." I always was one to go where my emotions led me, but this was different. This was taunting a dragon full of fire, one that everyone thought was asleep, but I'd seen the spark behind his eyes. Bastian had smacked my ass in the dark of the night like a man who owned the world even if he stood here now trying to appear docile.

Rage coiled around him. Every feature on his face hardened, ready to strike out at me. Still, he murmured, "Not here. Not today. You get this day, Morina."

I bit back a retort, not wanting to make more of a scene than I already had.

He sighed and pulled a little glass bottle from his pocket. When he held it out to me and I didn't move to take it, he gripped my wrist gently and set it in my hand. "It's a mix of rose, lavender, and chamomile oil for healing and comfort."

"You ... Where did you get this?" I stuttered. He'd only seen me use the oil on my food truck the one time, but he'd remembered like I mattered to him.

"I believe the oils are from Europe. They use sustainable operating procedures and it's organic." He cleared his throat and glanced around. "I researched it to be sure."

"For me?" I squeaked out, completely confused.

"For your grandmother passing, yes." He straightened his tie as if he was uncomfortable. "Anyway, I want to make sure this town is taken care of. Please don't fight me on it, Morina. I'd like to see you at the reading."

"This town can take care of itself. It isn't ruled by anything but the people in it," I said as I pocketed the oil, trying to forget our odd exchange.

"It's a small town surrounded by a lot of big ones, *piccola ragazza*." He rocked back on his heels, the name he called me in his native tongue suddenly felt like it was filled with condescension.

"Honestly, Bastian, I don't care about this at all right now. I don't care about the date or time or the will in general."

"I think the will is a little more important than your grandmother made it seem."

I stepped up to him fast, my boots clomping on the cement. "Are you calling my grandma a liar on the day of her funeral?"

"I'm calling her a caring woman who wanted to protect her only granddaughter a little while longer. There's a lot of responsibility you're about to take on."

People didn't listen to their gut instinct when biology and nature tried to tell them something. My heart pulled to Bastian in a way that it didn't with most men. I couldn't figure out if it was simply attraction or something more. All I knew was that, although my heart gravitated to him, my gut screamed for me to run the other way.

The sun shined on him like some higher power knew he held more authority than the rest of us. This man walked in a dimension I was not familiar with. And I didn't want to be familiar with it. I wanted to move with the wind and water and leave the convoluted dimensions to men like him.

"You and your suit, along with your security team"—I looked at Dante who was still in the car but stared at me with a look of remorse—"and your Rolls-Royce, can go to the will reading without me. Or shove the will up your ass for all I care."

He started to say something, but my body veered off its natural course.

"I don't want any part of the will. I don't want anything. All I want is the food truck and for you to leave." I waved my arms about like a child, my bracelets jangling as I did. "This is completely unnecessary. They can mail me the information for all I care, Bastian. But the only place I'm going is home. I'll be there for days. I don't think I need to do anything after losing the person I love most in this world. So, you can expect whatever you want, but I'm not going to that will reading."

"Morina." His voice came out low and menacing, not at all gentle like it had been before. It was a warning, meant to snap sense back into the chaotic blood running through my veins. His eyes darkened, his face changed. Gone was a man willing to negotiate. "Get your ass to that will reading tomorrow. Or I will personally be at your home to drag you to it."

CHAPTER 11: MORINA

I heard those words all through the night.

After tossing and turning for hours, I grabbed my phone to read the signs.

My horoscope was a freaking bitch.

It literally read, *Listen to the omen given to you yesterday. It will serve you well.*

Oh, shut up.

I purposely hadn't set my alarm. I wasn't going to wake to the sun or the waves either. I had every intention of sleeping in and missing the stupid will reading.

Still, something in the kitchen fell and woke me right at eight thirty. If my grandmother wasn't haunting me, she was at least trying to send signs.

I kicked off my weighted blanket. "Grandma, this is absolutely fucking ridiculous."

Somehow, yelling into the air made me feel better as I got ready. I didn't put on a nice blouse or even a cute dress. Instead, I threw on a black bikini with a yellow tank over it. I pulled on my board shorts and headed out.

I wasn't getting ready for any of them. I'd go surf right after the meeting and put the whole damn thing behind me.

I took my time, letting my old pickup idle along. Jonah had gifted it to me on my seventeenth birthday and it looked perfectly out of place in the law firm's parking lot. When I arrived at last, Bastian's eyebrows rose as he looked me over.

No surprise, he wore his normal navy suit, and Dante was

occupied on his phone. I rolled my eyes at them, but when I spotted the estate lawyer and another man sitting in the room, I almost apologized for my attire and the fact that I was right on time.

Of course, everyone else had been ten minutes early.

Instead, I took the last empty seat and presented my identification when asked.

"Well, I appreciate you all being here today. I'm Mr. Finley, and Maribel asked me to present the will to you all rather than mail it," the thin man with wiry glasses announced as he shifted some paperwork on his worn desk. "It's not under great circumstances, but your grandmother got this will together years ago and has updated it time and time again. It was important to her that you were all here to understand her terms."

My stomach flipped at his words. This was the one place Grandma didn't have me come with her. We'd done the funeral planning together. The banks and this part though, she'd said over and over, "I'll iron it out myself." Then, she'd send me off to the food truck or I'd try to go volunteer at the humane society.

"So." Mr. Finley's bony pointer finger pointed to the ceiling. "This is a will with a few quirks, which is why we also have Mr. Armanelli's lawyer here."

I narrowed my eyes and glared at my one-night stand turned nightmare. He'd brought his freaking lawyer? "How convenient," I grumbled.

Mr. Finley cleared his throat. "I'll be honest, your grandma's note to you explains everything in layman's terms, but I'll do that for you now as well." He handed me a letter.

"I'm sorry. This is from my grandma?" I gripped the letter a little harder.

"Yes. She wrote it specifically for you after she finished her final changes to the will."

The date on the envelope was only a couple of days before her death. "She died two days later," I whispered. This letter held words she'd never told me. It was a way to hear her thoughts one last time; a connection that carried past her dying. When I read this letter, I wouldn't be alone for those two minutes. She'd talk to me one last time.

A lone tear spilled from my eye, and I quickly swiped it away. When I glanced up, Bastian studied me with a frown on his face. Did he understand the pain of losing someone beloved? Of being all alone?

His frown fell away to an apathetic stare. Of course he didn't.

I turned away and sat taller in my seat. "I'll read this later. I'd like to hear the terms of her will so we can all be on our way."

"That's fine." Mr. Finley went over some legal jargon and stated that the will held the final say in everything. Then, he went into a story I'd never heard. "Your great-great-grandfather was the founder of Tropical Oil and Fuel. He ran the ports, the tank farms, and the transfers."

"My great-great-grandfather?" I raised my eyebrows, completely confused by the mention of the oil company that ran the town. We had no ties to that.

"Yes, he came from Ireland with a good amount of money already. He utilized that and his connections to start this business."

Bastian shifted in his seat, nodding to Dante, who pulled out his stupid phone.

"They formed a lot of partnerships. Your grandma was a woman who made things happen. She had ties back in Ireland. So, the partners let the company run this way. They won't do that any longer. They want the company sold to a specific shareholder, Ronald, who also owns their competitor, SeashellOil."

I scoffed at the name. The town knew it very well. SeashellOil wanted to make the tanks, the ports, everything corporate. They would push the terminals to their limits. "Well that's never happening. Tropical Oil hates SeashellOil."

"Your grandma hated them," he corrected me. "She had a majority vote, but without that, Tropical Oil will be sold to the highest bidder. We all know who that will be."

Pieces of my life fell into place suddenly. The way Grandma would watch the news on the oil plant with so much passion or how she'd be furious if something went wrong with it. I'd thought she cared about the town, and maybe she had, but now many more things made sense.

"But everyone hates them. I mean—"

"The board is willing to sell." The lawyer cleared his throat. "They want to sell."

I turned and glared at Bastian. "And you? Are you here to get your share of it too?"

"If she gave me some of it, Morina, I'm here to be a part of whatever she wanted me to be. I've made it known to everyone that I want those shares. I explained my plans for cleaner energy, for making your city thrive. I won't sell. I'll make the company better. I wanted to do it legally, without the partnerships you've all been nurturing."

"Nurturing?"

He looked toward the ceiling, a sure sign that he was irritated. "That food truck wouldn't be running without some Irish ties. We discussed this already. I won't work with them."

"That was hardly nurturing a partnership—"

"Your grandmother had more than that." Bastian cut me

off. "I'll buy your shares. Fair price. I'll take care of this city ... and you. You have my word."

Mr. Finley continued as if Bastian hadn't spoken. "So, your grandmother inherited these stocks and the company agreed to keep her identity secret. She moved from the city, changed her name. No one knew she was making large decisions for the company."

I grumbled and crossed my arms. This was bullshit. Grandma had left me to go in completely blind. My heart beat faster and faster as his words sank in. "Changed her name? Why?"

"It's a dangerous business." Bastian filled the silence in the room, like he filled every space he entered. "She wanted protection, probably for you and your parents."

Life had been simpler without knowing, and my simple ignorance bred a happiness I could live with. "I'm sorry," I wheezed, gripping the metal arm of the uncomfortable chair. The world turned on its axis. The water that normally ebbed and flowed with the tides, whooshed over and tore apart my carefully concocted simple life.

The whole world stopped. Even the water that I synced my breathing with. In that moment, I even believed the earth had turned flat and tipped over sideways, dropping me off a cascading waterfall.

Mr. Finley continued reading the will. I saw his mouth moving. I watched how he formed each word, and yet I couldn't make out a single one.

The only part I put together was the part I knew I couldn't handle. "She wants you to decide the fate of the company. She's giving you her majority share. She wanted me to state that these shares are somewhat dangerous to own." He glanced at Bastian. "You understand, right, Morina?"

"If Bastian knows what to do ..." I waved away the rest, then took a deep breath. "I'll do what's needed for this city. I'll sell to him."

The mob. I'd be selling to the mob. No one wanted to say we were surrounded by men who could kill us, but that was the truth.

Mr. Finley cleared his throat. "There's a stipulation."

Bastian glared at the estate lawyer. His voice held the threat of fury. "Go on."

Before he continued, Mr. Finley gulped like he knew it wasn't about to go over well. "So, to keep the city and Morina safe, the conditions are that she marry into the Armanelli family, of course. Your grandmother wanted me to put 'of course' in the writing." He chuckled like we all knew this.

"You can't be ..." I sucked in what oxygen I could. But I gulped in too much air. Or too little.

I stood up so fast, my chair flew back.

It never hit the floor because Bastian caught it, his gold Rolex peeking out from under his sleeve.

I stared at him as he set it back in place like he'd seen it coming, like he was two steps ahead of my every move. I wanted to scream at the smug look on his face.

"You're kidding." I shook my head, my wavy hair looking even more crazy as I glanced from one to the other.

"This is not a joke." Mr. Finley straightened his glasses, his knuckles cracking. "Maribel felt this would be most beneficial for the city and for you, Morina."

Would I be arrested if I jumped across the table to strangle the messenger?

"This is your fault." The words flew out of me before I could stop them as I turned to Bastian. I spat them like a viper ready to bite down on a victim. "You did this."

"No. Morina, your grandmother did this," he replied, irritation on his face too. "It seems this is an inconvenience for all of us."

"*Inconvenience*?" I screeched. "Are you kidding me? It's nothing to you. But to me, it's everything! I'm not marrying you."

"Nothing to me?" he whispered. Then, he stood slowly and straightened that stupid, stuffy suit of his. "I don't enjoy being around you. I need the shares, not some flippant girl who runs a food truck. I definitely don't want to be tied to you legally in any way, shape, or form. But the company is at stake."

"The company? What about the city?" I stomped my foot.

"That company runs this town." The words fell out of his mouth like dominos tipping one by one. "Half the people are employed there. You hand those stocks over to SeashellOil, and they'll get rid of this town. Hire the people they want and push that port to its limit."

"I don't want anything to do with this," I whispered.

The lawyer cleared his throat. "Your grandmother has written all the details in your letter, but I do want to read the rest of the terms here in case you do not accept them."

He motioned for us to take our seats. I huffed and plopped back down in mine, running my fingers over my bracelets. I tried to channel the energy from them. I needed at least ten more to get through the rest of the will though.

"If you won't marry one another, you may donate your stocks to SeashellOil. You will not get a vote on the outcome of the port, and you will not pass go and collect that two hundred dollars, Morina." Mr. Finley looked up at me. "She had me write that in."

If my grandmother were here, I would have strangled her. She always wanted me to marry, for God knows what reason. I swear this was her stupid version of haunting, and wow had she done a fan-fucking-tastic job.

"The stipulations are strict. One week to become engaged, one month to be married. You attend two quarterly meetings while married. At that point, which will be six months from today, Morina may sell or give the shares to whomever she wishes. Until then, they must belong to her or to SeashellOil."

"An ultimatum?" Bastian whispered under his breath and pinched the bridge of his nose.

She believed I needed a week's time for an engagement, then we'd move in together, legally get married, and I'd figure out if Bastian would be trustworthy with the shares in six months? "Why can't I sell to him now?" I asked, waving my hands about. He seemed to understand what businesses needed.

"You wouldn't be able to anyway," Bastian grumbled like he had all the answers and didn't like a single one. "There's probate and estate processing."

"So what?"

He shook his head. "You don't understand anything."

I wanted to scream that no shit, I don't understand. This is all news to me.

"This is the most ridiculous way of handling a will." I hoped Grandma's dead spirit could hear me. "I don't think it's even legal."

Bastian's lawyer chose that time to speak up. "There's a lot of legal jargon through this will, but I can assure you that everything Mr. Finley's saying is the truth."

I rolled the beads on my wrist over and over again as everyone waited in silence. I tried some deep breathing. I counted to ten.

Nothing worked. No answers appeared, and I definitely didn't feel calmer.

"There has to be a way around these stocks going to SeashellOil."

"Yes, you marry me, we have it be legal for six months, nothing more and nothing less. Then, I'll buy it from you for a fair price."

"Absolutely not." I wasn't marrying that man.

"Suit yourself." Bastian stood and glanced at Dante, who rose an instant later.

The man reading the will cleared his throat. "Make sure to put in paperwork to the courthouse on time. We don't want to break the terms of the will because of a mishap with marriage certificates if that's what you both decide to do."

He was hinting at Bastian's status, yet staring at me as if I were suddenly important.

I shook my head. "I don't know what you mean by that."

"The judge has some ties to the company just like the town does, Morina," he murmured like Bastian wouldn't be able to hear him.

I needed to get out of here. I needed some fresh air. "I can't do this."

The only person who seemed to get me or who would offer any type of helping hand spoke up right then. "Morina," Dante said in his deep, soothing voice, "your gut is pulling you in a lot of directions right now." I glanced at him, and the frown on his face suggested sympathy. "It's okay." He patted me on the shoulder. "Put your hand right on your stomach. Feel the heat and let it out."

It was a Reiki trick. I had practiced it before a little but had never gotten into it.

When I didn't move, he put his hand right over my belly. "Release all the negative shit flying through your head right here, right now."

I nodded and closed my eyes for a few seconds. He grabbed my wrist and put my hand over my stomach. I felt the heat, so much hotter than the rest of my body. Maybe the energy was passing through my hand to his, and he was getting rid of it.

The energy left me in some way or another, and a hint of calm crept in.

When I opened my eyes, I mouthed a thank you to him and took a deep breath. "I need a day. I need to think."

Bastian opened his mouth to speak.

I cut him off with my pointer finger in the air. "One day, Bastian. That's fair."

The muscles through the beautiful man I now hated rippled like every bone in his body wanted to disagree with me. He straightened that navy suit of his and closed his eyes like he needed his own relaxation method.

"I want to work with you. I want this to be an equal partnership where you understand I'm here to make the company better." His voice held genuine kindness.

Yet, we were on opposing sides of the world. How could I believe him? Hell, we weren't on opposing sides of the world—we didn't even live in the same world. His was more complicated, more astute; nothing at all like mine.

I grabbed my bag and walked to the door. Bastian grabbed my arm, right above the elbow. He spun me so we were eye to eye. His dark eyes pierced into my soul, into my fears, and peeled them back, shining light onto my vulnerabilities.

I bit my bottom lip to try to stifle the fact that his hand on me sparked a fire I'd tried so hard to squelch. Now, we were lighting it again, and I'd have to surround myself with that for six months.

"What are you afraid of, Mo? Of me? Or us? This will only be to your benefit," he whispered like he was trying to piece it all together. "I'll pay you fairly. There won't be many rules. We can make this work. It's just us."

"There is no us!" I shot back, my voice loud enough to show them all I was ready to go to war. I ripped my arm from his grasp and my bracelets jangled together, the black one stark against the pastels of the others.

Strength in my rage. I felt it now.

He let me turn so fast that my hair flared out around me, the drama was there for everyone to see.

"Morina." Bastian's voice stopped me at the threshold. "You need this more than I do. Your town needs this. I don't. But I'd like it. It's a partnership. And it's an opportunity to do things safely and legally."

"You're asking me to give up everything," I choked out. "And to trust you, a complete stranger who I know has a questionable past. Don't you get that I have a life? I'm happy. I have a job and maybe a guy or two who enjoy my company. I like coming home and watching what I want to watch and taking care of my grand—"

My grandma.

"Morina ..." He said my name softly, like suddenly he had some sort of soul that could feel something other than business transactions. He reached for me, but I jerked away.

"No." I shook my head as I squeezed my eyes shut. "I know. She's gone. It's just ... It was a slipup. And I ... I deserve time to think. Right? Someone agree with me. Dante? The moon is ..." I'd forgotten what day it was. Everything was all out of whack.

"It's about to be a full moon, Mo. It's all going to be fine. Breathe it in. It's the universe moving with you, huh?"

I nodded and breathed in. One more breath of the air he told me was calm, and my shoulders relaxed. I chanced one more look at Bastian and let my guard down. I needed him to understand. "I get this isn't a big deal for you. You've been tied to this way your whole life. My life is the complete opposite. I've been absolutely free. Probably to a fault. So, I need a day to think."

"You can't tell anyone until we decide, Morina." He arched an eyebrow as though making sure I understood. "The company being at stake will cause unrest. We need a plan. Take my number." He motioned for Dante to hand over his card. "Tomorrow, we make decisions."

I nodded and scanned the room to see who else would know this marriage was a sham. The lawyers, Dante, and him. That was all.

"I'll call you."

CHAPTER 12: BASTIAN

On day one, my phone didn't ring.

On day two, my phone was still eerily silent.

Of course she didn't call. She could barely make a damn meeting, let alone call me. I gave her those two days, which was more than enough. I waited patiently. And although I tried to be, I was not a patient man. I'd been running an empire since a young age. Now, I ran the country behind the scenes in more ways than one.

Businessmen like me didn't wait. No one even considered trying to make me.

And now I did for this girl who was barely a fucking woman. She didn't know the first thing about being an adult, and now I had to wait for her to make the fucking decision of a lifetime.

I ran the damn empire. I'd turned filth to gold and I'd made what was illegal legal. I'd Rumpelstiltskinned it all, and I would do the same here.

I didn't wait for people. She should've known better than to make that mistake.

"You're going to need to go easy on her," Dante told me on the drive to her grandmother's.

"Go easy on her? That's all I've done." I gripped my suit pants in anger and then consciously opened my fist so as not to make wrinkles in the fabric. I'd even went and researched oils for her and bought her one for a funeral. God knows why. It wasn't like we were friends. Still, I wanted to see those sapphire eyes of hers look at me without anger or frustration, just for a moment like they had on that jet.

I was going fucking crazy.

I grunted and told Dante, "She needs to realize I'm not going to baby her."

"She didn't grow up in this world."

"So she keeps saying."

"She's got her life and—"

"She's got new responsibilities now. None of us picked our lives, Dante. We stepped up to the plate when we had to. Her town is relying on her, whether they know it or not. She needs to grow up or decide to stay a child. Either way, I can't coddle her when her decision is one an adult has to make." I opened the window and breathed in the salty breeze.

Dante chuckled at me, and I swear to God, I wanted to resort to what I would have done years ago and punch him. "She's getting to you, and you're not even married yet."

"Fuck off." I turned the watch on my wrist one time and then again, trying to temper my anger. As we pulled up to the house, I glared at my friend. "Stay outside, jackass."

"Oh, that's good for your security." He rolled his eyes, but he was already texting someone. They'd have eyes on the perimeter as always.

"Like you're going to save me from her anyway," I grumbled because we both knew it wasn't my physical safety at stake, it was my mental health. She was going to drive me insane. All my muscles tensed as I walked up the path.

She swung the door open before I even knocked. "What are you doing here?" She was a little breathless and sweaty, with her hair in a messy knot on top of her head.

"Am I interrupting something?" I raised a brow and peered around her but she pushed the door to a crack so I couldn't see past.

"Look, can we talk later?" She bit her plump bottom lip.

What the hell was she doing in there? Then I glanced down and saw the sports bra, the way it hugged her curves, the sweat dripping down her toned stomach.

My dick twitched, and I took a deep breath. I didn't want her, I told myself. Even with her long, tanned legs and ample amount of ass to grab. Even if I'd had her once, she wasn't my type now.

Now, a legal partnership was on the line.

I wouldn't muddle deals or fuck them up in any way. My father had enough dirty deals for all of us. I'd looked deeper into Tropical Oil and my father's relationship with it. Mario Armanelli had always been a weasel. Although he'd never had a romantic relationship with Maribel, he'd swindled his way around the partnership and offered her protection in exchange for illegally bringing in products through her ports.

He'd screwed her over again and again. It was no wonder she hadn't trusted me. So, I'd make it right by changing this company into one that would flourish. I just had to prove it to Morina and become the majority shareholder. It meant leaving my libido out of the equation.

Easier said than done when, for some reason, even with all the complications and her attitude, my dick had an obsession with her. It jumped as she stood there, glaring at me. It didn't care that her maturity level was that of a teenager with wonky beliefs and that she was ten-plus years my junior. My dick was only interested in the fact that she'd answered the door in booty shorts and a bra, leaving little to the imagination. "You always answer the door in next to nothing?"

She reached her hand up in front of her face, closed her fist, as if grabbing something, and then pulled it down, letting out a whooshing breath.

"Are you pulling on air?" I asked, not amused.

She grumbled, "Dante would understand."

This conversation was off to a great start. "Morina—"

"I don't want to argue with you."

"I don't want to argue with you either." Good, we could be adults. "I'm here to discuss everything. Can we talk now?"

She looked a little concerned before she closed those big doe eyes. Her long dark lashes rested on her high cheekbones before she stepped back and said over her shoulder, "Bradley. We'll have to hang out tomorrow."

"Baby, third base is not a home run," Bradley, a tall dark-haired guy, said from her living room as he rolled up his yoga mat. "And we never actually got to yog—"

I walked around Morina and stared at him. The whining abruptly halted.

"Bastian, right?" He pointed at me and squinted as though trying to remember. "You're the suit who wanted a smoothie last week."

I nodded. Then my gaze ping-ponged between them. "Morina and I have a complicated relationship, one that goes way back."

"Not that far," she grumbled.

"Morina, *ragazza*, don't discount our relationship."

"Relationship?" Bradley looked puzzled.

Something burned in my stomach. I couldn't place the feeling. I hadn't had it in such a long time. It could have been frustration, pure and white-hot, with the fact that she'd been fucking around with a guy and had the audacity to call him here but couldn't be bothered to call me.

Or maybe it was that damn little green fucker called jealousy. I wouldn't place my bets on it quite yet though.

Still, the man was tall, well built, and seemed to know his place around Maribel's home. He ambled through the living room, straightening a few things as he waited for me to give more information.

"Well, Morina is supposed to be my fiancée, Bradley," I announced. "Which means she probably isn't going to give you a home run any time soon."

Her jaw dropped, and Bradley's practically hit the floor.

"Mo." He turned to her immediately. "Baby, you're free-spirited and go with what moves you. I get that. I love that about you, Mo. And you're hurting from your grandma passing, but you're not alone. You can't marry a suit on a whim, Mo. That's not—"

"Bradley." I cut him off with just his name, an emotion flowing through my body that I wasn't quite sure I could control even if I wanted to. "My fiancée and I need to talk. Please leave us."

It was his turn to look between the both of us.

Morina didn't immediately do anything. Her sports bra rose and fell rapidly with each breath she took, and maybe I'd shocked her a bit with what I'd said. Straightening suddenly, she combed a hand through that long wavy hair of hers and motioned him toward the door. "I'll call you later, okay? It's complicated."

"You know I'm here for you, whatever you need." He caught her gaze and held it, showing me he probably would have gone toe-to-toe with me if she told him in that second.

"She doesn't really need anything from you that I can't give her myself," I found myself saying.

Making allegiances in this town might be harder than I'd originally thought.

The man studied us a second longer, murmured to Morina

to call if she needed anything, and then walked out the door.

CHAPTER 13: MORINA

"Are you kidding?" I slammed the door and turned to him. "You can't go around saying stuff like that!"

"Like what?"

"I'm not your fiancée!" I shoved the chair that was sticking out an inch too far from our dining table. The wood clunked and the table legs shrieked across the floor.

It wasn't enough. I wanted to throw something at him. This would have been the perfect time to have my grandmother's ashes. She would have enjoyed knowing she'd knocked a big bossy asshole over the head even after her passing.

Except she wanted me to marry this one.

Technicalities, Grandma.

"Well, you could be if you'd just agree. Plus, you didn't say no quite yet." He shrugged, completely unfazed by my outburst. If he looked any more austere yet relaxed in that navy suit with its stupid gold cufflinks that I knew cost a fortune, no one would hold me liable for grabbing wine to pour on his head.

I turned for the kitchen. "I need a drink."

"I'll have water, considering it's only eleven in the morning." His footsteps followed close behind me.

"I'm sorry. Are you judging me right now? My grandma said you're all such gentlemen nowadays, but I'm not seeing it." I spun to meet him chest-to-chest and didn't back away even as we touched.

He stared down at me, scanning my face. I watched how maybe he lingered on my lips, how he assessed every feature like he could get something from it. "I don't think today is the day to judge you. Your grandmother was right. I'm trying to have a partnership with you, and I intend for it to be cordial."

Studying him, I couldn't see any lies. Still, this was the mob. I'd seen the movies, heard the whispers about them through the city. "My grandma didn't trust you all for a reason."

"Your grandma wanted to trust me. She held on to remnants of my father's fucked-up dealings. We have to work together."

"I just ..." I yanked open my grandmother's fridge and shifted my energy back to getting drinks. That's what I needed to focus on. Inside was Champagne and orange juice. Breakfast mimosas—perfect.

"This appropriate enough for you?" I lifted them up in a mock question.

"Again, I'll have water."

I slammed the bottle down on the counter and grabbed some ice and a glass. Bastian took that as an invitation to start uncorking the champagne. When the cork was almost out, he waited a second, showing he knew much more than I did about the popping of champagne, of etiquette and cordial business dealings. The top came out in silence, no champagne spilled.

He poured my drink without glancing at me, then grabbed a glass for his water.

"Thanks," I mumbled after a few sips in silence.

His brows knitted together. "So, we going to get married and save this little town you were so protective of the first time we met, or are we going to do this the hard way?"

"Okay." I dragged out the word, trying to corral the thoughts of mine that were running every which way. "You realize I didn't call you because I don't have an answer to that question."

"I do realize that. We don't have time though. The will doesn't give it to us and the board is going to start making decisions on Tropical Oil without you. Marry me and get this over with. Go back to your life in six months at the most. I won't even take much from your normal day-to-day."

"If we sleep together again, it won't have anything to do with this partnership. I won't change my mind about you," I blurted out. God knows why that was the first thing that came out. But it had been on my mind since the will reading. I remembered his hands on my ass, his voice in my ear, and his lips on my neck. If I was around him long enough, it would happen. We couldn't taint the partnership with it. And that was perfectly fine. I could keep business and our fake marriage separate.

"I don't want to sleep with you again, Morina." Bastian sighed as if I was dense.

It was like a garbage truck had driven up and dumped its trash all over me. He didn't want to sleep with me? I'd been that unremarkable to him, while he'd been that memorable to me?

"Good. Great." Of course it hurt my confidence even if I'd been the first to say it. I cleared my throat. "I mean, we might if we have to be together for six months, considering we've already tested those waters and we jibe fine."

"A fine fuck doesn't really seem like a good risk to take when I need you to understand I'm serious about the company. I want to buy those shares from you and prove there aren't any other strings."

"Are you nervous about strings? You scared to fall in love with me after just an okay fuck?" My voice sounded hurt, and I didn't know why I let the words even leave my mouth.

"Let's sit and discuss, huh?" He pointed to the chairs, all business with his perfectly ironed suit and his nice, soothing voice. This was a man who was made to make deals and smooth things over. "I never said *okay*. I said *fine*. That's very fine, *ragazza*. I'd bend you over this table and fuck you finer today too if it weren't for the will."

I nodded and gulped down half my glass, poured in more champagne, and then proceeded to sit.

He raised an eyebrow at me.

I lifted mine right back at him. "I think we should have a rule that you don't judge me during this whole thing because I feel a lot of judgment already." His mouth lifted a little. "I'm serious, Bastian."

"Didn't say you weren't." He took a seat and leaned back. When he looked toward the ceiling and sighed, I wondered if he ever really relaxed like I'd seen him on the jet.

Bastian Armanelli was a dragon waiting to be unleashed. I'd only felt the sting of his fire when he'd brought his hand to my ass. Now, he was buttoned up tight, but I could practically feel the coiled tension and the poise he worked so hard to maintain.

I sat across from him and gripped my glass like it was a lifeline. "If we do this ..." I hesitated when he looked at me because his eyes held determination and were hard with it. He wasn't going to let there be an if. We were doing it. "Would you force me to marry you?" I asked quietly. "What if I say no?"

"Am I that offensive to you that you can't live with me for six months?"

"I honestly don't think I could live with anyone for six months."

He hummed low and tapped a strong finger on the table. "I'm not in the business of forcing anyone to do anything. My father used to do that."

"And you didn't get along with him?" I wanted to know

more about his father's relationship with my grandmother, if nothing else.

"I wouldn't say that. We had a lot of different views as I grew up, but we got along sometimes."

"Do you get along with everyone?"

"I try to."

"Well, that sounds draining."

His smile came fast and whipped through our easy conversation. Suddenly, I wanted to back away from the genuine smile—and from the feeling it gave me, all fluttery and light.

I cleared my throat and glanced around. "So, if we do this, you have to know, I'm not like that. I'd rather keep to myself. I don't do the whole making allies and kissing asses thing. I have one friend and she travels the globe, so I barely talk to her. I live in my own world."

"I'm beginning to see that."

The beads of my bracelets jangled as I combed a hand through my hair to try and relax. "I just feel like you don't really know me and you're going to be disappointed with this partnership once you figure it out."

"Well,"—he shrugged—"good thing it's only for six months then."

"Right." I folded my hands together. "You said the public needs to see us. Why?"

"You need to be protected. An old tradition is that a woman who marries into my family is an Untouchable. No gang or family or syndicate will do you harm. I'll essentially claim you as mine."

Mine. I needed more to drink. The word mine rolled off his lips and lit a fire at my core. Bastian sounded like a god when he talked of control and possessions. He enjoyed it even if he didn't like to acknowledge the fact. He could say he was an ally all he wanted, but I saw the king in him.

I twisted the stem of my glass. "So, do we act like you're living here?"

"No one would believe that."

"Why not?"

"Because I'm not a person who lives with security issues."

"What's wrong with this place?"

"Well, for one, I could kick in the door and be standing over your bed in two seconds if I wanted to. And the windows give easy entry points along with eyes on you in pretty much every room. I could probably catch a glimpse of you showering if I tried."

"Oh my God. That's not true. My grandma—"

"Your grandma was protected, Morina. We need to be protected too. In most circles, I'm a well-known businessman. I've been photographed around the country. People follow me all the time."

I sat back, eyes popping wide. "People follow you?"

"You don't pay attention to the entertainment news, but I own enough that, yes, people are watching. People will be watching you too, those who knew your grandmother. I'm sure there are families and syndicates paying very close attention. Your identity as a partner in this oil port could spark concern in underground gangs, in greedy businessmen, and some overall very dangerous people."

"I don't think so. They already knew my grandmother was a partner, I'm sure." But my mind was racing. Had she organized protection for me? What did protection even mean? I gulped down some of my diluted champagne and eyed the bottle again.

"Your grandmother had my father. She had ties to other syndicates and families. All that protection died with her.

Through all this will business, she basically assigned me as your protector." He waited a beat. "I'm not happy about it. I'm sure that's the case though."

"So, what? I have to move in with you to be protected?"

"Or simply because that's what normal engaged couples do. They find a place for them both to stay. We can go look at penthouses near the port tomorrow."

"What about this place?"

"Keep it or don't."

"I can't make up my mind."

"Do you live somewhere else?"

"Mostly, I live in the food truck now." It was a quiet confession. Only a few people knew I slept there. "I store my board there and there's a little bed above the food level. It's pretty amazing."

I didn't see any judgment in his dark-brown eyes. For that, I was thankful.

Then he asked, "Have you read her letter?"

"Um, I haven't gotten around to it." It was a terrible excuse, and I winced even as the words came out of my mouth. That brow that questioned all my actions lifted, and I felt a little ragey. He didn't say what was obviously on his mind though—that I'd had time, easily. "I mean, yes, Bradley was here this morning, but I've been busy with the food truck, and I volunteer at the humane society."

I waited for him to say he understood, but the man lifted his other brow too. It was a total accusation even if he didn't say a word.

"I'm sorry I don't think about business all the time like you, Bastian." I threw the accusation right back at his brows. He deserved it.

He nodded and glanced around. "I guess it's only

believable we'd be fooling around at first. So, Bradley shouldn't be a problem. People get cold feet all the time."

"Well, what about when we're married? Do you honestly want to be celibate for five months?"

"I think we can navigate just fine."

"Navigate a fake marriage? Do you hear how crazy that sounds?" I bit my lip.

"Your grandmother came up with the idea, *piccola ragazza*, not me."

"That's not a good nickname for your fiancée, Bastian."

"You were perfectly fine with it on my jet."

"Oh my God. Don't bring that night up. Ever. Again."

"I'm happy keeping our sex life in the past." He shrugged. "Six months of us putting on a show, Morina. That's it. Is that something you can do?"

"I have a feeling I'm going to hate your condescending tone by the end of these six months because I already dislike it."

"It's not condescending." He straightened his cuffs and stood. "I don't have a lot of time to sit and chat. We can schedule some time to be seen together and then move your belongings into a place near the company over the next week."

"Week?" I squeaked out. "That's fast. Let's just see how it goes."

"Okay." He nodded like I was delusional but would appease me for now. "Happy wife, happy life."

"Please don't say that." My stomach flipped in what must have been rebellion and fear.

"Anyway, Dante's waiting for me in the car."

"Next time, have him come in." I shrugged.

"We need alone time, Morina. We need to appear as a couple."

The charade seemed ridiculous. "I wish I could understand

why you think so. People get around these wills all the time. We can get married but live separately and do what the will says word for word, not vow for vow. This isn't really until death do us part." He hummed, straightened his tie, and didn't agree with me. The man didn't want to concern himself with more conversation and bickering. Fine by me. "Look, I'll text you, and we can iron out details."

"You really going to do that this time?"

"Of course." I put my hand to my stomach to try to contain whatever energy Dante had told me about. I needed to research it more.

"I'm going to do everything in my power to have this go on without a hitch." He nodded and stroked one fingertip down my cheek. "You're a good girl, Morina. I want this to work out for both of us."

Then his touch was gone. And, spinning on his heel, so too was he.

The breath I didn't know I'd been holding whooshed out of me.

"What the fuck, Grandma?" I said to the house in case she was there.

Bastian had looked at me like we could do this, like I could be a partner in this with him. I wanted to believe him but there was no actual way I could be that person. He came from that questionable background. Yet, my grandmother trusted something about him or about his father enough to place us together.

I sighed as I went back to the bedroom I wasn't sleeping in. I'd decided the food truck was a much better fit for me after Grandma passed. I had never enjoyed staying with her anyway. Now, it felt wrong. I came here every day to straighten up and get the mail. Then I'd jet off to work and to volunteer.

Now I sat on the corner of the spare bedroom's bed and stared at the white envelope. Her chicken scratch wasn't at all ornate. I didn't expect any hidden treasure when I opened the envelope.

Morina,

You're reading this, so that means I'm haunting you. Or trying my best to do so. Jesus, I hope I went fast and didn't make it too gory for you. Anyway, straight to the point: You're marrying Bastian because it'll keep you alive and it'll keep our town alive too.

Mario and I did a fine job keeping our business under wraps. I had ties to him and to a couple people in Ireland. They won't keep the partnership thriving, Morina. They don't care like they used to. They want the oil and the ports and to expand it into our city. Ronald, that crochety old man, is champing at the bit to get his hands on these shares. And oil refineries everywhere want in.

Bastian may want that too. I'm not sure. He seems to have other ideas. I want to trust him, but it's our town, Mo. We have to be sure. Six months isn't that long. See if he cares about that port enough to clean up what his family dirtied, what all the families and syndicates want to dirty.

This was the only thing I could come up with. It protects you and the town for a time. You'll have to figure out the rest. You get on a surfboard and go with quick decisions every day. Remember that—you can do that here too.

Oh, Mo, you're mad at me. I know you are. But you're strong like your father was. Surprised that I'm complimenting him? I hated him at the end, but he charmed anyone who met him before that addiction. And I will say he loved you and your mother. He stuck with her always, and I think he taught the whole town to surf. He always said to be quick and commit on the surfboard. He was something before those drugs took them both away. We have to forgive them for their addiction, right?

Charm and strength with that Bastian man on your arm will be enough, I think. Go to the company. See his vision. Take the time to see if you believe in him. If so, give him the shares for all I care. Your marriage will protect you. It makes you a wife of a Mafia king. As long as he's in power, you'll be safe, Morina. I needed to do this for you as much as for the town. He'll protect what's his, even if he has no interest in you whatsoever. It's a pride thing. Men measuring their dicks and all that.

As for you, this town is what you love. I didn't want to ruin what you loved without giving you a chance to save it. I kept it going for you. I don't care about the money. I care about the people here and about you most. I did all this for that very reason. Well, and because I wanted you married, of course. You can be a noncommittal little brat sometimes. So here I am, pushing you over the edge in death. Here's to hoping you follow those vows you say to him and don't part until death.

Don't be so scared to commit, Morina. I wonder if you're so scared because you lost your parents at the end or because you had to lose them over and over. I'll never forgive them for that, you know? I'm hoping I get to smack them both now that I'm dead. Just remember, not everyone is like them. Look at me. I only left you in death.

Hopefully just like Bastian.

'Til death do us part, right?

Sincerely,

The Grandma Who Haunts You

"You want me to burn down your house, don't you?" I asked her as if she was sitting across from me. "You want me to burn this letter too?"

God, she was such a controlling witch sometimes. I loved her and hated her so much all at the same time.

I hated that she'd left me with this huge burden.

I crinkled the letter as one tear fell onto it. "I just hate that you left, Grandma."

The waves crashed down on the beach in their familiar rhythm. If there was one thing I'd committed to, it was the water.

I threw on a bikini and grabbed my board in a frenzy, leaving the letter behind. I wanted nothing to do with the burden it brought to my life. I wanted to catch the wave, to ride what should've been unrideable. I ran into the ocean like it was the center of gravity and dove in, letting the cold rush all around me.

Water flowed over my face and combed my hair back. It soothed my hot skin and fought me just enough to show who was in control. This is what I'd married. I'd belonged to the waves since I could remember. This was where I worked hard enough to forget everything else in my life.

I'd forget how I felt when my parents would leave on yet another quest to find themselves. I'd forget about a bad date or a lost friendship. I'd forget about the time my grandma sat me down and said Mom and Dad weren't coming home because their small bus had crashed into a wall in an unknown city.

Some people in town had said it was for the best.

I remember running to the water where I could get swept up in a wave. The current took me out fast that day, and I'd stayed there for hours like I was now. I rode wave after wave after wave.

My body ached with each stroke, pushing myself hard enough to find the speed to turn a liquid to a solid, to shove my body up high enough that I could snap my legs up beneath me. I pushed my fatigue so I didn't have to feel anything else.

Grandma had called me noncommittal. But I was committed. I was committed to this town, to the water, to the food truck. I'd do whatever I had to.

I trudged up to the food truck, so drained from the water that I didn't even change. I dropped the board on the hooks outside, unlocked the door, and grabbed a night shirt from the corner. One sniff told me it'd do. I changed in the dark and shoved the ceiling hatch to the side. It was a little hidden gem that the roof had an addition not many people knew about. I crawled up the pull-down ladder, and it snapped back up when I rolled onto the mattress. I pulled the sliding hatch closed and drifted off to sleep.

I dreamt of men in my food truck, looking for me.

I woke up to something very different.

CHAPTER 14: BASTIAN

"What do you mean 'get to the food truck'? It's five in the morning," I bellowed into the phone, but my brother Cade was always a tweaked human being. When he called, you answered and did what he said.

"I'm saying I turned a traffic security camera on that section of the beach. She went in there and stayed the night. Hours later, three guys broke in. You should send someone over to check."

As he talked, I got dressed and went to bang on Dante's door. We were still staying in a hotel minutes outside of the town.

I had already looked over pictures of a penthouse, confirmed one for us as a couple after reviewing, and paid for it. I had people furnishing and decorating it at that very moment. That seemed best now that it looked like Morina would be moving in with me sooner rather than later.

Dante came out of his bedroom as I slipped shoes on and followed suit as I talked. "Did the men leave the food truck? How long were they in there?"

"Not long. I'm guessing she's fine. She changed and climbed up into some hole."

"She changed? Did you watch?" I ground out.

"I watch everything, but it's not to fucking jack off, dumbass." His voice was muffled.

"Are you texting someone right now? I hear you pressing fucking buttons." My blood boiled. He wasn't taking this seriously. I motioned for Dante to follow me to the car, and we took an elevator straight down.

"I've got this irritating glitch I've been trying to figure out," Cade said like he didn't care at all that the girl I was supposed to marry might have been murdered in her van. "Some hacker is fucking with me and you—"

"I'm going to strangle you when you get here." I was dead serious too.

"Well, you're going to be waiting awhile to do that. I'm working on new software for the businesses and—"

I hung up on him.

"Jesus fuck!" I pounded the roof of the Rolls-Royce before I got in. Dante didn't even blink. He just folded into the car and started it. We were well on our way toward the beach before I'd settled down enough to speak. "Why does nothing go right in this town?"

"Because we don't have it under control yet. It'll get there."

"Your optimism is infuriating right now, Dante." I dialed Morina's number. She wasn't going to answer. "Why the fuck would she answer?" I said more to myself than anyone. She'd been the most irritating woman I'd ever met in my life, and there was no reason for her to change her ways now. "Drive faster," I commanded, but Dante just laughed.

"I'm going fifty in a twenty-five already. I'm not risking a pedestrian's life."

"So you're willing to risk Morina's?"

"Oh, we care about her now? Or is it the company we're concerned about?" He picked up speed though.

That was good enough. I wouldn't argue with him. There was no use to trivial bickering when it was the source of our frustrations anyway.

We passed palm trees and the little brick road in the center of their city. The town hadn't woken yet, but the sun rising on the beach gave it an allure that most places would have envied. I understood the pull of the touristy community. Welcoming locals, a beautiful landscape, and oil terminals and farms near enough that many could get a great job and return home in good time.

Yet, like every little town that surrounded a big one, it came with underground filth. People like my father were always trying to get ahead, and they didn't care who they had to trample on to get there.

Before Dante even parked the car, I told him to watch the perimeter and was out and pacing toward the food truck. The back door had been jimmied open. It would have made for a pretty silent break in. When I opened it, I found they'd ripped open a few cabinets, knocked over her dishes and smashed up her blenders.

"Morina?" I tried to sound authoritative and kind at the same time. "Morina?"

After some rustling above me, a board slid away from the truck's ceiling.

Hair sticking every which way and pillow lines imprinted on her face, Morina peered out.

"What are you doing here?" Her voice was groggy from sleep. She disappeared for a second before her long sculpted legs swung down and she lowered herself.

She rubbed her eyes and blinked at her surroundings. Her nightshirt was practically see-through, and she didn't have anything under it because I saw everything I didn't want to see.

She crossed her arms over her chest where my stare undoubtedly lingered and bit her lip when I shot my gaze up to hers. "So, I'm guessing my dream wasn't a dream last night."

"Depends on what the dream was."

Her frown deepened as she looked around. "I was so tired after surfing that I just passed out. At one point, I heard banging and someone saying they swore I was here. My heart was racing so fast in that dream but I remember thinking not to move except for throwing the dark blanket over my head in case they found my roof bunk."

"My brother's going to figure out who did this."

We both stared at her belongings.

"I guess I won't be opening the food truck today," she murmured.

"I can help you restock what you need in here."

"I don't need help," she shot back, then shifted in her nightshirt and rubbed her forehead. "Sorry. I'm really tired, and I know you're trying to help, but I need a couple minutes. I'm not a morning person unless I'm in the water."

"Should we go to the water then?" I didn't know why I asked.

"I ..." She squinted at me. "I think that might be nice."

I opened the back door for her, and she stepped out, not even pausing to put any more clothes on. It wasn't the time to tell her that I could barely have a conversation with her in that nightshirt, let alone feel good about her walking around the beach where others could see.

Yet, the beach was empty, with the sun just starting to rise beyond it.

She pushed her small foot into the wet sand and let the tide roll in to submerge it. I stood on the edge of dry land, not sure if I wanted to remove my shoes and step in with her.

My phone rang, making her jump. I slid it from my pocket and switched it to silent.

"You can answer it."

"No, I can't." I shook my head. "I forgot to silence it."

She breathed out like me turning off my empire for a second eased her. "Thank you."

We let the minutes pass by as the sun rose.

"So, we get another sunrise," I murmured. We'd agreed not to discuss that time. I knew it, but my mind went to where we got along. It was how you built a base to trust on. I needed that with her, and she needed it with me.

"I get the sunrise over the beach a lot. Your island was pretty too."

"I get why you love the town. This is a definite perk."

She sighed. "I guess I'll be moving sooner than I planned." She breathed in the salty air, and I did the same. It was fresh in a weird, warm way, like it could wash away all your sins and still give you something to live for after.

"Because of the food truck?" It would be better to let her come to terms with the arrangement instead of forcing something from her.

"Maybe. Or maybe because I read my grandma's letter." She wiggled her feet deeper until they were almost completely sucked down by the sand. "I think you're right that she was trapping you into protecting me."

"Now we see how smart she was to do so. No one would have ever attempted ransacking my girlfriend's food truck."

She turned to me. "You're that powerful and well-known?"

"Outside this town, *ragazza*, I'm a god."

She squinted into the sun like she was trying to see something way out there. "Do you think if there really were gods, they would enjoy it? The decisions, being responsible for lives, moving mountains maybe when they were tired?" Her sapphire eyes cut to me. "Do you get tired, Bastian?"

I didn't answer her. If I opened my mouth, I'd say something I didn't think either of us could handle. Morina could see somewhere in me that I didn't want anyone to see. She asked questions and rolled with things in her mind no one else would. Her thoughts put into words so quickly were dangerous.

At least to me.

The wind blew her dark chocolate waves off her shoulders, and the sun had risen just enough to kiss her tanned skin. The silhouette she created against the sea and sunrise was one an artist should have captured.

She cleared her throat, perhaps realizing I wouldn't answer. "Anyway, you think I'm stupid for not giving in right away, for not taking your hand in marriage immediately. Maybe I was. I needed time to adapt."

"I understand that, but you haven't got the time."

"Well, I'm starting to get that." She grabbed for her wrist, perhaps seeking the beaded bracelets I'd spotted before, but they weren't there. She still ran her hands back and forth, trying to find comfort without them.

"Should I get someone to pack for you?"

"Pack for me?" She chuckled. "I wonder how many times you've moved over the years and had someone pack it all up for you."

She liked to point out our differences. It created a barrier that she felt like she needed. I was okay with that. We'd need boundaries anyway.

"If you're fine packing yourself, I can have Dante drive you over when you're ready."

"I have a pickup truck. I just don't use it much." She cleared her throat. "I can look over some buildings with you. I don't have access to everything with regard to rent yet but I can owe you for half of wherever we stay."

"I already own a building near the company." I'd only recently purchased it but I didn't feel the need to tell her that.

Why I was going to such great lengths to make her comfortable, I didn't know. No one was going to be scoping out our living room. "No need for rent when I'm as invested in this venture as you are. I'm hoping to stay in your good graces enough that I can buy out your shares when the time comes."

"I need to trust you'll keep this city safe and thriving, Bastian. My grandma—"

"She didn't trust me."

"Well, right."

"My father wasn't as good to her as he should have been," I admitted, knowing that my only reason for being here should have been to make sure I cleaned up that business now.

"Okay." She dragged out that same word, a tell that she was uncomfortable and didn't know how to proceed.

As the wind picked up and she shivered, I couldn't help but be irritated with her lack of clothing. I unzipped my hoodie and handed it to her. She frowned and took a step back. "I'm fine."

"You're shivering," I pointed out.

She shook her head as if my hoodie was extremely offensive. I held up the hoodie again. "Seriously?"

"Then you'll be cold. Plus, I'm in shock that you're not wearing a suit. A hoodie was one thing, now a T-shirt?"

The way she said it with a straight face, in utter disbelief had me looking down to make sure I actually looked all right. Then, a laugh burst out of me. "Are you kidding me?"

"No!" She snatched my hoodie as I continued to laugh at her and stuffed her arms in the sleeves. "It's unnerving that someone wears a suit so much but seeing you out of it feels unnatural."

"Well, I was sleeping when I got a call about your break-in."

"Did you run here to save me?" She blinked with wide eyes

and a smarmy smirk.

"I'd think you'd be thankful," I grumbled and turned back to the food truck.

"I'm a little perturbed is what I am. I won't be able to open the food truck, and they didn't even do a good job of finding me. I mean, wasn't this an attempted kidnapping?" She stomped after me. "They didn't have to wreck my equipment."

Making light of the fact that they probably would have tortured her had my mood shifting, but I kept up my quick pace to the truck.

"I would have appreciated a note or maybe a call with some polite questioning instead. Who knows, maybe we all want the same thing?" She sounded so nonchalant.

She was young. She hadn't lived my life, I reminded myself the same way Dante had a few days prior.

"I don't get why we all can't work something out. Instead, we have to act like a bunch of crazy people with all these ridiculous stipulations and have people break into our property."

She was on a tangent, grumbling to herself now, but it struck a nerve. "Your food truck was ransacked, Morina," I growled at her, turning.

She stopped abruptly and my hoodie hung from her shoulders, so big it was halfway down her legs, the zipper flapping open in the wind because she hadn't bothered to zip it up.

She looked a rumpled mess, the same way she'd looked on my jet, and the idea had me bordering on furious.

I tried to keep my sanity with her but I was failing.

They'd have taken her like this, and they'd have been tempted.

They'd have torn apart every shred of innocence and love she had left for this world.

I stalked up to her and grabbed the zipper.

"What ... what are you doing?" she squeaked as I pulled it all the way up to her chin.

"Covering you up and keeping you warm."

"It's not that cold."

"Yes, but you're that exposed." I didn't stop at the zipper. I pulled the hood up over her head and tucked some of her hair into it. "You were too exposed in that truck. I can't have that on me."

Her eyes narrowed, and she searched my face. Her hand came up to it and she smoothed my jaw. "I think my grandma was right about you. You want to do right by everyone." Then she shook her head and pulled away. "I don't need you for protection, Bastian. You shouldn't have the burden of all your father's wrongdoings on you. My grandma shouldn't have put my safety on you either."

Why did her saying that make me actually want to do it? I knew she was right. I knew her life didn't fall on mine. Yet, in my business, everything fell to me. I had a family that relied on me too. "Blood and lives have been on and in my hands since the day I was born."

No one had ever said they weren't. For her to do so made me care for her in a way I shouldn't have. She was a tiny little storm, but she could turn into a tsunami for me. I could so easily care for her, and I didn't want that.

We'd started on a beach, sharing a moment. Here we were again, sharing pieces of ourselves we shouldn't have.

I stepped back. "Let's get this ball rolling, huh?"

"Right." She nodded, her hand dropping to her side. Then, she pointed to the food truck, now mere feet away. "Well, I can stay here for a few more nights and clean it up."

"Stay where?" I stared around. She couldn't really think

she was staying in that tin box another night. Not after what happened. I gave her the opportunity to change her mind.

"Well, I need to clean it up and it'll give me time to—"

"All you've been given is time." The words burst out of me. "You're not staying here even if I have to drag you to our place today."

She blinked as her mouth dropped open.

"I swear to God, Morina. I'm not in the business of being told no. I make efficient and reasonable demands for that very reason. I've been more than gracious with you."

"Gracious? You're asking me to move in with you in a week's time and then marry you when I don't know anything about you."

I dragged my eyes up and down her body. "You know a few things about me." She'd pushed my buttons and instead of taking the mature route, I pushed hers back.

"Oh, screw you! That was supposed to be a one-night stand and now we're in a once-in-a-lifetime hell together." She stomped her foot. "I need time."

"You don't have it." I glared at her. "You're not staying in the food truck again in the next six months. You'll be my Untouchable soon, and I won't risk your safety even if you're willing to gamble with it. You're too valuable."

"What?" She crossed her arms. "Because of the company?"

"Well, that's obvious, isn't it?" Standing outside at the ass crack of dawn made it not so obvious for me, though. Was she something more to me?

"Will you find out who did this? I think they should be held accountable." She glared at the mess.

"Yes. They will be." They could have kidnapped her and that thought alone had me wanting to hold them all more than accountable. "I protect what's mine. And that's you. My fiancée."

She huffed and pushed past me to her food truck. "Fine. But I'm doing this for my town. You know that, right? Otherwise, I wouldn't do a single part of it. I'd donate these stocks. I'd get rid of the burden this is. It's ridiculous that you'd do all this for money, Bastian. It really is."

I watched her storm inside. She threw things into a bag, not paying me any mind.

I completely agreed with her.

Money didn't matter.

For me, it was never about that.

It was about the family, about making my legacy something better than my father's.

I breathed it and lived by it and suffered for it. I didn't take my responsibilities lightly.

She would have to learn not to either.

I peered into her food truck to ask, "Would you like me to call Mr. Finley to tell him we're engaged or would you like to?"

"Why don't we do it together?" she sneered. "Since we're a couple now and all."

It took patience to deal with that attitude of hers. I liked to think I had a little of it. "Tonight then. I'll leave Dante here to watch your truck while you pack. He can drive you over when you're ready."

I left her at the food truck and called a driver so that Dante could stay with her.

As I stood waiting, I knew I'd have to deal with finding the men who did this. The respect of my family and Morina's life was at stake.

The uncomfortable feeling that she could have been hurt didn't go away when I called Cade to tell him that I wanted action taken against those who'd wrecked her truck.

"What type of action, bro?" he chuckled. "It's not like we're going to throw them in a river. We haven't used force in a long time. I'll talk to the syndicates in the area to make sure they're aware you're now engaged."

"See that you do." I pulled at my neck and tried to get the kink out of it before the next words fell from my lips. "And, Cade, I want an example made. Use some force this time. She could have been seriously harmed."

My brother didn't say anything back for a moment as I heard rustling on the line. "You okay, Bastian?"

"Yeah, I'll be fine once this shit is over."

CHAPTER 15: MORINA

I needed more time on the water ... or on my own.

Nothing felt the same.

Bastian looked at me like suddenly the weight of my safety was on his shoulders and nothing about that sat right with me.

He'd been exposed to something so different in his life. I could see it when he looked over my food truck again and shook his head, the way the line between his brows deepened when he called someone to make sure there were eyes on me.

I didn't know how they accomplished any of it or how I was going to deal with people following me around for the next six months, but I knew I had to try.

I waved to Bradley as I pulled my board up and hooked it to my truck. He ambled over, water droplets still falling from his dark hair. His sculpted body flexed as he rubbed the hair back and forth, trying to shake it off. "You opening the truck soon?"

"Nah, not today." I stared at the window, contemplating how I'd put across my closing. I should have had a social media account or website to give those updates, but I figured it would have lost some of its small-beach-town charm.

"Well, that's a shame." He crossed his arms over his chest and stared at the window with me. "What're we looking at?"

"I need a sign that says I'm closing."

"Oh." He turned on his heel. "I got you! Be right back."

He sprinted toward the parking lot, not asking any questions or wanting any more details, just happy to help. I smiled at his back, not understanding why I'd never pursued more with him over the years. He'd been a great friend, a good lay, and was as noncommittal in pursuing a relationship as I was. Maybe that's what made us work so well together.

I sighed as I saw Dante idling in the parking lot too, knowing my life was about to be much more complicated.

Bradley jumped in the back of his red Jeep and popped back up two minutes later with a wooden sign. It looked like a box lid of some sort with pine slats nailed together and he'd used black spray paint to write Closed until Further Notice.

The man beamed when he approached me with his handiwork. "This work well enough for you?"

"I'm not sure whether to be impressed or concerned that you have all that in the back of your Jeep."

"Impressed, Mo. I'm a damn problem solver." He leaned the sign on the counter window and mumbled, "I can nail it in later. I'm guessing you're about to be on your way with that suit in the parking lot?"

"Yeah. It's complicated." I sighed and he came to stand next to me without prying for more information. "I don't know when I'll open again."

"That mean you also don't know when we'll be sleeping together again?" He smirked.

His question was justified, especially since Bastian had thrown around the fiancée word yesterday.

"Yeah, probably that too." I combed a hand through my hair. "Again, it's complicated."

"I hate that word, but I'm here for you if you need me."

"I think I need to beat you in catching a couple waves every morning still." I chuckled and nudged his shoulder.

What would I do without a friendship as easy as his? Or a town as perfect as this one? I turned to watch the ocean once more before I locked up the food truck and waved goodbye to Bradley.

Dante ended up coming over from the parking lot after giving me some time alone.

I dragged sand and water into the car with me, along with a half-empty suitcase.

"You need to stop at your grandma's?" he asked while watching grains of sand sprinkle onto the expensive carpet.

"Sure. I have to grab a few things. I'm guessing we can move furniture later. Or does Bastian already have a style?"

He chuckled. "He definitely has a style."

"Care to enlighten me?"

"It's ..." He glanced back at my feet and shook his head once before speeding off toward my grandmother's. "It's clean. Let's put it that way."

"Great." I slouched into the seat.

"It'll be fine." He tossed a file back to me. "That's some documentation you should look over. There's a prenup and other information that pretty much protects both you and Bastian. Also, Tropical Oil is having its meeting soon. You need to read up on the company, understand the oil business, and probably familiarize yourself with the board members."

"Okay." I curled my lip and glared at the packet. It looked big. Too big. Like a stack of homework I didn't want. Didn't they know I was a college dropout? Actually, I hadn't ever gone. I'd been offered a spot at one of the state universities, and on the first day of classes, I decided I wasn't made for the pressure of all that.

The words about commitment in my grandmother's letter flew back to me.

Other than my food truck and the humane society, had I committed to anything longer than a couple months?

Right on time, my phone went off.

Dr. Nathan: Pups miss you and I'm thinking it's because Tiffany keeps mixing up their toys and food.

Morina: I miss them too. I can come by tomorrow. Life has been crazy.

See, these were my passions. People committed to what they loved and believed in.

"I don't think I'll have time to read all that." I scratched the side of my face and shoved the papers to the other seat.

"Honestly, I feel the same way you do—go in blind and figure it out as you go. That's what people in the past did. Yet, Bastian handles most of the business side of things, and he's adamant that it's important."

I snorted, not agreeing to anything.

When I got to my grandma's, Dante came in with me and sat as I packed another suitcase. I grabbed too many crystals, a salt lamp from the spare room, my bracelets, and lots of toiletries. A couple weeks of clothing was all I would need for now. I'd be back to change things out.

I glanced at a few plants I'd told Grandma I'd water before she passed. They were all shriveled up. I groaned and shoved two pots under my arm and the other on top of my suitcase.

"I'm ready."

Dante glanced up and nodded before looking over the living room. "You'd get a good price on this place right now if you're interested in putting it on the market."

I turned on my flats to try to take an objective look. Granite counters. Hardwood floors. She'd maintained her home without aging it.

"Yeah," I said softly. "I don't know why I'm hesitating, but it feels like she's still here. I don't know. It hasn't been that much time."

"I get it." His voice matched mine, and when he clapped a hand on my shoulder, it was warm with comfort. "Don't rush things. The universe will work with you."

I nodded. For all the crystals and beads and salt lamps I had, I knew I should believe him. Dante was a man who probably could Reiki the hell out of someone. He'd done it to me days ago. I wanted to trust the universe, and maybe having him as a friend for six months would help. "This whole arrangement is going to be a hell of a lot, huh?"

"Probably." His chuckle was deep as he took the suitcase and plant without so much as toppling the pot. He walked toward the door and pointed at the plants under my arm. "It's going to be hell trying to get Bastian to keep those too."

"Oh, come on." I blew a raspberry. "They'll bloom right back up when I give them some water."

His chuckle turned to a laugh as he came back to grab my salt lamp. "Let's go dirty up the man's place, huh?"

We loaded the Rolls-Royce and left, passing the company where most of the town worked.

Twenty minutes later, we'd arrived.

"Is there a parking spot for me?" I asked as Dante keyed in a code and the garage opened. "I'd like to get my pickup here so I can go when I need to."

"We'll make sure you have one. It can be right next to Bastian's here."

He drove to a spot surrounded by metal walls and another set of doors. I wide-eyed it all. "A garage within a garage?"

He shrugged. "Bastian likes his privacy. This gives access

to a private elevator too."

"Private jets and private elevators. A lot of things the man needs to hide."

Dante's dimples popped out with his smile. "He's not really hiding all that much from you specifically. He was followed as a child because his father was infamous, Morina. Bred to be a leader. Homeschooled for security purposes and then made enough partnerships that even the paparazzi follow him now."

I scooted toward the door, and Dante opened it for me. I didn't know how to take what he said, so I kept quiet. Bastian and I didn't grow up at all alike. We'd had one fun night, and now we had to try to merge our lifestyles for months.

We lugged my stuff out of the car.

Dante left the suitcases. "A doorman will bring up everything."

"Well, I'm taking my plants and salt lamp." I hugged them closer.

"Glad to hear it." He ushered me into a small elevator lined with mirrors on three sides. The other featured a floor-to-ceiling window.

I gulped and contemplated gripping the railing as we got higher and higher. "How far up does he live?"

"*You'll*"—he emphasized—"be living on the fiftieth floor."

"Jesus," I whispered as the doors opened to a white penthouse. The wall-to-wall ceiling-to-floor window view was the first staggering thing I laid eyes upon. As I approached, the landscape unfolded until I could see all of the ocean, all of the city, all of my town. I knew my jaw had dropped. I didn't even try to hide my astonishment. I'd been inspired by small towns and small things my whole life. The ocean was the monster that I submerged myself in. Now, I got to look down at it, and it did not disappoint.

And yet, standing so far above it, away from everything I held close to my heart, my perception shifted.

I spun to tell Dante that this was some different type of universe I was in and that I wasn't sure if it would work for me, but he'd gone to the open-plan kitchen while Bastian stood right before me.

His eyes fell to my plants right away. "No."

That's how he greeted me.

"What?" I whispered, not really taking in what he said. I was staring at him in this place, in his natural environment. In his universe.

All clean lines. All navy suit and brown leather against a white, pristine background. The frown on his face cut perfectly with his strong jaw, a total contrast from those soft lips. Everything about Bastian was hard but appealing, dominating but desirable.

"No, we will not have pink lamps and dead plants in here."

Before I could sound off, Dante snickered into the refrigerator behind us and a woman with literally the best body I'd ever seen walked out from the hallway on the left. She wore all black. A cropped top ended just below her breasts, and tattoos kissed her mixed skin tone. "This her?" She pointed to me with a red manicured nail.

"Katie," Bastian pinched the bridge of his nose. "Why are you still here?"

I almost dropped my plant. Was he having relations even when he was expecting me to show up? It was within his rights, I knew that, but it didn't stop my stomach from clenching.

She walked up and patted the side of his face pretty hard. His jaw ticked and she smiled. It was a little bit of scary and a lot of beautiful all mixed into one. "Because I'm always welcome here? You said that stupid shit. Not me."

Bastian's eyes ping-ponged between us and then he pointed to her. "She's a colleague. Nothing more, nothing less."

"Oh, I mean, he almost fucked me." Katie walked over to the fridge where Dante grumbled to go easy on me. "What? It's true. Although now I refer to him as a brother of sorts. He's not *only* a colleague. Maybe a friend who knows not to fuck with me, huh?"

Bastian shook his head as we both looked at her and Dante standing next to one another. Dante bit into an apple, and she leaned into him like she was really that comfortable with these men.

"I'm Katalina. I head up the bratva and partner with your soon-to-be fiancé. I intend to clean up the ports if he can't. So, please make sure you both do."

"I'm ..." I looked at Bastian and raised my plants and salt lamp for him to look at. "So, this is a lot when I'm just moving in, right?"

Right when I thought he might agree with me, his doorbell rang because why wouldn't his penthouse have a damn doorbell instead of someone just knocking? He spun to let in the doorman who had both my suitcases. The red color against his white marble flooring almost had me wincing.

"Yup, this is a lot," Katie agreed before she walked to the door. "I was leaving anyway. My husband is a fucking feral dog if I don't hurry back to him and my kid. So, just know I'm here. Not for you to reach out to and be friendly with, but more like I'm here, watching you if you fuck up. I don't exactly want to come clean it up. So. Don't."

"Fuck off, Katie," Bastian grumbled.

Dante followed her to the door. "I'll drive you to the airport. These two don't need me with the security here anyway."

With that, Katie slammed the door behind them.

I looked like a frumpy deer in headlights with her leaving me in the dust after that warning.

"Her bark is worse than her bite." He thought about that for a second. "Nope. It's as bad, but her warning was directed toward me."

"Mm-hmm." Why did I suddenly want to burst into tears? I was overwhelmed. I was straight up in shock, I think. More than that though, they all interacted like a family that I was going to be part of.

"I can't act like that." I glanced at Bastian. "I mean, I'm a little bit of everything but I'm not strong enough to stand my ground the way that woman does."

"I don't expect that from you."

"What is your expectation then, because I'll tell you one thing, I'm pretty sure I've avoided a lot of situations in my life to avoid anyone expecting anything from me, and now I think you all might need me to uphold something I can't. Dante gave me this file and—"

"Take a breath, Morina." He approached and outstretched his arms as if to take the plant and lamp from mine.

I gripped them tightly, not letting them go. "What are you doing?"

"I'm taking these from you."

"No." I stepped back. "These stay, Bastian. They'll live. They just need water."

He peered down at the offensive plants. "It's dead, *piccola ragazza*," he said in a voice that was probably meant to pacify me.

"It's not dead." My heart squeezed hearing him call me that. Why did I resort to thinking about how he'd cared for me during a meaningless one-night stand? I took another humongous step back. "Do you nurture plants back to health?"

"I ..." He paused over his words, probably because my line of reasoning was somewhat outrageous at this point. "Of course I don't nurture plants back to health."

"Then you wouldn't know!" I stomped over to his granite countertop and placed the plants in the center.

"Morina, no." His jaw worked as he stared at the dark pots full of dirt so dry it would surely crumble if either of us touched it.

I ignored him and floated over to an end table where I set the salt lamp.

He combed his hand through his dark hair. "Look, you get to add things to this place however you want ... mostly. I'm going to try to stay out of your way, and I'd appreciate it if you stayed out of mine. This place is more than big enough for the two of us."

"So, then you're fine with the plants there." I waved over to my newest favorite things. I took great pride in the way Bastian looked literally itchy while staring at them. He needed something to ruffle his feathers because God knew this whole situation ruffled mine.

He stuck his hands in his pockets, and I thought I saw the fists they made under the expensive fabric. "Fine," he said through gritted teeth. "Salt lamp and suitcases in your room though."

"Suitcases. The salt lamp stays. I need peace when I'm out here."

"Peace? I'm not even going to be here."

"You're here now. And this place isn't peaceful."

"You don't like it?" His voice was suddenly pained.

"Does it matter?"

He dragged a hand through his hair. "No, I guess it doesn't. I'll help with your suitcases and show you to your room."

"So, we'll pretend we're together when people come over and that I sleep in the same room?"

"The Queen and King of England had different rooms," Bastian said, like it wasn't a completely preposterous idea.

"Not one of my friends would ever think I'd live with a man if I wasn't sleeping with him," I grumbled but that was sort of a lie because I didn't really have any close friends anyway.

"Who? Linny? I have yet to see that woman since the first night I met you." He scoffed like he knew me better than everyone already.

"Linny travels a lot." I crossed my arms. "Fine. Would your friends believe that?"

"Katie lived with me for a while."

For some reason, that grated on my nerves, and I probably should have let my feelings about it die, but my mouth ran away with itself. "And she just said you almost slept with her!"

"It was complicated."

I told my curiosity to shut up and ground my teeth together to keep from asking further questions.

Turning to the left, he ushered me into a room that was bigger than my grandmother's whole house. The views were sweeping and again looked over my town, while the bed and walls were decorated in soft pastels.

I trailed a hand across the oak dresser and circled the bed to get to the opposite door. It led to a bathroom with ombre mosaic tile all the way up the shower walls and mirrors framed in gold to match the faucet.

My fingertips dragged against the deep blue tile. "It's like a wave."

"I figured you'd like it."

That one comment had me turning back to study him. "What do you mean?"

He cleared his throat. "There's another room too. This one though, I think, suits you."

I hummed. I wanted to tell him that he didn't know me, but I was starting to think that maybe we knew one another a little. He was putting me in new situations and witnessing me in such a vulnerable state, it caused me to question all relationships I'd had up to this moment.

"I think this will work out fine." I nodded as he placed my suitcase on the ground near the dresser. I folded my hands together, although I was itching to get my crystals laid out. "Want to give me a tour of the rest of the place?"

"Sure. Guess you'll need to see where we pretend to sleep with one another," His tone was light, but my body was on some sort of high alert being alone with him in his natural environment.

Bastian was one of those enigmas who didn't belong in our world. He was too appealing but elusive enough and powerful enough to stay away from. He walked through this place like he owned it, and I wondered if he felt like he owned every single thing in the world.

Maybe he almost did—he was certainly much closer to it than I was, even with the prospect of owning some of this oil company.

The hallway stretched on and on with two more double doors that Bastian pointed to. "Spare bedroom and spare bath." We passed another sliding door, and he mumbled that it was closet space.

"Should I stock paper towels there or something?" I asked. "I need to know our chores too, because I'm not very domesticated."

He pulled at his neck like he was uncomfortable saying the next part. "A maid comes through daily to make sure we have what we need. You can tell her if you'd like something even if it's a shirt. Just let her know your size. A chef will be here every now and then to cook, but he mostly stocks things in the fridge."

I couldn't hold back my scrunched up face. "A maid and a chef?"

"It sounds ridiculous, but I didn't know how we would operate together and this just makes it easier."

"Is this because of me though or do you always have these things?"

He glanced toward the last door at the end of the hall. The arched doorway and double wood doors told me that was the master suite. "Does it really matter what I have in other places, Morina?"

"Well, if we live together for six months—"

He cut me off. "This place is big enough that you'll probably barely see me. I travel a lot too."

"Hence the private jet," I grumbled and turned to the main suite. I didn't know why I was annoyed with him for separating us and reminding me of how different our lives were.

Maybe I was irked that this life seemed easier, and I wanted my life to seem easiest, uncomplicated. I didn't want to want anything in the world. It made for unhappy thoughts about greener grass on the other side.

I knew the allure wasn't true, but I didn't need temptation brewing for six months. By the water in my town was where I found happiness, but luxury had a funny way of presenting itself as the most appealing thing in the world.

I gripped both handles of the large doors and glanced over my shoulder. "Shall we?"

The left side of his mouth tipped up a little. "You shall whenever you want."

I don't know if I imagined it, but his eyes trekked down my

face and paused at my lips as I licked them. I shoved the doors open and ignored the butterflies in my stomach.

The bed in the middle of the room overlooked more of those sweeping views. The windows spanned the whole room and wrapped around to the bathroom. There wasn't much to say except, "Wow." I whispered it as I walked on plush carpet around the bed and up to the window. Bastian came up next to me, so close I sucked in a breath when he reached out. I thought he was going to pull me to him, that we were going to continue our one-night stand.

The fact my mind went there when I'd told myself we couldn't ever go there again was proof enough that I needed to do some self-reflection in my own room.

Yet, he didn't reach for me. His hand went right past me to push the window and it moved quickly, extending out a few inches before sliding into a pocket in the wall.

He stepped out and beckoned me out to stand over the city on the terrace with its glass balustrade.

I shook my head.

He tilted his, confused. "Are you scared?"

This was new for me. "I guess I am."

"I've had coffee out here, Morina. It's completely stable."

"I mean, you say that, but I'm pretty happy where I'm standing."

He put his hand out. "Come on. One foot, at least."

"What for?"

"Maybe to prove to yourself you can do it. You can try something new."

"I surf and try new things all the time."

He nodded like he didn't believe me at all.

I took a deep breath and stepped forward enough that half of my foot was on the balcony. The threshold between the two had me wobbling a little, and I immediately grabbed his hand.

The electricity that shot through me scared me as much as the balcony. My gaze flew to his and a little smirk rose on his full lips.

Nothing more and nothing less.

Did he feel it too?

Or was he trying not to laugh at my fears? I set my other boot on the balcony and shifted my weight. "If we die, and I can make your existence hell in the afterlife, you bet your ass I'm going to."

"If we die, your grandma and my dad will make both our afterlives hell."

I chuckled. He was probably right. A twinkle lit in his eyes, and the wind ruffled his hair enough that he almost appeared approachable, like we were on equal footing.

Maybe that's why my words flowed more freely than they should have. "I don't know if I'm scared of this marriage or scared I'm going to take all this on and not be able to finish it. I don't finish a lot of things I start."

"Why do you think that is?"

"Might be that my brain's wired a little differently. My grandma always said I had a jumpiness to me. My teachers claimed it was an attention issue, but I think it's that everyone's different and, in the end, it makes us all the same. I struggle to keep my attention on one thing long enough to see it through."

"Well, we'll just have to switch it up every now and then."

"Or we can power through these six months," I suggested, uncomfortable that Bastian had so easily accepted something about me that I was normally embarrassed about.

"Sure, Morina," he murmured, "sure." He waved me back inside and told me we needed to dial Mr. Finley.

We sat in silence as the phone rang and rang.

When he answered, Bastian gave him the news and I confirmed it.

"I'll check that off the list and make sure we legally document this milestone. Congratulations."

Or condolences.

After he hung up, I announced I was going to my bedroom. What else could I do in a place with a stranger?

Later that day, I heard the front door open and close.

I didn't see Bastian for three days after that.

CHAPTER 16: BASTIAN

"What the fuck do you mean you're on the way to my new place?" Why did I yell questions at my brother every time he was on the phone?

"I want to do a security sweep of the place and make sure the cameras are all doing what I need them to."

"You can't do that from Chicago?" I pointed to my driver and mouthed, "Home." He was quick to steer in that direction. I probably would have gotten a smart comment from Dante but he'd gone to handle a job across the country.

"Well, no." There was a pause. "Plus, we used a little bit of muscle for this Morina girl. I'm coming to meet her and, well, I'm babysitting."

"You're what?"

"I have our niece with me," he grumbled, like he knew that omission would send me into a rage.

"Don't tell me you have my niece on the jet right now." I ground out. "Her parents will kill you. Please tell me you called Katie."

"Well, no. They left me with her for half the day. What did they expect?"

"You're fucking asking to die. I swear to you, Katie is a damn bratva queen." I lowered my voice, used to talking in secret when it came to how our family used to operate. "She's married to our enforcer. Do you understand the concept of babysitting for them?"

Rome and Katie had met when we were all just kids. As

we'd taken our rightful places in powerful positions, their love had grown enough that they'd brought a child into the world. That four-year-old was our pride and joy but also the thing we were most protective of.

"Ivy asked to go to an amusement park. They have one down there with characters and shit. We'll go for a few hours."

"You have to plan for a trip there, Cade. They book the damn park out!" I fisted my hand, trying to wrangle the fury I had with my brother's flippant behavior. He was the youngest. He didn't know responsibility like I did and he had a knack for doing things before he thought about them.

"Well, I hacked part of the system while we were flying."

"Of course you did." I sighed. "You can't go today. Ivy is going to be too tired. And you better have my niece's seat belt on."

"Technically, she's not your niece. Rome's our cousin, you know."

"Of course she's our niece. We're Armanellis. She's *famiglia*, you idiot. Did you say that shit in front of her?"

"No. She's squealing to go to the bathroom. I'm just trying to piss you off more, see if you'll explode before I get there."

He was making me go back to that damn penthouse and under these conditions. An explosion was warranted. "When's the plane landing?"

"About thirty minutes. I intend to be there in an hour, and we're going to be hungry."

"I'm not within an hour's distance. Go eat somewhere first. I got Morina there and I haven't ..."

"You haven't what?"

"I'm not really there." I pinched the bridge of my nose. I didn't need Cade questioning how I was handling this situation.

"You serious? You gotta play hubby and wifey and you

154

aren't even getting to know her? That's not like you."

"What's that supposed to mean?"

"It means normally you can find common ground. You have a knack for making alliances, obviously. Is she that bad?"

"She's not bad at all." I defended her immediately and then tried to backtrack on that statement. "She's just in my space."

"Kind of what a wife does."

"You know this is a legal marriage, that's it, right?"

"Well, sort of. You have to fake it enough for it to look real. If someone believes she's not an Untouchable, that puts her in harm's way again, right?"

I punched the back seat of the Rolls-Royce. The pressure of Maribel's damn will shouldn't have been on me. "I'm so sick of carrying Mario's shit on my back."

"Dad was great at building shitty partnerships."

I cleared my throat. "Morina doesn't know he was importing illegal shipments, okay? I need that kept out of the equation. I'm working on showing her that we're here to shift Tropical Oil to clean energy and that it will help her city thrive. We'll clean up the other shit quietly. Got it?"

"Why not? We ended the drug imports years ago when Dad died. She should be thankful."

"Maribel didn't trust us enough to sell those stocks to me for that very reason. You think her granddaughter is going to want to sell them to me if she knows our father lied to her grandmother?"

"Right." Cade sighed. "I'll wipe it from as many places as I can. The dark web might have some mention of the drugs that were coming in."

"See that you do. I don't want any more complications. This marriage is a big enough blip on our radar."

"It's for damn sure not something I was expecting." After a

beat, Cade cracked up. "I never would have thought you would be the one getting married now."

"Why?"

"Man. I don't know. You're the head of our family. It's enough work as it is. You have to right all Dad's wrongs, and you take it way more seriously than you should." There was rustling. "Ivy's back. We're going to eat a snack. A little advice, bro. I'd start letting your fiancée know a bit more about what's coming up. You have a damn charity gala to attend for the oil ports in a week. Does she know?"

"There's nothing to know. She'll get dressed and go. We can announce our engagement publicly and put together a small ceremony a week later."

"You're planning all this without your bride like it's going to go over so well." He chuckled into the phone. "I'm excited to see how it all crumbles."

"You're a sick fuck most days, Cade."

"Proud of it too." He mumbled something to Ivy and then said to me, "Be a pal and let Katie know we're safe and sound if she calls you."

Then he hung up.

Not twenty minutes later, Katie's number popped up on my screen.

There was a time way back when I thought she and I could be more than what we were. She was this powerful girl who didn't bend to anyone. We found out she had ties to the bratva, and slowly she chipped away at all their businesses and ours. She'd become one of the most influential people in the world, and I loved that we had a great relationship, the type between colleagues but also like a family. We all worked together to make sure our businesses ran smoothly, that our families stepped in line.

"Yes, Katie?" I answered on the fifth ring and eyed the tall building that my penthouse was located in. We still had another thirty minutes of traffic to navigate before I arrived.

"So, your brother says his fucking flight just landed with my child." Her voice was filled with venom.

"I had nothing to do with this."

"I don't know if I believe that. Except, you're probably hiding from your soon-to-be fiancée and so that may just be the case. Either way, you now have everything to do with it. Ivy can't stay up all night flying back on a plane. So, she's staying with you and Morina. Take her to the park, feed her well, and watch her like a hawk. Those parks have got to be crowded. Cade needs to get a team together if it's to be safe." She paused. "I can't get there fast enough, Bastian."

The concern at the end of her commands put out all the fight in me. "I got her, Katie. She's fine. We'll have fun, huh?"

"Oh, you won't have fun. It's going to be absolute hell. If she comes back unhappy, though, I'll break all the bones in your body before I skin Cade alive."

She was the second person to hang up on me that day.

I didn't flinch at her words. I'd been threatened enough times. I knew she meant what she said. I also knew that I would die before anything happened to the little monster that was about to tornado through my penthouse.

I told the driver to speed the rest of the way, but we still didn't get there in time to intercept my family. Instead, I'd have to face the woman I'd been avoiding for days with my brother and niece there to witness the awkwardness.

As the elevator ascended to my door, I swear I could smell her scent already. She wore something spicy enough that it had lingered in my jet for days. I'd thought I'd be happy when it started to fade, but instead, I remember contemplating asking someone what the smell was.

Now, I'd get to smell it for six months.

That had to be some sort of rude karma that she probably believed in.

I shut my eyes, frustrated with myself for being irritated with her. Her grandmother's will wasn't her fault. The fact we'd slept together and I couldn't stop thinking about her bent over naked as fuck wasn't her fault either.

I didn't dislike the girl's company. I simply thought I'd never have to see her again. She was young and shot off at the mouth and wasn't at all what I needed for this venture. It was my last one. The last loose end my father had left for me. And he'd left a lot over the years.

This was the one thing I needed to right to give the family a new, fresh slate. It meant I was doing this clean as hell. No hiccups.

No loopholes.

If Maribel had willed that she wanted a marriage for me to prove I was going to make this company thrive, that's what she would get. Morina would see I meant business.

And no pleasure, even if I'd watched her hand drag across that mosaic tile and wanted it to be my dick instead. The way her bracelets jangled as she did it and her clean nails grazed each piece with a delicate touch, she was enticing.

And infuriating. I didn't need the complication of wanting her. So I stayed away.

Now, my brother was forcing a damn reunion even if he didn't know it.

When I exited the elevators, Ivy was running around my waterfall island with all the nearly dead plants directly in the middle. They were a complete eyesore. And the salt lamp was on as if it provided some sort of natural element to the space.

It didn't.

Morina believed in hocus-pocus. None of it made sense to me, but instead of being completely fine with her bringing it into the penthouse, I'd lashed out immediately.

That wasn't my usual nature, but with her, it was. Normally I would have agreed, set on us getting along.

She stirred some emotion in me that I couldn't control, and that only infuriated me more.

Cade winked at me when Ivy came running, her long curls everywhere. I was ready to catch her when she jumped right at me.

I might not have been a great person for Morina to live with, but I was a good-ass uncle. I caught Ivy before she was even halfway in the air. "My little poison Ivy. How did you get here?"

She squished my cheeks together and giggled. "On a plane, Uncle Bastian. You're so silly."

"Silly?" I lifted a brow in mock terror. "I'm not silly. I'm your very serious uncle."

She thought about it for a second, looked back at Cade who wiggled his tattooed fingers at her, and then pulled me close. "You're right. Cade's sillier than you."

I nodded solemnly. "Someone's got to be the oldest."

"That means you're the boss too, right? Mommy always says she's the boss, but I think maybe Daddy and you are bosses too." Then she leaned in and pulled my ear out way too hard for it to be comfortable. I didn't even wince because the little girl with her gray eyes and big dark curls had my whole soul, and I wasn't wiping that smile off her face for even a second. "Cade's not the boss though."

"Careful, you little monster," Cade said, even though he was looking into his phone now. "I hear everything. It's my superpower, and it might just make me the biggest boss of all."

She giggled and shook her head which turned to a full-body shake in my arms.

The girl had infinite amounts of energy, and I wasn't sure we were all ready for it, but we had her for the day and would just have to deal. I threw her up in the air, and she squealed in delight.

Then I plopped her on one of my hips. "What are you hungry for?"

"Your friend Morina fed me." She pointed over to the woman I still hadn't acknowledged.

I should have said hi or told her thank you, but we needed to have such a big conversation about what lay ahead that I decided we didn't need one at all.

We could just follow my lead. She could step in line like most people.

Like Ivy said, I was the boss.

Or one of them.

"That was very nice of Morina," I said softly to Ivy while looking at the woman I hadn't seen in days.

Her wavy hair was, as always, a mess that somehow worked around her face. She wore a tank top that was much too loose, with a picture of a hand making up a peace sign. She'd paired it with a blue sports bra that left little to the imagination. Her ripped jeans fit over her ass much better than I remembered, and she glared at me with a face I found I was starting to really like.

I set Ivy down and motioned for her to go play with Cade. He swooped her up into his lap and they started playing a game on his phone.

"Sorry for the visitors today." I slid my hands in my pockets, not sure how to approach the awkward phase we'd stumbled into.

"I like tiny visitors actually." She smirked toward Ivy who looked up and wiggled her fingers at Morina, always half-listening. "Ivy kept me company for a little bit while I made grilled cheese. The chef had the fridge stocked with lots of different cheeses, I'm guessing after they found out I eat that."

"Right." I cleared my throat. "We're going to head over to the amusement park first thing in the morning. Run her around there, and then she'll be going back home."

Cade's head popped up. "Not today?"

"Cade, you can't go to the park in the middle of the day. There are rides that take hours to get onto, and even if you hack every system that lets you skip lines, we still won't see everything. You want to start your time at the park with a half-tired child *and* with the knowledge you won't get to show her everything?"

Ivy nodded and looked at Cade with big puppy eyes. "I want to see everything, Uncle Cade."

"Of course you do." He hopped off the barstool with her. "Guess we need to go mess up Uncle Bastian's house then. We need to build a fort for our movie night."

"Yay!" Ivy screamed, but instead of skipping over to me to give me a high five, she skipped over to Morina. "You'll watch a movie with me, right?"

"Um ..." She glanced at me and then back at Ivy. "Sure. I think. I just ..." She wrung her hands together. "I have to go take care of some dogs first and then I'll be back to watch whatever you want."

I swear Ivy's whole body, even her curls, straightened at the mention of dogs. I shut my eyes in defeat and Cade slapped a palm to his head. Morina mouthed "What?" to us over Ivy's head.

"I want to see the dogs you take care of," Ivy announced.

Scratching the scuff of my five-o'clock shadow, I waited to see how Morina would navigate this one.

She glanced at me like she was caught between a rock and a hard place.

Yes, woman, you did this to yourself.

I looked away and ambled toward the fridge. She could figure out how to tell the cutest thing in the world no.

"Um ... well, I think your uncles probably want you to stay with them."

"Oh, they'll come with. Uncle Bastian, you have a car to drive us, right?" She turned those misty eyes toward me, and I didn't even hesitate.

"Of course I do, monster."

Morina's jaw dropped. "You ... you can't come."

"Why can't we all come, Morina?" I blinked real big like a little kid.

"I mean ... I guess if you want to hang out, but you haven't wanted to hang—"

"Yay!" Ivy cut her off and barreled into Morina's thighs to hug her.

She patted the child's back awkwardly and then side-eyed me. "I'm gonna change, then I guess we can get going in ten minutes if everyone's ready. I have to do a quick sweep of the kennels. I'm not going to be there long."

"But there's going to be dogs for me to pet, right?" Ivy asked, a tiny little pointer finger up in the air as if she needed to be clear.

"Mm-hmm." Morina started down the hallway to her room. When Ivy followed, Cade glanced at me, and I shrugged.

"Jesus Christ," my brother mumbled, then called, "Ivy, we're making a tent in Bastian's room while Morina gets ready and talks to Uncle Bastian."

The little girl shot off down the hall, and Cade ran after with a roar.

Just as he did, Morina turned into her bedroom even though she'd heard Cade announce that we would be talking.

I sighed and made my way to her door. With it being cracked and my being right behind her, I didn't think to knock.

When I cleared my throat, she spun away from her closet. "Do you think you could knock next time?"

"Knock?"

"Yes. This is my room." Her tone held anger and accusation.

It immediately put me on a defense I didn't need. "This is *our* room. Just like this whole place is our place."

"Wouldn't know it from who is in it all the time."

"Are you mad I haven't been here?"

"Nope." She said the word so loud it ping-ponged off the walls.

"I work and I told you I wouldn't be here much. I'm giving you space." I crossed my arms.

"Great. I'm happy with it." She didn't sound happy at all.

"I come home after three days and you immediately are gallivanting off to the humane society. So, that proves the point that we don't want to be around each other."

"Yup, that proves the point."

"Are you going to say anything you mean right now?"

"No!" She stomped her foot. She breathed fast, holding her fists tight at her sides. "I don't want to talk to you right now."

"Care to share why?"

"Because you're annoying me!" She winced when the words flew out of her. "I don't ... I'm not comfortable here. And I have my crystals and oils, and I surf to stay comfortable. I live in comfort, Bastian. I don't do luxury or chefs or white countertops well. I have to figure out the will because I can't buy food processors for my food truck to make money so I can buy more ingredients to sell and make more money. And I can't do any of that because I'm out of my depth."

"Out of your depth?" I repeated, trying to catch up with all the words she'd just thrown at me faster than a peregrine falcon diving for food.

"And this stupid packet of a million words and pages is like a different language. And it's boring, Bastian. Like really boring. And I know we don't know each other except for some not-boring sex on a plane, but I can't do boring. I'm not ... I don't think I'm—"

"Stop." Her eyes darted up to mine and she suddenly looked her age. A decade younger than me with big sapphire eyes that were scared and vulnerable. I always assumed she didn't care or it was no big deal for her because she acted nonchalant and told me exactly how she wanted things. But ... I took a deep breath. "Jesus, you talk fast, huh?"

"I normally don't."

I squinted at her. "When's the last time you were really nervous about something?"

"What type of question is that?" She wrung her hands like she had in the living room.

"Never mind." I had a feeling we were both going to get to know ourselves a lot better in the next few months. "Let's not do boring right now, huh? Let's go see the dogs and then watch the movie and act like children at a theme park. Then, we'll do boring."

She peered over at the paperwork lying on the bed. "It's really *boring*, Bastian," she whispered.

For some reason, I cracked up with her admission and the lines on her forehead disappeared as she smiled big.

Brilliant. Beautiful.

And brutal.

That's what that smile was.

She'd wreck my world if I wasn't careful.

CHAPTER 17: MORINA

We got to the humane society just as Dr. Nathan was locking the doors. With a grin, he swung the door open again, but his smile faltered when he saw I had a posse in tow.

"So, I brought extra volunteers tonight." I began introductions immediately so he wouldn't worry. "Ivy's almost five years old. She has eight more months to go, but she really wants to be a veterinarian when she grows up and loves dogs. Bastian and Cade are, um, good friends and Ivy's uncles."

Dr. Nathan's shoulders relaxed when he heard that Ivy's relatives were with her. "Nice to meet you all."

Technically, there was paperwork each person would have to sign to see animals, but Dr. Nathan looked tired, and we rarely printed copies of those forms anymore. We had a town of two thousand people and most of them brought their kids in every now and then just to pet the dogs.

"Dr. Nathan, if you need to get home to your family, that's fine. We'll feed the pups and do a walk-through. I need to check who needs nails clipped, and it was Moonshine who was having some issues right?"

"She just needs some love, is all. She's young and confused. I would have stayed with her longer, but it's actually my wedding anniversary tonight."

"Wonderful. Congratulations." Was it wrong of me to not ask how many years? And I had too many thoughts of Grandma's letter running through my head. She truly wanted to haunt me in some way, and that letter with its judgments on my ability to commit was a perfect example of why I couldn't get on board with marriage.

"Thanks. I like to tell her it's a feat she's stayed with me this long, and she likes to tell me that if it weren't for the humane society taking up a good portion of my day, she would have divorced me a long time ago."

The candidness had me giggling. Maybe I wasn't the only one not completely on board with matrimony, and yet they were making it work in a way I envied.

He patted my shoulder. "Thanks for stopping by. The animals miss you."

He shook hands again with Bastian and Cade and told Ivy she could grab some dog treats from the bowl on the counter.

Ivy skipped over to the rounded front desk, ringlets bouncing with her.

"So." I grabbed two boxes of toys from a side cabinet and shifted. "You guys can play with a couple of the dogs in the visiting area. I have to do some quick checks on a couple of our rock star dogs."

"Rock star dogs?" Bastian raised his eyebrows.

"They need and get a lot of attention, hence the name. Secretly, I call them our problem children, but most get adopted." I waved them along so we could get moving. The motion sensor lights flickered on down the speckled-tile hallway, setting off the puppies barking and the cats meowing. "This is the visitation room. There's toys and more treats on that table."

"Do you know which animal will be best for Ivy to play with?" Cade asked, his eyebrows pulled together. The brothers' stares were completely serious, and I melted as I witnessed two very good-looking men unleash their protective-dad stances on me.

Inside, my ovaries woke up after being in hibernation for a very long time.

Ivy with her uncles would do that to any female. She was cute and bouncy and had so much positive energy vibrating through her that you wanted to soak in as much innocent love as you could.

"I have the perfect girl for her to meet. She's a rock star, but only because she wants constant love. She's the one the doc was worried about. He texted me that she's been really depressed, but I bet it's only because she's lonely. She was the last in her litter, we think. The family that owned her ..." I hesitated. "They had a rough time after a car accident."

As I rambled, Bastian and Cade sat in the metal chairs and Ivy bounced excitedly with her little fingers threaded together.

"As long as she's safe," Bastian said, his eyes on his niece.

"I'll be right back." I rushed to the back kennel and grabbed a sleeping little rottweiler mix. We'd calculated she was probably only seven weeks but she was already chunky. Her short legs, big belly, and sweet brown and black markings had us all cooing at her right when she came in.

The pup cuddled into my chest as I brought her into the visitation room.

The moment Ivy saw her, she turned into a different little human. Gone was the jumping and screaming and in its place was a soft-spoken girl in love. "She's so small," she whispered.

"She is." The puppy squirmed in my arms at seeing more people. "She's just a baby who probably misses her mom and dad and brothers and sisters."

Ivy nodded, a frown on her face. "I'll be your sister if you want ..." Her gray eyes turned up to me. "What's her name?"

"Right now we call her Moonshine. When a family adopts her, they might change it."

"That's not ideal," Bastian blurted out.

"Seems confusing for the little girl." Cade waved his hand at me, looking at the pup. "Give her here."

I held her little pot belly while she perked up and whined. "She's really hyper and wiggly, okay?"

Cade nodded and took the dog like a pro, his tattooed hands gentle on the tiny animal. He petted her and cooed at Moonshine like they were best friends already.

"She likes you, Uncle Cade." Ivy patted her uncle's back like she was really proud of him.

I bit my lip. This was the part I loved and hated most about the visitation room. People falling in love with animals I was already in love with, them becoming a part of someone else's family permanently. I knew that wasn't the case with this family, that Ivy and Cade were only playing, but the idea was the same.

I took two steps back. "I'll go run through my tasks real quick. You guys enjoy Moonshine."

My heart hurt too much to look at any of them. Moonshine would go to a great family. She'd be just fine. That dog, though, when I held her, I felt more connected to her than the others. She always calmed in my hands and licked my face way more than anyone else's.

Dr. Nathan had said, "I think this one might be yours." But I'd just shook my head. I didn't need any pets.

"I'll go with you." Bastian stood, his suit somehow not at all wrinkled. He unbuttoned his jacket and slipped out of it, placing it on the back of a chair. Eyes on me, he undid his cuffs and rolled them up his forearms. "An extra set of hands for help, right?"

I cleared my throat, unable to look away from the tattoos on his forearms. He hid his markings from the world so well,

I forgot he had tattoos there. The way they snaked up his skin, weaving around the veins that popped up had my mouth dry.

Jesus. I needed to get laid. I grabbed two plastic boxes of equipment, trying to clear my head.

He followed me out of the room.

"It's really fine to stay with your brother. It's nice they're here to visit, and I do this by myself all the time."

He hummed. "Well, tonight, you have me."

"I feel like this is a one-eighty from how much time we've been spending together," I grumbled more to myself than him. I couldn't help that my heart beat too fast and how hyperaware I was of him walking behind me, probably assessing how I looked from that angle.

I stepped to the side and pointed to the kennels. "Some of the dogs aren't as friendly."

"I'll be fine." He slid his hands in his pockets and eyed the boxes in my arms. "Can I carry something for you?"

"I'm good." I sped forward, but he still beat me to the door and opened it for me. The barking drowned out most of my crazy thoughts, and the way the pups leaped onto their wire cage doors had me rolling my eyes. "Oh, don't act like you're deprived, you guys. I haven't been gone that long." There were about ten dogs that needed my extra care tonight. I pointed to a little white dog. "Tito needs a warm blanket and petting while he eats. Otherwise he won't touch his food. Can you do that?"

"Is that what's most helpful?" Bastian asked, completely accommodating.

I didn't get his newfound desire to help or be a part of my day. I tallied my pups. Most would be a pat on the head and quick fix. "Yes, I have to clip nails, let out Darcy one last time, give a few pups some pills with food. Tito is the most time consuming."

"I'll sit with Tito then."

I pulled keys from my pocket and opened the kennel door, eyeing his suit pants. "Maybe, um, I can get you a chair."

He tsked and plopped down right on the cement floor next to Tito. "Don't be ridiculous, Morina."

I gasped. "Those pants will be ruined."

"I'll buy more."

"It's such a waste of money."

"Not when I'm helping my new fiancée," he singsonged without looking up at me.

Was this the new and improved Bastian who had finally decided to commit to this process? Did he expect me to do the same?

Our vows wouldn't be true, our marriage would be a sham, and our lives would be under some stupid, weird contract. I set a candle from my box on a shelf near one of the windows. Lavender in the candles helped to soothe the animals. I lit it and played some rain music on my phone.

Breathing in the scent, I tried to tell myself I could do this with him. Faking should be easy. Except with him here now, in my space, I wondered if we could handle each other in such close proximity. Why my body reacted to him sitting on a urine-stained cement floor, ready and willing to suddenly make this work after days, was a mystery to me. It was one I didn't want to solve either.

The nails that I hadn't manicured or painted in months looked much too ragged as I peered down at them, trying to think of something to say to Bastian.

I mumbled a quick thank you as I walked past and got to work on the animals.

Each had a different personality. The kittens sprang up and purred for as long as I would stroke them, some purrs so loud that they shook the kitten's whole body.

Some of the pups, on the other hand, didn't even lift their heads when I came in to pet and feed them. Darcy actually pranced away from me. The poodle in her was proud enough to avoid even the little bit of attention she got from me. Still, she wagged her tail when I took her out back to go to the bathroom and threw the ball a few times.

Finally, once the kennels had calmed from our company and all the animals were taken care of, I returned to Tito's cage. Bastian leaned against the brick wall with Tito curled up in his lap. He rubbed the puppy's head back and forth. Both had their eyes closed.

Glimpses of what Bastian must have been to those he loved showed through his absence of these past few days. Suddenly, I was warm all over staring at him.

"He needs someone to sit with him, and it seems you don't mind a pup sitting with you either." I leaned against the kennel's metal doorframe.

"He ate all his food," Bastian murmured, still rubbing the dog's head. "You're right though. Wouldn't continue eating unless I was petting him."

Why was I more than warm now? Did big, masculine men showing love set off an internal beacon for women?

I stuck my hand in my jeans pocket and felt around for the small blue crystal I'd slid in there. This was supposed to push tranquility. I was hoping for more like tranquilizers for my libido. "All pets have their quirks, I guess. Just like us humans have ours."

"What's your quirk, Morina?"

The question shouldn't have meant much, but Bastian was analyzing me.

"I probably have so many quirks that my quirk is having

too many." I cleared my throat and pushed off the metal frame, picking up Tito. He whined as I set him down in his bed and covered him with a little blanket we'd made for dogs that liked to snuggle in. "We should go get Cade and Ivy. I'm all done here."

"Why don't you have a dog?" Bastian still sat on the floor like he was in no rush to move and wanted to chitchat with me all day long.

"Because ... I don't need one. I have all the dogs and cats and pets when I'm here."

"Sure, but then they go to a permanent family. Do you get attached?" His large hands threaded together, and the big gold ring he always wore glinted under the flickering lights.

"I mean, yeah. I like all the animals, but I don't have enough time to give them a good home like the families who come in here do."

"You told me the first time we met that you don't travel." He managed to rise up from the ground like a god.

My eyes narrowed. "So what?"

"So a dog can be at home for eight hours while you work the food truck. That's the norm for a pet, I would think. What do you mean about not having time? Or is there another reason?"

"I ... does it matter?" My arms crossed over my chest as I rolled my eyes. His questioning made me itchy for some reason.

"I think it matters, yes. I need to know you if we're going to live together for six months, and I can't quite figure you out."

"Well, good thing you're barely around."

"Did it bother you that I was gone so long?"

"I told you I don't feel comfortable in that place." I threw my hands up and spun on my heel to go back to Cade and Ivy.

He grabbed my elbow. "Wait."

I turned and looked at him. "What?"

"You said you're not used to the space and you're uncomfortable. You didn't say you wanted me in it with you."

"Well, I don't know. You're the only person there I sort of know, and I don't like being alone in weird, luxurious places where I feel like I'm going to break something or mess it up. Your dining room table is literally glass. And there're no spots on it anywhere. I thought about making a shake, but the blender looks like it's made of crystal. I didn't want to break one of your appliances and—"

"Our."

"What?"

"*Our* table, *our* appliances. You live there with me now. None of it is *mine*."

"Fine. Whatever. You know what I mean."

"It's six months, Morina. That's a long time. You need to get comfortable with the place and that means you need to stop thinking about it like it's all mine."

"But it is all yours," I almost screamed. I ground my teeth together and stepped away from him. Back into my pocket my hand went. "Tranquility," I murmured.

"What?" he asked.

Sighing, I pulled the crystal from my pants. "I carry crystals sometimes. They're supposed to help center me."

"Am I uncentering you, Morina?" His eyes flicked down to my jeans pocket but then they trailed up slow.

It was torture for me to watch how his lashes lifted and then paused at my lips. I bit the bottom one before responding. "I don't think you mean to. I honestly believe that you want us to work through this thing well together. But I don't think you consider much past yourself."

He lifted a brow. "That would classify me as a narcissist."

I blew a raspberry at him trying to be offended in something he knew I hadn't called him. "We both know that's not the truth. A narcissist wouldn't have sat with that puppy and would be able to say no to Ivy. God knows a narcissist wouldn't have gotten me off as many times as you did on—" I slapped a hand over my mouth and shut my eyes. "Forget I talked about that."

His response was to tug at a strand of my wavy hair until I dared peek back at him. When he caught my gaze, he smirked. "A narcissist wouldn't have made you scream my name that many times though, right?"

"Oh my God." I backed away and pointed at him. "You're making jokes about the night now?"

He shrugged. "It was just one night, Morina."

I crossed my arms and hugged myself. "I know that."

"We need to be comfortable around one another. I misstepped when I avoided coming home to the penthouse."

"Okay." Where was this going?

"We have to put on a show for the world. Might as well be relaxed while we do."

"Of course." I rolled the crystal between my fingers as I started back to Ivy and Cade.

"Do you always carry those crystals?" He pointed to the fingers moving in my pockets.

"Why are you asking so many questions?"

"Oh, get used to the questions. I intend to be around a lot more now."

"Why?"

Suddenly, Bastian was too close to me, and I was too exposed. "Because you're my fiancée, Morina."

I didn't correct him because it was no use. To the world, that's what we were.

I snuggled Moonshine close when we returned to the visitation room. Ivy told me how Moonshine was the sweetest dog she'd ever met.

Smiling into Moonshine's fur, I nodded.

I left them to put Moonshine back in her cage where she whimpered. "You're fine, little girl. No one's going to hurt you here. It's your home, and I'll find you the perfect one just as good as your comfy bed too."

She turned on her bed twice before plopping down. I blew out the candle at the window and led my fiancé and his little family outside.

As I locked up, Bastian stood next to me. "When you come here to lock up in the future, I need to be with you, okay?"

I stared up at him, cloaked in darkness, hovering over me like a guard. The idea that I couldn't do this on my own was a little stifling. "I've done this for years, Bastian."

"You did the food truck for years too. I'm not risking it."

I hummed and didn't answer one way or the other. There would most likely be nights when he wasn't home. I'd have to go if they needed me to close.

"Say you'll listen, *piccola ragazza*," he murmured. His voice combed through my body, leaving heat in its wake. Just a few words, and he almost hypnotized me into agreeing.

I bit my lip as I stared at him. "I'll let you know if I have to go. Is that fair?"

He stared at me like he was contemplating a million things before he touched my hair. "Fair enough."

CHAPTER 18: BASTIAN

Morina was the one person I wanted to actually force to do something. She needed someone with her in the middle of a dark night, and I would force that if I had to.

She didn't make any sense.

The way she wanted to do everything on her own and keep everyone at arm's length told me she was smart enough to be scared of something that could emotionally hurt her. I'd watched her with that little Moonshine puppy. She'd frowned and at one point even turned toward the door to wipe her eyes. She loved that little dog even if she was avoiding taking it home. Yet she'd go in the dark of the night to close up a building on her own, not at all caring about her physical well-being.

She'd almost gone by herself but Ivy, thankfully, had brought us all here which showed me how dangerous it was for Morina to go out on her own.

She didn't look around or protect her back while she locked up.

Reckless.

And naïve.

That's who I was marrying, and if I didn't take care of her, she'd be dead soon.

As we watched the movie, she twisted her wavy hair around her fingers, and when that wasn't enough, she moved to playing with her beaded bracelets. Did she really feel like those crystals in her pocket had some effect?

Was she more tranquil now?

"Our tent needs to be much bigger for us to fall asleep," Ivy announced as we stared at some princess singing about a magical house.

"We're all going to sleep in beds, Ivy," I told her.

"What about we sleep here for a little bit after the movie and then we go to our bedrooms?" Ivy tried compromising.

Cade chuckled, probably because he knew my appreciation for negotiation.

Morina watched me with those piercing eyes of hers, waiting for a response. When I nodded sure, her mouth dropped.

Morina thought I was something I wasn't, and I had to prove her wrong. We needed a united front when we went out in public, and she had to trust I would do right by the company. The only way to do that was by winning her over.

My father would have illegally wormed his way out of this one. There would have been fear, coercion, and threats.

I wanted this to be of her own free will. A business transaction we both agreed on.

"Why can't we have a singing house, Uncle Cade?" Ivy pointed to the movie.

Cade glanced up from his phone, and his hand fell to her curly head, rubbing back and forth. "That's not real, Ivy."

"But aren't we going to see a real castle tomorrow?" Her voice was high with concern.

Morina glanced at both me and Cade like we were going to ruin the experience. "Well, the princess castles are real, of course," I corrected before Cade could kill her dream. He wouldn't pick up on the social cues. He'd grown up too isolated from them. "And Uncle Cade made sure you're going to get to them as quickly as possible tomorrow."

Cade muttered when Ivy went back to watching the movie.

"The theme park has some high security. We'll have to get fingerprints into my tablet tonight. I'm working the system though. I've also sent a message to the CEO. If they see it, we'll be good. Worst-case scenario, you call him."

"Call him for what, Cade? To get my niece into a park? That's a little ridiculous."

"Not ridiculous, Uncle Bastian," Ivy singsonged.

We all winced. The girl had the uncanny ability to be listening even when she wasn't. She'd grow up a fantastic multitasker.

We watched more of the movie, and Ivy's eyes drifted shut as she snuggled next to Morina. Cade meandered off to grab his laptop and retired to another room.

Morina lifted her head to stare at me. "Why do you even have the CEO's number?"

Morina didn't understand that I was a man who had most people's numbers, especially if they were in the business of making money. "He was a friend of my father's."

"What exactly did your father do, Bastian?"

The question made me tense. The muscles in my neck that were rarely ever this relaxed coiled tight again. "We were all in the business of growing businesses."

"Or protecting your own, right?"

"Does it matter?"

She leaned in close. "I think if you're doing something illegal and threatening companies like my grandma said your dad used to, it does matter. I have to marry you and be tied to you for six months. You want this to be believable and for me to understand your intentions?" She glanced down at Ivy. "Are we safe around you?"

"More safe than you would be *not* around me. Your food truck was ransacked with you in it." I held back a wince at the reminder.

Morina was like one of the naïve princesses in the cartoons. She knew something was up, and yet, I swear she avoided it at all costs. She avoided everything except maybe goading me.

"Ivy is a sweet kid." She tugged at the little girl's curls softly.

"Yes, and she'll remain a sweet kid." My voice was low. Was she insinuating I would hurt my niece?

"I'm just saying, if something happened to any of you because you were all doing something illegal—"

"Morina, my father did illegal dealings long before I was born."

She kept staring at Ivy. "So, you are all the mob? I'm marrying into the mob instead of getting further away from it."

"It's not what we consider ourselves anymore." I pulled at the back of my neck and looked toward the ceiling, searching for the right words. "I'm cleaning up his businesses slowly. We've got families too. We're products of this shitty life he brought us into, but I'm on the cusp of having everything clean. I just need ..."

I couldn't tell her I needed to confirm that no illegal imports were coming into her grandmother's company, even as she stared at me, completely willing to listen. She was studying me, her dark-blue eyes swimming with questions.

"I need you to trust me. We need to work as a team."

She chewed on her bottom lip. "So, I need to read that packet."

Something about the fact she'd brought that packet up while we were talking about millions of dollars and people's lives pulled a laugh from deep under all the stress of this situation.

"Yes, Morina. You need to read the packet."

She sighed. "Maybe keep this movie on in case she wakes

up while I start that?"

She stood and stretched her long legs and toned stomach. The movement went straight to my dick. It remembered how smooth that skin was, how smooth every part of her was.

When she pursed her lips at my staring, I smirked. "Can't blame me, *piccola ragazza*. You're still the woman I slept with a few weeks ago."

"You said no more of that, daddy." There was her goading.

I hummed low, and her blue eyes flared.

She stomped away, walking around the tent we'd made from Egyptian cotton sheets draped over the couch and barstools. I watched her ass the whole way.

We were going to have to figure out a way for us not to take the path of least resistance and end up sleeping together again. It would complicate an already complicated situation.

She returned with the files and plopped down next to me, leaning against the couch while Ivy slept.

"I'm going to read it out loud in hopes I can focus." She cleared her throat. "Sometimes I have a hard time keeping my attention on things like this."

I shrugged at her admission, not caring at all that she thought this was boring. "It's a lot of information."

She wrinkled her nose. "I'm not that good with focusing sometimes."

I shrugged again as she blushed in embarrassment. I didn't know what for. "Everyone has their strengths. Can't hold this one against you since I don't particularly enjoy combing through data either."

She beamed at me and then got to reading. When she'd read about two pages into the oil company's daily processes, her eyes started to droop.

"Did you write this?" she grumbled.

"No." I straightened. "I compiled some of it and Cade pulled some from the internet. We had a few people work on drawing up the documents."

"Do I really need to know all of this? I find it hard to believe my grandma did."

"She didn't. That's the point. If we want to clean this company up, we need to know everything. You want your town running in a way that it can stand the test of time, right?"

"Of course I do, Bastian." She set the file down and got up in a huff before filling a cup of water. "I just don't think I can provide any good insight. Tell me what you want to change and why."

"You'll take my word for it?" That wasn't smart business practice.

"Oh my God, can you wipe that look off your face?" She poured the whole cup of water into the plants. I winced. That wouldn't help them thrive at all.

I took time to cover Ivy up on the floor before going to meet Morina by the kitchen island. "You can't water the plants in anger like that."

"Huh?" She glared up at me. "I'm not angry."

"You're frustrated. And you dumped a whole cup in one spot. How's the orchid and its roots way over here going to get anything?"

She rolled her eyes, but then she watched as I got more water and trickled it in, circling the plant. "You said before that you don't nurture plants. Was that a lie? Maybe you should water the plants."

"I can do that."

"If you're here, that is."

I chuckled. "Fair comment, Morina. You get one more. I'm sorry for not being around."

"One more? Then what?"

The way she questioned me, I had half a mind to take her over my knee. I glared at her, ready to tell her precisely what a punishment from me would look like.

"It's fine," she sighed out before I could and slumped onto the counter. "If I can have friends over or—"

"Do you have many friends?" The girl was a free-spirited loner as I was learning. If she couldn't take home a dog and she hadn't called a girl since I'd been around her, I doubted she had many. "What's the name of that girl you were with the first night we ...?"

I stopped talking when she side-eyed me. "Linny's busy a lot."

"Linny let you go on a jet with a man you barely knew."

"You were very convincing, Bastian. And Linny will trust any human in the world. She travels and believes in the good, not the bad. She once took a cab in the middle of Mexico with three men who were twice her size by herself without a cell phone." She poked my chest and smirked. "Also, don't discount that you have a way about you. You gave her your card and everything."

A lot of men could have done the same. I hummed low. "Don't trust a man when he does that."

"No other man's ever done that. I normally just go find a private—"

"I don't want to know." I shook my head as something twisted in my stomach. I returned to Ivy and sat on the couch. "Want to watch the rest of this movie?"

"The princess cartoon?" Her eyebrows lifted.

"Don't you want to see how it ends?" I was ashamed of how much the film intrigued me.

She yawned but shrugged. Before she came over, she

grabbed a lighter and pulled a stick from a little vase she'd placed on the counter. She inserted it into a wood plate with a lip.

"What's that?"

"Just a bit of incense. It's supposed to—"

"Do you believe in all that?"

"Of course. The oils have proven to be great in diffusers and this incense is soaked in citrus and peppermint. You liked my shake, right?"

I nodded. They were probably the scents I couldn't get off my jet.

"Well, you can get the same effect with smells. Taste and smell are tied very closely together."

"Did you read all about those oils in one sitting?"

"Yes, but ..." She paused. "Are you going to say I need to read that offensive file again?"

I didn't hold back a smile. "Come on. If you're not interested in the movie, you can read while I watch and ask me questions."

She stomped her foot like a petulant child, but she meandered back over and placed the file on her lap.

I gave her credit. She got through another page before looking up. "There's a lot of money here if my grandma really owns all that stock."

I nodded. She glanced up and down the page, her midnight eyes trying to decipher something. "You are seriously going to pay me that much money for some shares in this company?"

I didn't hesitate. "This is the last company my father had his hands in. I've changed hundreds over the past five years. I've righted illegal dealings, I've cleaned up shitty organization, and I've made my family a profit we won't ever see the end of. I'm cleaning up my legacy."

"You want this for something other than profit then?"

"I have enough profit if I'm able to buy these shares, right?"

She sighed and combed a hand through her hair. "Can you explain to me what you want to do to my city?"

"Sure." I sat back and told her what I pictured. "The UK has done this, and I think we have all the workings to do it here. I've talked with engineers. We have plans drawn up in that file but essentially, we want to transition to clean, green energy. It'll be more secure for your city and all the skilled oil and gas workers in the long term. We'd be giving them a foundation to work on for years, and we'd get government buy-in. We need the board to vote that way. Ronald, the owner of SeashellOil and part owner of Tropical, won't do that. Without your vote or mine, they'll push more oil at the risk of causing a spill or something catastrophic."

I stopped, giving her time to process even though I wanted to keep talking.

"You really believe in this, don't you?"

"We converted in California, and it's gone very well."

"My grandma wanted this?"

"I think so. She didn't trust me though."

"Why?"

"My father was a shifty man, Morina. He didn't shake your hand and keep his word. He crept around at night and stabbed you in the back."

She bit her lip and stared at me, then nodded. "I believe we can be better than the ones before us. After we're married, let's go to the plant, and I want to hear you make those calls to the government. We get that started, and I'll hand over the shares to you."

"I'll pay you."

She smirked. "It won't change my life, Bastian. I have what I want out of it. I simply want what's best for the town."

With that, she went back to reading and got through another five pages before her head slumped onto my shoulder and her eyes closed on a long blink. They didn't open back up.

How quickly she'd trusted me like she knew me, like I was a man of my word. I had been to everyone I'd done business with. I'd bent over backwards to be different from my father. I'd always been furious when people compared me to him and didn't trust me immediately.

Yet, with her, I wanted her to push back. She shouldn't be barreling into just handing over that much money. Was she crazy?

Or was I crazy for wanting to make sure I dotted every i and crossed every t in making this a perfect transaction? If she wanted to dive headfirst into a shit deal and get nothing out of it, all the better for me.

Right?

Except Morina was becoming something more than an obstacle to be tackled. She was nice and weird in a way I wasn't used to. She was trusting and eccentric with her beads and her incense.

She lived in a beachy land of sandcastles and surfing and cuddly puppies.

That packet held the greed and viciousness that came with money.

Something dark like oil would pollute Morina's pure water, and I wanted to get her out unscathed.

My father never did that.

Yet, now it was all I wanted.

The movie ended with the girl finding magic in being herself. I sighed and turned to Morina, who breathed heavily on me.

I needed to get her to a bed and Ivy to one also.

"Morina?" I whispered and she stirred against me. "Want to go to your bedroom?"

She shook her head and with her eyes still completely closed, crawled onto my lap. Somehow she folded into a little warm ball and snuggled against me.

Jesus, her ass rubbed right on my dick, reminding me how good it had felt to sleep next to her.

"Uncle Bastian," a little voice whispered. I snapped my attention to my little niece who stared at us with stars in her eyes. "She's your princess." Ivy's chin rested on the back of her threaded hands as she sighed at what she thought she was witnessing. "I love her with you."

Then the little girl plopped back down on the floor and pulled the covers up to her shoulders.

"Fuck me," I groaned just as Cade came and scooped Ivy from the floor.

"I'll take her to the spare and take your bed, considering you two don't seem to be moving any time soon."

"Fuck you," I grumbled but Cade was already laughing his ass down the hallway with our niece in his arms.

I let my head fall back and closed my eyes.

It might have been minutes or hours later when I felt her slide and pull me down with her. My eyes shot open, my hands at her hips immediately. Those sapphire gems sparkled in the night's dim light as she stared at me, biting her lower lip.

"Morina," I warned, my voice low.

"Yes?"

"Don't tempt me, *ragazza*. Our marriage contract is too important for that."

"Your cock is the thing tempting me right now, Bastian." She arched and her ass pressed against my sweatpants. "Plus, I don't think the company has to get mixed up with our pleasure.

I'm too wound up and used to getting some somewhere. You think we're really going to hold out for six months? We could ... you know ... just this once or twice. It's not like we haven't before."

"Morina Bailey."

This time she smiled, a mischievous languid look in her eye. She was still a mixture of subconscious sleep and reality. She'd fallen victim to what she thought the dark could hide.

"You'll regret it in the morning." I closed my eyes and attempted to go to sleep.

Rustling made me open my eyes again. Her hand was between her thighs, and her night shirt had ridden up. Suddenly I needed to know what was under it.

"Fuck, woman," I ground out.

She didn't stop, just arched her back and pushed her ass into my hard dick as she rode her own hand. Her gaze, blue as the deep water, locked over her shoulder onto mine. "Bastian, please ..."

She might have been lost in her own ecstasy and dark dreams, but now I was lost to her in the dim light, a siren of beauty who had hooked me. I gripped her hips but she slid my two fingers into her wet pussy.

"So wet for me, Morina?" I whispered. She gasped but didn't answer. "Tell me it's for me now so I can let you come." I needed to hear it.

"Only for you." She turned and whimpered into my neck as I slid another finger into her. I let her ride me as I stroked her clit and she bit my neck when she got off on my hand.

When she finally came down from her high, I don't think she wanted to lift her head to meet my gaze. I saw the blush staining her cheeks even in the dark, even though she tried to hide just below my chin.

I slowly removed my hand. "*Ragazza*, look at me."

She sighed, her breath small and soft before she did.

I made sure she caught how I put the fingers that got her off in my mouth. I tasted her finish on my skin, salty and sweet and fucking perfection. "You taste divine, love. Don't ever be ashamed of that."

Then I kissed her forehead.

"Bastian, I ..."

I shook my head, my resolve about to snap. "I'm not having sex with you, Morina. You need to go to sleep."

"You don't want to get off too?"

Fuck me. "I want to slide in and out of you over and over again. I want you to scream my name instead of muffling your gasps against my neck. But I need you to trust me, *ragazza*. Now go to sleep. *Please.*"

With that, I closed my eyes and pulled her thigh up around me. I'd sleep as close as possible to the woman I wanted but couldn't have.

If I tempted myself enough, maybe I'd become immune.

Maybe in the morning, I'd rethink my plan of staying here. Morina was turning into the damn storm I'd been trying to avoid.

The morning would come and wake me from the fairy tale of Morina's little world.

We'd be back to reality very soon.

CHAPTER 19: MORINA

I snuggled into his chest even as I heard a little voice squealing from the kitchen area.

Chest?

Snuggled?

I snapped one eye open and realized I was tangled up on the couch with Bastian.

His strong tattooed arms held my waist like a vise, and his scruff nestled into my neck.

Goose bumps flew across my skin as he exhaled right on a sensitive spot near my collarbone.

My God, the man smelled good even in the morning, and he felt even better with all his muscles up against mine.

He must have covered us up because the warmth of a blanket was draped all the way up to my shoulders. Thankfully, it hid what was happening underneath, which was a win considering Ivy would have seen my thigh wrapped right around Bastian's midsection. The way his hand was gripping it near my ass was a little too X-rated for a four-year-old.

In the kitchen, Ivy squealed at Cade, who seemed to be putting together breakfast as I tried to quietly extricate myself from Bastian.

How could I have fallen asleep on him and then climbed him like that in the middle of the night?

And I'd lost my mind completely, trying to get myself off.

Except, God, I'd needed it.

In my defense, the files probably pushed my subconscious

to its limit. I needed an outlet. I hadn't surfed or hooked up with Bradley or done anything to relieve stress in days.

So, I'd done this instead. He could have indulged too. I wouldn't have minded.

My thigh brushed up against Bastian's length, and I found myself biting my lip. I hadn't forgotten how that felt inside me.

I whimpered a little at the thought of him licking his fingers clean last night and knowing I'd have to be around him for six months without any relief.

Bastian's hand squeezed my thigh, and his eyes snapped open. All honey and molasses and caramel-colored goodness.

"Whimpering when your body is against me, Morina, is asking for me to give you something to whimper about."

Jesus. His voice. "Oh my God. This is unfair," I whispered and poked him in the chest.

"What?"

"I shouldn't ever have to wake up to a man when I'm not getting all of him. And why does the man have to be you with your voice dripping sex first thing in the morning?"

A rumble that must have been a laugh came from him.

I licked my lips, even more frustrated that his laugh sounded as good as it did. I shifted, ready to push off him and get up, but his hand squeezed my thigh again, signaling for me not to move.

I stared at him, and then my eyes bounced between the kitchen and him. "What are you doing?"

"Trying to sift through the part of my brain that's screaming I need to take you to my room for a second alone with my fiancée."

"Oh my God. What happened to me trusting you or the fact that not too long ago you told my grandma I was a little girl no one in your family would want?" We needed to de-escalate in any way we could.

"You know damn well I didn't mean that little girl comment when you were riding my dick not a week before, Morina. I licked your pussy from my fingers last night." He slid his hand right up to it.

I shouldn't have even been contemplating sleeping with him. That was the problem with morning grogginess though. Some part of the human conscious was still sleeping while the animalistic, basic-need side was ready to fulfill all desires.

I rolled my hips on him, and his eyes flared. Caramel and chocolate turned to lava and fire.

"Uncle Bastian!" Ivy screamed when she rounded the couch and saw us both awake but still under the covers. "Breakfast time, and then we get to go fly on carpets and ride fast boats and Uncle Cade said there's a pirate ship battle we'll get to see!"

At the mention of his name, his hand flew from my ass and his eyes turned right back to honey while he watched his niece vibrating with excitement. I scooted off him while being kind enough to leave the bunched up sheet on his lap. I straightened my night top as I hopped off the couch. "I'm just going to go freshen up and shower. You guys eat without me."

The shower was where I got myself back together. I let the water run over me and reminded myself I needed to get back on a board after I finished reading that file. Supposedly, I had meetings and galas to attend soon according to the papers. We'd have to put on our married game faces and falling down a rabbit hole of lust with Bastian wouldn't be good for either of us.

He was right.

I couldn't risk indulging emotions, especially when the city needed me to iron out the company's future.

This was a good first step.

I would be seen out and about with Bastian and his family. That would mean something.

"Hey, do I need to wear something better than this?" I asked as I came back out to the kitchen, suddenly concerned about being photographed.

"Why would you ask that?" Bastian growled.

Cade studied me though. "That'll do just fine."

"What are you talking about?" Bastian swung his gaze at his brother.

"They're going to judge her with you." Cade shrugged and handed me a plate of eggs and bacon.

"Thank you." I eyed the perfectly cooked bacon that had enough grease to make my mouth water. "This looks amazing."

"It's eggs and bacon." Cade chuckled. "My mom would have scorned us if she saw what Bastian had in his fridge to feed you, honestly."

"Shut up." Bastian grabbed a plate without saying thank you to his brother.

"Mom would be mad. You and I both know it."

Bastian and Cade, two men I'd swear could have melted the hearts of all the women in the world, stared each other down. The story of their family was one I'd wondered about. Curiosity was a bitch I needed to keep in line though. It wouldn't serve me well.

Ivy leaned over and whispered, "Daddy says Bastian doesn't like talking about his mommy because she's not here anymore. Bastian doesn't have a daddy either." She ran her hand down my face as if soothing me could soothe Bastian too.

I glanced at him, but his eyes were trained on his little niece.

"I like talking about her, *bambina*. Don't say that, huh? I loved her very much. I just don't talk about her because she's gone now."

"He means she's dead, Morina," she informed me as if I didn't know. I shoved more eggs in my mouth so I didn't have to be a part of the conversation. "And I guess when people die, Bastian doesn't talk about them anymore." Ivy frowned at her uncle. "We aren't supposed to talk about them, right, Uncle Bastian?"

Cade smirked and folded his arms. "Yeah, Bastian, please explain that to us. I'd like to know too."

Bastian's jaw worked up and down and up and down. Before he answered, he grabbed a water bottle from the fridge and chugged a few sips. He slammed it down harder than necessary onto the granite countertop. "Ivy, my mother was a really nice lady. She loved my daddy and us more than life itself. When your daddy would come over, she'd make cannoli, and we'd sit with her and laugh and laugh. She was very nice. But she has passed away. We have to move on."

"But she's your momma." Ivy sounded so confused that I put my arm around her and glared at Bastian, who in turn glared at me.

"And I have family here now that she'd want me to enjoy, huh? Let's eat." His command held no room for argument.

Maybe Bastian was more broken than I'd originally thought. His brother lowered his eyes, and I did too.

We ate in silence until Cade announced the drivers had arrived. The elevator took us to the car I thought we would all pile into, but two black SUVs awaited us, surrounded by security guards and men in black suits. I froze, not sure if I was going to die right there.

I glanced at Bastian, and he rolled his eyes like he knew my thoughts. "They're here to walk the park with us. We got Katie's kid, and she's infamous in certain parts. She wants her child protected."

"Jeez," I whispered. That was momma bear on another level. Yet, every aspect of this excursion was getting more and more stressful. "Are all of you that infamous?"

"In some circles, yes." He hesitated, like he was weighing what to tell me. "You know, we'll be photographed today. The theme park with my family is good though. It will solidify our relationship. No one will bother you after today."

We got there in good time considering it was a few hours' drive. Bastian groaned about us not taking the jet most of the way. "It takes away from the experience," Cade told him.

"Get real. You haven't had a real experience in decades with your head in that phone."

His grin was one of a Cheshire cat. "You'd be surprised, brother."

When we arrived at the park, the SUV dropped us at the line for people who already had tickets. When we had to scan in, they took our fingerprints.

My normal life didn't involve my heart hammering about getting in somewhere. If they said no, we'd go to the other line and buy tickets. Just more waiting. Cade's skills must have been golden though because we got that green light and went through the gate without a hitch.

Ivy danced around us in a little dress that fluffed out at her waist. I eyed it. "Who got her that outfit?"

Cade shrugged. "She's got a million dresses back home like this. I packed a few for her."

"You're the perfect uncle, I think." I elbowed him and he nodded.

"I probably would have been the perfect husband too. Sorry you got stuck with my brother."

Bastian grumbled as we walked in but didn't pay us much

mind. He was probably happy he didn't have to make small talk with me.

"I see the castle! I see the castle!" Ivy screeched. "I'm going to be a princess! I'm going to be a princess!"

Bastian and Cade stared out at the park, and I think the gravity of it hit us all at the same time. People swarmed in and out every which way like herds needing water.

"Have you ever been to this park?" I took a deep breath.

The guys shook their heads, but Cade grabbed Ivy's hand with a smile and they skipped ahead.

Before we could continue our conversation, he looked back at us. "Phones on. I'm going to get a stroller for our princess here. We'll do some rides and meet up soon."

"Why don't we just go with him?" I asked Bastian, but my wonderful arranged partner was already waving them goodbye.

"We've already got eyes on us. We need to play up that we're having a good time together."

"What?" I glanced around. I didn't see anyone who looked suspicious. There weren't any cameras in bushes or people holding microphones like they were going to come ask us a question. "I don't see any cameramen, Bastian."

He pinched the bridge of his nose, and I waited for him to calm down.

The crowd fanned out around us as they entered the park. The place was big but still not large enough to accommodate the massive swarm of excited theme park fans. People were dressed in character, some ran in like they needed to catch the best rides, and others snapped picture after picture of the castle in the distance.

"Most use phones now. And there are underground gangs, crews, other businessmen following us. They want evidence and the media want photos."

My eyes darted uncontrollably around, trying to spot spies.

"You won't see them, Morina. Cade's good at security, and so he knows."

"So when he said I looked nice today ..." I trailed off realizing my question had been stupid.

"He means you look like you should. We're supposed to be dating. Hand-holding and whatnot, okay?"

"I don't know if I want to hold your hand."

"Sure you do. We can go shopping together and try out a ride or two."

"Do you like these sorts of rides?"

"I didn't go to theme parks growing up," he shrugged, "and haven't had time for them as an adult."

"I'm sorry about your mother," I said softly. "I know that doesn't really help to say because people have said it to me over and over again. Sometimes, I want to punch them or scream that words don't help. Still, I don't know what else to say."

He nodded and pulled out sunglasses from his suit pocket. It was a great way to mask that emptiness every orphaned child felt. "I'm older now. It doesn't hurt so much anymore."

"Were you close to her?"

Chewing his cheek and sticking his fists in his pockets told me before he answered. "My mother held the family together. We were actually pretty happy and normal with her there. My father took her soul, though, and sucked her dry until I found her with a bottle of pills on the bathroom floor."

I cleared my throat. My heart hurt for him like it hurt for myself. "She OD'd."

"She died of a broken heart, and a man as evil as the devil took her life. My father deserved to rot in hell for that." Bastian murmured the words, but they came out violent and full of hate.

"Then, I hope he is." I patted his shoulder as he stared off into the theme park.

"If he isn't, he's rolling in his grave now seeing me reconstruct his whole empire and make it mine."

"For your mother then?" I asked and did a fake cheers. "Guess we're going to be saying these vows for her?"

He chuckled. "Sure, Morina. Sure." Although his aviators were reflective, I felt his gaze snap to mine. "How did your parents die?"

I stepped back, not wanting to discuss them either. "Their bus crashed."

He hummed. "Death is a fucker. I'm sorry you lost them too. Did they ever take you to the park?"

"No." I sighed, not ready to share with him that my parents had been addicts. People judged them too quickly, not realizing that they'd still loved me when they were around. It wasn't much, but it was something. "I don't know that we didn't have the time to go. I just didn't have parents who—"

"Left town?" He chuckled, thinking my parents had been just like me.

"No. They left all the time." The admission was a painful one because they blamed me for their leaving. I heard the fights at night with my grandmother about how I was too hyper, too much to handle. Sure, they loved me and I loved them, but they needed a break. My grades were mediocre and teaching me anything drained them.

They got a break by partying, doing drugs, and leaving town.

Every time they left, my grandma assured me it wasn't because of me. Yet, it had to be. Why else would so many parents stay when mine always left? The reports from school every semester were the same. *Attention issues.* It turned my stomach sour just thinking about it.

I went to stick a hand in my pocket to grab a crystal, but Bastian caught the hand and threaded my fingers with his.

"What now? I didn't piss you off already, did I?"

I cleared my throat and watched the large carousel of unicorns with families riding it round and round. "I don't talk about them much."

"I understand that." He squeezed my hand, and I wasn't sure if it was for the cameras somewhere or because he wanted to comfort me. "I don't talk about my father and mother either."

"I could tell from what you said to Ivy." I threw the joke out, but it didn't land at all how I wanted. "I'm sorry. It's ... you actually did great with her today. You make a great uncle."

"You do great with her too. You like kids, I can tell. Do you want them one day?"

The questions he asked felt like he really wanted to know me, like we were becoming friends. "I do. I loved the time I had with my parents when they were there. Sure, I have resentment some days about random things, but I loved some of my time with them. I want to drag my kid out to the ocean at sunrise like my dad did with me some day."

He hummed. "You'll be good at it."

"You would too." I nudged him as we walked. "Seriously, Ivy loves you."

"I always try to be honest with her." He shrugged. "My parents weren't always honest with me. It's what ended my father's life."

That made me freeze and stare up at him. He waited, staring right back. I wouldn't ask the question, not even if he wanted me to. I knew what it was like to be asked about my parents. Were they high when their bus crashed? Did I miss them even if they were never there in the first place? Of course they must have been drinking, right?

None of it mattered.

They were gone.

"Well, it's good we're here." I turned back toward the castle covered in lights that made it shine in broad daylight. "Let's see what the universe throws at us."

"The universe isn't concerned with us, *piccola ragazza*." He pointed toward a roller coaster, and we made our way over.

The finality of his words sank in. Bastian didn't think I was big enough for the universe to care about, but every speck on this planet moved the universe in a different direction.

CHAPTER 20: BASTIAN

Nothing about this park was tranquil. Cade texted to say he'd meet us in an hour as walking with the stroller took longer than he'd anticipated. The man thought he could control everything with technology, but some things he had to still navigate in real time.

Luckily, he'd managed to get us passes to skip most lines. Morina and I decided to take on the biggest ride in the park. It was well known and took pictures of the riders.

After checking the signs, I ushered Morina to the faster line. We needed our cards and fingerprints to get through but Cade didn't disappoint and they worked fine. Even so, we waited about ten minutes.

Taking in the park while we stood in the shorter line was an eye-opening experience. A man told his son to stretch taller and taller just to get on a ride.

Morina watched, wide-eyed. "Do you think he'll make it?"

I shook my head when the devastation occurred. The park employee, dressed in full getup, told the son and father he still wasn't tall enough. The father yelled, and the kid's face fell.

"Oh, jeez," Morina said, like it broke her heart too. Her hand left mine after literally minutes, and now it turned those beads on her wrist.

I wanted to punch the father, if not for the kid's sadness, then for Morina's.

That emotion wasn't one I should've had, but it looked like one I'd need to deal with for the foreseeable future.

"He shouldn't be held accountable for something he can't control," I mumbled more to myself than anyone else.

My father had. He insisted I answer for things a child has zero culpability for. It stuck with me far more than I wanted it to.

Morina heard though. "No, he shouldn't. His father is human too though. He's probably working through something himself. At least they're here."

I glanced around while the theme park music played softly on speakers above us. All these parents navigated one another, pushing their kids around in strollers, doling out food from backpacks, all with smiles on their faces. They were definitely different from the parent Mario Armanelli had been. My father would never have brought me here. This whole park was full of parents who wanted to do right by their children.

Mario wanted to train me, not love me.

"Yeah, this is not a place my family would have ever come."

Morina moved up in the line. It was supposed to be a roller coaster that splashed us halfway through. I wasn't looking forward to getting my suit wet but the pictures would serve us well.

She thought about it for a second, her leg jutting out so she could tap. "Maybe my parents would have if they hadn't been so preoccupied with their own stuff. Not sure."

She didn't seem bothered at all by this admission the way she had been before. "Were your parents ever not preoccupied with their own stuff?" She glanced away. Ah, there it was, the past pain we both had. "I guess we'll tackle family relations later in our marriage."

The word had her snapping her attention back to me. "I think we need to decide when that should happen." Her hair blew in the wind, flying back enough to expose her neck. There was a hint of blush there, like she was embarrassed to bring up our arrangement.

I found myself wanting to bring that color to her skin more and more in a very different way.

"Your file said the board meeting is weeks away and the will says we need to get this wedding planned," she pointed out.

"We're building to that." I should have discussed the plan with her. "I've got it figured out. The timeline I have in place will work well."

She nodded and glanced at the family ahead of us. One kid on the mom's hip screamed and the other pulled on the dad's leg, whining about hunger—we were fine, they weren't paying any attention to us. "So, it might be nice to include your fiancée in the planning of that timeline."

"My fiancée? My fiancée doesn't really want anything to do with planning a *fake* wedding, does she?"

"Well, I don't want to get stuck doing something I don't want to." She gripped the metal railing. "This gala is where we're making our public entrance?"

"I think that's best. We can go separately or together, whichever you prefer. Maybe make a display of it."

"Display how?"

"People need to know I won't let anything happen to you."

"Because your dad did that for my grandmother?"

"Essentially." I winced at how easily I lied. He'd taken advantage of her partnership, but he'd also protected her in some capacity.

"Why can't we have the same understanding?"

"You'll never be as protected. Your grandmother had ties to people overseas and refineries around the world. Now, you're one lone woman with one ally."

"And that's you."

"That's right."

"Grandma should have let me sell the stock to you immediately." She rubbed her forehead like this was all frustrating and confusing at the same time.

"I agree. I'm good to my word." Even if Maribel hadn't believed me.

"Yeah, well, Grandma wasn't stupid either. Yet, she only spoke highly of you. I'm guessing she wants us to fall in love and make the decisions together."

"She was a tad delusional," I grumbled and walked forward, almost at the ride. "The love aspect was far-fetched. But she was right about protecting you and it will ultimately benefit me. I'll get an understanding of the company before I buy in."

"Are you considering not buying in if you don't like what you see?"

"No. I'm considering changing what I don't like and evolving the port. This gives me time."

"Couldn't you buy out some other shareholder?"

Although Morina was young and acted like a free spirit with no attention span, her questions were on point.

"Curious today, huh?"

"I'm always curious. It's a curse of mine. I wouldn't fall down rabbit holes if I didn't inspect everything."

I chuckled because as she said it, we stepped up to the ride platform. We weren't given many instructions as we boarded a log shaped boat on the channel of water. I pulled a bar over our laps and wiggled it over Morina's hips.

She froze as my hand grazed her thigh.

My jaw ticked and every muscle in me tightened. Just a small touch set both me and her off now. I hadn't been sleeping around or pursuing other women since the will reading.

I probably needed an outlet.

Six months was going to be a long time, and we were still only counting down to our wedding. The marriage aspect would make it hard, if not impossible, to find another woman I could indulge with.

The feeling of her smooth skin on the back of my hand as I confirmed the security of the bar made me not even want to think about another woman.

I had silky soft flesh here, and she knew exactly how to make my cock feel good.

The ride started, and into the lair of psychedelic painted creatures we went. Bears ate honey with loud music pounding, and my mind ran away with fucked-up ideas like how the honey would taste on Morina's skin.

"This is a whole different type of aura," Morina whispered, her blue eyes wide. "Oh my God, Bastian, look at that!"

I leaned back and watched her turn into this bouncy girl, completely entertained with a kid's ride.

Her hands fluttered around, and the rings she'd put on today glittered with topaz and other jewels I had no understanding of. "I thought this was going to be hokey!"

It was definitely hokey, but they'd put in more detail than I'd expected—probably more than most parks. And who was I to ruin her fun? She bounced next to me and our shoulders knocked together enough that I put my arm on the back of her seat.

We'd have looked like a couple to anyone watching, but no one was. They watched the moving plastic creatures and the bright colors, and if anyone did glance at us, they'd have been caught up with the stars in her blue eyes.

After a while, the boat tilted backward as the bottom hooked onto the ramp that inched us up, up, up to the big drop.

"This is going pretty high!" she squealed and glanced at

me. Her face fell a little. "Oh, right. This is probably where they take the picture too. I'll just ... lean into you here, I guess."

Something about her face falling, about the way she lost the little girl inside to take on her responsibilities had me wanting to bring back the emotion. Or just feel an emotion with her.

I gripped her chin in a way I shouldn't have. I murmured, "Smile for the cameras, Morina."

"Bastian." She whispered it like she knew what was coming, like she had any ability to stop it.

I leaned in and took her lips in mine.

Morina's aura was rubbing off on me.

Her kiss ran through me, those lips so soft they reminded me how soft she felt everywhere. My finger dragged down her neck, and she shivered and nipped at my lip right as the boat went over the edge. She gasped, and I pulled her closer, taking the opportunity to dive deeper.

I was in the psychedelic state of Morina.

And I needed to get out of it before we found ourselves in a fucked-up situation.

CHAPTER 21: MORINA

He kissed like he owned my mouth, the ride, the butterflies in my stomach, and the whole aura around us.

I went with the flow. I tried not to get too riled or feel anything too deeply. It was easier that way.

Yet, Bastian captured a moment on that ride where I was feeling a little too alive and then he injected himself into the equation, amping my emotions to catastrophic levels.

I'd dropped forty-nine feet with one of the most powerful yet questionable businessman in the state making out with me.

I didn't even feel the splash of water at the bottom.

I was lost in the way his lips commanded the kiss, the way his hands tracked down my throat and then gripped onto me like he had a right to.

My heart beat like a jackhammer on high speed, and that jackhammer chipped away at the idea of having him as a fake husband for six months.

His mouth would be so underused, and his hands—so strong as they gripped my neck in our kiss but gentle when he dragged his fingertips over my collarbone—wouldn't get to make anyone feel that good for a long time.

I moaned as I shifted in the seat, aching to get closer to him. We'd passed the point of the photo, and now I was simply being greedy as my fingers threaded through his hair, and I kept taking what really wasn't mine.

As the songs faded and we emerged from the cave of wondrous animation, returning to the sunlight, Bastian pulled back.

I snatched my hands back and covered my mouth, looking away.

"Sorry." I'd taken it too far by biting his lip and trying to practically climb him, despite the bar in my way.

As it lifted, I jumped out like the ride was on fire. Our part of it was.

I didn't even glance his way as I hurried toward the exit. I shouldn't have expected us to be able to forget and avoid the topic so easily though. As we weaved through barriers on our way out, there on shiny big-screen TVs were the photos of the drop.

"Guess we didn't disappoint in taking advantage of that moment, huh?" Bastian pointed to us.

His hand was on my neck and mine were in his hair. We looked absolutely, disgustingly in love. Nothing in me should have twisted and coiled around the idea. I chanced a look at him. That set jaw, the lines of concern on his face, and his pursed lips definitely weren't showing any signs of enjoyment as he stared at us.

"There are a few people behind us who will most likely buy that photo."

"What, like for evidence of us being together?" It sounded absurd.

"Exactly." He nodded. "Want one for our penthouse? Could put it on the fridge for guests."

I bit my lip. This display was beyond a show for me, and that exposed something I wasn't sure I wanted to stare at frequently.

"I don't need it if you don't."

He hummed, his signature sound as his hands went to his pockets and he rocked on his heels. "Why don't you go get something in the little gift shop for Ivy? She'll probably want a snack and a toy by the time we meet up with her. I'm going to go fight the cameraman to make sure our photo stays up for a few more people to see."

I nodded and took him backing away as a sign that he wanted a little time on his own. Fair enough since I'd practically mauled him.

I hurried to a sliver of mirror near some cheap sunglasses on display and smoothed my hair down. My lips looked swollen and happy. The blush on my cheeks appeared fresh. "Get it together," I grumbled and went to find a stuffed animal for Ivy.

Bastian met me at the counter and handed his card over before steering me out of the store.

Cade and Ivy met us with smiles on their faces. Cade's tattoos on his hands and arms and up his neck were probably one of the things that deterred people from us. It could have also been that following Cade and Ivy were three large men in suits.

While I stared at them, Bastian leaned in. "They're completely unnecessary. Most everyone here is trying to make sure their kid doesn't scream to go on the next ride before the line moves. We're surrounded by families and that's not a place for anyone to do anything."

"Would you be nervous about that otherwise?" I tried to gauge what my grandma had said to me before—these were businessmen now, not vicious, ruthless men.

"Not really anymore."

"The food truck?" It still presented to me like something out of a movie. Would they have tortured me or gotten straight to killing me?

"That wasn't someone like us. Underground and completely unorganized. It's been taken care of."

I didn't ask further questions. I let our day unfold instead.

"Uncle Bastian, will we stay for the fireworks tonight?" Ivy asked about a minute later. "The castle lights up and then fireworks come and another little girl said they play all the music from the movies."

"We did a lot of talking with another family in our fast lane before the ride." Cade nodded.

"I think your mom and dad are going to want to see you before then, kid." Bastian patted Ivy's head when her face dropped.

"But Mommy and Daddy could meet us." She huffed and plopped into her stroller. She had the four-year-old attitude down pat.

"I see she's quickly adapted to that stroller," Bastian grumbled to his brother. "I'll push it for a few. You want to run surveillance and see if we've got any business updates?"

Cade wheeled Ivy over to Bastian, but I stopped him. "I can do it for a while."

He nodded, and I took the stroller to push Ivy as we walked and they talked. After a few minutes, a man bustled by and knocked me so hard I gasped and whipped around to see what his problem was.

Instead of apologizing, he glared at me and said, "Watch where you're going, bitch." Then, he tried to hurry on.

I thought that was the end of it, but my fake fiancé caught the man's arm as he was passing Bastian behind me. Bastian stood much taller, bigger, and more menacing as he whispered, "Say excuse me to my fiancée."

The man glanced around and his eyes widened. "What?"

Bastian grabbed the man's face and turned him so that he had to look at me. My heart was beating fast at either the display or at the man defending my honor. Bastian mushed the man's cheeks together, and I could tell the grip on his arm must have been painful from the frown he had on his face.

"I won't tell you again. Say excuse me *and apologize* to her."

"I'm sorry. Excuse me," he stuttered out as he saw how the black suits had surrounded us.

"Watch where you're going around women and children, motherfucker," Bastian said and then shoved him away like he was garbage.

I bit my lip, trying not to kiss him for sticking up for me and women everywhere as he came over and put his hand on my lower back. He leaned in. "Let me take the stroller for a while, *ragazza*."

So vicious and then so gentle, all for me.

I looked up at his eyes all gooey and warm, and I stepped back fast because if I didn't, I'd do something stupid.

He hunched over and pushed the little umbrella stroller as he continued talking to his brother. I didn't hear a thing coming out of their mouths. The sun shone, families bustled around with smiles on their faces, happy music played from speakers on every corner, and Bastian pushed a pink stroller.

The man was all suit and muscle and tattoos peeking out from under his cuffs, yet a tiny pink stroller was his top priority right now.

He navigated the crowd with ease, or maybe they navigated around us–either way, we made our way through the park quickly.

With the FastPasses, we were able to get on most of the rides. I had a feeling Cade was glitching the system though, because I overheard other families saying they could only book rides at certain times. With us, that wasn't the case.

Ivy rode the flying carpets and went higher and higher on the elephants with Bastian at her side.

The little girl loved her uncles, and they loved her too. There wasn't a moment of hesitation throughout the day until they realized Ivy had to go to the bathroom.

Bastian said he would walk her to the guy's bathroom and she could use a stall, but I rolled my eyes. "Ivy, want to go to the girls' bathroom with me?" I held out my hand. She nodded, handed over her giant lollipop to Cade, and took my hand with a big smile.

The park held magic that I knew children would remember for all their lives. Yet, I think a lot of the adults were here to remember the faces of their children too. Just like Ivy's face in that moment, their innocence was the magic of it all.

Ivy fell asleep as the sun set, and we navigated through the crowd back to the entrance.

"She doesn't need to see fireworks. I'll bring her back again when Katie and Rome aren't down our throats." Cade shrugged.

Bastian even stopped to consider it. His eyes bounced from the castle to his little niece curled up on his suit jacket that he'd bunched up as a makeshift pillow. I knew it was thousands of dollars, but he hadn't even hesitated when her neck looked kinked. "She had fun right? This was good enough?"

The man was asking me.

As if I knew any better than him, I glanced down at her too. "She looks really tired."

"Right." Cade nodded, still staring at her.

We all stood there as guilt coursed through our veins at skipping the fireworks. The magic of this park was that adults were pushed to give kids everything too. It was a great marketing scheme.

"Sir, Rome and Katie are waiting in the parking lot back at the penthouse," one of the security guys announced to Cade.

"That makes the decision for us then." Bastian sighed,

the muscles in his shoulders falling like that had removed the burden of having to choose.

We got Ivy into her car seat in the SUV and made our way back to the penthouse.

As we entered the garage, even more black cars joined us. I wondered if businessmen ever drove anything different.

Cade unbuckled Ivy as she woke up. Another car's door opened, and the little girl screamed as loud as she could, "Mommy! Daddy!"

She wiggled out of Cade's arms and ran straight to Katie who swooped her up and spun her around. The woman was all black tattoos and cut-up clothing, but the smile she gave her daughter radiated pure love.

A man with bigger muscles than even the security guards stood behind Katie, watching like a wolf protecting his pack. He turned a cold stare to Cade. "You fucking want a bullet in your head?"

"Oh, fuck off. She wanted to go to the damn park."

"You fly my daughter without my knowledge again, I'll drag you to hell," he growled at Cade.

"Yeah, yeah, yeah." Cade waved off the vicious warning and walked up to the man like nothing was wrong. My eyes widened, my whole body tensing. The man was going to punch him or something.

Instead, Cade pulled him in for a hug. "You're getting soft. I thought I had a gun to my head coming with that warning."

A deep laugh rolled out from Ivy's father as he hugged back, and I let out a breath.

Bastian smirked at my side. I'd forgotten for the first time in a while that he was near me. "He's a lot of bark but not much bite when it comes to family."

I dragged out an *okay*, not sure how to take all this in.

Katie glanced at me. "Meet my husband, Rome."

Rome walked up and shook the hand I extended immediately. "Welcome to the family."

"Oh, I'm just ... I mean ... thanks?" Was I meant to be pretending with them or not?

"We're heading up. We have to plan some things," Bastian said after he hugged Rome too. There was no exchange of how are yous or other niceties.

I didn't know whether to apologize for Bastian leaving or not but I opted not to say a word. This was his crew, and I probably would never see them again.

"Morina, right?" Katie stopped me as we started toward the elevator.

"Yes?"

"Thank you for taking care of my daughter. These two dumbasses are untrustworthy."

"Morina took me to the bathroom, and we washed our hands together," Ivy announced, and Katie's eyes softened as she looked at me. Then they snapped to Bastian's, a look of determination there. "Take care of her, huh?"

I didn't know if the sense of foreboding I got as they left was only from her words.

That night, Bastian and I made a little small talk, but we both retired to our own bedrooms.

It didn't stop me from thinking about him under the same roof as me. Or halt the way my mind drifted back to our kiss on the ride.

He hadn't kissed me again that day, but he'd held my hand here and there, enough that it almost felt real.

Except it wasn't.

It was all a charade.

A touch shouldn't be that complicated, yet, my mind liked

to run away with an idea.

I rolled over and tried to picture anything else.

CHAPTER 22: BASTIAN

"Good evening, Morina. How was your day?" It had been a week since the theme park, and I'd made it home every night. I split my time between businesses in Chicago, LA, and New York. Making it back to Coralville, though, proved to the world we had something going on.

Was I doing it to prove something to them or because of her outburst about feeling alone in the penthouse? I wasn't sure.

I scrolled through my phone while lounging on the couch as the woman ambled down the hallway to greet me. Entertainment news had caught Morina and I together numerous times leaving this building, and the theme park trip was everywhere.

She grumbled something about a day of napping as she walked by, her sleep shirt rumpled and hitting at mid-thigh. She pulled off messy well, like she belonged that way.

"It looks like people have caught wind of our relationship." I held up my phone.

She glanced at the screen. "Surprised they didn't use our splash-roller-coaster kiss as the photo."

I didn't comment. That photo wasn't for the world to see.

Yet, pictures scrolled by of us holding hands, of her staring into my eyes. Each one appeared intimate.

"They really do an amazing job of making us seem in love." Pointing, she chuckled. "Except this one." She giggled and plopped next to me, close enough that I knew she'd loosened up over the past week I'd been home. "This one looks like I'm getting scolded." She lowered her voice to sound like a news anchor. "Bastian Armanelli and Mediocre Mo fight already."

I took note of the news outlet while she scoffed at the nickname.

"Would have sounded much better if they'd written 'Daddy Bastian Puts Little Miss Mo in Her Place.' And, oh my God, are they guessing my weight? My ass alone weighs much more than that."

A chuckle escaped my lips, and the tension in my neck loosened. The woman truly didn't give two fucks about the media. Her nonchalance had me wanting to grip her hips and knead said ass.

Desiring her shouldn't have been in the cards, but I still joked with her. "If only they knew how big and not mediocre your ass was."

Her tanned skin blushed immediately, and she licked her lips like she would be ready to go if I asked. When she turned her hips just a little, my hand acted on its own accord to graze over her hip bone. The phone in her hands clattered onto the table. "Bastian ..."

Her moaning my name had my hands flying off her. I'd talked of my mother with her, and I remembered how Mother had fallen so in love with my father, how she'd lost her passion for the world to that man.

Morina was just as vibrant, maybe even more so. She was young and full of life, and I wasn't pulling her any closer to the mob family I was trying to fix.

"Sorry." I shook my head. "Sorry, *ragazza*. It's time for bed."

"And here I thought you were so much older than me." She smirked, goading me to bend her over my knee.

I sighed, my restraint ready to snap. "Get your ass to your

bedroom, woman."

She laughed all the way down the hall like this was just some fun. To her, it might have been.

To me, I needed to keep my sanity and make sure she had a clear mind to sign those shares over to me. It meant clean energy and a clean family legacy. Even if I wanted her ass, I'd have to find another outlet. And it wasn't only her body. I found myself liking Morina more and more. I had to be careful with that in the future.

I went to bed frustrated and thinking about her ass.

When I woke up, I almost knocked on her door to see if she wanted to do something about it.

Instead, I made coffee and read the paper. I took care of her plants and researched the damn orchid that didn't want to bloom again. There had to be a solution.

She slogged down the hallway to the kitchen and mumbled something about needing water, and I turned, getting her a glass of it.

"No, no, no." She waved it off. "I need to surf to wake up. I told you this a couple days ago." We'd had a few conversations here and there in the days since Ivy and Cade had left. Most of the time, I was on my computer and she tinkered on her phone or with things around the penthouse.

Yesterday, she put up a painting of Buddha. When I asked if that was her religion, she laughed and said no. When I asked why she had it, she said she passed the picture in a discount store and thought he looked cute.

That was Morina. A free-spirited loner with a need to indulge every gut instinct and feeling to its fullest extent.

"Why do you need to surf in the morning again?"

"Because if I don't, I'm like this," she hissed. Her voice directed malice at herself, though, not me.

The girl flew toward every feeling she had with a drive that wasn't healthy. Right now, she'd veered into hating-herself land and combed erratically through her tangled hair with her fingers.

The first time I met her, I'd wanted her on my dick and today was no different. Even with no makeup, Morina was beautiful, maybe even more so. Her full lips pouted out soft and pillowy above her strong jawline, and her blue eyes pierced my soul through dark, thick eyelashes. Her face would've been striking to anyone, even when she tried to hide it behind a mass of wavy black hair.

Her body tempted me, even in a baggy sweatshirt. This one was monochrome, a black and gray design of characters from the theme park. She liked shirts two sizes too big, and the fact Cade had bought that sweatshirt in exactly the right size irked me for some stupid-ass reason.

On top of all that, I could still see her full chest straining against the material. I shouldn't have been looking.

I probably studied her much too long because those azure eyes glared at me like I was dumb and deaf. "Are you even listening to me?"

"Of course. Do you want to go surfing this morning?"

Her smile lit up the room as she went to the top of the refrigerator to grab her lighter. The incense smoke curled up around her face as her face soured. "Today, I woke up with the need to finish that file."

Ah, that was the true culprit of her bad mood. Morina hated that file like a sculptor might hate being given paint instead of marble. She was the type of person who thrived in action, not in reading about it.

"I'll do it with you." I shrugged and took a sip of my coffee.

First, a grin spread across her face, then it dropped like a ton of bricks. "You should work."

"Should I?" I grabbed the plates of food I'd made while she was sleeping. "Here are some crepes and strawberries."

"Strawberries and what?"

"Crepes." I nodded to the thin, folded pancake.

"Okay." She dragged the word out like she always did when she was unsure. Still, she went to fill two glasses with water and set them beside each other on the island counter. Then, she turned to me and winced. "Are you eating with me? Sorry, I assumed because it felt like you–"

"I'm eating meals with you as much as possible from now on."

Combing a hand through her long dark hair, she sighed before grabbing us silverware and laying them near our waters. "You honestly don't have to. I know I was a little crazy a week ago, but I'm okay."

"Well, it's good for us to get to know one another. We can go over the rest of our arrangement timeline." I went to sit on the stool beside her. "We need this all laid out. That's why we're going to go over the rest of this file together. No issues, okay?"

She cut into the crepe and shrugged as she put a piece in her mouth before continuing the conversation.

Except the conversation came to a screeching halt when the woman moaned over my food.

"Oh my Lord, what is in this?" Her eyes rolled back like she was in ecstasy.

It was a thin pancake with a little vanilla extract, powdered sugar, and maybe a few hidden ingredients. Mom had taught Cade and me well over the years.

And a little piece of me was pleased that she followed her emotions head-on in this exact moment, because the woman made the best sounds of pleasure.

My dick immediately recognized them.

Jesus, the way her skin glowed when she was happy, that hint of color on her cheeks—I believed she responded in honest satisfaction with each of our encounters.

Morina was free spirited and indulged probably like I did. I just had more years of experience.

It made her even more appealing, the fact that she knew what her body wanted and yet hadn't even begun to understand what I could do to her.

Jesus fuck.

I wasn't doing anything more to her.

I was marrying her and doing this hand off legally. That was all.

I cleared my throat and shifted in my chair, trying to calm my damn dick down. "It's just a thin pancake, Morina. I can give you the recipe if you want."

She nodded, staring at her plate with pure adoration. "Yep. I'll take it. Normally, I'd say no. I don't cook that much. Just shakes, you know? But this ... this, I will take. I will master it somehow because it's so good. So, so, so good."

My dick wasn't calming down to save my life. I shoveled my food down and didn't say another damn thing. I let her eat while I went to find the godforsaken file.

I plopped down on the couch and said over my shoulder, "Let's summarize where possible. I'll give you the highlights, and then you can forget about this damn thing hanging over your head."

"It's a very large thing." She held up her fork like she needed to point it out. "I still don't understand what I should and shouldn't be doing."

"Do you want to make a plan for the rest of the six months?" Her nose wrinkled like the word *plan* made her physically ill. I chuckled. "It's not that complicated or binding, Morina. Don't look that appalled."

"I ... Plans make me crazy. They always veer off track or someone lets somebody else down."

"Did someone let you down?"

"No." She answered way too fast. "Just tell me, how are we going to pull this off? I'll do whatever. I just need to know."

She was flowing down whatever river I wanted her to. Honestly, the girl was a little too trusting and free-spirited. Until it came to certain things. God forbid I try to take her salt lamp or grandmother's plants out of the damn house.

The plants were coming back to life after our talk though. Or maybe after I'd taken to watering them instead of letting her do it. I was quite pleased with how much better the orchid looked after some research. I told myself she needed them alive for her grandmother and to feel comfortable here, but her smile when she looked at them was reason enough for me.

"We will attend the charity gala like the company does every year. It will be a great place to announce our engagement. We'll make sure to get married quickly, live here, get through the legal probate of the will. You can attend board meetings and work at the food truck once we're married."

"I can go back to the food truck?" She stopped eating for that.

"Yes. We found the guys who ransacked it." Cade had tracked the underground gang down. "They won't be a problem again."

Her blue eyes widened. "Please tell me you didn't ..."

I smirked at her hesitating to ask. "Kill them?"

She bit her lip.

"What if I said I did?" I tilted my head and waited. I'd wanted to kill them, I'd admit to that.

"Well, I don't know." She dropped her fork and threw up her hands. "It's concerning, that's for sure."

I chuckled. "I didn't kill them. I did have them beaten badly enough that they won't make the mistake of touching anything that's mine again though."

"They touched my food truck, not yours."

"What's yours is mine, love." Thinking of someone harming her now made me want to destroy something, made me want to resort back to violence in a way I hadn't wanted to for a long time.

"Well, I guess all these plans and me going back to the food truck, like we're living normally, is great for the cameras." She sighed but waved away her disdain. "Okay, you said there's a gala with some of your *business associates*." She emphasized the words like she felt they were complete fiction. "The board will also be there. And we're making a statement. If you're proposing there, what's pushing you to do that so fast? I mean, they've only seen us living here and visiting the park. Seems sort of quick."

"What makes a man act quickly then?"

"My grandma always said men are about pride and measuring how big your ..." She turned back to her food.

"My ego is, Morina?" It was a small tragedy that I didn't get to see her skin blush because I knew she was thinking about my dick right then. She'd teased me about it on the plane that first night. I remembered the way her mouth had dropped open, how she'd taken it down her throat so well.

I adjusted my trousers. "We can figure out the logistics later. The fact is we need a proposal there. We need to marry within a week after that, and then you'll attend the first board meeting."

"Can you come to that?"

"They're old school. Spouses come, especially if they're

men." Equality in business wasn't exactly fair. I didn't know if Morina really cared one way or the other.

"Well, that's shitty." Guess she did. She got up and rinsed her plate. "Anyway, what do I need to know about the meeting? The terminals run fine, right?"

"Refineries are getting antsy to push more oil here. I don't think it's necessary. We need to fully restructure. That means—"

"That means the potential for cleaner water and air."

"Yes, over time." I explained more as she came and sat on the sofa next to me. I handed her the file when she reached out. "It's a long road. I want ports open to that throughout Florida though. This state, and others, need to go greener."

"Why?" She narrowed her eyes at me. "You'll lose partners and make enemies that way."

"I intend to make allies on the other side though. I want to right what my father wronged."

"Did he wrong all of us?"

"My father wasn't a good man. He wronged everyone."

"But my grandma—"

"She probably didn't know."

"My grandma wasn't dumb," Morina stated, her voice stronger than normal. "She would have done a lot, even if it was bad, to save this town."

I nodded. I wouldn't argue with her on that. I wouldn't elaborate on her grandmother's votes over the years either.

Cade had hacked into records enough to know Maribel had made deals with the Irish and then with my father over the years. She'd made some terrible votes, and I could only imagine they were because of her partnerships.

"So, I'm voting on what? Can I see the ports beforehand?"

I cleared my throat and thought that over while she folded her knees to her chest and pulled the sweatshirt over them.

"We have to be married first. Then, you get access to everything according to the will. We go to this gala. We put on the show. We get married in the next week. It needs to look real if we're to maintain your protection. The media will cover us, and other businessmen will look into you. Do you understand? This has to be the plan, and it has to be executed right."

Morina wriggled in her baggy sweatshirt, her eyes darting around like she was antsy with the whole thing. "Sure, sure. That sounds good."

"It'll be fine."

"I'm just not used to it." She cleared her throat and waved her hand in the air.

"I'll help you get used to it, okay?" I knew my change in subject would calm her. "Want to go surfing now?"

"Can I?"

"If I go with you."

Her eyes grew even wider. "You said you have to work today. Also, I ... I don't think it's a good idea for you to come."

Now I was intrigued. "Not a good idea. Why not?"

She chuckled. "Well, you can't surf, can you?"

"I'm sure I will catch on fine."

She laughed and laughed, and then her smooth brown legs slid out from under her sweatshirt. "Okay, Bastian. Let's see."

That was easier than I'd expected. For a woman not set on enjoying anything with anyone, she was suddenly fine with me coming along.

I did have to work. I had to call a few companies and attend a virtual meeting regarding my investments. Still, I could maneuver around them.

Today, I had to show a little girl that I knew how to swim. That's all surfing really was. Swimming and balancing on a damn board.

CHAPTER 23: MORINA

He wouldn't be able to get on the board if his life depended on it, I was sure of it. I asked if he'd been paddleboarding or anything. He said he'd be fine.

I tried to hide my surprise when he emerged from his room wearing a gray T-shirt and board shorts. Of course he still looked much more put together than I did in my Hendrix "Excuse me while I kiss the sky" oversize T-shirt. It might have technically belonged to one of my guy friends rather than me. Either way, it hit below mid-thigh and was perfect for a quick car ride to the beach.

When we got there, I hurried from the car, desperate to get on the water. It'd been too long. "You know, as a child, my father almost had to save me a few times out there. He used to say to be cautious. She's beautiful but if you're not careful, she'll eat you alive."

Bastian smirked. "Maybe he would have said the same to me about you."

"What?" I squinted at him as we approached my food truck.

"Morina Bailey, you're like the ocean. Pretty without trying, alluring without knowing, and I think you might be just as devastating. You could probably eat me alive."

I laughed at his assessment, not sure I could take it as a compliment. Still, Bastian's words warmed me even when I tried to ignore them.

I pulled my board from my abandoned truck, then rounded to the other side. "You can use Bradley's spare board."

I think part of him was a little irritated. "You store a board here for him?"

"I'm close to the water. I've stored for other people too."

"Except, his is here routinely."

I shrugged and slid the board from the hooks. "Sure. He usually surfs with me in the morning if I'm out."

I hadn't been though, and it was totally like Bradley not to reach out with questions. We had that lazy sort of friendship. He might not show for a week, or I might not. This time, at least he'd had warning I'd be gone after making me the sign.

"Mo, you back?" My old friend, Jonah, ambled up, his worn body on display in his swim trunks. For a seventy-year-old, he rocked his surf bod better than any of us could.

"Not to make smoothies, Jonah. Sorry. It's going to be a few more weeks."

He glared at Bastian. "You stole her from us?"

I chuckled. "Someone trashed the inside of my food truck, actually."

Bastian placed his hand on my back. When I glanced at him, he winked, his eyes full of determination suddenly.

A display was in order, I guess. "We're also sort of dating," I mumbled.

Jonah nodded. "Word gets around." He shook out his shaggy gray hair. "Hope this man is good to you. And remember, I need to make sure I get more smoothies soon." He patted my shoulder and walked on, undoubtedly chasing bigger waves down the beach.

"We're going this way." I pointed toward a smaller surf area. "I've never encountered riptides here but don't fight the water if you go under."

His brow lifted. "Don't fight the water?"

"Yes, the water can feel overwhelming when you fall. Never panic. I always say if you go with the flow under there, it's a fun, safe sport."

"And if I don't do that?"

"Well, you can't dominate the ocean, Bastian. And you can't reason with it either. The ocean is the boss. Treat her that way."

"Her?"

"Sure. Only a woman could handle all these men riding her and come out on top every single time, right?"

He laughed at my joke, but I believed it. The ocean would have been a beautiful woman; one with power and depth and darkness that held secrets no one could imagine. She took all the waste of the world and still came out looking stunning.

I pointed out at the sparkling horizon. "Did you know the Gulf of Mexico has four thousand offshore oil and gas platforms and pipelines? So much drilling and pollution in that water. I think we'd all be better off without it. I want that. I mean, the whole town had to help clean up the spill a few years ago. It was hundreds of thousands of barrels of oil. How do you recover from something like that? The animals ... It was just so bad."

"I won't argue that." He stared out, and I glanced back at my food truck.

Bradley's sign had already faded, the spray paint not holding up against the ocean air. "We have a love-hate relationship with the port and terminals. We make a living off it, but it ruins the beauty."

"I think we can all work together to bring change to that," he murmured like he believed it.

I nodded. "Well, then, I guess I need to get the truck up and running again if this town is going to be thriving soon, right?"

He turned to me with a question in his stare, but something shifted in his gaze before he asked anything. "I'll get a crew to clean it out and have security come when you want to work."

"I don't need security."

"That's the only way I'm going to let that happen, Morina."

"Let it happen?" The statement rubbed me the wrong way, like someone stroking a cat from tail to head.

He watched a seagull fly by, white against the blue skies. "It's a matter of safety, not control."

With a sigh, I conceded, not sure I wanted to fight him on that front. I didn't know how much it would cost him to have the food truck secured, but I wanted to make my small amount of money, and I missed my customers, the feel of the beach, and the smoothies too.

We walked to the edge of the water in silence, each probably unsure how to broach the subject of our marriage and the ridiculous measures we had to take so these port shares could be easily transferred to Bastian.

Before our toes hit the water, I dropped the board near me, and he followed suit. "So, Bradley might be a little bigger than you. The board will be fine though."

Bastian's eyes narrowed at my assessment. As I stared at him, his shadow engulfing me, I reassessed because Bastian was a whole head taller than me.

He slid off his T-shirt, the movement unhurried.

I didn't look away. Instead, I sucked my bottom lip in between my teeth and stared like a hungry dog. He was muscles on top of muscles and abs over abs, and that vein on his pelvic area that dipped under his swim trunks was much too distracting.

I'd had him before.

I knew how it all felt. How big he was and how well he maneuvered his size.

"Morina." His voice was thick and full of gravel. He dragged a finger from my collarbone up to my chin, tipping it up so I could look at him. "You're staring where you shouldn't be, *piccola ragazza*. Don't do that, love, unless you intend to do something about it."

I stepped back and cleared my throat. The way I wanted to take him up on the offer wasn't at all healthy. He and I both knew that. "Sorry. You're normally in a suit and not so ..." I waved at his abs. "So on display."

"Only reason you're looking?"

"Sure," I said, moving on from the uncomfortable questioning. I'd been holed up in that penthouse for way too long. He was running around for work and probably still indulging in women. I couldn't possibly bring a guy back.

It was a topic we'd have to discuss later.

The idea caused a fire in my stomach, hot and worthy of fury if I thought about it. Instead, I whipped my own shirt off, and when I looked back at him, he was staring exactly where he shouldn't be too.

Good. I wasn't the only one. I'd expected that and honestly hoped for it. I'd worn a smaller bikini, and it was a bright coral instead of the normal black and white ones I wore.

I don't know why I needed to get his attention that day, I just knew that I wanted him to look at me like I was attractive enough. Maybe it was the fact that I was all too aware of his beauty or that I wasn't sure if I'd simply been a girl in the right place at the right time that first night.

I wasn't a diamond like most of the women I was sure he dated. I wore baggy clothes with the color fading. I didn't do my nails, and I didn't even try to act girly. I embraced astrology and the smell of essential oil in shakes for a living.

To most men, I was easy, not unique. I was there and willing, not rare and one of a kind. I was okay with that because they were the same for me. I didn't want anything more or less from the men I'd hooked up with in the past.

Now, I had six months left with a man I actually enjoyed as a sort of friend. I know I enjoyed his crepes, that was for sure.

Standing at the edge of the water, I explained the basics of surfing. He didn't seem to get it when I told him it was going to be difficult.

He smirked in my face like the cocky boss he thought he was here.

Oh, dear Bastian, your dick is big in other areas, but no one rules the ocean.

So, I let him dive deeper and deeper into his cockiness until he tried his first wave.

He sputtered, coming up for air after being knocked off by the monster that was the sea.

Somehow, he still managed to look like Poseidon, all muscle and anger and ruthlessly glaring as water dripped from the strong lines on his face.

I can admit, I was a bit distracted by the six- or eight-pack of abs he was carrying and didn't exactly give him a great lesson. Yet, he kept trying and trying. At one point, he popped up from the water with a scraped arm, his tattoos pouring blood.

"Jesus, you hit the floor?" I winced, realizing we were closer to a rock bed than I'd originally anticipated.

He shrugged. "It's fine."

"There are sharks," I grumbled because the man didn't seem to know when to quit.

"And you think out of all this water, a shark is going to pick me?"

"You're bleeding."

"Isn't that a myth?" He floated, leaning his arms on his board.

"Probably," I sighed. "I think we need to call it."

"Because you think I can't do it."

"You can't right now." I swam languidly around my board, flipping onto my back and letting the sun hit my skin as the water made me rise and fall. "You'll get it if you keep practicing."

"So, when should we practice again?"

I turned and stared at him. Glaring at the board as he trailed his big hands up and down it, I saw the look of a man not used to failing.

"I'll bring you whenever you want." I tugged his board close to mine, dragging him with it. "You did good, Bastian. You've outperformed more than most. The first time Bradley came out, he said he was quitting and that it was a dumb sport."

"And you?" He squinted into the sun as though wanting to catch every movement of my face.

I glanced away. "My dad was a good surfer. He had a little bit of Samoan and Haitian in him. He didn't talk about his parents much, but I know they practically lived in the water. I took after him."

"He teach you?"

"Teach is a strong word. We all just sort of came here to be. My mom and dad loved the beach, and all three of us surfed for as long as I can remember ... until we didn't anymore."

"Okay," he said softly. Bastian never pried. He didn't ask questions about my family. I think it was because he didn't want me to ask about his.

We tiptoed around our pasts because we didn't really have a future, and so it wasn't like our knowledge of the past mattered.

Still, for some reason, I almost told him. My heart wanted to.

I found myself struggling with that. It was the first time in a long while I didn't go with the flow of my emotions. I pulled them back, completely scared of what might happen.

"Should we head in? The sun's about to set." I pointed up and started to swim back to the beach.

He followed without argument.

CHAPTER 24: BASTIAN

Mother Nature, or Mother Ocean, had proven she could overpower me. I wanted to scream at Morina that I would be staying in the water all night.

But I would follow the woman in her tiny bikini anywhere she wanted me to go. I drove us back home and didn't even consider the fact we had our wet asses on the leather seats of my Rolls-Royce.

My mind had shifted into unknown territory in that water, watching her today.

Morina truly could have been a mermaid in another life. And the way she jumped out of the water like a freaking goddess who walked on the stuff. The surfboard didn't carry her, it floated with her, and her muscles didn't look like they were straining.

She'd ridden the wave to the end, then turned and waved to me like it was the easiest feat in the world.

I had to give her credit—she'd told me it would be difficult to learn and that the ocean was dangerous. I could have blamed the board or the waves or anything, but I knew the truth. This was something I wasn't good at.

There weren't many of those things in the world.

I could coerce most men into doing as I told them. I learned from the very best in each industry I got involved with, and when I couldn't get something done, well, my family knew how to force it.

"You're quiet." Morina twisted her wet hair around her

hand, tying in a knot. "Are you mad?"

"I'm frustrated." No sooner had I spoken than I wanted to snatch back my words. Still, they hung in the car as I drove through her small town to go back home.

She nodded but didn't push. She seemed to know when to pick her battles, and this wasn't one she wanted to fight.

We silently existed with one another for the rest of the car ride and retired to our separate bedrooms to clean up once we got to the penthouse.

Cade called with an update on the day. His rambling about different issues within our businesses realigned my priorities. I commanded attention here. I was able to fix those problems with ease.

It was a good reminder. Our worlds didn't mix outside of the small one we had created for the time being, and that was fine.

I hung up and a weight lifted from my chest. While she tinkered in her bedroom, I grabbed some flour, eggs, oil, and a dash of salt. She'd tried to teach me to surf, so I'd return the favor and cook for her.

My mother would have been proud. I told myself I was just hungry though. This was an easy solution and a nice gesture, considering we needed to be on great terms with the upcoming gala.

She peeked around the corner in another baggy T-shirt that I swore she wore to drive me insane. I wanted to know if there were shorts underneath or if she just wore panties that would be easy to slip aside.

The friend zone we hovered in was becoming my least favorite place.

"You okay with pasta tonight?"

"Are you making it by hand?" She rounded the corner and

beelined for me. I felt the heat of her instantly and guessed she didn't have a bra on from the way her body moved on its way over.

"I think it's the best way to make it, don't you?"

"This might not be a good idea." She shook her head but still stared at my hands kneading the dough.

"Why not?" I asked as I tried not to smell her wet hair. Since the woman moved in, I'd been acutely aware of her scents everywhere. From the incense to her shampoo, I was overstimulated and stressed. The supposedly calming aromas had the opposite effect on me. Every time I smelled her damn hair, I wanted to wrap it around my hand and tell her to get on her knees.

"I think I'll fall in love with you if you keep cooking for me, Bastian. That, or I won't be able to get on a surfboard. I'll literally burst at the seams, and I can't go to a gala looking ten pounds heavier than I already am."

She said it with such honesty, I wondered if she believed that.

"We're going in a couple days, Mo. You won't gain too much by then. Even so, I'd love you on my arm either way."

She smirked up at me, those blue doe eyes filled with disbelief and condescension. "You'd be fine taking what your colleagues would surely classify as a big girl to an event and then proposing to her?"

Maybe it was her blatant skepticism or the way she genuinely thought I'd have a problem with it that had me turning to the fridge and pulling out a cannoli the chef had made.

I held the dessert out in front of me. "Open wide, love."

Her eyes narrowed, and my dick jumped when she whispered, her voice suddenly husky, "I know that phrase."

"I wasn't joking the first time I said it, and I'm not joking now."

She licked her lips and opened.

I slid my hand into her hair and slowly placed the cannoli onto her tongue. "Bite, *ragazza*."

She did and, of course, whether she wanted to or not, she moaned and closed her eyes. I gave myself a second to listen to her before I brushed a piece of frosting from her lips. She stared at me sucking it off my thumb.

"You can eat anything you want," I told her. I meant it, too.

She nodded in the same trance that had taken me over.

If I kissed her, would she indulge?

I knew the answer and knew we also needed to find a boundary. At this rate, we wouldn't make it to the gala.

I returned my attention to the dough.

She glanced at the plants and before I knew it, she'd grabbed a cup and started pouring water carefully in each one but only after feeling the soil.

"You're learning." I nodded, then grabbed a sharp knife and sliced thin strips for the noodles.

"Only because I had a great teacher." She walked into the living room, turned on her salt lamp and sighed. "Much better."

I hid my smile.

She still caught me. "You can question it all you want, but don't you feel better when it's on?"

"If I do, it's only because you're in a better mood when it's on."

She rolled her eyes and folded up her sleeves as she came back to my side.

"What can I help with?"

"If you want to put some water on to boil, that'll help. I'll start browning the meat for the ragù. We have some sauce in the fridge."

"Is it homemade?"

"The chef made it, but it's my mother's recipe. Does that count?"

"I'll take it." Her hip bumped mine, and she smiled.

We worked in harmony in that kitchen, like we were somehow made to be in it together. When we sat down to eat, I glanced at her. "If you don't like it, I won't be offended."

She glared. "*I'll* be offended if I don't like this. You're crazy."

With that, she dug in.

I waited for her moan but there was complete silence as she chewed with her eyes closed.

Maybe I'd lost my touch.

Then her head hit the table. "No. I can't stand it. I'm dead."

"What?"

"I'm in love with you now. I can't believe I get this cooking for six months. Oh my God."

She didn't even glance up as she moaned a long list of different deities.

Fuck, I needed an outlet. The woman's voice was sex on a stick to begin with, and now I was reminded of how good she sounded with her mouth around my dick.

"Morina, don't be ridiculous," I ground out. "Eat your food."

She turned her head on the table and opened one eye. "I'm not being ridiculous, Bastian. How can you eat anything but this all day long?"

"I like variety." I knew my cooking was as good as my mother's. She would spend hours in the kitchen and had recipes from Italy that no one else would be able to match. We put love into our food and that took pride, patience, and a learned touch.

"What will I do when our six months is up?"

The pain in her voice and how she completely embraced

the fact she'd be sad when we left one another had me agreeing to something I never thought I would. "I can teach you, love."

She sat up. "Seriously?"

"Sure." I pointed a fork at her. "You can teach me to make a smoothie too, huh?"

That smile shot across her face and straight into my chest. I didn't like the way I was starting to care for her or the way she smiled at me like I could do her no harm.

Our worlds were different. And you didn't mix a man born in filth with a mermaid, not tainted yet by the pollution of my cities.

CHAPTER 25: MORINA

Bastian was talking to me over his food about the gala. Three days until then. More acting and faking. At this point, it was him faking and me being completely and utterly confused.

And even so, I couldn't seem to focus on his words.

The man made pasta.

With his big bare hands. He'd smiled at me when I said I wanted to learn, and he'd asked about the recipes for my smoothies.

Then his phone rang, and he didn't bother getting it. He silenced it instead, like I was more than his business.

I got up put the dishes in the dishwasher, but he followed and helped rinse them off before stacking them into the machine. His body was close when he asked if I wanted to watch a movie.

I pressed the dishwasher button and when I turned to look at him, his eyes were all ooey-gooey chocolate colored, and his lips begged for me to lean in.

I could have run down a list of reasons why I shouldn't, but I didn't think about the negatives or hesitate in life. I just went for it.

Quick decisions.

I took his lips in my mouth and pulled him closer by the collar of his shirt.

Maybe I expected him to pick me up and lay me out on the counter and ravage me. I definitely expected him to at least wrap his arms around me.

He did neither.

After a moment of him letting me kiss him, I pulled back.

"You kissed me." He said it almost like a question with a slight hitch in his voice. But somehow it was also a statement.

Normally, I didn't turn red, my blush would be hard to see under my sun-kissed skin, but I knew he could see it now. It rose from my chest to my cheeks, burning with embarrassment.

"I ... I'm sorry. I thought ..."

He rubbed at his lips, and his frown led me to my own conclusions.

I rushed out an explanation. "It's just you've been here these past couple days. I mean, I went to a theme park with you. We kissed."

He nodded. "We kissed for the cameras, Morina."

"I know that was for show. But we slept on that stupid couch together and you ... well, you know! I know it was because of me and being sexually frustrated and ... oh my God, I don't know. The freaking pasta and there was something in the air."

He tried to speak again but I was on a rant now. "I felt cooped up, and then we surfed and, Bastian, you were decent at failing out on that board. And then I thought I wanted to tell you stuff about my family, and normally I would have just done it because we know I *just do* everything, but I didn't. That's a large sign something's off for me."

He stared at me. "So you kissed me?"

"It wasn't a good idea!" I threw my hands out and beelined to the fridge and reached on top of it for my lighter. I needed a scent in the air to calm myself down or something. "But I'm here and you're here and I keep thinking, well, I can go to the food truck and work and get away from you, but if I go to the food truck, is a mobster going to come and ransack it? And if I go surfing, is someone going to drown me if you're not there? I know that sounds ludicrous but, well, is it?"

He stared at me like he was waiting for me to work it all out for myself.

I leaned in and whispered, "Those stocks are worth a ton of money, Bastian. Millions."

"Yes, Morina. How do you think your grandmother had the majority vote? With thousands of dollars' worth?"

"Well, okay, in my defense, I didn't think she had any vote until the day of the will hearing." I wanted to smack him for being logical. "And then, I guess I didn't put two and two together. I—"

"You avoided it because the idea scared you."

"Don't say that like it's what I do all the time. I do everything and anything. I go with the flow."

"Until you're scared of the flow."

"I resent that statement because I'm doing this fake marriage stupid plan with you even though it scares the ever loving hell out of me. My gut said no. I usually go with my gut. And can I also say, it hasn't been a walk in the park, okay? I just ... you were gone, and I felt alone. And now you're here, and it feels like you're everywhere. You're everywhere and nowhere at the same time. You're in my space with your food and your voice and your body everywhere and I had a very healthy sex life with Bradley and guys that were—"

"I'm going to stop you right there." His jaw was granite, sharp edged and flexed. "I don't need to know about your sexual history, Mo." He sounded mad, and maybe even a little disgusted.

"Well, I'm just trying to explain. Normally, Bradley comes over or I go out. This is a tourist town, mostly. Men want a fling and I enjoy—"

"Stop." It was yet another time I heard more emotion in

his voice than his usual stoic persona. He pulled at the collar of his shirt and then rubbed his forehead. "Maybe you need an outlet."

I narrowed my eyes. What he could possibly mean by that? Did he want to be the outlet?

He sighed and ran a hand through his hair. I considered grabbing it while he went down on me and was immediately okay with the idea of him stepping in for a roll in the hay.

"I'm serious," he grumbled. "I can't have you around me, ready to go all the time, without delivering on it."

What a dick! I glared at him as I set a hand on my hip, ready to give him hell.

He covered my mouth before he leaned in, taking a step closer. Suddenly we were chest to chest, body to body. I had to look up to meet his eyes. My embarrassment at his words deteriorated as I felt the length of him against my stomach. He was long, thick, and rock hard.

He whispered in my ear as he retracted his hand, "Maybe I need an outlet too, okay?"

I bit my lip to keep myself from doing something stupid again. He was so close. I breathed in while he breathed out. Both of us fighting an attraction we really didn't need.

Especially when his attraction was probably only because I was a warm woman who'd come on to him.

His allies and his business associates came first. He lived his life based on rules, and I lived mine on desire. We were a match made in hell. Tonight, when I lit my candles, I'd remind my grandma of her terrible matchmaking skills.

He took a deep breath and in turn my chest rose with my own inhale. His pupils dilated as he glanced down. My shirt left little to the imagination while his dick twitched against my stomach and sent my imagination running wild.

He picked at one of my tangled waves. "I guess no one really knows what's going on."

He mulled it over, and I watched how he tried to remain completely professional. He dropped my hair and stuck his hands in his pockets. "It could work. You've been in and out of the penthouse. We've had a whirlwind relationship, so the tabloids have said. Let's draw attention by attending the gala separately, and you do what you want beforehand."

"Okay." I drew out the word, frustrated that he was distancing himself rather than fucking me on the countertop.

If he was willing to go and discreetly do something with other people, we could go ahead and really cause a scene. I glared at him. "Why don't we actually go to the event with whoever we like? You can get your fix, and I can get mine. I'll take Bradley."

His face hardened. "Bradley?" Did he feel the frustration too all of a sudden? He cleared his throat and his features. "If that's what you want to do."

I'm sure my eyes widened. I spun away from him and grabbed a wipe to clean the counter. I needed something to do to get rid of this ball of tension that had built in my gut. "So, I'll ask him then. We can do whatever we want discreetly beforehand. It'll be perfect."

"Perfect?" he whispered, like he was shocked at my line of thought. He'd started them though. He could end them too with a few words.

Just ask me to go with you.

I stared at him, and he licked his lips. The man was holding steady to his original plan of us not being together and this being an easy six months.

I guessed the six months would be a bit harder with us attracted to one another.

"Okay, do you have a plan for the end of the night? Want to profess your love after seeing me with another man or something?"

"That would actually be believable," he murmured, but he wasn't looking at me anymore. "You should attend with whoever you'd like. The date will end with us together though. Do what you want discreetly beforehand. I'll ask you to marry me by the end of the night publicly."

"Just me?" I pointed to him. "You should bring someone too."

His whole face contorted like I was ridiculous. "I don't want to bring anyone, Morina."

"Oh, like you don't have some woman you can bring? This is good for us." I was convincing myself and him at the same time. "I need you to bring someone, Bastian. It's only fair that we both get some and have an *outlet*."

His jaw worked up and down, up and down. "This isn't going to end well."

"Of course it will," I said it with confidence. "And once we're well into the six months, we can separate officially. It can be public enough that we can date other people. That can still work right?"

He sighed and pulled at his neck before he answered. "If people know we respect and care for one another, everything will be fine. You'll always be an Untouchable. We can discuss the oil company, and I'll go through the rest of the file with you. I'm happy to take you to the terminals and show you what I have planned for them too."

I shut my eyes. Bastian was appeasing me and compromising for the good of the company. His words twisted my gut into a ball of frustration and something that felt a lot like a letdown. Why had I wanted him to say we could get together instead?

We'd done it once before. Why not do it again?

I'd kissed him. I'd scared him off, and instead of wanting anything more with me, he wanted to distance himself with others in between us.

It was the right thing to do. Logical even.

Still ... "I don't need protection like this, Bastian. It feels like we're both sacrificing so much now. If you're worried about me, I'm fine. The sheriff knows about the break-in at the food truck, and I can ... I don't need you to sacrifice for my protection—"

"I'm here, aren't I?" He lifted my chin and waited for me to open my eyes. Why was it that whenever he was nice to me, he looked just about my age, just about as mature as me, like we could be together, like he was a man I would be attracted to? "It was my decision to get engaged to you. I want this company to thrive, and I want a hand in it. We can sleep with other people and still be married. Couples do that all the time."

The coldness of his words, how he so easily tossed me aside even though I'd given him the go-ahead had me nodding my head.

"Okay."

"Okay?" He narrowed his dark eyes and searched mine. I turned away and grabbed a glass from the cupboard to get some water. I needed him to back up, which he did immediately. Without him near me, I would be able to think more logically.

"Yeah. I think it's a great idea." I downed the liquid and set the glass by the sink. Then, I stalked off to my room.

I texted Bradley and confirmed he would be my date to the gala.

The wheels were in motion.

I just hoped my heart wouldn't get derailed.

CHAPTER 26: MORINA

"I'm sorry I couldn't be there, Mo." My friend sounded so broken-hearted over the phone. It was our one call every couple months while she traveled the freaking world.

"Don't worry about it." I brushed off her apology because she shouldn't have felt bad. It was for no good reason. I'd cried enough for my grandma, and now I was pissed at her.

"She played Eminem at the funeral."

"What?" She burst out laughing. "You're kidding. That woman was epic."

"I know." I sighed. "But she left me a huge mess and she knew it. She wanted to haunt me, I swear."

"Just like Maribel." We were both quiet for a moment. "I'm still sorry you lost your best friend, Mo. I'll be your second, not-very-present one always, okay?"

I smirked as I added some shadow to my eyes. It was the night of the gala, and I was almost ready.

"Anyway, I'm going to a gala for Tropical Oil tonight."

"Oh my God," Linny squealed. "Because of that stallion you're dating? Who knew my dare would have gotten you here?"

She didn't know the real story, but she thought she did.

"Have you been approached by the media yet? They freaking love you guys. I see your face on fucking magazines, Morina."

She was much more excited about it than I was.

"It is what it is," I mumbled as I finished my look off with some lip gloss.

"Oh my God. Seriously, though, can you even walk? You must be banging the shit out of that man."

"What? No," I screeched. But most people thought this was for real. "I mean, we're taking things slow."

"Slow? You moved in with him, Mo! It says so in a magazine."

"The magazines are wrong. I'm only staying here a few nights a week." The news would explode with our engagement soon, but I was going with Bradley tonight and that was our story.

"You'd better be fucking that man every day. Don't get all weird on him. You're committing. He committed by getting that penthouse. Maribel is probably dancing in her grave right now."

I wanted to tell her all the details but now wasn't the time. Maybe next year when it was all said and done. "That's not commitment, Linny. He already had this place." I scoffed and cracked my door open.

"No. What? I read the tabloids. Girl, I know how much your place costs. He's got it bad."

I cleared my throat. I needed to do a Google search, but I wasn't going to admit that, since his fiancée should've known the cost and when he bought it. The tabloids lied about that stuff though. Bastian surely had this place before me.

This conversation was painful but good practice for me, I guess. Even if I felt a little bad for lying to my friend, she'd forgive me one day when I got to tell her the whole truth after my divorce.

Divorce. I sighed at the thought of that word.

"Is something wrong in the bedroom or something?" Linny took my sigh for something it totally wasn't.

Nothing was happening in the bedroom. That was the real problem.

248

"We want to keep things slow."

"Is he holding out now or something?" She mumbled something to someone. "I'm about to jump on my connecting flight. I have just the thing though. I'll send it to you. I have your address but need the penthouse number. Text me, chica. Love you! Bye."

She hung up before I could even protest. I wasn't going to, anyway. She'd find a way to get my address if I didn't text it, so why fight it?

Bastian tapped on my door before pushing it all the way open. "Will you be ready in an hour?"

"I could have been naked."

"That's what I was hoping for." Bastian Armanelli stood there clean shaven, in shoes that must have been shined and a suit that cut to his physique from a skilled sculptor. The man looked devastatingly hot.

I rolled my eyes and stood to twirl in the silk midnight-blue dress I'd ordered online for the event. "Not naked. Actually, I'm about ready."

He'd been smirking, but as his eyes trailed down my body, he leaned on the doorframe, and his smile disappeared.

The slits up my legs were high enough that my thighs would be on display but the dress hugged my waist and breasts in all the right places too. His stare raked up and down once, twice, three times and hovered where the dress fit snugly. "The blue matches your eyes, *ragazza*. You're breathtaking."

I yanked my heart back from running toward him when he murmured his compliment. "You have to say that after I spent hours in here getting ready."

"I don't. But I want to anyway." He took a large breath and closed his eyes with his next admission. "I won't enjoy practicing restraint tonight."

"What do you mean by that, Bastian?" I asked, wanting to make sure I didn't do something stupid like kiss him again.

He shook his head. "Nothing. Nothing. What more do you have to do to get ready?"

Back to the man who kept it all together. I sighed and turned to my drawer to pull out five crystals. "Do you think we need poise tonight?"

"For the board members?" He shrugged against the doorframe.

"Sure." I didn't wait for him to answer and swiped two back into the drawer. "These three will do. Sexuality, beauty, and determination."

"Sexuality? Really?" His brow slammed down like he had something more to say about that.

"Well, yeah. For being on men's arms. I need to look better than the women on your arm in the past and look good on Bradley, right? I'm selling the view, am I not?"

His jaw worked before he backed away from me. He didn't comment. He just mumbled that a driver would be downstairs for me when I was ready. I left the penthouse without saying another word to him.

I rode quietly in the back of the SUV to get Bradley, and he stood there in a black suit that didn't quite fit the way Bastian's always did. He'd never been good at wearing them. He belonged on a beach in board shorts and not much else. "This good?"

"It's great, Bradley." I patted his shoulder as he entered the SUV Bastian had arranged for Dante to drive. "Thanks for coming with me."

"What happened to your guy?"

"It's complicated." I almost combed a hand through my hair, then remembered I'd curled it around my face for tonight. No beaded bracelets or boots to wear either. I wore strappy black heels and had a small purse that fit my phone, a few cards, and the crystals.

"Does being complicated mean you're still with him, Mo?" Bradley asked.

I glanced away and wrinkled my nose. "I'm probably using you a little tonight."

"What, like a rebound?" He chuckled. Then he held up a finger. "No wait. Please tell me this is a revenge fuck. I'd love to get that out of it."

Dante sighed from the driver's seat as he maneuvered onto the busy roads.

"Bradley." I rolled my eyes. "You should feel bad I'm doing this. I feel bad I'm doing this."

"What for?" He shrugged and put his arm around me to pull me close. "We've always used each other for sex. It's not like that was going anywhere. You're too much like me for that."

"What do you mean?" I jerked back to glare at him. "I'm not like you."

"Of course you are. We'll never move away from the water, and we're not quick to commit. You're a lot like your parents in that way. They never said they'd do anything. Remember the way your dad would navigate out of any responsibility, and no one even knew he was doing it? He was such a charming guy. Man, I wish I had that same skill."

He laughed at the memory. I winced at it.

So many times my dad would sugarcoat an exit with offers to bring me back candy or a jacket or something I'd been begging for months. I'd loved him so much when he was there. Both he and my mom looked at me like I was their world. I'd believe it too, until they'd pack a bowl, shoot up their arms, and then take their bus somewhere new.

Even that last time they were home, I think I'd held onto

hope. My father had said he'd be home in a jiffy, and I was fifteen, but I still asked to go with.

I'd begged them, but my grandmother was done. She'd quit talking to them. She took my arm and pulled me inside. I heard her telling them to stop the bullshit and not come back if they couldn't stay. I screamed at her for that.

Then, only days later, I cried with her when she told me that they'd crashed their bus.

"Like my parents?" I whispered, not able to let go of his words. They sliced at me, leaving a wake of pain.

He squeezed my arm. "Hey, I didn't mean anything by that."

"No. It's fine." I shook my head, knowing the town had dealt with them as much as I had. "My father wasn't good for any deal, and my mother sucked the life out of everyone. I get what you mean though. They didn't agree to much because they knew they wouldn't follow through."

"Yeah, but they went with love, Mo. They followed their heart and their feelings. They lived even if they died doing it."

"They were addicts, Bradley."

"So, an addict doesn't have a heart?"

I didn't argue with him. I wouldn't. Some people in town loved my parents. I did too in my own way. But I resented them as well. I'd walled off the parts of my heart that reminded me of them. I avoided memories even if they might have helped me understand myself better in some way. If I dwelled on why they left, asked myself questions about why they couldn't commit to parenting me—if I wondered over and over what had been so wrong with me—I'd fall into the abyss and find myself in a darkness I couldn't escape.

"So, the party should be fun. It's a charity for the oil company. My grandma had ..." I hesitated. "Some stocks in it.

So, I'm going to rub elbows."

"She owned shares?" he repeated.

It wouldn't be long before everyone knew. "I think she had a majority vote."

He stared at me, his eyes wide. "That can't be true. That ... That company is worth billions, Morina."

I took a deep breath. "I'm aware."

"So that means ..."

"I don't want anything to do with the money, or even the company, but I want to make sure our town is safe." He nodded but I didn't think he took much in. "Bradley?" I snapped my fingers in front of his face. "She was a partner who kept her identity within the company hidden, and I will be until I get rid of the shares too."

"Fuck me, girl. You got a lot on your plate. Maybe you should have brought that Bastian guy with you. I don't know anything about rubbing elbows with these people."

I laughed. "I don't either. I'm here because I'm supposed to show up and the tabloids are getting wind of my situation with Bastian."

"All I can do is help you make that man jealous and provide the revenge fuck of the century." He laughed at his own joke.

I shoved him and laughed too. It was all a show, but in his mind, that's what it would be. I shrugged. "Sure. Maybe."

We reminisced a little more, and he was the best sport about me using him.

We exited the vehicle a half hour later at a large mansion on the outskirts of town. A large shareholder of Tropical Oil was hosting the event.

Hooking my arm in Bradley's, we navigated through throngs of people and the glass doors opened to a magnificent entryway. A woman who introduced herself as Ronald's wife greeted us. I didn't know Ronald or Patty and wasn't sure what to say.

Bradley took the lead and told her the place looked extraordinary.

She fluffed the collar of her dress because there were literal feathers spurting from it. Glancing around, I realized most women were dressed similarly.

Opulence, luxury, indulgence.

Crystal champagne glasses on silver trays whisked past, and a double staircase wrapped around both sides of the entrance hall.

We left Patty to welcome more guests, and Bradley's stare darted to mine. "You rolling with bigger people than even Linny now, huh?"

"I wouldn't say I'm *rolling* with any of them."

Skirting the crowd, we made our way to a quiet corner, and I scanned the whole scene. I didn't know anyone, didn't feel like I wanted to know them either. How would I go to board meetings with people like this?

A moment later, Ronald made his way over to introduce himself. He was an older man with a strong jaw, head full of silver-gray hair, and a winning straight-toothed smile.

"My wife tells me your name is Morina." He stuck out his hand. He had a gold ring similar to Bastian's on his finger. "I'm Ronald of SeashellOil and Tropical Oil."

Bradley's lips curled. We all knew Ronald had been blamed for some of the oil terminal troubles in the past. He pushed companies to their limits, and I now wondered if my grandma had been on board with that.

"Nice to meet you. I'm Maribel's granddaughter. I appreciate the invite."

"Well, you'll be a part of the family now." He glanced at

Bradley. "And you? You must be her lucky partner tonight. I was surprised after reading some of the tabloids."

It was a bold statement from him. Like a weasel, he wriggled in his true reason for approaching me. Bradley stuck his hand out to shake though, ready to play the game. "I'm Bradley. And I'm damn lucky, that's for sure."

He pulled me close as he shook Ronald's hand. The man smiled and his teeth were too white and too perfect to be real. All of this exchange felt the exact same.

Ronald continued talking to Bradley as if I wasn't there. He explained they were holding a silent auction down the hall, that there was a powder room that way too. He invited us to take a self-guided tour of his grand place and even explained his part in the company to us.

A friend of his, who was closer to my age than Ronald's, meandered over and introduced himself as Quinton. He shook my hand and stared at me with blue eyes and a smile that seemed a bit more genuine. Then he said, "By the way, Morina, I know your ex, Bastian."

"Well, nice to meet you here without him," I said as I pulled my hand out of his, not asking him to elaborate. I'm sure many people knew Bastian. This was his scene, not mine.

Bradley and I nodded and hummed at all the right times while Ronald and Quinton discussed how the oil terminals needed to be expanded and how our town had the ideal coastline for it.

"You know, your girlfriend here holds the cards, Bradley," said Ronald.

My friend was nodding and nodding but his mind had clearly wandered off.

"Bradley, why don't you get us another glass of champagne or some hors d'oeuvres?" I said.

He practically jumped at the chance, excusing himself and beelining to the other side of the room where butlers served alcohol.

I wanted to disappear with him, wanted to search the room for Bastian, wanted to be anywhere but here.

"Morina, I have to say that we've talked to government officials, and we could make all this a smooth transition, even without Maribel. I know this is a lot for you. Maribel didn't tell you, did she?" He patted my arm like I was a child.

I cleared my throat, stepping out of his reach and glared at Quinton and him. "It's a lot for anyone, but I'm excited to do right for the city and the company."

"Of course." He nodded vigorously and then leaned in to whisper, "Quinton and I are willing to pay you fairly and take all this off your hands. I'm happy to see you aren't with that Armanelli fellow anymore. He's been a bit of a thorn in our side since the whole thing with his father."

"What whole thing?"

"Oh, you know—"

"Ronald. Quinton." From behind, his voice cut through our conversation.

Shivers ran down my body at the tone, deep and low and totally in charge.

I turned to see the man I'd secretly been searching for since arriving. He stood tall in a crisp black suit with a navy tie that shined in luxurious silk. His collared white shirt popped perfectly in all the right places and his gold cufflinks glinted bright under the chandelier.

Bastian belonged in big houses with crystal flutes of champagne. More than that though, he belonged with an exceptionally beautiful woman like the one on his arm.

Tall and willowy, she stood on heels that put her body at

the ideal height for Bastian to lay his arm atop her shoulders comfortably. Her long deep-auburn hair rested against his chest.

He leaned down and murmured something to her as she smiled up at him, her red lipstick painted perfectly across her lips.

"Bastian Armanelli," Ronald almost sneered but his hand shot out. "Thank you for coming tonight."

"Absolutely." Bastian shook his hand and scanned our faces. He didn't wink or smirk or show any connection to me. "Good to see everyone could make the charity event. Thank you for hosting."

"Of course, of course. I'm happy you all could make it under these circumstances."

"What circumstances?" his date asked. Her voice was like a sex operator's, and I instantly felt the need to leave.

How had I thought Bastian would want to kiss me back or sleep with me over this stupid amount of time we were supposed to spend together when he normally had women like that?

"Well, Elizabeth, you've seen the tabloids." Ronald and this woman were obviously on a first-name basis already. She belonged in this society. I didn't. "You know these two, well, they have a history."

Ronald chuckled a bit like he was trying to rile Elizabeth, but the woman's delicate hand was on Bastian's chest as she looked up at him and murmured, "Oh, Ronald, none of us are worried about that. Right?"

Bastian smiled like a man in love and whispered something in her ear again, so close to her neck, I was sure they'd been intimate.

Suddenly, I needed air. Or a break. Or something. My hand went to my stomach as I breathed in deep. "I think I'll just—"

"Babe!" Bradley's voice boomed across the crowd. He was holding up champagne glasses and rushing my way. "Sorry. I had to talk to somebody real quick about our beach. They didn't know you surfed and that you're about to be part of Tropical Oil."

Bradley winked at me like he knew I needed rescuing. When his arm went around my shoulders, I leaned in. Bradley was the crystal I didn't have in my pocket tonight. He was my comfort in this foreign place where people had hidden agendas and masked themselves as good individuals when really they were trying to cut you down.

"I'm going to steal my date for a dance." Bradley pulled me away before anyone could protest.

"Thank you," I breathed out, following him as fast as my strappy heels would carry me.

Laughing, Bradley spun me in his arms as we arrived at the dance floor. "Did you see his face?"

"Who's face?"

"The guy you're trying to make jealous, Mo." He pulled me close. "Bastian was furious. He looked about ready to kill me."

"I don't think so." He'd looked just the same, no change in expression and no feeling at all toward me. "He's enamored by Elizabeth on his arm."

"Well, most men would be. The woman is hot, Mo."

I tried to step on his feet. We both moved well on the dance floor, having done our fair share of drunken tiki bar jukebox dancing. He sidestepped and I didn't catch him. "Just shut up and dance."

We did that for a whole song while the orchestra in the corner of the grand room played jazz. More people joined in. An emcee encouraged more to do so before the silent auction closed. Bastian and Elizabeth made their way over. When he turned her in his arms, she curled into his chest, like she belonged there. His dark stare was on her before it snapped up to laser in on me.

I didn't get any indication from him that this was a show. He must have known that woman, he must have slept with her by the way her hands went to his neck and then his hair as she whispered sweet nothings into his ear and burrowed into his neck.

My heart hardened toward him. This truly was an arrangement. We'd had fun but I wasn't falling over a cliff of love or enjoying him more than I should ever again.

Bastian belonged with her. I belonged with a man like Bradley. Two worlds didn't collide and mesh perfectly. I had the ocean, pure and cleansing, while he had his cities full of mob money and dirty luxury.

Bradley murmured in my ear and Bastian took that moment to lay a soft kiss on Elizabeth's neck.

Gentle didn't suit Bastian. A peck instead of a bite wasn't his normal MO. My gut twisted as I realized I didn't know him as intimately as I thought. I'd kissed him, I'd gotten myself off in front of him. I'd probably done all that when he'd had Elizabeth the whole time.

No wonder he'd hesitated.

Bile rose in my throat, and my whole body stiffened.

Bradley nestled into my neck. "Mo, that girl is pretty. I know I said as much, and I know you know that. You're stunning though. She's got nothing on you. Bastian knows that too. Don't let them get to you."

I stiffly nodded, trying to take his words to heart. Yet, I grumbled, "Says the man who knows his only chance of getting some tonight is with me."

He laughed but when I didn't join in, he tickled my hip as

we slow danced. I jumped and broke eye contact with Bastian as I chuckled, then squealed for Bradley to stop his assault.

"Lighten up, Mo," he murmured to me. "It's only one night, okay? Remember, you can still go with the flow. You just have to decide to do that, right?"

His words struck something in me. They echoed my grandmother's letter. I made quick decisions on the water all the time.

I rode the wave.

I took the risk.

Suddenly, I was done dancing, done staring at a man who didn't want me, done not indulging. I grabbed Bradley by the hand. "Let's take that self-guided tour."

"Self—"

I pulled him off the dance floor and down a hallway. We passed a powder room and the silent auction set up on a large oak table in a grand dining room.

We turned a corner and found a door cracked open. I pulled us inside. Books lined the walls, all maroons and greens and hardcovers that must have been first editions. The desk in the middle of the room sat on a Persian rug and would do just fine.

Pulling Bradley against me, I kissed him hard. I backed up to the desk so my ass could slide onto it when the time came.

He tasted of comfort and safety, like Bradley always did. He smelled like the ocean, where I felt at home.

I clawed at his back, wanting more of a rush, wanting to feel what I felt with Bastian. I wanted Bradley to grip me hard like he owned me and tell me I was his.

None of that happened. Bradley idly stroked his tongue over mine, caressed my arms up and down, like we had all the time in the world.

I bit his lip, and he smirked before pulling back. "You sure you want to do this with me, Mo?"

"Of course I do. We've done it a million times before." I hopped up on the desk and pulled him between my legs. "We can have some fun on this old guy's desk and then leave this terrible party."

"It's been fun enough." He lowered his mouth, kissed me again, and I ground my hips into him and moaned.

Bradley tried. He really did.

We made out a little longer, but when I unbuttoned his pants, he stopped me.

"You don't want this type of revenge, Mo. I can tell. You're stiff as my surfboard. I'd take the revenge fuck, but I don't think you'd enjoy it half as much as I would."

I slumped on the desk and shut my eyes. "Bradley, I wish you were more of a jerk."

He chuckled and pushed some of my curled hair back from my face. "I'm gonna catch a ride back to the tiki bar soon. Take a minute, then you go find that suit and tell him to stop fucking around, okay? I'll see you out on the waves another day."

I bit my lip and nodded as I stared down at the silk of my dress.

I pounded a fist on the desk, my frustration bursting. This was the point of tonight, to release the tension between us with someone else.

I wasn't supposed to want Bastian. I needed to want anyone.

The problem was I still felt his hands on me, still craved the sting of his palm coming down on my ass, and still remembered exactly how he gripped my thigh and squeezed it the morning after I'd got off in front of him. Bastian owned my sex drive, and I wanted to take it back.

Glancing at the large door, I noticed that Bradley had pulled it mostly closed.

My fingertips grazed the silk of the expensive dress I'd bought. So sleek and soft, it slid like caramel over my thighs. Just the way Bastian's caramel eyes would look at me, would caress me with a stare.

I made another quick decision. I wanted my own release, and I was going to take it. I moved fast, slipping a hand into the slit of my dress and under my panties.

It only took a minute of imagining Bastian's lips on mine, his rough hands running over my skin, and his grip in my hair when I hit a high.

Eyes closed, I moaned out his name, seeing the stars I reached for.

I could do this for a couple more months. I could get off and be done with all of this sooner rather than later.

"You enjoy yourself?"

I jumped off the desk and stumbled on my heels right into Bastian. "What the hell are you doing in here?"

"You wanted to have an evening with other people and we did. Did you enjoy him?" Bastian's question came out callous, his tone harsh.

"How long have you been in here?" I hissed, ready to meet his meanness with fury.

"Long enough to know you didn't like him enough, *ragazza*." His nickname for me sliced through the air.

"Did you watch?" My eyes bulged. Had he seen me get myself off? I hadn't even considered it. "Where's your date? You have fun with her?"

I tried to smooth a wrinkle in the silk dress as I waited for his answer.

"Of course I did. She's good at what she does, unlike yours."

Something pierced my heart, it cut through so quickly I almost didn't feel it, but the bleed out was painful.

"Great," I whispered and it came out like a deflated balloon. I wasn't going to stay here and let him gloat. I wanted to get home, and I wanted to wash the night off me. He could have all the women he wanted.

I wasn't doing this marriage for him anyway. I had to remember that.

"I'm going to grab my jacket." I tried to rush past, but he caught my arm.

"You always gasp my name when you come, *ragazza*?" His words whispered over me and my whole body tightened for him.

"Excuse me?"

"You heard me."

"You heard wrong." I lifted my chin defiantly. Fuck him and his ego. I'd never moan it again after this. "I don't moan for a daddy when any hot guy can get me off."

"Come on, Morina. Don't lie." He yanked me back and spun me so my front was pinned against the wood desk and my ass was against his cock. "Want me to show you how it's really done?"

"You've had your fun with someone else tonight." I gasped as his hand shoved my dress to the side.

His five-o'clock shadow rasped against the nape of my neck. "You wanted dates, not me. It was your idea for Elizabeth to be on my arm."

"You agreed," I panted out as his hand dragged up my side.

"I didn't have her, Morina. I wouldn't when all I wanted was you. Here. In this dress." He kneaded my thigh. "Instead, I had to watch you kiss another man. Don't you know I don't enjoy sharing?"

"Sharing what?" I whispered.

"Anything," he growled. Gone was the playfulness. His touch was possessive, and his gaze held menace as his thumb flicked fast over my panties, brushing my clit. My body was in overdrive, sensitive after my own orgasm but completely ready for him all the same.

"Bastian, this is an arrangement," I countered, like I suddenly had to defend myself. Something was different in his touch though. The man on the plane who'd smacked my ass and called me his was back. In this low-lit room, Sebastian Armanelli, the head of the mob, had come out to claim what was his.

We were in uncharted waters that I didn't know how to read. As he hummed against my neck and ran his hands over my body, I said, "You wanted it to remain professional. This is the best way. Both of us are getting a release somewhere else. I can find other men—"

"You won't find the right one, *ragazza*. You know it. So do I. You're wound tight and can't find a release with anyone because you've finally had me."

"Bastian, this wasn't the plan," I said over my shoulder.

His tongue slid across his teeth like he was shining them before taking a bite of my resolve. "Isn't it though?"

Then, his head descended onto my neck as he pushed my panties to the side. He bit at my sensitive skin as his finger entered me so fast, I had to catch myself on the desk, bending forward as I moaned, scared I would crumple to the floor.

I was falling, falling headfirst for a man who was perceived as an accommodating businessman, but here in this darkened room, he was a boss, claiming his property.

"Someone might come in, Bastian."

"That's the point, *piccola ragazza*. To make it known you're mine."

I couldn't decipher fact from fiction, pretend from reality. Was he doing this for publicity? My mind spun webs of tangled happily ever afters and temporary arranged marriages and got confused.

"I'll only be your wife for a couple months, Bastian," I choked out, riding his hands faster, almost there.

"Yes, but maybe I need to ruin you, like you're ruining me. I can't fuck a woman without seeing dark messy waves or sapphire eyes. I can't grab an ass unless it fits perfectly like this one in my palm." He squeezed one cheek hard before sliding his hand to the back of my head where he gripped my hair. "What type of fiancée will you be to me, huh? I want you and can't have you, but you'll spread your legs for another so fast, I'm not sure we can keep this little charade going."

Possessive and cruel.

"Sebastian Armanelli." I gasped his full name, and he laughed like a madman behind me.

"You say my name like you've just met me."

"Haven't I?" I whipped my hair over my shoulder and glared at him, rolling my hips into his dick. This was a different man from before. He and I both knew it. This was the man that I could have cowered from or faced head-on.

Quick decision again. I only wanted this one.

His eyes dark, furious, and full of something else, he responded with his voice low. "That's right. The leader of the Armanelli family. About to get you off and do you a favor so you won't have another man risking his life to do the same."

Another finger slid into me, so hard and long that I immediately rode his hand, barely listening. His rhythm was magic, his cock at my ass was foreplay, and his voice was vicious with compliments and then obscenities.

"I can do my own favors," I breathed out as I rocked against him. I couldn't stop if I tried. I wanted his favor much more than my own.

"No one can do it like me, baby." He took his hand from me right as I was about to scream out his name. "Remember that."

He undid his trousers as I watched and sheathed himself with a condom from his pocket. Before he entered me, he held up those fingers that had been in me moments before.

"Open, *ragazza*."

I was lost to him at that point, lost in my own fucked-up world where nothing mattered but him being in me even if he was commanding me. I opened like he belonged there, and when he placed his fingers on my tongue and leaned in, whispering, "Now suck," I did exactly as I was told.

I tasted myself mixed with him, a salty slickness that I knew he'd created within me.

"Good girl. You taste good, don't you? Sweet. Wet. And all mine. That's what I do to you."

I whimpered, and he took back his hand and slid it under the slit of my dress to grip my thigh and lift it before he plunged into me, thrusting hard.

He cursed and cursed as he fucked me, like he couldn't believe he was doing so.

I couldn't believe it either.

This wasn't the show we'd planned, and yet I fucked him back because I couldn't stop myself.

Sebastian Armanelli.

He was the one thing that could keep my attention.

And he had all of it.

CHAPTER 27: BASTIAN

Morina Bailey had pushed me over the edge in a matter of weeks. It'd taken this little free spirit only that amount of time to do what no one else had ever done. I wanted to punish her and fuck her all at the same time.

Her MO was to go where her gut pushed her, and she'd decided that meant following her anger down the path of attending the gala with other people.

When I'd suggested we go separately, I was only trying to create a professional distance, one where we were still friendly with one another.

She'd thrown that in my face and suggested another man like she could insert anyone between her legs and be fine.

She probably would've been because I wasn't about to hurt her. But I'd kill the man. I wanted.to put a hit out on Bradley for that very reason.

I'd seen red when she'd left the ballroom with him.

Maybe it was a pride thing. I had to tell myself it was. Mixing business with pleasure and staking the family's legacy on something as frivolous as my feelings for her was unacceptable.

Bradley had shaken my hand tonight and smiled while on the arm of the woman he'd heard me call my fiancée a week before.

I didn't care what she'd told him. In another life, I would have shot him just for that. Had I been like my father or anyone else in the mob, he would've been dead already.

I still wanted him dead even after I'd had her.

His lips had been on hers, and he'd dragged his hands across her hips.

It didn't matter that he'd stopped. It didn't matter that she'd called my name out while getting herself off.

Lost in something that wasn't even jealousy at this point, I took her pleasure the way I wanted it.

Reason wasn't present in that room with her. She'd called me by my full name. Sebastian Armanelli, head of the mob. The last name that signified violence and danger. In that moment, the name fit me perfectly.

Fuck.

She shoved me away once we'd finished. I let her go. I couldn't be held accountable for anything I did at this point in the night.

She breezed by me, her blue dress flapping with how fast she left the room.

I pounded the wall with a fist.

"What are you doing?" I whispered and then spun around, pacing back and forth.

We weren't even a month into this arrangement.

I needed to marry her. Lock it down. Get this shit straight and stop indulging. She trusted me enough already to sell those shares, and she'd be an Untouchable. It would be complicated, but if we kept ourselves in line, it could be clean. This company didn't need feelings involved. She needed to trust me without my cock in her.

I called my brother. "I'm marrying her tomorrow. If the papers aren't ready, prepare them."

"Tomorrow? I thought we had another—"

I hung up on him, then called my lawyer and told him to get the courthouse ready tomorrow too.

I was done tiptoeing.

I stalked back into the ballroom. She stood at a small table on her own that looked over the dance floor.

A man approached her and my temper flared again when she smiled.

Morina didn't seem to understand that we were bound now in a way she would never be able to shake for as long as she lived.

My Untouchable.

Her sapphire eyes locked onto mine as I stalked closer. I didn't wait for an introduction. Instead, I took her fingers in mine and ran my hand over the box in my pocket.

Leaning down to her ear, I saw the bite mark I'd left. My cock stirred. I whispered in her ear, "Smile, *ragazza*."

Then I got down on one knee.

I spoke in Italian to her. I told her she was as beautiful as the sea, that I would never really be able to have her like I wanted because who could bottle the beauty of the ocean.

She wouldn't understand, nor would anyone else.

I opened the box and dark velvet swaddled her ring. At the center sat a princess cut diamond, but the surrounding stones were crystals. "Rose quartz, howlite, and some other stuff I'm not sure of at this point, *ragazza*. Same as your crystals and beads."

I told myself I went through the trouble so she'd be comfortable wearing it for the remaining months.

The smile she'd pasted on her face dropped away. "My bracelets, Bastian?" she whispered. Then a lone tear fell from her eye. Then the real smile, the one I really wanted, shone across her face.

That was the real reason for those crystals in that ring, you dumbass.

I took the jewelry and slid it on her left ring finger.

The crowd clapped. The cameras went off. The news was made.

Our arrangement had officially begun.

She gripped my hand, hers so small in mine as I thanked everyone who congratulated us and steered us toward where our coats were checked.

"Your date gone for the night?" I asked her, knowing I'd sent Elizabeth home.

She nodded, apparently not willing to engage in any sort of conversation with me. She was probably shocked with the night's events. Or embarrassed.

And I knew that was on me. I should have been embarrassed too for fucking her in the library of someone else's home. Yet, I couldn't bring myself to find much remorse in it.

We drove home, silent for the first half of the ride. She turned that engagement ring on her finger over and over again.

"Thank you for the crystals," she murmured finally.

I nodded. "I figured you'd need them in times like these when you decide not to wear your bracelets."

Her hands folded into her lap. "I'll get you a ring too."

"Not necessary." I tapped my gold ring on the window, the one that held such weight and responsibility. "I have this one. It's fine."

"That's not a wedding ring."

"It's for my family. It's what I'm truly dedicated to."

"Well, you're dedicated to seeing this marriage through for a few more months to get the shares, aren't you? It means you can wear a wedding band from me."

She wanted to give me back something that I didn't need. I didn't even want it. "I don't need a reminder, Morina."

"A wedding band isn't a reminder. It's a symbol of trust or something. We need that. We need something after what happened tonight."

"And what happened?" I eyed her in the dark of our SUV.

Goose bumps popped up on her arms. "You fucked me in public like you owned me, Bastian! The night was a shit show. You don't even want to fuck me. You were the one that put the brakes on it in the first place."

I humphed and kept tapping on the window. "Your friend knew we were involved."

"So what?"

"So he shouldn't have kissed you."

"The whole point of going with other people was for us to screw them discreetly and release our sexual tension before we were engaged." She slapped the leather of her seat.

"I don't think that's an option for me when I see you with other men who know you belong to me."

She screamed in frustration, balling up her fists. "You wouldn't even kiss me a few days ago!"

I nodded, knowing I sounded insane. "I still don't think we should. It's fucked-up that you're in my head this much, that I'm around you and can't feel, smell, imagine anyone else, Morina. Do you know I considered checking my horoscope today?"

"You're insane," she grumbled. "I can't talk to you right now. You're so fucking insane. I just want to go to sleep."

"Great."

I did too. I wanted to wake up tomorrow and screw my head on straight because tonight I was losing my mind.

CHAPTER 28: MORINA

"We get married tomorrow." He threw his suit jacket on a hook and loosened his tie as we walked into the penthouse. His voice made me jump, we'd been silent for so long.

He moved quickly, slipping his shoes off and not making eye contact with me at all.

"Bastian?" When he didn't look my way and started down the hall to his room, I yelled, "Bastian, what the hell?"

"'What the hell?'" He whirled around, molten rage brewing in his gaze, singeing me as he approached. He got right in my face and grabbed my hair at the nape of my neck. "I said, we get married tomorrow. You and me. My fiancée. Tomorrow, you'll be my wife. Do you understand?"

I searched his eyes. "You have the audacity to be like this? Mad and all pissy?" His jaw ticked. "You have the audacity when you had that woman on your arm, whispering things to you all night. You laughed at her jokes. You nestled into her neck. I saw you. And you even said she knew what she was doing before you fucked me." I poked his shoulder as the grip in my hair got tighter and tighter.

"None of that matters, *ragazza*. We marry tomorrow, and that means you're not spreading your legs for anyone after that."

We both stood there, breathing fast, stewing, our furious gazes locked on one another. If I'd lit a candle, it would have been blown out by the anger and jealousy flying through the room.

"All about what you own, huh? Am I your property now?" I

didn't give him time to answer. "Fuck you, Sebastian Armanelli."
With that, I smacked his hand away from my hair and stormed
past him into my bedroom. I slammed the door and screamed.

He didn't come after me like I thought he might. I heard
his door close not long after.

Good.

He could rot on his side of the penthouse for all I cared.

Except, all night, I felt like I was wasting away. My mind
ran through every scenario and then stumbled upon the most
pressing one.

I was getting married tomorrow to a man I didn't love,
without friends and family, a dress, or even shoes.

Quick decisions would have to be made.

"Right about that, Grandma."

I probably drifted to sleep trying to conjure up a way for
her to haunt me in my bedroom so I could throw something at
her, but none of it happened. She didn't even come to me in a
dream.

I woke and read my horoscope, the Sagittarius in me
ready to be stubborn and vengeful toward Bastian for dropping
our wedding date on me without even twenty-four hours of
planning. I knew we would be going to the courthouse, but I
pulled a white baggy T-shirt from a drawer and slipped it on
over a bikini. I looked like I was going to the beach, not going
to get married.

When I walked down the hallway, he had breakfast on the
island for me. Those stupidly good crepes sat there folded and
perfectly covered in a delicate sprinkling of powdered sugar.

He washed dishes, suit on, completely ready for the
madness we were about to go through with.

When he turned and scanned me, I was ready for the fight.
Sebastian Armanelli was going to come out of his shell and tell

me to go change.

I braced for it as I sat at the counter.

He grabbed a glass, filled it with water, and slowly poured it into my grandmother's plants, circling the stems to make sure it was distributed evenly.

The control he had in the daylight was out of this world.

At night, though, we both knew he had none.

"So, our appointment to sign papers is in two hours."

I rolled my eyes and took the fork he'd left me. Nourishment might help get me through the day.

As I took a bite, he reached above the refrigerator and grabbed the lighter. He lit a stick of my incense, then sat down next to me as if this was totally normal.

"So, I'm sorry about last night," he breathed out.

My fork clattered onto the plate. "What?"

"I'm sending mixed signals." His eyes were milk chocolate and molasses now. Sweet and accommodating Bastian was back.

"You're telling me!"

He cleared his throat. "I should have given you more warning about the marriage ceremony today, also."

"If we're going to the courthouse, it'll be fine," I grumbled, not quite sure how to react to the change in him.

"I can take you to the terminals today. I'll show you my plans."

I narrowed my eyes at him. "You fucked me last night, Bastian."

He nodded. "I'm aware, Morina. It shouldn't have happened. You need a clear head when you make decisions about these shares, and I'm not giving that to you."

"Oh, God." I rolled my eyes. So, we were back to business transactions and professional relations. "Sex isn't going to muddle my brain all up, you idiot. I can fuck you and keep our business separate."

He stared at me, then swore when his phone lit up.

"Is someone calling you right now? Do you have it on silent?"

He slid it back in his pocket. "Yeah, sorry."

"You can answer your calls. I don't care." I shrugged. He was ever so present when he was with me, and for what? We were simply business associates.

"I do," he countered. "You deserve my full attention when I'm here. And I'm serious about this conversation. We should right the ship and try to be friends through this transaction."

"Okay." I nodded. All of that made sense except, somehow, my brain couldn't get past him putting his businesses on hold for me by silencing his phone. Something didn't quite compute, and yet, I couldn't figure out what.

But Bastian sat before me, alert and on point this morning, making complete sense, while I was a jumbled mess. Someone had really slept much better than I had. He looked refreshed, cleaned up, and completely dedicated to what he was saying.

"I'll go change after I eat this." I dug into the crepes, not wanting to show that I was such a mess. I focused on the way the sugar melted in my mouth, the fluff of the thin pancake, and how its taste blended perfectly with the strawberry jelly he'd folded in.

"Morina."

I glanced his way when he sighed my name. His hand was fisted; his jaw flexed.

"Yes?" I stared at his dark eyes boring into mine. Our chemistry clashed around the room. Did he feel the pull and the need like I did? Or was it a one-way street?

I shot up with the half-eaten food still on my plate and

went to the sink. He didn't answer after saying my name, so I changed the subject. "I'm guessing someone will be outside those courtroom doors to take our picture today, correct?"

He stared at my plate. "You didn't eat all your crepes."

"Yes." I dragged out the word. "I'm full."

His brow furrowed. "You moaned like you loved it a second ago. Was something wrong with it?"

My cheeks heated. Sometimes the fact that I loved his cooking so much I got lost in the taste of it was straight up embarrassing. "It was fine."

"Bring it here then and let me try it."

"What?" I glanced at the food in my hand. Then set it on the counter. "No. That's not ... I'm not eating it because I'm trying to not appear bloated for cameras today."

"You what?" He stood, his chair screeching behind him before he rounded the counter.

"They'll put our picture in the tabloids, and I don't want to look like I ate—"

He picked up the fork and stabbed the rest of the crepe onto it while a string of Italian flew from his mouth. His other hand went to the nape of my neck. "Open, *ragazza*."

"Bast—"

He pushed past his name with the fork, and the food was in my mouth before I could protest. I didn't. The taste was absolutely delightful as always. I grabbed his wrist and pushed it back to remove the fork though and shook my head at him as I chewed.

He watched my mouth the whole time, then pulled me close, his hand combing down my locks. "I want you this way. Full. Bright eyed and free. Don't change anything. Not your clothes. Not your hair. Nothing. We go in twenty, huh?"

With that, he released me and disappeared to his room.

He left me speechless, my heart pitter-pattering over and over again, loud enough to drown out all my reservations about the day.

I flew back into my room and cut the thread of a bracelet of flattened stones. I pulled most off the string and then retied it just big enough to fit a man's finger.

Sebastian Armanelli would wear my ring too. He might belong to his family as Bastian, the man who accommodated most, but Sebastian, with his commands and his possessiveness, was pulling me to him. Like Grandma had advised in her letter, I was making a quick decision to figure out where he'd take me.

* * *

The ceremony was fast, most likely because we both stood there with our hands folded in front of the judge, not willing to recite vows. None of those things mattered. We were dotting the i's and crossing the t's to ensure I'd get the shares so I could sell to him.

As we walked out of the courthouse, flashing lights bombarded us. Questions flew from every direction as a hoard of paparazzi descended upon us. Even if Bastian hadn't cared, I was happy I'd changed into a flowy white beach dress.

Someone had tipped them off. Bastian pulled me close and pushed through the crowd. Suddenly, suits surrounded us, escorting us to the Rolls-Royce. Bastian's hand was on my back as he made sure I got in the car safely. Then he turned and actually smiled at the men and women photographing us.

"Morina Armanelli is beautiful, isn't she?" He waited as they threw out more questions. His voice carried through the crowd. "She's beautiful, and she's mine. Now and forever. Make sure you write the last part everywhere." Then, he folded into the seat beside me.

The security got into another SUV, and as our driver maneuvered the car away from the crowd, I breathed out.

"Jesus. That was all a bit over-the-top." I turned to Bastian. "Especially you."

Bastian didn't respond. Instead, he told the driver to go to Tropical Oil.

"Guess we're right on schedule." I turned the ring I'd made on my thumb over and over again. I hadn't given it to him in the courthouse since I wasn't sure what to say in front of a judge who pretty much knew this was a marriage of convenience.

"It's the perfect way to get the word out, Morina. You're an Untouchable now. The media will tell the syndicates and families."

"Right." I shoved my hand into the pocket of my dress, not sure I wanted to give him the ring on my thumb at all anymore.

"It was an honorary title for a very long time. In my world, it still is."

"Did your parents marry?" I asked, not really sure I wanted to know, but he talked about his world like I might have something to learn about.

"My mother ..." He sighed. "Yes. My mother loved my father and agreed to marry him after only a few months. He wasn't a good husband, but she was a good wife. She even called my father *amore mio* on her last day alive."

"So, they loved each other?"

"Yes. And that's probably what killed her." Pain laced his words, like maybe a part of him had died with her too.

People left, and we left them in death. It wasn't always a choice. I reminded myself of that every day.

"She loved you, too, though. I can tell."

"She should have loved herself enough to leave. And she

should have taken us with her," he ground out. "Sometimes, it pays to be bold and go against the people you love most."

Did he truly believe that? "Have you ever done that? It seems you do all you can for the people you love, including running the family business."

"I killed my father, Morina." He dropped each word as he stared at me, the darkness growing in his eyes. "I took his life to bleed out the filth in my family."

My mouth opened, but I didn't respond. I tried to.

No words came.

Sitting across from a man who killed his father robs you of your voice as fear snakes through you. Sitting across from a murderer who you think you understand and most likely care about morphs your soul into something you're not ready to face.

I changed as I sat in that car on the way to see oil terminals and farms. My body vibrated with fear but also arousal, adrenaline, and a need to comfort him even if I feared him.

This man had just married me and confessed one of his darkest sins without hesitation. Now he searched my face, looking for my reaction.

He shook his head at my silence. "You're stunned. You should be. You like to play, *ragazza*. You think sex with me and marriage to me isn't dangerous or serious."

I bit the inside of my cheek to keep from arguing with him.

"You shouldn't goad a man like me. I say that only to you because you seem to know exactly what match to light to set me on fire. I don't want to kill again for the good of my family."

"Are you threatening my life, Sebastian?" The words came out so quietly, I wasn't sure he heard.

His body instantly recoiled at my question. "*Piccola ragazza*, you think so little of me that it actually pains me. I'm never going to hurt you. I'd kill for you. You're my family now.

Your life is precious, love. It's safe with me. But the men around you? I'd put a bullet through their skulls faster than you could murmur *daddy*."

"That's over the top, Bastian." I couldn't stop myself from saying it.

"It's the bottom line. We're married now."

"Speaking of ..." I turned the ring on my thumb again before sliding it off and holding it out to him. "It's just one of my bracelets. I made it smaller but it stretches and the beads are made of black tourmaline. It's supposed to block bad energy and protect. It also gives you strength."

He stared at it in my hand, his face contorted, like he was confused and disgusted.

I pulled it back and fisted my hand around it. "I didn't have anything else. It was a quick thought—"

His hand snapped out like a viper and snatched my fist back toward him. He tapped my knuckle. "Open."

God, when he said that word my body reacted in a way it shouldn't. I lifted my fingertips, and he took the ring.

He turned it over, removed the gold ring from his left ring finger and replaced it on the right, then rolled my flattened beads down his finger until they sat snuggly where they should, showing he was a married man.

We both stared at that marker, that symbol, and then he murmured, "My mother would have done anything for my father. I didn't understand because he never would have returned the favor. She used to say if you care for somebody, you do it even if they don't care for you. I think I'm starting to understand."

My heart hurt for the boy who'd tried to understand and for the man who now lived with the boy's pain. "To love and to be loved utterly the same is a hard thing to find."

"Yes, *ragazza*." He took a deep breath and gulped. "You know, my father gave her an ultimatum, and she beat him at his own game. He said, 'You leave me, you die.' She did exactly that but didn't give him the glory of doing it himself. It was for the best though. Marriage to him was a death sentence in it and of itself."

I took his hand and tapped the ring on it. "Marriage to you won't be the same. I know that."

He squeezed my hand. "No. It will be protection, Morina. Protection."

I took a deep breath and went with what I was thinking. "I'm sorry she was never really given a choice to leave him. As a boy, that must have been painful for you."

Bastian took to turning the new ring on his finger. I hoped it would give him strength.

We pulled up to the oil terminals. The metal beams and massive storage crates and tanks along the coastline were a good reminder of why we'd come here.

We showed our IDs, then walked the property. Bastian pointed out where they'd expand if I didn't sell him the shares. "If you decide to sell to Ronald or keep them for yourself, know that they will be pushing government funding here. They want to expand into the city. It would be a great thing for the community in the short term. More jobs, more money, the potential of a few grants here and there. You'd solidify partnerships with oil refineries too."

He began with what I could gain, considerate as always. He wanted to give me a fair choice.

I was starting to see why this man accommodated everyone but himself first.

"Great. And why don't we want to do this?" I prompted.

"Like the UK, we could morph all these terminals into

clean energy. We could repurpose the farms, and the whole plant could be lucrative without expanding into the coastline. This would require more workers, but it would create more energy and an increase in profit after the first nine months."

"You go over this some in the file." I nodded.

"Yes. It's easier to see, isn't it?" He smirked at me like he knew my attention span and that file didn't get along.

"You're right." I smiled as a man passed us.

He eyed us, then changed course, coming over. "You're Bastian Armanelli, right?"

Bastian didn't answer but his stance changed. He moved a little in front of me and looked the man up and down. "Eyes everywhere. Two guns trained on you now. Don't try anything you shouldn't."

The man sucked on his teeth. "Seems you know when you see a family man, huh? My Irish blood isn't here to bleed out. I'm here to tell you some of us want what you want. My family loves this city, and we'll back you if the partnership comes along."

With that, he backed away, keeping his face to us until he went out of sight behind a tank.

"What the hell?" I whipped toward Bastian. "Two guns? What are you talking about?"

"It's security, *ragazza*."

"Do I have two guns on me?" I screeched, my heart beating louder than drums in a marching band.

"You will always have a sniper watching out for you if that's what you're asking. I won't risk your safety again."

"You're being overprotective. Actually, you're insane. The food truck was one time."

He turned to the car. "One time was enough."

I hurried after him in my combat boots and white summer

dress. The match we made would have been an iconic picture. I could picture the tabloids now: "The Suit and His Hippie Wife Arguing." They'd come up with something catchier, of course, but the point remained. We looked out of place together.

I didn't even argue with him on the way home. Instead, I asked, "So, when I start working at my food truck tomorrow—" He tried to cut me off but I held up my hand. "Tomorrow because you said I would be protected after we said I do. Will there be someone watching me then?"

"Yeah, the fucking paparazzi and everyone else. You can't work the food truck right now."

"I want to go back to work."

"No."

"Are you joking right now? Don't you have to work?"

"Yes, and you can stay at the penthouse while I do it."

I crossed my arms. "I'm so happy this isn't 'until death do us part.'"

"Are you so sure?" he threw back. "Maybe I won't divorce your smart ass and you can deal with me for all of time."

"What wonderful vows. I'm so proud to be your wife. I should recite every vow possible just so we're clear." I stomped my big boot on the car's floor. "I vow to stand beside you for the remaining months. I vow to have only myself to hold during that time and never you."

"Don't forget sickness and health."

A giggle burst out of me. The vows were always a ridiculous aspect of marriage in my opinion, but ours could be so twisted.

"In sickness, I vow to lock you out of my room so I don't catch it too. For richer or poorer, well, we know you're rich and I'm poor until the end of this, so do with that what you will."

Bastian's face finally cracked into a smile, then broke into a laugh.

"I vow to make you as rich as you need to be, *ragazza*." He chuckled. "You can have and hold me any time you like too."

We both laughed at that, knowing we had a twisted sexual relationship.

My head fell to his shoulder as our laughter sobered. "I really do want to vow one thing though." He nodded and smoothed my hair, something he was starting to do a lot more. I cleared my throat. "I really do vow to trust you, because I believe in what you're doing. I hope you know that."

He turned and kissed the top of my head. It was platonic, soft, like a friend greeting another. Still, I wanted it to be more, and I probably imagined it was more. "My vow is to protect you, *ragazza*. Even if it's from myself."

CHAPTER 29: BASTIAN

Weeks later, Morina *Armanelli* fluttered around our penthouse like a new person. We'd found a weird sort of harmony, one built on odd partnerships and a marriage that didn't quite look like any other, but it was working.

She buzzed into the kitchen that morning like the weight of the world had been lifted from her or she'd had some come-to-Jesus moment.

She thanked me for turning on her salt lamp and making breakfast, something I'd started doing every morning. The lamp provided light, nothing more, but it had a weird, nice glow to it, and I found it meshed well with the sunlight in the morning.

I read the newspaper that was delivered every morning and made small talk with her as she lit some incense and fiddled with a diffuser thing she had ordered online.

"So." She said the word with caution before she continued, "I'll go clean up my food truck today and buy some ingredients to start blending again, I think. It's been almost two months, and I need to get back to work. I'll be out of your hair in about an hour."

"Out of my—? I'm working from home for you." Two months? It meant we'd been married and worming around each other for three weeks without a fight.

We had a routine. I woke up, made meals, and worked. She put together bracelets and mixed oils and studied the file. She'd pop her head up every now and then with a question, but other than that, we lived together like it was completely normal.

I didn't mind working from home. She was good company most of the time. Quiet, lost in her own world, then sometimes she'd meander over and tell me to smell something because I was stressed. Her read of my emotions was eerily on point most of the time.

At night, she'd tell me about some horoscope she'd read and go on and on about it.

The woman had the amazing ability to get lost in a hobby or thought and be completely engrossed for about twenty minutes. Then, she moved on to something else.

"Morina, you said you felt alone here about a month ago. So, I rearranged a ton of things to be working remotely."

"Right, but now, we're married. And things have died down. So, I should get back to work."

"Why?" I studied her as she turned the bracelets on her wrist.

"I think we've been getting along so well and ..." She took a deep breath. "I'm pretty sure I'm done with the file and understand it now. I've read it all, and I got the research in. I get all the points. I didn't want to do anything else until I knew I understood it. Now that I do, I have nothing else to do here all day, Bastian."

"You finished it?" I smiled at her. How could I not? "Morina Armanelli, you told me your attention span wouldn't let you finish something you didn't want to."

A blush crept across her cheeks. "Don't make it a big deal."

I stood from the table and folded my newspaper. When I approached, her blue eyes sparkled and her chest rose and fell like she was excited. Stopping right in front of her, I touched her hair the way I'd been wanting to for weeks. "You did it, *piccola ragazza*. And it *was* offensively boring."

"So offensively boring," she whispered.

I stared at her lips. Fuck, this woman was something I wasn't sure I could keep avoiding. "I'm proud of you."

She nodded and took a step back. I let my hand fall, knowing I needed to take caution with our interactions. We were in too good a place not to.

I returned to the table and opened up my newspaper. "So, you need to clean up your food truck?"

She didn't. I'd had people do it for her. I just hadn't told her that.

"Well, I need to get back to work, and now that we're married and I'm done with the file, I'll be ready for the board meeting in a month. So ..." She shrugged her shoulders in her baggy, worn shirt. It was way too big for her, fit her like a dress, and had Jimi Hendrix on the front.

Probably an old boyfriend's shirt. Instantly, I wanted to tell her to take it off.

After the good weeks we'd had, I knew I couldn't.

"I don't think the food truck is a good idea." This was going to be enough to push our day into negative territory anyway.

Immediately, the energy shifted in the room and on her face.

The fact that I was even thinking about energies was a problem.

"I have to work, Bastian."

I straightened my newspaper and turned the page. "You really don't. You're about to be a multimillionaire based on those shares alone. You could also sell your grandmother's house."

Considering she hadn't moved on it yet.

"Oh, that's smart." Her tone was sarcastic. "Where will I live after all this ends then?"

"Here, of course." Was she dense? I wasn't going to be living here.

"This is your place. I wouldn't continue to stay here."

"This is our place, *ragazza*."

"For now." She plugged in a little ball that spurted her essential oils into the air or something. When the mist puffed from it, she squealed. "Perfect. It smells like lavender. We're going to be so relaxed."

I took a deep breath, hoping the air was wafting my way to calm me down right now. "If it's just mine, how do you expect me to get the scents out of here when you leave?"

"I don't know. You could sage the place or something. I didn't even do that when I moved in. I probably should have, considering you've probably slept with women and brought bad—"

"I didn't live here before." I slammed the paper down.

"What?" Her eyes bugged out and she froze by the island counter that she'd practically morphed into a wellness station.

I sighed at my omission. "I bought the place for us."

"No. I came here, and you walked me through it ..." She shook her head.

"I'd just purchased it. I figured it was close and that you'd like tiles that look like the ocean." I sounded idiotic, like I'd been pussy-whipped from the beginning.

"The bathroom tiles?" Her jaw dropped. "Bastian, I can't pay you back for that."

"I don't want you to." I rubbed my eyes. "It's just ... I'm saying it's here if you need it once we're divorced. That's all."

She walked over to me as I lifted the newspaper back up and put her hand on it so we could stare at one another. "I don't expect you to keep this place for me, but thank you for buying it in the first place."

Something was happening between us even if we were on good terms. I was falling down a damn slope into wanting Morina as more than my arranged marriage partner of six months. I didn't know how to stop the descent. I didn't know if I could.

She took a breath and clapped her hands, stepping away from me. "Anyway, I'll be back from the food truck this evening and—"

I guess there was no getting around her going back to work.

"My driver will take you to the food truck and back." I looked back down at my newspaper. "He can also be in the food truck with you for security purposes."

"You want someone in the food truck with me?" she asked like it was ridiculous. "No."

I stared at my hand holding the newspaper and the ring now on it. She'd listened to the story of my parents and hadn't shrank back in disgust when I'd told her I ordered my father to be killed. She'd accepted a part of me that sometimes even I couldn't accept.

For that alone, I'd protect her even if she didn't want it. "Yes, Morina. Don't argue with me for no good reason, please. What does it hurt you to have a person with you?"

"Well, for one, it's small quarters in the food truck, and also, is he going to help me make shakes?"

"If you want him to, I'm sure he will."

She threw up her hands, then went and placed them on the salt lamp. She closed her eyes and stood there for a few seconds before opening them and staring at me. Those midnight blues were soft and appeasing. "Only because I've started to like you will I agree to this."

I smiled, and she rolled her eyes and skipped down the

hall.

I watched her ass the whole way in hopes that T-shirt would ride up a little further. "Wear shorts to work, Morina." It was for my own sanity, but I also found another reason quickly. "There will probably be paparazzi."

When I looked up to see her flying out the door in a black bikini and board shorts a few minutes later, I was proud I didn't scream at her to go change.

I sat there a whole hour without calling her, and I even made myself coffee before I went and got my board shorts on.

The woman should have worn a shirt. She meant to drive me insane by not, and I didn't care what anyone else said.

I took the Rolls-Royce there faster than I should have, and when I walked up to the food truck, I had to actually wait in a damn line because her just being there with the sign down caused a stir.

Some of them were paps with cameras around their necks, but a lot of them were locals telling Morina they'd missed her.

She was a mercurial loner by nature. I didn't think I'd ever heard her on the phone with Linny, but they all seemed to accept that about her.

I let the crowd die down before I went up to the window. The smell that hit my nostrils was rich and aromatic. "Are you selling coffee today?"

"Yes." She narrowed her eyes at me like I shouldn't argue. Normally I wouldn't have. I was in the area to make alliances. It worked best. I'd done better than my father in that arena time and time again.

"What happened to the shakes?"

"Well, it's winter, so this is a good idea, but that's really not the point. The point is I'm making coffee because ..." She spun around and waved her arm behind her. "I have a whole coffee appliance area, Bastian!"

The smile across her face was as brilliant as the sun on the water, bright, bold, and blinding. I didn't see the roadblocks ahead of us or the obstacles when she looked at me like that. I only saw Morina Armanelli, free and beautiful and full of life.

She leaned out the window and grabbed my shirt and pulled me close. "You did this, and so I'm doing this now." She covered my lips with hers and kissed me without reservation. Nothing held her back as the salty breeze blew over us. She made out with me over a food truck window, and then she shoved me back and squealed.

"I'm fucking in love with it all, Bastian. There's a blender too! State of the art. And someone stocked essential oils up here with a freaking shelf. Did you tell them to do that?"

"I told them to make it functional, *bellissima*." I wasn't admitting to it. I watched as she showed me every single new thing she was excited about.

She shook her head like none of it mattered and her wavy locks flew back and forth. "It's more than functional. It's perfect! And now, I get to make you coffee. What would you like?"

I groaned, knowing I was never going to get a good cold smoothie now. "Can you make me a shake today?" Hopefully that would cool the fire starting inside me.

She sighed and combed her fingernails through her dark hair. "No. That's not what's for sale today. Check the board." She pointed with her brows lifted as if to say, Isn't it so new and shiny? It was. They'd installed a larger chalkboard for her to write menu items on. "We can brew coffee, tea, even make a mocha."

"We live in a warm climate, *ragazza*," I said softly, trying to break the news to her, but enjoying the fire growing in her eyes.

"Yeah, and you're on a beach with a girl who will only make you coffee." She crossed her arms. The black bikini she wore dipped low, showing off her generous cleavage. "You want it iced? I can do that."

"This isn't the way to run a business."

Someone came up behind me and peered around me, whooping when he saw Morina. "You're back, baby!"

"Marco! I am! Get up here."

The man didn't even glance my way. He just skipped me and pulled Morina in for a hug through the window. Jesus, she was selling something here and it wasn't only her fucking shakes. The men loved her, and it pissed me the hell off.

"I thought the life of a celebrity was going to take you away from us."

"Oh, shut up," she threw her head back and laughed.

"I saw your face on a magazine cover one day and thought to myself, *no shit*. Your face might belong there, but it belongs here first."

She rolled her eyes, and I wondered if he knew her husband stood right behind him.

"Anyway, Marco, I'm selling coffee today."

He groaned like he only wanted the same thing as me—a damn shake. "Can't I have a smoothie today?"

"Fuck off, Marco. Coffee or nothing."

He chuckled like this was completely acceptable. They were all waiting to talk to her. "Mo's in a mood today, huh?" he grumbled to me.

He didn't get out of line, just paid for the coffee he hadn't asked for.

He meandered away, telling her to come to the tiki bar soon.

Once he was gone, she placed her elbows on the window

frame, cupped her hands under her chin and stared down at me, her eyes bluer than ever and her lips the color of cherries.

I found myself leaning in to hear exactly what she was going to say.

"It's my business. I run it how I want to." She licked her plump lips.

"Give me a damn iced coffee then."

She bit that lower lip, dragged her teeth over it and looked me up and down. My dick jumped. How could it not when she'd been kissing me moments before? Then she spun and tinkered for a minute before returning with my coffee.

I moved to pay her but she rolled her eyes, glanced at the security guy by the door, and before I could stop her, she hoisted herself out the window.

"Jesus. There's a damn door." But my hands were at her waist immediately as I caught her and set her on the ground.

"What's a door good for when I got you to take care of me?" She winked and pointed to the security guy. "Plus, he goes out that way and makes a big scene about checking every angle. Now, we don't need to."

"Are you done for the day?"

"I'm taking you surfing again, Bastian, because it's the only way I know how to repay you for the food truck. That, or I'll fuck you right here in the sand, but someone might get that on camera, and we can't have them saying the hippie lost her mind, right?"

Her mind went ten different directions at all times, and I found myself chuckling as she fetched two boards off the truck.

The beads on her bracelet banged together, all different colors and materials around her arm. That along with her bikini was a bold sign, one that said she wanted the world to know that she was free to wear and do whatever she wanted.

It made me wonder if she would be that way in a few months, if I honestly wanted her to be.

"Hey?" I yelled to my guy behind her. "Close down and lock it up. We got other eyes. You can go."

We got to the water, and I grumbled about using Bradley's board again.

"If you want, buy yourself one, but you're not out here enough to spend that much." She shrugged, combing her hands through her hair and threading it into a loose braid.

She didn't realize coming out here once was enough for me to purchase a board. I wouldn't continue riding another man's things.

"He doesn't ever use this one anyway," she added.

That wasn't the point at all.

We entered the cool water, and she explained how I should snap up as the wave rushed toward us. I listened and tried again and again half-heartedly. I was more concerned that Morina was surfing with only a bikini like last time. This time, I wanted her wrapped up more.

Honestly, I didn't think it was possible to surf with a bikini on. Sure, they did it in movies and during competitions, but those people were the best in the world.

Morina wasn't the best in the world.

She was supposed to be an average girl on a board that had grown up around water.

How the fuck she even got on the board after I tried and failed so many times was baffling to me. How she did that and kept scraps of material covering her tits was a goddamn miracle.

Why the hell I was out here torturing myself in the first place was an even bigger mystery.

"Mo, I'm done." I bobbed up and down in the water next to my board after another failed attempt at standing up.

"What?" She jumped off her surfboard as she rode past. When she surfaced, she shook her head. "No! You're almost there."

Her smile was infectious. It stretched across her face in a way I'd never seen before. There weren't any frown lines when she looked at me, and the smile raised her cheeks even more than usual. The sun glowed on her smooth skin, and the water glistened on her nearly bare chest like a mesmerizing game of where not to look.

Fuck, she was pretty out here.

Now, more than ever, I wasn't immune to her. She radiated a light I wasn't used to. All my life, I'd been around darkness, business, pain.

My father bred me to take his place, and I was damn good at that.

How to handle a woman so genuinely naïve of that darkness was baffling, intoxicating.

She vibrated with energy as she swam to my board and wrapped an arm around it. "You almost got this. I'll give you anything to master it today."

"You'll what?" I cocked my head. "Today? You're kidding me. People don't get up on a board for weeks after they start trying." It pained me to admit I'd researched it after the first time.

"But you're so close, and I've never taught anyone to get on it and ride in less than a week of lessons. And I don't teach often, but come on! This could be epic for me."

"For you?" I pointed at her. "You realize this is supposed to be about me, the student."

"Okay. What does the student want from the teacher?" She squared her shoulders and had such a completely straight face that I couldn't help but give her hell.

"Teachers give gifts now, huh?" I chuckled and looked around. The blue water rocked us back and forth. The sun burned our skin, and the air smelled so damn fresh I almost forgot why I was irritated about being out here.

Then I looked at her and remembered people were eyeing up my wife.

"I'll give you one thing."

"You wear a one-piece next time you're out here."

She glanced down at her tits and back at me. Then, she burst out laughing. "Never happening, Bastian. My boobs, my display."

Fuck me.

"Fine. I'm done then." I pulled the board with me and made my way out of the water.

She chased me down. "Oh my God. Let's compromise! Jesus, you're such an old man sometimes. You realize people go topless here half the time? There's a topless beach right up the road. Want to go?"

"Don't fuck with me, Morina. You're my wife now."

She rolled her eyes. "I know. I know. Fine. I'll wear a sports bra next time. That's better, right?"

Compromises.

I made them with others.

With her, I was thinking I might cut up all her bikinis and throw them in the damn garbage.

Still, I stayed.

I got up on the board.

And she said if I'd asked, she would have gotten on her knees and praised me.

I almost let her. Her free spirit was rubbing off on me.

CHAPTER 30: MORINA

Another whole month together and Bastian was still home pretty much every night. He left sometimes for work, probably flew around the country in a day, but he came back.

I worked at the food truck.

I went to the humane society. Dr. Nathan told me Moonshine was growing and no one wanted her because they didn't love pit and rottweiler mixes. I petted my little girl more than I did the others.

Bastian and I lived in a weird harmony. My horoscope even said I should continue it.

I prepared myself and went to the board meeting alone, even though Bastian swore up and down he should come with. I hated the old ways, the world trying to make it so that women needed to rely on their husbands. I stood my ground, and his driver took me.

The meeting bored me to death while Ronald made small talk with the board members who were mostly my grandmother's age. Today they weren't voting on the government funding— whether it would be oil expansion or clean energy. Yet, Ronald rubbed the right elbows and even tried to rub mine.

He came over after the meeting, smiling with those fake white teeth. "You'll be at my next event, right, Morina? We're going over to Tybay Beach." The one and only topless beach in the area. The way the man glanced down at my tits gave me a perfect indication of the man he was.

"I'll think about it."

"Great. Great. I'd love to talk more about your shares. I know you and Bastian are married now, but they're still your call, right?"

Digging for information subtly wasn't his strong suit. I smiled and waved as a couple of the board members left. Bastian hadn't let me go alone. My security lingered in the corner, of course.

"It's a call I'll make with my husband." I turned on my heel and walked out. A quick decision, one my grandmother had known I'd make throughout my life, was to leave that man in the dust.

My shares were going to the right place. Bastian wasn't slime like Ronald. He'd felt the ocean. He knew my town's beach. He'd smiled in the sun and surfed a freaking wave.

I teased him that he deserved a reward other than me in a one-piece. God, I knew I was falling for him. The way he shone as a businessman who wanted to be everyone's friend in daylight, then I got Sebastian Armanelli when I pushed him over the edge on a rare night—the man behind the suit, tatted up, vicious, commanding, possessive.

He'd held back for awhile, and I had too. Held back against all the gut feelings I'd normally fly headfirst into. I'd only kissed him once on the beach, and I would have kissed literally anyone who suited up my food truck the way he had.

We'd been good.

He thought it was for the benefit of my sanity and his and the contract as well. He wanted a clean sign-over of my shares to him.

He'd get it either way.

I didn't know if my sanity would get out so clean though.

When I got home, I told Bastian how the board meeting went. I left out all of Ronald's sleaziness but told him the next event would be in a couple of weeks at the beach.

My husband searched my face like he wanted to dissect every word I said. Then, he grabbed a small spray bottle from the side of the plant that hadn't been there when I'd left.

"What is that?"

He went to the sink and tested the water before filling the spray bottle. "I bought it for the plants."

"You what?" I whispered, unsure I could handle what was about to happen.

The man shrugged in his collared shirt rolled to his elbows and stood there in complete bafflement at my shock as he held up a freaking spray bottle to water my grandma's plants.

"I got it for the orchids. We keep dumping water in and it's not evenly dispersed." He tsked and went to the island counter to mist the damn flowers.

I almost orgasmed right there.

The head of the freaking Mafia misted my grandma's flowers like it was the most normal thing in the world. He turned the leaves with such gentleness that I almost cried, holding back my orgasm.

Why was this man such a fucking god? A walking, talking, sex-on-a-stick, gentle-but-possessive-and-crazy god?

Placing one hand on my salt lamp, I took deep breaths and tried to absorb some negative ions or whatever would calm me the hell down.

"You still think that thing helps you?" Bastian motioned toward the lamp with his stupid spray bottle.

"It can release negative ions, Bastian. Those same ions are released near waterfalls and oceans. I figure the ocean soothes me, why can't this?"

"There's no scientific research to back that."

I narrowed my eyes on him. "So, you looked it up?"

He cleared his throat. "When's this beach event?"

"In a couple weeks. It's on the beach, so I don't think we need to really prepare."

"I need to fly out for a few days, but I'll be back by then."

I nodded and bit my lip. Bastian slept in the other room, but he still came home to eat. He silenced his phone. He talked with me.

We'd become married friends.

"Right. That's fine." I turned his ring on my finger, then shrugged. "I have to be at the humane society and man the food truck anyway."

"I'll have a guy go with you. Just call the number I text you."

I cleared my throat and looked down the hall. "Great. I'm going to rise with the sun, so I'm off to bed." I hurried down the hall, not sure what to do about the fact that my heart tightened at the thought of him not being here with me for a few days.

Even without sex, Bastian was muddling my feelings.

Quick decisions about the man with the spray bottle were most likely going to happen, and I was most likely going to regret them at a later date.

"Thanks a lot, Grandma. This is still all your fault," I grumbled and went to bed.

CHAPTER 31: MORINA

"It's a freaking topless beach, Bastian." I stomped my foot.

Bastian didn't even lift his head as he sprayed the fucking plants. "I really don't care, Morina. Wear a T-shirt or dress or one of those cut up tops you always wear. You're not going there in a bikini."

"Well, quite frankly, I think I should go topless."

That had him looking up, his chiseled jaw flexing up and down.

Good. He wanted to be a jerk this morning, I would too. We could both be pissy about this event.

It was the morning of Ronald's Winter Warm-Up event. Since the board meeting, it had been a week of him not here, then another week of him working a ton with his security following me around everywhere. I tried to go to the tiki bar one night, and they'd called Bastian, who'd told me to come home.

We'd been on such good terms that I conceded, but now I was irritated. What did he expect me to do once we divorced?

Never go out?

Was this the life I'd signed up for?

"I'm wearing the bikini." I stomped off to my room while he swore in Italian.

Too bad.

We drove in quiet anger to the event until I threw out the question that was bouncing around in my mind. "You can't leash me all the time. I'm going to do what I want. What do you expect after we're over?"

"You're an Untouchable forever, *ragazza*. You'll need to act like one."

"We'll be divorced." I punctuated the words. "I've been to topless beaches and tiki bars before. I'm going to go again."

"Well, use discretion in the future." He shrugged and then had the audacity to pull out his phone.

It was a direct slight. He never looked at it and always kept it on silent when we were around each other. I did the same.

"In the future, I'm going to go wherever I please, do whatever I please, and see whoever I please—because that's what divorce means."

He slid his phone back in his pocket, and his gaze jumped up to mine.

Fury glinted there now. Dominance.

I'd lured Sebastian out of hiding.

"I guess the honeymoon's over, *ragazza*. Couple months into this marriage and you're discussing what you'll do after our divorce."

"The honeymoon never even got started," I grumbled. Not only was I pissed, I was sexually frustrated near him *all the time.*

He hummed and his eyes tracked over my body, staying on my tits for far too long. My nipples tightened, and his jaw worked overtime, no doubt seeing how thin the fabric of my top was.

"I have half a mind to turn this car around."

"But you won't. You'll go and put on a good show for all your business associates. And I'll smile like all is right in the world. Or maybe I'll start our descent into divorce. Give the media something to talk about."

He narrowed his eyes. "Interesting play, *ragazza*." Then he sat back and combed his hand through his thick dark hair.

"Maybe you have the right idea."

He didn't say another word to me through the car ride, and I stared out at the coast, stewing.

When we arrived, I got out of the door he opened for me but didn't thank him. I straightened my sheer black skirt as it wafted in the wind and waltzed away from him.

My black bikini top was much less revealing than what half the women at the party wore. Ronald had decked out the beach with umbrellas and gold tables. Completely nude women covered in gold paint stood on platforms around us, shimmering in the sunlight.

I immediately grabbed a drink from a gold serving tray and downed it as an older woman from the board came over.

"I knew your Grandma Maribel," she croaked. She wore a skirt that only came half down her thigh. That was it. She'd embraced the topless theme like half the crowd. I wanted to hug her for it because she pulled it off better than most, even in her sixties. "And she hated these parties."

I watched everyone schmoozing on the beach, not one of them taking in the beauty of the ocean just feet away. "I can see why."

The woman with dyed blonde hair patted my arm and smiled. "I used to hate them too until I decided to hell with it. I'm going to do whatever I want. Now, I love them."

I nodded, not sure what to say. I wouldn't be coming to these events much longer.

She pointed to a man who couldn't have been more than a few years my senior. "See that guy over there? Last time, I slept with him in Ronald's spare bedroom."

My eyes went wide at her.

"What have I got to lose?" She shrugged. "I'm not married and I don't have kids. I'm doing what I want."

"That's great." I took a gulp of my drink. What was she getting at?

"You should too. That's what Maribel would want. She had you marry that man so you could do exactly that. She said you were a girl who stayed in this city and didn't commit to anything because your parents messed your mind up."

"Um ..." She had way too much information. I glanced around, hoping no one was listening.

"Oh, don't worry. No one's paying attention to me. I'm the crazy old bat. But Maribel wasn't. She thought you loved your parents too much, and then when they left over and over, it ruined you for commitment."

I tried to cut her off but she held up her hand.

"I know she forced you into this arrangement. Perfect plan, in my opinion. Now, follow through and make sure you kick Ronald right in the balls by handing that stock over to Bastian. Don't let us down."

My eyes bulged at her confession. They'd all told Ronald his idea was great, and I thought Bastian would be going against everyone. Turns out he was still winning the board members over one by one himself.

I turned to find Bastian as I patted the woman's shoulder and thanked her. I needed to tell him that we were doing it, that this was all going to work in the end, that my city and his legacy would all be fine.

Then, I saw him.

And Elizabeth. In pink bikini bottoms with no top.

She turned and brushed her chest against him as she said something.

He didn't back away, instead his hand was on her back as he led her over to another couple to speak to.

Maybe the pain was in their perfection. They looked like a

painting with the ocean as their backdrop.

My ocean.

My beach.

They tainted it standing there.

Then he looked over his shoulder, and we made eye contact. He didn't back away from her. He stayed right where he was.

She shouldn't have been on his arm. He knew it and so did I.

I was his wife. Maybe my free spirit had deceived him. I might've been younger, dumber, and not as good looking, I could admit that. Yet, Bastian was still my husband.

My heart shifted like the earth under the ocean, and a tsunami surged. Underwater earthquakes, hidden beneath the sea, were the ones that caused the pain, the suffering, the suffocating power of those huge waves.

When I was young, I dreamed of riding one. I wanted to ride in on the power and see the world below.

I would do that with my own world. Bastian must have made the decision to move forward with our public display of starting a separation.

So I would too.

I wouldn't care that he stood next to another woman. No, instead, I wanted to rock his world. I wanted to drown him in jealousy and make him feel what raged inside me.

He wanted me to blend in and not draw attention to myself as his Untouchable. I never blended in. I flowed through the town and breathed life where I went. I may not have ever committed to anything, but I was committed to being me.

Free. I sank my feet into the sand and breathed in the salty air. The waves washed to shore again and again. They were slow and tranquil, unlike the one building deep in my heart. The tsunami was about to crash, and it would feel like hell. Riding a wave like that would be dangerous. Falling in love with Bastian was the same.

A surfer always wiped out, and I knew this would be the biggest wipeout of my life.

Still, I was ready to hit every high point before then.

I glanced at a man who had been at the board meeting. "Quinton." I smiled at him and pulled the black string at my neck. "Can you help me?"

I turned slowly, and he didn't hesitate. He untangled that knot like a man on a mission to defuse a bomb.

The thin triangles over my breasts fell. Instantly the sun warmed my skin and my nipples puckered.

He didn't even look down at them because he was smiling so wide as I faced him again. "You're going to cause havoc with Bastian today, aren't you?"

Quinton had introduced himself to me at the gala not too long ago, and it seemed he knew exactly what we were getting ourselves into. From his smile, I knew he'd play along. I swung a leg over the lounge chair and sat down. I took my time unfolding onto it, closed my eyes, and waited.

Let the chaos happen around me. I was on top of my wave. I was above them all now.

If Bastian found his way here, fine. If not, I had others who would talk to me.

Most importantly, I was back to myself. This was me and would always be me. I wouldn't be an Untouchable forever, not in the way Bastian thought.

The sun reminded me who I was. The ocean spoke to me, the seagulls cawed at me, and the sand between my toes grounded me.

"You're really pretty like this, Morina." Quinton's voice sounded from above me. I cracked an eye to stare at him.

His eyes were a deep blue, almost like the midnight sky, and his hair was that dark blond I imagined a Ken doll would have in real life. "I'm not sure what you mean, Quinton."

He tsked. "Your husband is watching. His mouth slammed shut, and his hands fisted the moment he figured out what you were doing."

I didn't show any emotion, but my stomach knotted up and my heart pounded. I closed my eyes again so as not to give anything away.

My husband was obviously flirting with the woman on his arm and had probably already been with her. I'd been the naïve one sitting in our penthouse as if we were creating some bond.

Instead of trying to pursue any more conversation, I said, "Interesting."

My mind was all tangled up with new feelings, and I wasn't sure how to act now that I knew Bastian was watching.

"What's really interesting is how he hasn't made his way over here yet."

"It's mostly about pride and appearance," I told him and myself. Bastian didn't care what I was doing but he did care if I was making a fool out of him.

"Is that what it's about for you?" Quinton asked me quietly.

I stared out at the water and waited for the waves to rock and soothe me with their rhythm, the rhythm of the world. It didn't work this time, my heart beat too fast and my frustration roared to life in my veins. "It has to be just that for me."

He nodded. "Well, then, I'm here to entertain. And honestly, I'm here to stare as long as you'll let me."

I laughed at his honesty. Most men would have tried to keep their eyes above my shoulders or been creepy about it. Somehow, him admitting that it was fun to look let me relax a bit. In another world, I would have liked him. I would have wanted more with him.

In a world without Bastian.

"When did you get the tattoo on your shoulder?" Quinton asked as he took a seat in the lounge chair beside mine. He offered me a bottle of oil, and I rubbed it over my chest and stomach before answering.

"I got it when I was sixteen after I came to terms with my parents being gone." I closed my eyes and tried to enjoy his company, even if it wasn't the company I really wanted.

"Where did they go?"

Something about today had shifted my heart, and something about this man being so honest with me, had me wanting to be honest with him. "They were always runners. They would leave me for weeks at a time. When my mom was home, she was vibrant and full of life, and my dad adored her. Then, they'd say they were going to the grocery store and not come back again for weeks. I didn't really understand it until I was a teenager ..." I stopped because I was babbling.

"So, what happened? Don't stop now. I need to know the whole story."

I sighed, eyes still closed. "They were addicts, and I sort of hated when they came back. They would blame my being hyper or not doing well in school on them leaving over and over. I resented them and myself."

"I hope you learned different." Quinton sighed, like maybe he understood some part of it.

I shrugged. "Maybe I sometimes still blame myself. I don't know. Then, one day after they hadn't come back, we got a call to say they'd been in an accident a couple states away. It wasn't big news. Everyone wrote it off as another sad story of how drugs overtake people. And I agreed. Except I was still a kid. I still felt like they were coming home for a long time. When I finally understood they weren't, I got the tattoo."

Quinton sat and listened intently, even though I was topless in a lounge chair at this stupid party.

"Morina." Bastian's voice sliced through the air in a way that said I'd finally gotten a reaction from him. "Time to go."

My eyes flew open, and I met the dark stare of my husband. His strong jaw was hard enough to cut stone. His full lips pursed as he broke eye contact and scanned up and down my body.

It felt like lava on my skin as he perused every curve. I lifted my chin, ready to fight if that was what he intended. "Bastian. This is a great spot on the beach. Quinton and I were just enjoying the view."

"I have a feeling you were enjoying different views."

The man behind him chuckled and unfolded from the lounge chair. "Morina, next time you need company, feel free to give me a call."

"My wife has my company, Quinton. Don't be disrespectful."

"What is respect, Sebastian?" Quinton countered. "Letting another man entertain your wife and not coming over yourself? Or is that neglect?"

I saw the moment Bastian's stance shifted. His muscles rippled in a way they didn't usually. Quinton must've witnessed the transformation too, because he stepped back, raising his hands.

"It was a pleasure meeting you, Morina." He backstepped, leaving me with a man who never got angry, yet here he stood seething.

"It's time to go," Bastian said through clenched teeth, without looking at me. His stare was on the water, where mine once had been. The wind pushed the waves higher.

Angry waves.

The tide picked up like it knew Bastian owned the ocean

too.

Strands of my hair stuck to the sheen on my shoulder and across my breasts. I brushed them away, but my skin reacted to my own touch or maybe to Bastian's gaze that suddenly followed my hand.

My nipples tightened as he licked his lips, and his eyes narrowed. "Morina, I swear to fucking God, you are beautiful in your fury, and you have a right to it." His voice came out low like someone threw it through gravel. "But if you keep this up, I will throw you over my shoulder and carry you out of here, even if you are kicking and screaming."

My hand slid down my stomach, inch by inch. I arched and bit my lip, stopping right above my bikini bottoms. Both of our stares paused there too, his was furious and mine was wanting suddenly.

I wanted him to possess me, wanted him to feel the jealousy and the desire I felt for him at the same time. "Why are we resisting others' advances, Bastian? We could both be enjoying ourselves, working toward legal separation."

He pulled my string bikini top from his pocket. He must have picked it up from the sand. He threw the balled up piece of fabric onto my chest. "Put your top back on."

"It's a topless beach, Bastian. Everyone is—"

His large hand shot out and was under my hair so fast, I didn't see it coming. He gripped it hard at the base. When he knelt beside me, his other hand gripped my jaw and I was trapped. So easily, he had an advantage as he pulled my ear close. "I'm happy to make a public display of how you're my wife right here, right now if you want to. No separation of any sort. You want to enjoy someone else's touch, *ragazza*? I'll make you beg for mine on this beach."

I stared at him, suddenly something a lot like fear slithered through me. Bastian was supposed to be the one who made allies with everyone, who was soft where his father had been hard.

Bastian was gone.

The head of the Armanelli family held me in his grasp.

The shake in his hand, the wild look in his eyes was something like I'd never seen.

I opened my mouth, ready to agree. He didn't let me though.

"Don't say a word," he whispered calmly. Yet, that grip, the grip in my hair bordered on painful. "Pick up your top and cover what's mine."

Why did my body want so badly to defy him, to push him past the point he could control? He must have seen my hesitation, because he jerked my head just a little and ground out, "Now."

I cautiously brought the strings to my neck where he raised my hair enough for me to tie a knot right below his grip.

Before I could adjust the triangles of fabric, one of his hands trailed down the string on my neck. The other dragged over my breast, his thumb rubbing over my tattoo, his fingers curling around its curve. The thin fabric was no barrier.

He squeezed and rolled me in his hand forcing a gasp from me before my hand flew to my mouth.

No. He didn't get to pull a reaction out of me. He didn't deserve that; yet, my body was already giving in.

"Why can't you work with me, huh?" His question came out like he was far away. "Why goad me with other men when you know you only have to be good for a few more months?"

His hand slid down my stomach, following the trail I'd made. The slick oil was warmer now, heated by the sun or my body reacting to the beautiful man holding me hostage on the beach. It didn't take any more from him to have me arching into this touch too.

I'd been without for so long. I'd dreamt of his touch, burned for it. I'd beg for it at this point. Even if I knew it wasn't healthy, we'd end up crashing down in a destroyed city after.

The tsunami of us was growing and swelling, becoming a monstrosity.

Fingers at the edge of my bikini bottoms, he nipped my ear. "Should I make you plead with me in front of them all? Is that what you really want? To get what you're dying for in front of all these people?"

"Bastian," I whispered and shook my head. "It's a public event."

"Where you took your top off, right?"

This was my punishment. This was him showing his power. He might have had a hold on the whole world in one way or another, but his hold on me was sexual. A bond of possession and possessor. He wanted me to understand respect, to understand that I was his.

I squirmed when his pinky dipped under the fabric.

"You wouldn't," I hissed.

The smile that spread across his face was vicious.

His hand dove into my bikini bottoms. I don't know who was watching. Most everyone was behind him, a little ways off where the gold women posed and the alcohol was being served.

Still, anyone could have walked over.

Formal Bastian was gone though. And the woman who would have thought better of riding a man's hand in public, well, she wasn't around either.

I bit my lip and arched as his finger slid in.

A tsunami always started small. The shift in water, quick. This was his earthquake, and he intended to make me feel it.

He was on top of the tsunami and I was below, staring up in awe at the man inside the business suit. He ruled all of us, and he ruled me too.

"Willing to take it anywhere, *piccola ragazza*. I should tie you up and keep you locked away."

"If only you could, right?" I moaned and gripped his wrist as I gasped and took what I wanted fast.

He leaned down and whispered in my ear, "Say your husband's name when you moan, *piccola ragazza*. Tell them all who gives you pleasure you can't bear to wait for."

I stared at him as he slid another finger in and curled them, his thumb rubbing over my clit. I gasped out, "Sebastian Armanelli."

"Till death do us part," he murmured, and I didn't correct him.

CHAPTER 32: BASTIAN

Elizabeth shouldn't have been on my arm, but Morina took it too far.

Fuck.

I still wanted to drag her across that party and scream she was mine to each and every person who looked her way.

Now, we sat in my car on the way home as she grumbled about wanting to go to the humane society.

That place calmed her, and she probably used it a lot of the time to distance herself from me.

I didn't want distance anymore. I wanted Morina, with her crystals and bikinis and baggy T-shirts, to be only mine. I'd watched her on the beach with Quinton, and I knew she might not belong to anyone, but I was going to belong beside her at the very least.

Fucking mine.

That was the difference between her and others I'd been with. I hadn't realized before. She was an ocean that moved and rocked with the wind. She couldn't be owned by anyone but me. I'd be Poseidon if she was the ocean. I wasn't letting her go so easily.

The company shares would be worked out.

We could work things out together.

I veered toward where she volunteered.

The animal shelter was probably more for her than the animals. I found she came back happy, full of life, and smiling every time she went. She told me about the dogs and how Moonshine still hadn't been adopted but she would be.

I had my doubts.

"What do you need to do there tonight?"

She didn't answer, just glared at me. "I want to go by myself."

"Too bad."

"You're such an asshole. You know that? You do everything for everyone else. You smile in their faces and accommodate everyone's demands. And with me, you don't try at all."

That was probably true.

I didn't give a fuck.

I let her stew. I'd stew too. She'd gone over the edge, and I wasn't willing to climb back up to sanity with her right now. She stormed out of the car, and I sighed and pounded my fist on the dashboard.

You're going to have a heart attack from a woman who probably wants you to drop dead.

Then I followed her in and watched as she packed up her little box at the front desk and stomped to the kennels. I observed her lighting each candle with care.

She soothed animal souls with that spirit of hers. Why did she rattle mine instead?

I was hanging on by a thread after seeing her let Quinton pull her top off. I should have seen it coming, though. Elizabeth had been too bold in her advances, and I shouldn't have put my hand on her back. I hadn't even glanced at Elizabeth throughout it all. I wouldn't have been able to tell anyone the color of her outfit, if she'd worn heels or not. I could only describe the pain and fury in Morina's eyes and knew they matched mine. Still, had a man been as close to her as Elizabeth was to me ... Well, I was already contemplating killing Quinton.

She'd told *him* the story of her parents. That had pushed me completely over the edge.

Morina murmured to one of the dogs. "Should we play some music or let the silence descend on us?"

They didn't answer her, but she still put on a thunderstorm. Moonshine whined, and Morina opened the kennel and scooped her up. Her hair fell over her face and covered the dog too. The pup was almost too big for her to hold.

She went down the line, catering to each of the animals with the same amount of care, her attention never drifting back to me.

And my attention was solely on her. She'd been abandoned again and again by her parents and then one final time. She hadn't told me they'd done that to her.

I understood her pain better, and it was only because another man pulled the information from her.

"Why didn't you tell me your parents were addicts?"

She glanced back and then rolled her eyes. "So you were eavesdropping too?"

"Answer the question, Morina."

"Because there's nothing to tell, Bastian. I told you they left now and then. You didn't ask much else, so I didn't share much else."

"They left you."

"So what? Everyone leaves when they die."

"They left you over and over again, you said. And you thought it was your fault. You don't think that's something you should share with the person you're in a relationship with?"

"A relationship?" Her eyes flared, burning blue fire as she suddenly paced past me, box under her arm, toward the front of the building. "What relationship?"

"We're married."

"Are we?" She shoved the box away. "Is that why you let some woman rub herself all over you and whisper in your ear?" She whipped the fire of her words at me fast, and with her hands on her hips, I knew she was ready to burn me down.

Fine. We would end this now.

"You started that with your snide comment about a public separation on the way over."

"Oh my God. Do you make all our marriage decisions on your own now?"

"As if you would want to plan any of those decisions," I grumbled, pissed that she was right.

"That's bullshit. I've gone above and beyond in this stupid arrangement. I've listened to you about oil and green energy and terminals and gone to visit the company. I've done the board meeting. Don't act like I'm not involved."

"I'll agree to that. You've done great." I nodded, ready to let the whole thing go. "We need to keep working together."

"Work together? Right. Work together." She shook her head like she couldn't handle it. "Bastian, Bastian, Bastian. What a guy. Always working with everyone. Too bad he doesn't know how to make a goddamn real move and risk it with me. So I get you in the dark when no one's looking, like I'll forget in the morning. It's bullshit."

"What?" I whispered, sure I heard her wrong.

"I don't want Bastian. I want Sebastian Armanelli, the man who knows how to take what's his and claim it. But if you're not him, then fuck you." She spat the words at me and turned to leave.

She shined light on my flaws, cut them up, and handed them to me on a platter. I wanted to punish her for it and then fuck her quiet while I made love to her for calling attention to what no one else could. She stirred the devil and the sinner in me, the man who was the head of the Mafia. I didn't want to hide him with her. Not anymore.

My hand shot out.

Bastian was gone.

CHAPTER 33: MORINA

The man pulled me to him and ravaged my mouth, devouring my anger.

He gripped my face in his hands like he wanted to hold me forever, and then he kissed down my neck where he scraped his teeth over my skin like he needed to inflict pain to remind me I was his.

"You're driving me insane, *bellissima*."

Italian flew from his lips as I wrapped my arms around his shoulders, trying to steady myself. His body was firmly against mine, his hands on every part of my back and my ass.

We lost ourselves as we clawed at one another, trying to make up for weeks of frustration and wanting.

"Please, please, please," I begged, not sure what I was begging for.

He pulled back, holding me at arm's length as he searched my face in the front office's dim light.

Before I could say another word, he threw me over his shoulder.

"What are you— Where are we going?" I stuttered out, now upside down as his hand stroked my thigh. I wasn't fighting it. I wanted to have him.

Here. At home.

Anywhere.

This was long overdue, and I knew the consequences would be a broken heart in just a few months but I didn't care.

Quick decisions needed to be made.

"I'm going away from the front doors in case someone wants to drop off a dog tonight."

"Hm, all of a sudden daddy doesn't like an audience," I taunted him with what he'd done earlier today in front of so many.

He smacked my ass. "I don't like anyone seeing anything about you, Mo."

He tried to go into the front room with all the animals, but I pointed and said, "Back room. No dogs to bark at us." I rolled my pussy right into his shoulder, completely ready to drive him wild now. He groaned as he strode through the swinging doors. He slid me down his body and took his time dragging his hands over it, as he set me on the floor.

"This body is mine, Morina," he murmured.

I bit my lip as his hands left heat in their wake. "For a few more months."

"Are you so sure?"

I nodded slowly. "Like you said, we're married until then. But just remember"—I circled him once and then tapped his finger where my makeshift ring sat—"you won't have to wear this after that day. You'll be free, and so will I."

"Until then, you're mine."

I shrugged and looked at my nails like I didn't care about his rules. "It's an arranged marriage, Bastian. All for you to get some fucking shares in a company."

The words were hurtful, but I was still mad.

He was too. And I wanted this side of him. I was ready to have Sebastian with me all night long. I wanted his pleasure, his pain, his torment.

I wanted what he hid from everyone else.

Bastian showed his teeth, slow, as if he was smiling. Yet,

something was off. There was no happiness. My comment had pissed him off even if he tried to hide it. I wasn't being a good wife, or a wife at all really. I frustrated him instead.

Before I knew what was happening, he pulled me close and kissed me as he backed me against a kennel wall. I took his lips—so soft and yet so demanding—with mine and enjoyed what I hadn't been able to for weeks now.

Suddenly, he shoved me back, and a jolt of surprise ran through my body. He wiped his mouth with the back of his hand and moved quickly around the kennel's gate. I stepped forward, but he slammed it in my face.

We stared at each other through the chain link, and I gripped the steel wire as I narrowed my eyes at him in question. "What are you doing, Bastian?"

"Locking you up so you can think about what you said."

I chuckled at the ridiculous notion. "I have the keys to open the kennels."

"You mean these keys?" He opened his fisted hand, and I stared blankly at a key chain that looked eerily like mine.

The light above us buzzed and flickered before going out. This was my punishment. Of course, the lights would go at this very second. Only the moonlight from outside now shone in.

Bastian, the man of allies and good behavior with everyone else, stood before me like a devil shadowed in his fury. The angles of his cheekbones and the lush mouth that I knew kissed much harder than it looked were sinister all of a sudden.

"Ha, ha." I shrugged like it was no big deal. "Joke's over. Open the gate."

"Morina, I don't intend to open the gate. You have to work for me to do things like that. Show me you've learned."

"Learned what?"

"Learned how to talk to and treat your husband."

"Because of what? Saying this is arranged?"

"You can add that to the long list of shit you've done wrong today."

"Are you still mad about Quinton?" I smiled as I dropped his colleague's name.

"I'll forever be mad about that, *ragazza*."

"Bastian, it was a topless beach." I rolled my eyes. "Let's not forget you letting Elizabeth hang on your arm."

"Jealous now, are we?"

"No apologies for that?" The hitch in my voice let some of my hurt show through, and he stared at me long enough to probably see it.

"You don't get it, do you, Morina?" He shook his head, and he swore in Italian. "I shouldn't be apologizing for a woman flirting with me. I should be apologizing that you even care enough to be jealous about it. I wanted to keep this arrangement clean, but I dirtied it."

"What's dirty about this? The fact that you feel something for me? The fact that you can actually show me that feeling?"

His finger traced a metal wire. "You go with every gut instinct and emotion, love. I can't do that."

I shrugged. "You can with me."

Like a whip, his gaze flew to mine. We stood in silence only a gate between us. "You sure about that, *ragazza*? Today, I wanted to rip a man's eyes out for looking at you without your top on."

"Oh, I'm sure." I lifted my eyebrows. "Maybe I should have had him look longer."

"Do you not understand that I'm your husband? That he stared at what's mine for far too long?" Ah, so this was a respect thing to him.

He wasn't really jealous. He didn't really care.

I don't know why that hurt so bad. Maybe because I'd seen how another woman looked so much better on his arm than I did.

"We aren't actually married." I threw out in pain. "A real husband of mine wouldn't have let another girl hang on his arm."

He searched my face and then put his forehead on the metal wires before whispering, "I hurt you."

I nodded once and went with honesty. "You did."

He winced at my admission like I'd physically wounded him. "You mentioned separating, and I reacted poorly. It's not an excuse. For that, I'm sorry, Morina. I see now I don't want your pain, not when it looks that devastating in your eyes."

His words broke away the anger around my heart. Even in his frustration, the man still found a way to show he cared about me. He hated my plants, yet he watered them. He didn't believe in the salt lamp, but he turned it on. He hadn't left even when I was the one person annoying him through the day.

I might only have a few months left with him, but it made me want all of him even for that short amount of time.

I sighed and kissed his forehead before I teased him. "It's okay, *daddy*."

His gaze narrowed as he looked at me, a small smirk on his lips. "Want to go home, *ragazza*?"

"Of course. Open the gate." I pointed to the lock.

His lips rolled between his teeth before he said, "Show me you know who your husband is and I'll let you out."

"How am I supposed to do that, Bastian?" I stomped my foot.

"Since I apologized, I think you need to also."

"Oh, really?"

"Yes, Morina. Get on your knees like a good wife." His

voice held menace, and I wondered if I'd ever been turned on like this before, because my adrenaline went from zero to one hundred, the shock of it like lightning fast and electric.

I bit my lip but didn't really hesitate. He'd see who his wife was. He'd see that I had dirtied and muddled this arrangement as much as he had, that I owned him like he owned me.

If this was how I'd finally get to have my way with him, I'd take it. I'd slept with enough men to know *Sebastian Armanelli* was the one I wanted.

I'd pushed him over the edge. When we'd hooked up before, it had been a fling, something to get out of our systems. I'd tapped into his hidden emotions, the place he wanted to keep confined all to himself.

In marriage, nothing is a secret though.

He slowly unbuckled his belt, and I watched how the prong slid from the brown worn leather. His moves were deliberate, like he was waiting for me to tell him this was wrong and disrespectful.

"Is this what you want, Morina? For me to command you all the time, for me to take what's mine, to make you see every fucked-up side of me?"

"I want the real you," I murmured, licking my lips as I waited for him to move on to unbuttoning his slacks.

"You're going to get more than you asked for."

"We'll see if you can really deliver on that threat."

"Crawl to me, *bellissima*. Come. Right. Here." He pointed to the spot in front of him. I moved slowly, my eyes on his zipper as he lowered it.

His cock sprang free, thick and so big I wasn't sure he'd fit it through the diamond-shaped mesh.

Yet, he slid one hand through the space between the gate and the post and threaded his fingers through my hair. With a yank, he brought me right up to him.

His other hand pushed his dick through the chain link so I only had access to that part of him.

"Open, *ragazza*."

I stared up at him. We warred with our gazes, and I almost didn't, the defiance in me strong.

"Your choice at the end of the day. Decide who you want."

That quick decision, the one to choose him or his soft counterpart, Bastian.

I opened for Sebastian Armanelli, and he shoved my head down on his dick faster than I was ready for.

He was so big, I almost gagged, but I kept my mouth open, taking all I could. I ran my tongue over his veins, the pre-cum salty in my mouth. He throbbed against the roof of my mouth, and I swirled him like I couldn't get enough.

I stared at his face, how his neck tightened more and more as I went up and down faster and faster.

Moaning on his dick gave me all the power even when I was on my knees, hands clasped on a kennel cage, locked in.

"*Ragazza. Bellissima. Amore mio.* My wife. My love. Mine." He strung all his words together as he fucked my mouth, his hips thrusting faster and faster.

And just as he was about to come, he pulled my head back so far I arched my back, putting my breasts on display in the bikini top. He let the cum spurt over my chest and across both of my breasts as he moaned my name.

His forehead fell to the kennel wire and his hand slid from my hair, grabbed the keys, and unlocked the door.

In a daze, I didn't move as he picked me up off the floor and carried me like a baby to the humane society's washroom.

He placed me on my feet long enough to grab paper towels and dampen them before turning me in the mirror to stare over my shoulder at me.

His seed dripped from my chest, there to mark me.

"If I could leave it, *ragazza*, I would." His head fell to my neck as he placed gentle kisses there and rubbed away the evidence of him on me.

What a sight we were.

Suddenly, I wasn't sure I could forget him in a few months. I found myself completely and utterly frightened by the idea that I'd be ruined from this.

What man would lock a woman in a kennel, and what woman would enjoy every second of it?

"I won't enjoy divorcing you," I murmured.

He looked up and assessed my chest before he did anything else. It was all clean, every piece of our encounter wiped away.

"I won't enjoy it either, Morina."

I took a shaky breath. "Will we still be friends?"

He kissed my cheek. "Sure, *ragazza*. Sure. Let's go home, huh?"

CHAPTER 34: BASTIAN

Morina and I went to our own bedrooms quietly that night. I waited to see if she'd invite me to hers, but she didn't.

Rightfully so too. I was the man that had locked her in a cage and marked her.

Rising before the sun, I got dressed quickly, and left to start my day. I needed to fly to Texas and meet with an oil refinery that wanted to push more oil our way. We could handle it for the time being, but I was set to propose funding from the government soon.

"You tell Morina yet?" Cade asked over the phone.

"Tell her what?" I asked as I stared out the window on my flight. My mind wasn't focused on business. Instead, it was thinking of a girl with hurt blue eyes that handed me a part of her heart the night before. I think, at this point, she had all of mine, even if she didn't know it.

"That you're looking to partner with the refinery until you get the green light from the government."

"Why would I tell her that? She doesn't care about all this. She wants what's best for the town and is happy to hand the decision-making over to me."

"If you told her about the clean energy push, I thought you would tell her about this too."

I straightened my cuff links and brushed off his assessment of the situation. "I'm not starting an argument with her for no reason." Our relationship was too fragile at this point to do anything of the sort. "The refinery's proposal won't last long.

It's not something that will even be brought up until she's gone, and then I'll be nixing the idea as we move forward with reconstructing the oil terminals."

"I'm just saying these guys are who Dad partnered with in the past. We need to walk a fine line with every one of them."

"Agreed." My brother knew his shit and was looking out. Still, his advice had me coiling up in defense as I got to the meeting.

Quinton sat at the round table, along with Ronald and a few others. The head of the refinery, Mr. Crow, shook my hand, his sweaty in mine. A gold ring on his finger glinted. We all wore them. Irish, Italian, Armenian, Russian, and more. They had different markings but they meant the same thing.

Family. Filth. And money. The families came to this table because the money was at it.

If he could have called in, even the president would have.

"I'm wondering if we start this now or wait until Bastian is a permanent shareholder of Tropical Oil." Mr. Crow chuckled.

Ronald sneered. "That's not set in stone. I have it on good authority there's a prenup involved, and she doesn't have to sell to you at all."

"Ronald, don't pout." I cracked my knuckles. "Losing never suited you, but I intend to keep our business thriving even if it isn't the way you want it to be."

"We'll see if I don't outbid you with her first." He humphed but sat down in one of the plush leather chairs around the large wooden conference table.

John, another shareholder of the refinery, waved us to our seats. "Now, now. This shouldn't take long. Let's discuss other matters and make sure our alliances are in order. I've had a few of my guys mining digital currency, and I want to make sure we cover that too."

A few of them grumbled, but it led to a heated debate about who was monopolizing what and if they were scamming the others.

Ruthless sharks sat at this table. We were the heads of our families, and we wanted to make sure they had enough food to eat.

One man raised his voice about how the Armanellis must've been doing something I wasn't sharing with regard to mining. We'd pulled in much more than most of them.

I shrugged. "There isn't a trick to it other than hiring the best of the best. Cade grew up doing this."

"You can't be the best and have the best of everything, Bastian," Mr. Crow said. He sat there in a checkered suit and wire-framed glasses, eyes narrowed at me. He was the one at the table we cared about. He owned the refinery I'd have to break ties with at some point.

"I'm just here to work with everyone, Mr. Crow. That includes you."

"Ah, so you've come to agree to more oil at the ports then? I can't have Tropical Oil underperforming."

The room went quiet. Most knew my stance on this business, and they knew I didn't want any more to do with it than necessary. "What does that do for me?"

He leaned forward and twisted his mustache like there was really something to consider. "Well, I can pay you more."

"I don't need money, Mr. Crow."

"Oh, now, everyone needs more money," he scoffed, then straightened his bow tie. "What more do you want? The terminals don't mean much to you. Let us have our fun. Go back up north where it's cold. We know how to handle our Gulf."

"Well, you see"—I leaned back in the leather chair and took them all in—"I have a wife there now. She loves the ocean, and she loves that company. I'm invested." Around the table, grumbling ensued. "Are you importing anything else?" I didn't break eye contact. I held his with a grip so strong he wouldn't look away either. If he did, I'd have my answer.

"If you want part of imports—"

I cut him off. "I want any illegal imports to stop."

"They're essential to my—"

I stood. "They stop or I walk right now." This was where I wouldn't bend. Every single person in the room knew that.

"Fine." Mr. Crow straightened, jumping at his chance. "You increase our limits on the terminals receiving the oil, and I'll stop the imports."

His hand stuck out over the table. I stared at it. Sometimes a handshake carried a lot of weight. Here, it would carry millions. I'd have to hold off on clean energy for months, and I didn't even have the shares to do that yet.

But the imports had to stop. The last piece of my father's legacy had to be torn apart.

We'd have a clean family business, one my brother and my mother always wanted.

"Done." I shook his hand.

I'd have to tell Morina later. She'd understand.

CHAPTER 35: MORINA

Bastian was already gone when I woke, but he'd left me crepes and switched the salt lamp on.

I went through my daily routine and tried to forget about what had happened the night before. We'd pushed each other over the edge, and in a flurry of emotions, we'd lost control.

That was it.

Nothing more and nothing less.

Except I ached for him like I had no other man. He'd become more of a friend to me than even Linny.

After I went to surf and sold a couple of smoothies, I called her in hopes I'd catch her between flights.

She answered without a hello. "You're lucky I stay up late. It's midnight here."

"Where are you now?" I asked as I got ready to lounge on the couch.

"If you'd follow my Instagram, you'd know I was in Germany. It's sort of cold, but I went to see Berlin's Brandenburg Gate, which was spectacular."

"I'll have to look at pictures when you come home."

She mumbled about her Instagram again, knowing I wouldn't go on there. "Anyway, what's up? You having Bastian's baby yet?"

"Oh my God. No. Never. Why would you even say that?"

"I don't know. It felt like the only reason you'd call. You call me like once a year unless there's an emergency."

"Well, there's no emergency. I'm ... Do you think I'm meant

to be alone?"

"No. You're married. That means you're never going to be alone again."

"We could get divorced." I knew that was coming anyway.

"You're not getting divorced. I see the magazines. Bastian looks at you like a fucking werewolf ready to rip someone apart for you."

"Did you just finish a paranormal romance?"

"Yes, and it was so good." She said it like she was taking a bite of the best ice cream.

"Lend it to me. I need a good one."

"So, are you guys fighting?"

"No, we're just ... I'm ... I know what I want finally. But I never really wanted anything before him. And I never used to hesitate, and I never used to have this problem. Why am I second-guessing everything?"

"Because you're actually going after something that's hard. Love is hard and relationships are too. You run away from those things, Mo."

"I don't run away. I've never left anyone—"

"No, because you usually make sure there's no one to leave. You kind of go with the flow and avoid everything that's hard." I shook my head, ready to tell her it wasn't true. "Your parents fucked you up. I get it. I think your dad did the same to half the town. They loved him and then hated him every time he left and took your mother with him. She was a freaking shining star and brightened up the whole town up, right? He came in and charmed her away."

The days I remember her smiling at me and hugging me tight were some of the best ever. My father would sneak into my grandma's house after months of being gone and hold up a surfboard at dawn. During those moments, I loved him more than the ocean, the sand, and my board combined. We'd have a few good months, and then they'd leave again without a goodbye.

"I'm probably a little more scared of commitment than I thought."

"You overcame it. You're married. Give yourself some credit. And remember, you're not on drugs, so you're doing better than them."

It shouldn't have been funny. It wouldn't have been with anyone else. Except Linny and I had grown up together, and her parents had been addicts too. She'd seen the shit my parents pulled. "Oh my God," I said. "Remember that one time they got so high they tried to rob the tiki bar for alcohol? Not money, alcohol."

Linny cracked up with me. "They couldn't even walk and the sheriff locked them up just to get sober."

"He should have kept them there forever."

Linny sighed as her laugh died down. "I mean, they probably should have locked all our parents up. Mine haven't been seen in years. My mom called me like two weeks ago, and I couldn't understand a thing she was saying."

"What the hell? Is she okay?"

"Who knows?" I heard rustling on the other side of the line. "Look, if you're questioning things, remember, it's the people that mean the most to you that make you do that. He means something to you. Don't run from it. Embrace it. Now, I gotta go. Don't forget to check your mail in a few days. The package took longer to get ahold of but it's coming. I love you, bye!"

I sighed and hung up, not really sure why I needed to have that conversation with her in the first place. I'd committed and I hadn't run away, despite the terrible situation this was.

Yet, now, I wanted to stay, and I wanted to tell him that too. My heart had fallen, and I'd tried to jump in after it and pull it back up to the land of sanity, but it kept falling down, down, down, into the dark abyss that was Sebastian Armanelli.

I wanted to submerge myself down there forever and find every piece of hidden treasure. I knew it meant I'd have to do the hard thing first.

I'd have to walk the plank of telling him I didn't want a divorce and hope to God he felt the same. Fear pulled at my self-confidence though. Enough that I wasn't sure what would be worse, missing out on someone I loved or finding out they didn't love me back.

We had two months. Two months of planning our separation if I didn't tell him, and two months until the board meeting where I could potentially announce he was buying the shares. We hadn't discussed the plan, and yet now was probably the best time to do so.

I just had to figure out what the plan was.

I, the girl who hated plans in the first place, had to decide a multimillion-dollar company's future and what my broken heart would look like—one of rejection or one of regret.

Turning on the salt lamp and lighting incense to burn while I wallowed and waited seemed like the only thing I could do.

At 10 p.m., I wondered if Bastian was ever coming home. He never left me overnight without telling me.

I fell asleep on the couch.

The next morning, I woke up in my bed with the blankets tucked in around me.

Bastian Armanelli, sweet and accommodating. I threw the covers off, wishing I'd gotten Sebastian instead, wishing he'd taken advantage of me.

I stomped out of the bedroom in my worn nightshirt and found crepes again.

No Bastian.

This went on for two more days.

I passed the time doing my own thing. I made new shakes and even called Bradley just to talk. He didn't answer but I still chattered into his voicemail.

Finally, as the sun went down on the third night, I gave in.

> **Morina: Are you coming home?**

He answered immediately.

> **Bastian: Why wouldn't I be?**

> **Morina: It's later than you normally get here. I haven't seen you in days.**

> **Bastian: Do you normally time me coming in and out of the house?**

I rolled my eyes at his playfulness, a weight lifting that I hadn't known was there.

> **Morina: Shut up. When do you plan to be here?**

> **Bastian: We're stuck in traffic for about another thirty minutes.**

> **Morina: I'll try to stay up. No promises though.**

Bastian: Maybe I'll wake you then.

Morina: Doubt it. I get carried back
to my bed, gentle as can be so I'm not
disturbed even when I want to be.

Bastian: Ragazza, tempting a man
like me won't end well.

Morina: Like, I'll be punished or ...?

Bastian: For that statement alone,
yes. I'll redden that ass just to hear
you beg for forgiveness. First, we
have a conversation though.

My stomach dipped low. Did he mean that? Were we finally past tiptoeing around one another?

I didn't know if I should respond or wait for my spanking, so I sat there without a single thing to do and stared at the door.

My attention had never been so focused.

I sat on the sofa in my T-shirt thinking about what he might say, my foot waggling back and forth.

Maybe we could try sleeping in each other's beds from now on, sex and everything.

Or maybe he wanted to discuss the start of the legal separation.

When the lock turned, I jumped and grabbed my phone to look a little less desperate when he walked in.

Instead of the fabric rustle of him unbuttoning his suit jacket to hang, though, a whine came from the door.

"What the—?" I looked up and leapt from the couch when I saw ... "Moonshine?"

Bastian stood there in his navy suit, brown dog hair on him, and a red leash attached to Moonshine. In one hand he held the leash and a plastic bag filled with toys, and from the other he dropped a big bag of dog food next to the door.

"Bastian ..." I backed away, shaking my head. "Why is Moonshine with you?"

"What do you mean? You told me Moonshine was struggling to find a home. I told you she would."

"Okay ..." I let the word linger, my heart thudded way too fast. "Where is she going?"

"Well, nowhere now. I let her piss out front, and now she probably wants to go to bed. I figure our third bedroom is fine for her. She doesn't need a dog bed if she has a real one."

"I'm sorry ... Can we please back up? Why is Moonshine here?"

"She found her forever home with us."

"No." I shook my head again, stunned. I took another step back and stumbled against the corner of the couch. "No. Nope. Okay, you can call the humane society. We'll take her back."

Moonshine whined and strained on her leash, trying to get to me. I knelt down and called her over. Her big body was more and more like a rottweiler and less like a pup. "You have to get back to the kennels so we can find you a good home," I whispered.

"What's wrong with our home?" Bastian inquired and pulled a dog bowl from the plastic bag.

"Are you out of your mind?" As soon as he placed the bowl on the ground, I grabbed it and tried to shove it back in the bag. "Do you know how much a dog slobbers?"

He swung the bag away. "That can't possibly be a concern of yours, Morina. You probably make more of a mess than the dog."

"Excuse me?" The metal from the bowl clattered as I dropped it and stood, glaring at him. "I've kept my mess in my room since the day I got here."

"I saw your room last night, and the night before when I put you to bed. It's a mess."

"Well, don't put me to bed then," I yelled, and Moonshine whined.

"I'll put my wife to bed any time I want," he growled, suddenly in my face.

"I can't believe this." I spun around and pointed to the dog. "This isn't okay."

He scoffed and scooped Moonshine up, taking her to the third bedroom. I watched him walk down the hall with his perfect ass in his perfect suit trousers. He disappeared into the bedroom, and I waited for him to return so I could tell him how fucking terrible she was going to be on her own in there. After five minutes, he came out and announced, "She's fast asleep on the feather pillow."

I swear, his damn smile was the smuggest thing I'd ever seen.

I stomped over to the kitchen sink. "This is going to be so painful for the dog."

And for me. I didn't want to give her up, and the fact he'd brought her home had a little voice in my head that I didn't like to entertain screaming that I should tell him I loved him. Tell him I wanted to live happily ever after in a house with a white picket fence and a rottweiler mix.

"I don't think it has to be painful for anyone. Why do you think this is such a bad idea?"

"Well, for one, it's not sustainable. I'll be gone in two months and so will you. I don't want to get attached to her if I'm not going to keep her. I'm already attached."

He pulled his tie from his neck, set it on the counter, slipped off his shoes, and went to the refrigerator like I was the kind of wife who'd made him dinner.

"I didn't eat dinner, so there's no meal in there. Are you listening to me?"

"I ate already." He chuckled like he knew I was never going to attempt to cook him food. He was probably right. "And I'm listening. I just think we should calm down and discuss this rather than spiral into you talking twenty times your normal speed and us going off the deep end again."

I sighed and tried placing a hand on my stomach, hoping the Reiki technique would work. "Do you want a night shake?" I could actually use one, and it would calm us both to have me doing something with my restless mind.

"Sure." He nodded and sat at the counter, watching me pull ingredients from the refrigerator.

A state-of-the-art blender lived in the corner cabinet, and I liked how quickly it blended ice. I added ingredients and fruit as I waited for Bastian to say something.

"Let's start at the beginning, huh? We should probably discuss the other night because I don't see how, *ragazza*, but we've both woven our way under one another's skin."

I scoffed. "I know how. We had to spend a couple months together after we had a one-night stand on a jet. This has been the longest morning after—"

"We're not an extended one-night stand. You're truly my wife. I care about you. I stay up at night in my room considering dragging you to mine."

I hit the blend button harder than necessary and grumbled, "I wish you would."

When I turned it off and poured the ingredients into two glasses, he murmured, "This is our problem."

I set the glass in front of him. "What's the problem, Bastian?"

"You say things like that, like you think they don't affect me, like you think I'm immune to you."

"Aren't you though?"

"Are you saying I'm just indulging myself with you?"

"Why weren't you here the last three days?"

"Because I was working."

"That's it? Or were you creating distance after you indulged with me again?"

"I want this to be fair for you, Morina." He sighed and his jaw ticked.

I rolled my eyes. Fair wasn't any of this. Fair would have been me on another planet than him, because here with him, I couldn't deny myself. "I'm selling you the shares because I want to, not because you've coerced me into have feelings for you. And I actually take offense that you presume I can't separate the two at this point."

"I never said that—"

"Oh, whatever." I picked up my shake, took a taste, and slammed it back down on the counter. I was barreling toward insanity at lightning speed, and the thunder about to roll out of me would be just as crazy. "So, we're going forward with legal separation then? It's probably time we start pushing that to the media. We've had a few days away from each other, and I'm guessing you were creating distance for that reason. Let's plan the rest."

The words flowed out of me like I'd struck a match and dropped it on a line of kerosene. It spread like wildfire, hot, fast, and mean.

Bastian clearly felt the burn, his face contorting with my words.

Biting my tongue, I decided my shake could wait while I washed out the blender. I took it to the sink and scrubbed it hard, trying to get out my frustration.

I wasn't sure if he even wanted me. He wanted to be my friend through this, but I wasn't sure he wanted more.

How could he when he left for days after what we'd done in that kennel?

I scrubbed and scrubbed that glass. I wanted it spotless when I placed it into the dishwasher. The dishwasher wouldn't actually do any cleaning, rather it was double checking my work. It was also a way to avoid that man on the other side of the island, staring at me like I was going to respond to him being immune to me.

I wanted to wring his neck, tell him to go to hell, and kick him out. I was so sick of this charade, sick of faking something and then not being sure if I was faking anything at all.

I felt him before I heard him behind me. His hard chest pressed into my back as I scrubbed away.

"Mo, can we back up?"

I scoffed and grabbed another dish without looking at him. "Back up to what? Should we start over and just be friends? Forget that we fucked?"

It was official. We were bound by marriage, and we needed to unbind.

"What's got you so worked up, huh?" he whispered into my neck, and I shivered, instantly aware of how close his whole body—specifically the dick I knew was of life-altering size—was to me.

"I'm not worked up." It came out defensive and breathless. I couldn't stop myself from pushing him again and again. I knew how to get a rise out of him and now that was what I wanted. "I just want to get this plan out of the way. I hate them and you know it. So, I think we both go out a few nights here and there throughout the month. The media can take some shots of us with other people. We'll drop something to the news about us being separated. If you or I enjoy our dates, we can call each other to say we're staying—"

He cut me off. "You come home every night."

"I'm sorry. That kind of defeats the purpose of moving on, Bastian. You want me to have a clear mind going into this whole selling shares thing, right? Then I probably need to move on to other guys." I turned to him and wiped my damp hands on a dish towel.

"You can get off and come home, Mo." His turned red. "Are you a cuddle after you fuck type of girl?"

"So what if I am?" I put my hands on my hips.

"Then I'll fucking cuddle you." His palm slammed down on the counter. "You're not staying over at some guy's house when you're my wife."

"So, I can sleep with someone else, but I can't stay the night?" I crossed my arms as this got more and more ridiculous. "That makes no sense, Bastian."

"I'm not risking your safety. You'll have security on you too."

"Oh, no. I'm not doing that. You can't have Dante or someone follow me around. That would be weird for my date."

"Who is this date, by the way? You've got someone in mind already, I can tell."

"Oh my God. Let's just go to bed."

He chuckled and then scrubbed a hand over his face. "My bed or yours?"

"What?" I practically screeched.

His chuckle turned to a full-on laugh.

The corners of his eyes wrinkled, and the dimples I forgot

he had popped out. Bastian was always a good-looking man. He was handsome and unapproachable at the same time. Like a diamond in a museum that you knew was worth billions and admired from afar. But when he laughed in front of me like this, he felt attainable. Heart-crushingly attainable.

"I think you're going crazy." I shook my head at him.

He wiped at his eyes and sobered before walking right up to me. He studied me for what felt like ten minutes. His eyes darted all over my face like he was memorizing it or cataloging each tiny detail of it.

My heart beat louder in those moments than it ever had. All thought left my brain. I couldn't say one word, couldn't provoke him or console him or try to reason with him. Heat rose over my chest and on my cheeks. My stomach and core tightened.

His next words rumbled out, soft. "Turn around, Morina."

He hummed low when I did and his hands went to my shoulders. He rubbed at my knotted muscles, but the tension in them increased. I wanted to scream at him to move away from me but I was frozen. I didn't know where we were going but I knew that if he left again after this, I wouldn't be able to come back from it. We were teetering on the edge of no return if he indulged with me again.

He didn't get it. To him, I was a little girl he was protecting; but to me, he was a damn god who I wanted one more chance to fuck.

He pushed at a tender spot and I moaned. "Jesus."

He chuckled. "You're tense."

"No shit." He rolled a finger over the same spot, and the dish in my hand clattered into the sink. I gripped the edge of the counter. "I'm just ... I need ..."

Every sensation went on high alert. I stared at his reflection in the window in front of me and that smirk on his face told me he knew it too. "You need what, Morina?"

"I need to go to bed," I whispered but we both knew I didn't mean it.

"If you go now, who's going to take care of how wet you are?"

"Jesus, Bastian." I tried to step away from him, but his grip on my neck tightened. He pulled me up against his body and turned me into the island counter until I was pinned between him and the granite. His cock pressed against me, and I felt the length of it at my ass, hard and ready.

He took that moment to rip his hand away and step back. I immediately whipped my head around, about to stutter out his name, but I didn't get the chance, because he yanked my panties down and grabbed his tie off the counter.

I bit my lip, not sure what to do as I stared at him staring at me. His gaze trailed up my legs and stopped at my pussy.

"If you're going to leave again and act like we aren't fucking, I don't want this, Bastian ..." It pained me to say the words. It felt like I was ripping my heart out and giving him the knife to stab it.

"Oh, I'm not going to. I'm taking what's mine. You're my wife. I should have been fucking that perfect pussy of yours from the very beginning. You keep trying to let another man have what's mine, Morina, and I keep trying to be good to you and resist. For what?" He took my wrists as he talked and looped his silk tie around them.

I watched in fascination as suddenly he pulled one side tight, and my wrists slammed together, trapped. He turned me by my hips and pulled my wrists to the faucet, where he tied the other side of the silk.

I was suddenly caught, bent over, my ass half out for him

to stare at.

Then he slid his hand up my thigh to where we both knew I was wet. "Look at this. You enjoy it. You love knowing I own you. Why do I keep fighting that?"

I started to pant from the way his hand went to my ass cheek, the way he kneaded it over and over. "I've never asked you to fight it."

"*Ragazza*, you brought crystals of color into my world of white. This was supposed to be easy and clean."

"I've never been clean. Easy, maybe."

"Easy? You think living with you and having you mention another man having you is easy? You think I want to share you with anyone?" He gripped my ass harder. "You think every time you bring up handing your ass out, I'm not going to tie you up and redden it?"

His fingers were so close to my entrance that I rolled my hips in hopes I'd get him to graze right where I wanted. But his hand pulled away only to come down hard on my ass cheek.

Not once, not twice, but three times.

I'd never had a man spank me before Bastian. Then again, I was dealing with the head of the Italian Mob, the mob that ruled all of the US. The daddy of all daddies, even if he didn't want to be that.

I flipped my hair, quickly turning my head and staring him down over my shoulder. "Tying me up won't make me only yours. You have to say it, Bastian, or I could be gone tomorrow."

The little girl in me who'd been abandoned over and over again needed to hear it. Did he want me or did he not? Was this one more fuck or was this solidifying our relationship?

His jaw worked up and down, the tendons in his neck pulling taut. He was holding back, but in his eyes I saw the raging fire I'd seen the other night. Everyone thought Bastian's default was to make alliances, to be the most amiable godfather there had ever been. Maybe I was the first to witness the fury he'd locked away deep down.

My pussy clenched as we glared at one another. I was tapping into a ferocious energy that no one ever got to witness. Like the moon, the stars, the planets, or the sun, I moved with this man.

The powerful emotion in him was like the sun. So bright, so big. And still, I wanted to be near him, near that emotion. It would burn me, probably kill me and leave me in ashes, but I couldn't fight the allure.

"You're mine, *ragazza*. You spread your legs for another man, I'll hunt him down and kill him." He'd turned vicious, the way I wanted him. "I only want you. You'll have to decide if you want all of me too. I'm not a good man. I never was, but I'm going to try for you, *ragazza*. I'm going to try."

He got on his knees and made me scream his full name. I yanked at the faucet when he brought me to orgasm again by just fingering me. I told him I couldn't take it anymore.

He laughed against my neck. "You take what I give you. Take and take and take. I intend to give you the world. Now, keep screaming my name. It's all I want to hear for the rest of the night."

CHAPTER 36: MORINA

Time was irrelevant to me after that. Bastian carried me to bed and had me on my knees, gagging on his cock before he fucked me over and over again on my bed.

"Are you staying to cuddle?" I asked as he pulled me close.

"You got me now. Till death do us part."

I sighed and fell asleep with his tattooed arms against my skin.

I woke to Bastian jumping from the bed and running to let Moonshine out. She was at the door, yelping. It looked like she was semi potty trained from our work at the humane society.

I drifted off, figuring he'd be back to pull me close a couple minutes later, but I came to when he snuck into bed much later.

"Where did you go?"

"Moonshine didn't really have to go out. She just wanted a walk, I guess."

"Oh, you know what she wants now?" I chuckled.

"She yanked me around the building five times, Morina."

"Have you ever had a dog? You're supposed to be the boss. Yank back and tell her no."

His five o'clock shadow scraped at my neck as he nuzzled me. "You try telling her no. She has puppy eyes. I'm supposed to be a good dad."

"A dad or daddy?"

"Woman, don't start. We need sleep and nourishment before I fuck you again."

So, that's what we did.

And the day after that, we did the same.

Weeks of bliss went by. I even got into the habit of reading him his horoscope when he woke up. He didn't tell me his birthday, but he disclosed he was a Taurus, powerful like a bull and stubborn too. The thing about Bastian was he was dedicated and reliable.

When we stumbled from one of our beds each morning, Moonshine went to him. He was her daddy, and she, along with everyone else, relied on him. Cade called him. Rome and Katie did too. He handled everyone's business in the way they trusted him to.

A world full of people depended on him, and he didn't ever stumble. His emotions didn't seem to play into what he did, except that I knew his father had wronged his mother, and so he did most everything to spite the man.

One day in the kitchen, I stopped him as he spread sauce over pizza dough. "Did your father like how your mother cooked?"

He curled his lip at the mention of them. If anyone didn't like talking about their parents like I didn't like talking about mine, it was Bastian. "My father liked it and took advantage. He had her cooking for extended relatives all the time."

"I see." I didn't want him to remember the bad times; I only wanted to understand the dynamic of their family more.

"She taught me the recipes only weeks before she left us. I think she planned it. She wanted Cade and me to remember the food. It was her passion, after all. That and us."

"She sounds wonderful."

He nodded as he put the handmade pizza in the oven. "She would have liked you. My father would have liked you too."

"I'm sorry I didn't get to meet them."

He stared at me for a minute. "When I put out the hit on

my father, he stared at me, you know? The man who killed him asked me as he held the gun to his head. I didn't hesitate."

I watched Bastian relive the moment, the way he frowned and then rubbed his scruff showed me he battled with his choices even if he hadn't hesitated.

He continued, "He'd been trafficking women when he'd told me he hadn't. He'd done it to Katie and she was part of the family by then, probably always had been in a sense. I couldn't let him live for that. Maybe I'd loved him once, or tried to understand him, but that drained any respect I might've had clean away."

"Katie," I whispered her name because she'd been a ferociously beautiful woman to meet in the first place. Knowing her past made her all the more omnipotent to me.

"Katie had been furious. She wanted us to forgive him." He scoffed and leaned against the counter. "You'll decide, *ragazza*, if you can be with someone like me for longer than this arrangement we have. This is the life I live, one where I right the wrongs of the past and try my best to wash the blood off my hands for the future."

Rounding the counter, I took his mouth with mine. The kiss was slow and deliberate, like we were memorizing each other's real identities. I wanted him to know that I'd already accepted his. I'd accepted Sebastian Armanelli.

"My parents charmed me and then left me over and over again, Bastian. If you don't do that, I'll be here forever, waiting for you. It might be the only real vow I make to you."

We lost ourselves in the pretty words and promises we made to each other. We got mixed up in the fake married life we had and thought it was real. We called Moonshine our baby like we'd had her together.

Mixed up, tumbling around in a world we'd created on our

own, too blind with love to realize it was all a lie.

I worked the food truck and came back to screw his brains out.

Sometimes, he'd make me wait first because he had to spray the damn orchids or take out Moonshine. Sometimes, I told him I needed to make him a night smoothie, but he never waited.

I told myself he was falling for me and I was falling for him. We'd figure out the rest together.

That was my mantra. I let my horoscope point to anything positive and I blocked out the negative. The salt lamps, my crystals, and my bracelets worked overtime to protect us, and everything was perfect for a month.

CHAPTER 37: MORINA

"Mario Armanelli screwed your grandmother." Ronald leaned on the window frame of my food truck one day and shook his head. "Didn't she tell you any of this?"

As I wiped down the food truck counter, I felt the bone crushing weight of the city, of the well-being of children, of everything I didn't want bearing down on me. "That's not true."

"Look it up. We had a spill five years ago. You remember the one?"

Everyone remembered it. We even had animals brought into Dr. Nathan's office. We were a humane society but it was all hands on deck. I'd just started volunteering and hadn't understood the gravity of the situation.

Not until I had to use whatever soap we had to scrub the oil off the animals. Ducks and baby gulls and turtles all washed up on the shore. I remembered my hands, how I couldn't get rid of the smell, and how I'd washed a turtle for hours and hours only to find out it died overnight from poisoning.

I'd been young, but I'd known the toll it took on the Gulf. We couldn't surf, the shops couldn't sell because we'd lost tourists and vacationers, and my grandmother had cried.

She'd cried and cried, and I'd thought it was for the city, but maybe it had been something more.

"That was Mario Armanelli and your grandmother's doing. She was coerced, just like you are being. You want to make her same mistakes? Do you really love that man, Morina? Did he make you fall for him?"

It wasn't the first time I'd thought about that question but it was the first time someone had asked it out loud.

"He wouldn't do that to me." I stood tall but found my black bracelet for strength. This time, I didn't turn the ring on my finger, didn't touch it for any sort of energy.

"Sure. Sure. Except he was in Texas a little over a month ago shaking my hand and the same oil refinery's hand about more oil coming in. Have you asked him about his plan for the illegal imported cargo we still get?"

"You need to leave." I glanced back at the parking lot where I had told my security guy to stay. He'd finally started to listen to my commands over the past few weeks. He was on the phone, not paying attention to the truck. We both stood in plain view, though. Ronald merely looked like a paying customer from afar.

"Bastian plans to phase oil out for clean energy. That's what he's telling everyone, right?" Ronald's bright-white teeth flashed like a shark's. "Then why make a deal with the oil refinery in Texas, Morina? Ask yourself that question. I'm making no deals except with the government to expand. I'll pay you fair for those shares, and you know it. Add on ten percent."

He slid the check over the window counter, and I stared at all the zeros. So many.

Money I didn't care about, but my eyes still flared.

"Just consider it. Ask some questions. My deal stands for as long as you need it to." He left me with the check and walked away, his head held high like he was doing the right thing.

I closed the window, the wood slamming shut harder than I intended it to.

Had I been so naïve? I'd read the file. I'd asked questions and listened to the answers.

But it was his packet, and what if they were all fluff answers? Was he charming me, and was I as gullible as I had been all those years back when my parents had done the same?

Love made you vulnerable. Relying on others made you weak.

Someone strong would always be able to prey on that.

I sped home, not sure I wanted the answers to my questions but sure I needed to ask more. My city wasn't big; oil would clog it, destroy it along with the clean waters we'd taken so much time to purify after the spill. I needed reassurances and answers and more understanding.

Moonshine whined when I walked in, and I petted her head before I took her for a walk. I texted Bastian as I waited for our dog to go to the bathroom.

Our dog, as if this was a completely normal marriage.

What had I been thinking?

> **Morina: I need you to come home. We need to talk.**

He didn't text me, he called. "That sounds ominous, *ragazza*. What's wrong?"

"I talked with Ronald today."

"You what?"

"He came to the food truck and—"

"Where was security?"

"That's not the point."

"He shouldn't be anywhere near you. So, that is the point."

"Why shouldn't he be near me? I can have a conversation, can't I?" My paranoia lashed out.

"Of course." He spoke slowly and quietly like he was assessing the situation. "I'll be home soon, *ragazza*."

With that, he hung up. Bastian knew how to de-escalate, and he wanted to be here, in front of me, to do it.

My mind ran away with itself in those moments. I put Moonshine in her room so I could google oil spills and illegal imports and links between them all as I waited. In the corner of my phone screen, my horoscope app said something about heeding warnings.

My stomach twisted, the urge to throw up built and built as the conspiracies online tied the Armanellis to trafficking and drugs. Their partnerships with every big company in the United States suddenly felt questionable instead of respectable.

"Morina." I jumped when I heard him in my doorway.

"You scared me," I said, my hand to my heart.

"I didn't mean to," he said, walking over to kiss my cheek like he normally did now. When I didn't respond, he studied me, his hand in my hair. "You want to talk, love?"

"I think we need to."

"Okay, let's go in the living room. I'll make some food."

I followed him out like a woman trudging to her demise. I told myself I should have hope, that we could work through it all. Yet, a little voice screamed to run and run fast.

"Why don't you sit? What do you want to eat?"

I shook my head. "I'd rather stand. I'm not hungry."

"*Ragazza*—"

"Did you fly to Texas to meet with an oil refinery in the past month, Bastian?"

He narrowed his eyes. "That's very specific. I fly everywhere and have partnerships with everyone, Morina. Whatever Ronald told you—"

"Please answer the question." I held up a hand because I knew he would attempt to coax me down from my anxiety again. "Be honest. Did you shake a man's hand and say you would increase the amount of oil at our terminals?"

"That's the plan first, Morina." He nodded cautiously. "I

can give you details on that."

I spun the bracelets on my wrist. "You can give me details? You don't think that would have been a good detail to disclose early on?"

"I don't think it matters how we get to the end goal, Morina. We need to move things slowly with partnerships to maintain a good relationship. I intend to allow for this one time around while we confirm government participation in our green energy plan."

"And what if we don't get that participation?"

"We will." He said it like he had no concerns.

"You can't make that promise. And then you'll be tied to pushing those terminals again. *Again*, Bastian. You know why I'm saying *again*?"

"Morina—" His tone was consoling, for the child he must have thought I was.

"Did you know your father pushed my grandmother into voting for more oil at the terminals and it caused a spill?"

He glanced away and his dark-chocolate eyes, the ones I loved seeing rake over my body, showed guilt. It was all I needed to confirm the answer.

"Let's take a moment, Morina," he said, like his quiet voice would soothe me. He even stepped over to my salt lamp and turned it on, like that could change the damn mood. "Do you want to sit here?"

I knew he wasn't trying to mock the way I was. He wouldn't do that. He seemed to enjoy that I thought each crystal and salt lamp brought some peace into life. Yet, Bastian calmed and accommodated. He was trying to fit everyone into a box and make us all happy.

"Bastian Armanelli," I sneered his name as I approached the lamp. "You think you can have your cake and eat it too?

You think you can have the shares and still be partnered with a refinery that pushed my city to the brink? What happened to Sebastian, the man who could rule an empire and do exactly what he wanted?" I grabbed the salt lamp and raised it over my head. "You charmed me instead of being honest and being there for me." I threw it down and the crystal crashed on the floor, sending shattered fragments everywhere. "A marriage of convenience becomes a marriage of disaster."

"Morina!" He reached for me, but I jumped back. "You're overreacting."

"Quick decisions. My grandmother said to make them. Do you know how quickly I decide to overreact or indulge in my feelings, Bastian? Normally, it's faster than this. Normally, I go with what I feel. I stopped that with you. I went even though the path felt foolish."

"That's not true. You went down a hard path for once because you saw the risk but also the reward. It may have been a dark path, but—"

"Dark, unknown, and therefore stupid, Bastian. This was all so stupid." My heart galloped in my chest and suddenly, it ached. It ached like someone was pressing against it and the pressure had the potential to bleed me out.

"You can't overcome the darkness and reach your reward if you don't go down the path and find out what's there, Morina. We've got so much going for us." His brows knitted together, but he slid his hands into his pockets like he wasn't going to fight me. Or fight for me. I wasn't sure which.

"You go searching for secrets, and you'll always find them. These secrets are too big, Bastian. These lies and omissions of truth aren't worth it to me."

"What are you saying?" he whispered.

"I love you." I took a shaky breath, my eyes stinging from the tears I knew were going to come. Saying those words shouldn't have been like this. There should have been rose petals on the floor instead of shattered crystal. There should have been love in the air instead of mistrust. "I really, really love you. I thought I found someone who could accept my quirks and the fact that I run in ten different directions at the same time—"

"You did," he said, a frown on his face. "I'm standing right in front of you."

I shook my head. "But I can't. I believe you, but I don't. I want you, but I won't." I shook my head and my wavy hair fell over my cheeks. I backed away from him as the tears streamed down my face.

I left him in the living room around shattered crystals, shattered vows, and a shattered marriage. I went to pack my suitcases.

I couldn't trust him, and he couldn't put me first and fight for me instead of his companies, like I wanted him to.

We were broken before we even began, and if I didn't leave, I'd be lost to him forever.

CHAPTER 38: BASTIAN

Morina's heart turned on me like my mother's had turned on my father.

The look in her eyes mirrored the one my mother had when my father told her she couldn't leave him, that he would continue to do everything he wanted, and she would simply have to live with it.

She'd been so mad at my father about a shipment, and they'd argued and argued. He'd finally walked up to her and instead of trying to smooth things over, he'd smacked her hard across the face.

I'd just turned ten. I remembered the day because she'd made me a birthday cake the night before and when he hit her, she caught herself on the table, her hand landing in the cake. Fingers covered in white frosting and a cake ruined, she raised her face and shook her head at him in disgust.

Mario's eyes darkened, like he couldn't stand his wife realizing he was scum.

When faced with a stressful event, the automatic instinct for humans was always fight or flight, and in a boy, it was an even more innocent reaction. Gone was my fear of trouble or pain. I jerked forward, ready to stand between them. I knew my father's rage better than anyone. I knew he would hit her again. Yet, Cade caught me.

My little brother's brown eyes pleaded with me as he held my arm with both hands. "Dad's going to leave, and we'll take care of Mom then. You go to her now, and he'll drag you off with him."

I ripped my arm away and stormed into the kitchen. When I confronted my father, my mother started crying and, just as Cade had said, my dad dragged me out of the house.

I saw a lot of blood that night as he made me watch the real dealings of the mob.

His firstborn wouldn't be soft, he'd told me. It was better for me to learn now.

It changed my mother, and it changed me. Our family morphed from one that made the best cannoli into the head of the country's Italian Mob. That night, I came home and she said, "Bastian, my love, I'm going to teach you to cook."

The only farewell gift she knew how to give us was the passion in her cooking.

Now, I stood wondering if Morina would take something with her as she left me.

I would let her go.

Morina Bailey didn't deserve a man in the Mafia. She deserved a man who put her first, who didn't make deals with demons and wasn't the devil himself. Yet, as she rummaged around in her room, I still went to stand in her doorway. Over the crushed crystal, I walked to my doom, sure this was the walk of shame I deserved.

"Morina, I—"

"Don't try to explain, Bastian. I listened to so much explaining as a kid." She shut her eyes, and tears rolled down her cheeks. "Did you know I believed every single explanation? How gullible was I? Is that what everyone sees me as? This gullible, stupid girl who can't get it together."

"Morina, that's never what I thought. I didn't see the point in bogging you down with the details of—"

"You couldn't bog me down, why? Because you thought

my attention span couldn't handle it or because it hit too close to home? You can't possibly think having more oil brought over won't risk the water."

"There's always a risk," I threw back. "I'm taking a risk here with you. You took a risk the day you married me."

She slumped. "It wasn't supposed to be a risk of my heart."

"Don't say that, *ragazza*." Her words made me want to lock her up and keep her here. "I have to love my family, and it requires me to consider every decision I make. This was the best for everyone. We keep good relationships, we move toward clean energy over time."

"What if something happens, Bastian? What if that oil refinery does something wrong? You shook their hand when you wanted clean energy. How will that look?"

"Nothing will happen. I'm making sure of that. Can you just ... Let's go to get something to eat, huh? I'll explain it to you."

She stared at me in her baggy shirt and tiny shorts, her legs long as she stood up and narrowed her eyes at me. "I should say no but I want to say yes. So, I guess you'll get my full attention through one more meal. You should be happy that, for some reason, it doesn't stray when it comes to you."

She walked past me and put her shoes on. I mentally congratulated myself at the small victory. I could talk sense into her, I could make this work.

We drove to a little place in the city. The drive was silent, but tension swirled in the car. She breathed in and out, slow and even, and I knew she was doing some exercise as she twisted the bracelets on her arm. She didn't touch her ring, and it made me wonder if she ever would again.

Greenery scaled the restaurant's walls and ceiling with plants weaving in and out of blown glass structures. "We didn't go out to eat much over these past couple of months. I should have taken you out more."

"No reason to. This was an arrangement." She shrugged and looked at her menu, dismissing our relationship.

"You know that's not true, *ragazza*. This was more than an arrangement. It was a marriage and if you want it to be over, it will be, but don't discount it." My voice came out firmer than I wanted it to.

I took a deep breath and she rolled her eyes. "That's right, Bastian. Keep it all together."

Fuck me.

I would, even if she tried to make me lose it. I didn't need to become my father, and compromise always worked better. "In order to do what I do, Morina, a level head and compromise is necessary. You can't go with your gut all the time and hope it works out."

"Is that your fatherly farewell advice to me?" She lifted a brow.

I chuckled in irritation. "You like getting under my skin, and you're probably better at it than most. I swear to God if I didn't love you–" She gasped at my words. They'd slipped out in my irritation but I wouldn't snatch them back now. "I do love you. I don't think that's a question." I held her gaze as my heart thundered with the words. "I love your inability to finish a file without doing a million things in between and your complete disgust with my negotiation skills. I love that you adore the water and you go with the flow like the ocean. I love you. That's why I have to let you go for this."

She shook her head, her face falling at my words as she whispered, "You'll let me go?"

Maybe I would have changed my mind had I sat there and stared into those sapphire eyes that sparkled like the ocean she loved so much.

But Ronald, the man that should have never been talking to my wife in the first place, ambled over, his white teeth glinting in the dim light.

"Bastian, Morina." He stood over us, then grabbed a chair from behind him and pulled it up to our table. Security that I had in the corner moved, but I held up my hand. Let him make his bed. I wanted him to sleep in it. Permanently.

My body vibrated with an emotion I knew I wouldn't be able to contain. Keep it all together, Morina had said. But Sebastian Armanelli, head of the mob, knew that this man had gone against me, had spoken to my wife behind my back, and ruined the one thing I loved.

"Ronald," I said without looking at him. I looked down at that gold ring on my hand, the weight of a family symbolized in it. "I'm having a meal with my wife. I don't want to talk with you right now."

"She talked to me earlier, though. You must know. I hope it didn't cause any harm."

I tapped the ring on the table two times, trying to pull my anger back before I lashed out. I was a man of the family, a man who had done so well to create alliances everywhere.

"No harm." The words came out so quiet, I wasn't sure anyone heard. They were the last words of Bastian, he was suffocating under the rage of the other man I tried to keep hidden from everyone.

"Oh, good. Good. Morina," Ronald turned to her, "once this whole arrangement you and Bastian have is over, remember I'll pay you twice as much. You're for sale it seems."

Her fork clattered down onto her plate. It was the only sound before a voice that sounded foreign even to me rumbled from my mouth. "What did you say"—I rubbed my jaw, trying to calm down—"to my wife?"

He glared at us and didn't repeat himself.

"Apologize." It came out louder than it should have. Someone moved behind Ronald but my security took care of it. No one was coming to our table now. Ronald had to rescue himself.

He sat there with his hands fisted like he was struggling with his own pride.

Patience wasn't Sebastian Armanelli's virtue. Certainly not with an idiot. I was tired of being accommodating and working the system. So damn tired. And there was one place I wouldn't do it anymore.

And that place was with her.

The gun tucked in my back belt loop was the easiest weapon to access. In a second it was in my hand, and I spun the Glock so I held the barrel. I swung it at Ronald's face like a makeshift hammer as I grabbed the back of his head and brought it down on the metal swiftly.

He screamed as it connected with his face.

I let him have a moment as I heard commotion in the restaurant. My security was probably filing people out to leave. I didn't care. I leaned in and said to Ronald, "Next time it will be the other side of my gun in your face. And I'll pull the trigger, Ronald. Do not disrespect her again, you understand?"

Blood poured from his nose, and he whispered something, but it wasn't loud enough to make out.

"Bastian," Morina said softly, like she was trying to call that gentleman mobster back. *He's gone, ragazza.*

And Ronald, he wasn't begging for his life yet. Did he want me to kill him? He deserved it at this point. I spun the gun again and grabbed his gray hair as I pushed the barrel into his temple. "I should kill you." I stood and shoved it against his head. His eyes bulged in fear. "No one would miss you. And after that disrespect for my marriage, it's what you deserve."

He was pleading now, saying sorry over and over and over.

"Bastian!" Morina screamed, and when I looked at her, the whites of her eyes were showing, her face scared as she stared at the devil that was me. "You can't, Bastian, you can't."

I growled and drew my hand back before whipping it across Ronald's face. He cried in pain and I glared at Morina. "We're leaving now."

She nodded fast and followed me out of the restaurant with stares following us the whole way.

Silence again on the way home. She said my name softly once but I cut her off. "I don't want to talk about it."

When we got back to the penthouse, I stared at the shattered crystal on the ground, our marriage as broken as the rock, vows and promises and deals all destroyed.

"I'm sorry," she whispered as we stood staring at it all.

"For what?"

"I don't think I understand your way of life the way I thought. I think ... you have more responsibility than I ever had." I tried to cut her off but she held up her hand. "You're a Mafia king, Bastian, but you can't control everything by weaving in and out of partnerships. Your aura is all fucked up from it. I felt your anger back there, and it's catastrophic and brilliant at the same time. You have to be the bad guy sometimes or it will tear down not just a city, Bastian. You'll tear down much more than that." It sounded like disgust or defeat in her soft voice, and I wouldn't correct her because she was right.

Was that what she thought? "I've made sacrifices over and over again, Morina. I've trained myself to contain my emotions for everyone's protection. This is about my family, my legacy. It's about you needing protection too. I can't risk all that because I have feelings for you."

She winced at my words. "I don't want to be a concern for you. Your feelings shouldn't be a risk, Bastian. They should be the things you listen to because you need to be happy too."

"I'll take unhappiness if it means you're protected from all this," I confessed and meant it even as the pain in my chest suddenly felt catastrophic.

"I don't want your protection." She shook her head.

"You're an Untouchable, Morina. You can go anywhere in the world, and I'll be protecting you. I'll have eyes on you forever. That's the price I paid when I married you."

"The price you paid?" She stormed up to me. "I don't want your security on me. I didn't ask for any of this, and I don't want it. You need to focus on yourself. *Feel* something, Bastian. *Feel us.*" She took a shaky breath. "You almost killed a man, Bastian! That wasn't for nothing."

"And if you hadn't been there, I would have. Don't you think that's a problem, Morina?" The words bellowed out of me and Moonshine trotted to Morina. The dog might have acted like it had allegiance to me, but in the end, a pup knew its mother.

I stared at her, petting Moonshine almost unconsciously, and like a mom soothing her child, the innocent gesture stirred a protectiveness in me that I'd only experienced one other time in my life. "I won't keep you here like my father did with my mother. I won't ruin you because I love you too much. Staying with me would expose you to all the filth you don't deserve."

"Shouldn't I get to decide that?" Her eyes filled with tears.

"We need time away from each other, *ragazza.*" I wanted to reach for her, to tell her it was all going to be okay but I didn't trust myself enough to do so.

"You want that time to turn back into Bastian when all I

really wanted was Sebastian. I can't love you if I can't have all of you, you know?" She clutched at her heart.

"That's fair." I agreed with her because it was the right thing to do.

"Oh, shut the fuck up with your *fair*. You should try being unfair for once in your life, Bastian." She threw up her hands. "Go with the flow and see how it takes a weight off your soul. See where it gets you."

Caging an animal that was better off free never worked. Still, if I could have tied her to the bed and still had her love me in some way, I probably would have.

Instead, I had to let her go.

* * *

On the first day she was gone, I got a call from our lawyer. The shares were almost through probate, and Morina wanted to donate all of them to me. He could draw up the legal documents as soon as possible.

I hung up on him and tried to call her. I'd never take them for free. Morina had better believe I was going to set her up for life and do what was right and fair by her.

Try being unfair, she'd told me, and now she was forcing me to.

I grumbled as I took Moonshine downstairs to go to the bathroom. The dog had whined since her mother left, and she laid down on the grass now instead of walking around to piss. "You're going to have to go to the bathroom sooner or later, girl. We can mope together later."

She peered up at me with her brown-and-black fur shining in the sunlight and whined.

Petting her head, I whispered, "Remember how you took

your mom's side yesterday? I forgive you because I would have taken her side too. I'm a fuckup."

The dog sighed and looked away from me.

I needed a few days to make it right.

A few days of hell was what we got instead.

I got the call from my brother as I was boarding the jet to fly to LA for a meeting. "Mr. Crow's oil refinery is pushing illegal imports to another terminal. We got a boatful of women over there that the FBI just intercepted."

"I shook that bastard's hand," I whispered.

"I know. I think, fuck, man. I don't know. If I could, I'd kill him myself. They had kids on there that are Ivy's age."

"Katie and Rome with you?" I pinched the bridge of my nose.

Katie spoke first. "I want the whole refinery to suffer. I want to kill one or two of them myself."

Cade chuckled. "Bastian's not going to allow that. We need to be discreet and try to work out a solution."

My gut reaction yanked me one way. The immediate response was to shut it down but instead, I remembered her words. Morina made these quick decisions all the time, she went with the flow. She followed instinct rather than logical reason.

"I want the man dead," I said quietly.

"What?" Cade asked, his voice high.

"Rome, you're retired from this, I know that. You tell me the best man to do it, then, or I'll do it myself."

"Bastian," my brother said, "we can't—"

"Why can't I, Cade?" He'd been made an accommodating man because of me; now I had to unmake that man. "They're killing families all the time. Why can't I?"

"We're better than them," Katie announced. "You're better

than them. You do what we can't. You see the silver lining, Bast."

"Morina left."

"I know," Cade said. "You'll both figure it out though. She's an Untouchable now, and she'll understand."

"Understand that I shook hands with this man? It's specifically what she told me not to do."

Someone sighed over the line.

"What do you want us to do?" Rome said it like he was ready to spill blood again. "We'll do whatever you need." He had a little girl though and a family that needed him.

"I want his cybersecurity system breached for the oil refinery. Make it known it's us and infect the networks with ransomware. If he doesn't agree to pay five times what he's made on those families back to them, I will crush his whole business."

"That type of breach will be deemed a national emergency, Bastian. That's ... are you going to call the president?"

"The president can call me, Cade. I'm done fucking around."

CHAPTER 39: MORINA

Day two of driving up the coast and Bastian still hadn't called.

It was probably for the best, a clean break now rather than later.

I stared at palm tree after palm tree on a coastal road and wondered why I didn't miss my food truck more.

Instead, I was missing Moonshine and him. I missed seeing his face before I went to bed, and I missed waking up and smelling the crepes he'd made for me. It'd been two days away, and I was already considering crawling back.

Sighing, I pulled into another parking lot and hopped from my pickup. I'd been surfing from beach to beach, so I always wore a bikini. As I pulled my board out, the sun warmed my skin and I took in this new stretch of sand, not crowded with people at all.

When a black SUV pulled up, I sighed again. Security for life was something I needed to get used to. Bastian had said the words so seriously, I knew arguing was pointless. I had anyway.

I wanted Sebastian to take the reins, to tell me he'd handle everything, that we could be together and I didn't have to leave, that he wouldn't make any side deals.

Maybe it had been too much to ask, but I'd asked for so little before, and my heart had wanted it all this time.

All or nothing.

A quick decision that was mine to make. I made it by committing to a wave every day I was out on that sparkly water. I jumped up on that board and held my body up, trusting my balance and the water to let me ride. If I hesitated or half-assed it, I'd fall.

I was never good at school or jobs or anything, really, except that. My heart committed to riding the waves.

My tears mixed with the ocean water as I rode them again and again that day. I'd married one man and had gotten two instead. Bastian was a Taurus, strong and stubborn but always dependable. He wasn't going to let his legacy die or put his family in any type of jeopardy.

He'd submerge his love deep down in the water and suffocate it to make sure he completed whatever he set out to do.

I couldn't be with a man who did that.

I needed Sebastian Armanelli, stubborn and dominating. The man who knew what he wanted and took it.

My phone rang as I threw my board back in my pickup an hour later. I scooted into the seat, the sand still sticking to my legs as I stared at an unknown number on the screen. When you weren't with the person you loved, your heart dropped getting those calls.

"Hello?"

"It's Cade."

I took a deep breath. The mob didn't make house calls or small talk. "What's wrong?"

The words whispered out of me, but they built momentum in my mind, my throat closing from the thought of Bastian hurt or gone. Had he done something he couldn't come back from? Had his meeting with Ronald gone too far?

"Is Bastian gone?" I croaked out, tears springing to my eyes.

"What?" Cade cackled into the phone. "Are you crying right now?"

"What?" I glanced around, suddenly aware that he might be watching me. I swiped at my eyes. "No!"

"Oh my God. You are, aren't you? Why the fuck did you leave him then? You love him so much you're going to cry just thinking something happened to him but you left. What's it matter?"

"I still love him!" I said defensively and then shook my head. "He told you I left? So, he's okay then?"

"I mean he told me you left like I didn't see you walk out with your suitcase on the security footage," he said like we were a bunch of idiots.

"That's really creepy, Cade."

"Anyway, you need to get back to the penthouse."

"What?" I shook my head, then started to back out from my parking spot.

"You need to get back there. Or the security team can drive you or whatever. Bastian's on a call with the president right now, I think, but it looks like he's coming your way anyway."

"I'm not going back to him."

"You love him. Why not? You going to cry when he's gone but not enjoy him while he's here?"

"That's not— You can mourn the death of someone, Cade. It's different from protecting your heart. This is for the best."

"It's not."

"Why? Give me a reason." I needed a good one, or maybe just any one, because my resolve wasn't the best on this.

"You know, when my mom died, she'd only taught Bastian how to cook," Cade said. "I didn't care about learning, and she'd focused on him. He was the firstborn son in the family anyway. I think my dad punished him for that. He wanted every form of passion that reminded him of my mother gone from Bastian. But Bastian and my mother were close. She used to run her hands through his hair and say, 'You got my love for the world, Bast, and Cade got all our smarts.'"

I held my breath at his words as I sat in my pickup, taking in every detail he gave me about their childhood.

"I remember the first time Bastian came home from a deal that must have ended in bloodshed. He didn't say a word. He just cooked. Then he turned to me and said, 'Let's learn to make peace.' And he meant it. He doesn't want to fight anyone. But he will. He is. He's bringing down that refinery partly for you and partly because he found they were still illegally trafficking women. He'll kill the man if you don't go back. I'm sure of it, Morina."

"He can't," I whispered.

I got it now. The peace in him was his way of fighting.

He fought with alliances and peace and wanted happiness instead of hate. It was possible to rule with respect rather than fear, and I believed he was one of the only people who could do it ... But only if I took on his darkness behind closed doors.

I wanted Sebastian's pain and dominance and fury in the dark of the night where I could soothe him back to light by morning.

"I'll be back there soon." I turned the key in the ignition, ready now more than ever to go back.

"Thought you might say that. He should be at the last beach you stopped at. You can meet there. I'll text him."

I hung up and turned on the radio to try to calm down. The news didn't let me.

"The refinery was hacked only hours before, demanding compensation for trafficked families," the host said. "We have the votes going on whether we should commend the hackers or call them terrorists. I'm leaning toward commending them. Word is, this might be some sort of broken empire, with the mob families and syndicates fighting against one another."

The other host laughed. "I don't think it's the eighties anymore. Mob families are dead. This is just businessmen playing with their money and getting hacked by the people who want justice. I'm for it. I hope they end up having to pay that ransom."

I smacked the radio dial off. "Breathe, Morina," I told myself.

This time, I turned the crystal ring on my finger and drove fast enough down the coast to meet Bastian in half an hour.

The sun was setting as I parked, and I saw his navy suit out on the sand. He still looked completely and utterly out of place there, but it was picturesque, the juxtaposition of his luxury suit being dirtied by the sand and sea.

I stood too long thinking about us together, letting my mind run away with itself. I was too wrapped up in my own confusion and in my love for him that I didn't hear the man coming from behind me until he grabbed me by the neck so hard I barely got out a scream.

The cold metal of his gun pressed into my temple, but he wasn't the one who spoke.

A man with hair so inky it must have been dyed black stepped into view. "I really wish Bastian had held up his part of the deal so I didn't have to force this sort of transaction."

I wheezed just as Bastian whipped around.

Only about twenty feet separated us, but when a dragon broke from its chains and came out of the cave, the world felt it.

"Boss ..." the guy holding me murmured as my husband took a step toward us, his eyes fixed on the gun at my head. "He's trained. You'd better act fast because her security will be here any minute too. They'll be setting up snipers and he'll signal."

"You got a gun to this pretty girl, here, boy," his boss said to the guy holding the gun to my head. "Don't worry. He won't do a thing. He's a businessman."

"You're wrong," I whispered.

The man smacked the gun across my face. "Shut up. You don't know anything."

As black spots came into my vision and blood dripped from the lip he'd hit, there was something I was sure of, something I did know.

I knew that before me stood Sebastian Armanelli, the Mafia king. My protector. My lover.

Before the man could cut off any more oxygen from my lungs, my husband stood with the sparkling ocean at his back and moved like lightning to whip out his gun and pull the trigger.

I felt the hand slacken before my gasp even came out. The weight of a body fell from my back.

"Bastian," I whispered but he wasn't looking at me.

He had his gun aimed at the black-haired man. "Did you think you could come here to negotiate?"

"Bastian, please ..." He chuckled, his eyes darting back and forth. "I'm so sorry. That man, I thought he had the decency to talk. He's been an employee of mine but I didn't know—"

"Shut up, Crow," Bastian commanded. "Do I look stupid to you?"

"Of course not."

"Do you think my wife is leverage?"

"I thought it was just an arrangement. I was sure the stories I heard—"

"My *wife*, and no other woman for that matter, is meant to be dragged into this."

"Bastian, you pulled a pretty big stunt on my oil refinery.

Let's be fair—"

"Fair?" he asked, like suddenly the word was poison in his mouth. "*Fair?*"

He stalked up to Crow, and I knew I needed to intervene. "Bastian, hold on."

His dark eyes shot to mine, pain so deep I wouldn't have found the end of it, even if I swam in it for days. "*Ragazza, amore mio*, I could have lost you."

With that, his dark eyes turned to the hardest sort of crystal, and he pulled the trigger.

Another body dropped.

Closing the space between us, Bastian holstered his weapon and pulled me into his arms so tight, I lost my breath.

"I'm going to kill my whole security team," he grumbled. "And fucking Cade. What the fuck happened to his security?"

Burying my face into his neck, I couldn't answer any of his questions. I just needed him to hold me. Needed him to be with me.

"Are you okay, Morina?" He rubbed my back, no doubt feeling the shivers that wracked my body from the adrenaline wearing off.

"Please don't let go of me right now."

"I'm here to have and to hold, forever and ever, remember?" he murmured into my hair.

He kissed my cheeks where tears streamed down them.

"You killed two men." I closed my eyes not wanting to look.

"If I'd have lost my *ragazza*, I'd have killed a lot more."

"Jesus," I whispered, trying to digest what had happened. "You're going to jail, and I'm going to have to visit you there."

He held me at arm's length for a second and laughed like I was ridiculous. "Morina, that was self-defense. I'm not going to jail for even a day."

"That was pure anger and murder," I countered. "I saw your face!"

He smirked. "Ah, the fight's back in you already. Look at the color on your skin."

"Oh, shut up." I shoved at his arm.

His mouth closed, and his jaw ticked. Then, he lifted his hand and smeared away my blood from my chin and the tears from my face. When he brought it out in front of me, I saw how he studied it.

He sighed, "I'll always have a devil, Morina. This family is full of demons we can't lock up."

I held his thumb out in front of me. "Tell me to open, Sebastian."

His eyes darkened as he stared at me, reading and assessing and trying to figure out if this was fair for me. I let him take his time. I'd take a little bit of pain if I could have all of this man. I'd wait for him until death do us part. "Open, *ragazza*."

I did and licked the blood from his thumb before saying, "I'm yours. Your Untouchable. And every part of you is mine. The good and mostly the bad. I think the bad part of you chooses me every day, and I'm too insecure to want anything else."

The deep breath that came out of him as he looked down at his leather shoes held so much weight. "Morina Armanelli, you're like the oceans you love so much. Swift and beautiful in every decision you make. So fast, *ragazza*. And I wonder how an ocean can mix with sand and filth. You flow over all the jagged parts of the world, and I'm there like sand, moving over each one trying to smooth it over and make it right somehow. Yet, I'll always leave filth behind. I don't know if we can survive that together."

"Why can't we? The sand and the sea move together and

exist in harmony."

"You've always acted based on feelings, *ragazza*. I act based on overthinking. Today, I just felt. It's a dangerous thing."

"You told me once I'm in more danger without you than I am with you, Bastian."

He sighed, closed his eyes, and pulled his cell from his pocket and dialed. "We need a cleanup at my location. Get in touch with the media and the feds too. I have Morina and will be leaving."

He steered me away from the scene toward our cars. The man with his hand on the small of my back had just laid out two bodies for me. I should have been scared or wanted to mourn their deaths. Instead, I wanted to climb his body like a tree and tell him I loved him.

"Morina, you understand this is all because I ended the deal with the refinery obviously." He pinched the bridge of his nose and I saw the darkness under his eyes. "They forced my hand today, and the country will be better for it."

Nudging his shoulder with mine, I nodded up at him. "You did what you thought was right but you maybe followed your gut too."

"I did what my gut told me without even thinking. It'll make a bold statement."

"Can you handle it?" I knew he could but I wondered if he realized it.

He stared at me, then glared out at the water. "Yeah. I've pushed the president to move toward clean energy in this state. We'll do it fast. It'll work out."

"You've made enemies doing that today, though."

"I'll make more and more."

"You'll probably have to hold your temper better in the future."

"Morina, I'm fully capable of—"

"You're capable of anything." I said it because I truly believed it. "But you don't go down the right path all the time. Together, we can probably pick one or two good roads together."

"You want to stay?"

"I want and need to. My horoscope today even said to do what I want and need. And Cade told me you cook for peace."

His eyes turned to chocolate, and his hands went to my waist. "I'm not a saint. He thinks I am."

"He thinks you're his big brother who turned a broken empire into a golden legacy again. You taught him to cook, Bastian, and they count on you to bring peace. I'm proud you knew when to step up and bring war too. Don't discount everything you do."

He shook his head at my praise. "I should have told you about the deal, Morina."

"You should have. But then you served them all Sebastian Armanelli, the man who unleashes rage just for me."

He chuckled. "You'll always be risking something when you're with me, you know that?"

I hummed. "So, are you going to do what's best for me and let me go?"

Sebastian Armanelli smiled wide before he responded.

"Not a chance in fucking hell."

EPILOGUE: MORINA

"What are you doing?" My breath came faster in the living room of the penthouse that we'd somehow made a home. Bastian had bought my grandmother's house only for me to tell him to sell it. I loved living in the high-rise with him watering the damn plants with his spray bottle more than I ever thought I would.

"I'm tying you up," Bastian replied, as he wrapped my wrists in silk like his mind was already made up and this was the most logical thing to do.

I pulled my hands away, but they were already tied, and he yanked the end hard toward him. I stumbled into his chest, completely off balance.

Moonshine had already wandered off to her bedroom. The dog was a fucking princess when it came to her sleep schedule. She whined to get into her bedroom, and every night at eight o'clock, Bastian followed her down the hall, gave her a dog treat from the linen closet, and told her he loved her.

My hair fell over my shoulder, and I looked up at him through it. "You think this is fun?"

"If you don't like it, tell me to stop." He shrugged. "I'm here to accommodate my wife because it seems she needs someone to remind her she's loved even when she's being ridiculous."

"Ridiculous about what?"

He turned me with him and slid open the patio door.

"Oh no, Bastian."

"Oh yes. Morina. You need to come sit out here and enjoy

the salt lamps I installed on our balcony."

"I really appreciate that you did that." I pushed away from his chest, but he gripped the small of my back like I wasn't going anywhere. I tried yanking at my wrists, and he yanked back. "But I don't think I'll enjoy it as much as you."

"You will, *ragazza*," he whispered into my ear. Then, before I could stop him, he scooped me up to carry me out onto the balcony.

I squealed and gripped his shirt. The wind whipped at us both like it was telling us this was unnatural for a human to be this high out in the open.

I agreed. Shutting my eyes, I whispered, "If I die, I'm going to haunt you like my grandma haunted me. I'll make your life a living hell."

"Oh, what's there to worry about, Morina? The salt lamps are putting out negative ions." He chuckled as he walked us over to his oak rocking chair.

"That's not how it works, and you know it." I bit my lip as he sat down, scared the patio would suddenly give and we'd fall fifty stories to our doom. We deserved it after being so frivolous with our lives and stepping out here like we were gods of some sort in the first place.

"*Ragazza*, open your eyes," Bastian murmured and dragged a finger down my cheek.

I took a deep breath and reminded myself that this man had taken lives for me, had made me an Untouchable for my protection, tucked me in every night after a good amount of sex, and told me he loved me over and over. I cracked one eye open to only look at him, "I'm trusting you, Bastian."

"As you should." He nodded and then pointed, "Now look."

There were tiny crystals lining the railing and the overhang of our balcony that wrapped around the whole penthouse. They glowed a pinkish hue, almost the same color of the last rays of the sun in the sky. "We get our own sunset right here with the crystals," I murmured.

He nodded. "Maybe, but your ocean's sunset is better."

"Only because I have a husband who made sure it wasn't getting polluted." I kissed his neck, knowing that the wheels were in motion for Tropical Oil's new construction. We were turning terminals to green energy and the city was thriving just months after the deal had been solidified.

Bastian had rejected my donation of the shares only two days after Mr. Crow's death on the beach. He'd called the lawyer right in front of me and told him that he didn't want anything to do with the shares if I wasn't the shareholder.

I fought him the whole way. I wanted to surf and be a housewife, didn't he know? I enjoyed a lazy week, rather than one filled with packets of business dealings. Bastian had laughed at my confession and said he didn't care who owned what. He just wanted me happy.

Happiness had been him dealing with most of the planning and me still running my food truck. We'd had another six months of bliss and were nearing a whole year together as husband and wife.

Every night, we tried to be home by dinnertime. He made it a mission most days even though he sometimes traveled out of town on one of his ridiculous jets. Then, I watched him make dinner before I climbed him like a hungry cat. He had claw marks most of the time to show for it.

"I'm happy you're happy about it. We're six months into construction, and I think we'll meet the nine-month goal," Bastian murmured into my neck as I wiggled on his cock, not caring a bit about business talk at the moment.

"Can we go in now?" I stared at his lips, wanting to have

them even before we ate dinner or anything else that evening.

"What for?" He smirked down at me.

I gripped the baggy shirt that was bunched around my thighs. "Oh, I don't know. Maybe I want to thank you for this nice balcony gift?"

His gaze raked up and down my body before he said, "Something came in the mail for you today."

"Oh?" I shrugged. "What?"

He slid his hand in his chest pocket and pulled out a small metal ball. "Linny sent this to you. Her letter read that you'd need it since you were having so many problems in the bedroom."

"What?" I tried to grab it away, but he held it out of reach from my tied hands. "You opened a package that was addressed to me?"

"We're married, *ragazza*." The hand that held me at my back suddenly was pulling his tie above my head to the railing just beside the chair. He put the metal device back in his pocket so he could tie a knot quickly. Then, he slid the metal device back out to stare at. "You should know better than to think a package is solely yours."

"What? She put my name on it." I pulled on my restraints. There wasn't any give.

He turned it in his hand before pressing a small button that made it vibrate. "What's yours is mine."

Oh, God. My eyes widened as his dark eyes sparkled.

He took his time sliding his hands under my shirt and then said, "Be a good girl and lift your hips, *ragazza*."

I chewed on my cheek but knew I was going with the path of me getting off. I lifted and he slid my panties off to drop onto the ground. Then he took his time lowering the metal egg to my thigh and the cool metal slid up and shocked my system with each vibration.

"Bastian, we should probably go inside. We aren't going to do anything on this balcony," I said through clenched teeth, but my breath was already coming faster and faster.

"Of course we are, love." His middle finger grazed my pussy. "If we weren't, you wouldn't be wet for me right now."

"Your cock has been against my ass for the last five minutes. Of course I'm wet for you. That's not an indication that—"

I gasped when he slid the cold metal over my clit and then rubbed it over my entrance. "Bastian ..."

"*Ragazza*, call me by my full name when I'm about to get you off. Your husband likes the world to hear it on your lips."

I shook my head in defiance. "No one would hear me fifty stories up."

He grabbed my hair and pulled my head back to expose my neck so he could suck on it as he rubbed a thumb over my clit and let the device work me into a frenzy. "Then you better scream loud, *bellissima*. We need to let this city know you and your husband have no problems at all in the bedroom or out of it, right?"

I moaned when he went back to sucking on my neck. I wiggled back and forth on his dick, wanting every sensation I could take from him. He was pushing all my senses by bringing me out here, lighting up the night with salt crystals, and then vibrating my pussy into oblivion. "I need all of you."

He growled and then lifted and spun me so I was sitting on top of him, looking out at the town, the ocean, the horizon.

He moved my hair to the side so he could continue marking my neck, but his hands went to my breasts and clitoris. They worked me in unison to my high. I hit it fast with that device in me, and he murmured how beautiful I looked. Then he slid it out, turned it off, and put it back in his pocket before scooting me forward enough to unbuckle his belt. "I should take you back in to fuck you properly in a bed but if I don't have you with this as your backdrop, I'll never forgive myself."

With that, he plunged into me, one hand on my breast, the other on my hip. I gasped at the sensation, realizing right at that moment, we had no barrier between us.

I couldn't stop though, the feeling of my husband's cock bare in my pussy was too much. I rode him hard and met each deep thrust over and over again.

"You feel that?" He murmured against my ear. "That pussy belongs on my dick, nothing between us. I'll make an empire with you, *ragazza*. Give me a baby, huh? One I'll love just as much as you."

I froze and turned to search his gaze over my shoulder. "You mean that?"

His mouth lifted to a smile. "You said at that theme park a long time ago you wanted one."

I bit my lip. "You're giving me what I want?"

"Well, what I want too." He leaned in and kissed my cheek. Then he squeezed my thigh and flexed his dick in me. "Let's make a baby now, Morina Armanelli."

I rolled my hips on him.

"Fuck," He ground out and pulled my hair so that my ass arched harder into his lap. "Scream my name, *ragazza*."

His words sent me over the edge. He'd made the quick decision to make a baby with me, one he knew I wanted. I hit a high out there on the balcony that night with the man I loved.

"Sebastian Armanelli."

THE END

For bonus scenes and other content, sign up for Shain's
newsletter: shainrose.com/newsletter

ALSO BY SHAIN ROSE

Hardy Billionaires
Between Commitment and Betrayal
Between Love and Loathing
Between Never and Forever

* * *

Stonewood Billionaire Brothers
INEVITABLE
REVERIE
THRIVE

* * *

New Reign Mafia
Heart of a Monster
Love of a Queen

* * *

Tarnished Empire
Shattered Vows
Fractured Freedom
Corrupted Chaos

ABOUT SHAIN ROSE

Shain Rose writes romance with an edge. Her books are filled with angst, steam, and emotional rollercoasters that lead to happily ever afters.

She lives where the weather is always changing with a family that she hopes will never change. When she isn't writing, she's reading and loving life.

CORRUPTED CHAOS

USA *TODAY* BESTSELLING AUTHOR

SHAIN ROSE

**My enemy doesn't make the rules behind closed doors ...
Even if he's my boss.**

Cade Armanelli might be an infamous hacker with billionaire
status who operates better alone, but I earned my spot working
alongside him...
Whether he likes it or not.

It's precisely why I'm on the first plane to an undisclosed
location for our cybersecurity team retreat. I'm ready to prove
to our company that I can handle anything ...
Except sharing a cabin and a bed with my meticulous,
elusive boss.

He's antisocial.
Ruthless.
Enemy number one.

Unfortunately, he's also number one in tatted, dark, and
dangerous. I quickly come to find that not only are his hacking
skills perfection, but so is his performance in the bedroom.

Not that it matters. I have a job to keep, a heart to protect, and
our nation's data to secure.
Cade can't help me with any of that.
He's a distraction. One I have to avoid ...

*Even if it means I'm spray painting a red line down our bed and
keeping my boss on his side.*

FRACTURED FREEDOM

USA *TODAY* BESTSELLING AUTHOR

SHAIN ROSE

Is it so bad that I tricked my older brother's best friend into taking my virginity?

Maybe.

In my defense, it was Dante Reid—my crush, my first love, and the one I ended up pushing away.

Our paths split in opposite directions.

I went to college on one coast while he returned to work with the US Army on the other.

The end.

Or so I thought.

After graduating and attempting a bucket list of self-discovery, guess who I find standing outside the jail, bailing me out from a crime I didn't commit?

Dante freaking Reid—this time with more muscles, more tattoos, and more demands.

One of which is to move in across the hall from him so he can keep me safe. Like I need protection after a little felony mix-up.

I don't.

Unless it's from him.

Because Dante has been my downfall before ...

And living next to the guy I gave my innocence to a long time ago may actually end in my complete devastation.